THE
WEIGHT
OF
AIR

Books by Kimberly Duffy

A Mosaic of Wings
A Tapestry of Light
Every Word Unsaid
The Weight of Air

THE WEIGHT OF AIR

KIMBERLY DUFFY

BETHANYHOUSE

a division of Baker Publishing Group
Minneapolis, Minnesota

© 2023 by Kimberly Duffy

Published by Bethany House Publishers
Minneapolis, Minnesota
www.bethanyhouse.com

Bethany House Publishers is a division of
Baker Publishing Group, Grand Rapids, Michigan

Printed in the United States of America

Library of Congress Cataloging-in-Publication Data
Names: Duffy, Kimberly, author.
Title: The weight of air / Kimberly Duffy.
Description: Minneapolis, Minnesota : Bethany House, a division of Baker
 Publishing Group, [2023]
Identifiers: LCCN 2022037867 | ISBN 9780764240386 (paperback) | ISBN
 9780764241369 (casebound) | ISBN 9781493440672 (ebook)
Subjects: LCGFT: Novels.
Classification: LCC PS3604.U3783 W45 2023 | DDC 813/.6—dc23/eng/20220812

LC record available at https://lccn.loc.gov/2022037867

This is a work of historical reconstruction; the appearances of certain historical
figures are therefore inevitable. All other characters, however, are products of
the author's imagination, and any resemblance to actual persons, living or dead,
is coincidental.

Cover design by Kathleen Lynch/Black Kat Design

Author is represented by Spencerhill Associates.

Baker Publishing Group publications use paper produced from sustainable for-
estry practices and post-consumer waste whenever possible.

23 24 25 26 27 28 29   7 6 5 4 3 2 1

＊ ＊ ＊

To August, my sweet boy.
May you always remain rooted in God's Word
and remember what true strength is.
You only need to look as far as your father.

＊ ＊ ＊

PROLOGUE

❋

"YOU ARE SURE you don't want me to go with you to the station?" Bram asked.

Polly MacGinnis turned away from the tent being raised, its white canvas roof puffing and sinking like a deflated cheese soufflé, to look at her husband. "No, that isn't necessary. You are needed here. There is a show in a few hours. Let's not make Giuseppe even angrier than he already is."

Bram lifted his cap and scrubbed his hand through unruly brown hair. She'd offered to trim it before she left, but he said the extra length made him look wild. It was good for the act. "Must you leave? It's a long journey on your own."

"I can manage." She twirled her fingers through the air with a flourish and grinned, though he likely saw through it. "After all, I manage the trapeze and rope on my own."

"Yes, but Polly . . ." He stared down at her with those warm eyes she'd fallen in love with, and for a moment, just one insignificant beat of time, she thought he might see what she

7

used to be. Who she used to be. "What about the melancholia? If it descends, you will be alone."

She pinched her lips together and moved away from him. "I will be with my mother."

He followed her, his long stride easily eating the distance between them. At least physically. Nothing could bridge the divide created when she had brought their daughter into the world and nearly died.

"I want to say good-bye to Mabel. Where is she?" Polly spoke with brisk efficiency. There was no use dragging out the argument any longer. She would go to New York City to visit her mother, who would likely not survive another winter. Polly had been supporting her for a decade and wouldn't stop now just because Giuseppe Manzo needed his best aerialist to finish the season. Just because her husband thought her as fragile as spun glass.

"Where do you think she is?" Bram's words were gilded in proud amusement.

They headed for the menagerie, where Mabel would be found helping settle the animals. At only eight, their daughter towered over other children her age, but there wasn't anywhere a girl as willing or gentle. She had a tender heart.

Bram's fingers brushed Polly's arm as he guided her around a trio of clowns, and her spine tingled the way it always did— always had—with his touch.

Ahead, Mabel carried a crate above her head, and the Manzo Brothers Circus's prized Asian elephant, Meena, trailed after, attached to her waist by a rope.

"Darling, I'm leaving," Polly called, her words breaking in a way that drew Bram's concerned glance.

He swept the box, full of yammering monkeys, from Mabel's hands as easily as one would lift a dropped handkerchief. Bram MacGinnis, the great strongman, knew nothing about constantly trying to prove himself strong and capable.

Mabel turned with an enthusiastic shriek as the box left her grasp. She launched herself at Bram, flinging her arms around his waist, and craned her head back to look up at him. Meena snuffled and swung her trunk against the packed dirt, and Bram laughed as he set down the crate and worked open the knot at Mabel's waist. He tossed the rope to a passing bullman, who led the elephant away.

"Your mother is leaving," he said and chucked Mabel beneath the chin.

Mabel turned and blinked up at Polly, then approached softly, as though afraid to spook her. No gleeful abandon or affectionate displays. Only respectful deference. It grated against Polly's heart. Seared her chest until she thought she could spit fire like Luko, the flame-eater.

Her own relationship with her mother had been pocked by distance. Grief and overwork made any sort of closeness impossible. Polly had vowed to be different with her children.

But for the three days of labor that left her without even the energy to gasp. But for the months of recovery. The dark shadows that filled her mind and blunted the edges of her affection. The inability to nurse and the height that made it clear Mabel would no longer be able to train with Polly. Instead she moved to join Bram in an act that knit them together even tighter.

"You are going now, Maman?" Mabel spoke with too much restraint, and Polly wrapped her arms around her child in an uncharacteristic hug.

"I am, and I shall miss you soundly."

Surprise flickered in her daughter's serious gaze. Delight chased it. "Da said you must cross an ocean. Are you very scared?"

"Only a little bit."

Mabel tugged her lower lip between her small square teeth, then reached into her sleeve. She withdrew Isabella, the little French doll sent from America by Polly's mother.

"You told me Grandmother crossed the ocean when she left France for America." Mabel's gaze sparked with pleasure as she made the connection. "And now you shall cross from France to America with Isabella in the same way."

"Oh, but you must keep her. Grandmother sent her to you. She doesn't need her back."

Mabel reached for Polly's arm—not up or down, for they stood the same height—and tucked Isabella into the cuff at her wrist. "For courage," she said the way Polly always did before a show when Mabel shivered with nerves. "Isabella will be with you all the way."

Polly caressed the doll's tiny feet hanging from her sleeve. "I shall bring her back to you, and we will tell you all about our adventures in the United States. Be strong, Mabel, in all things you set your hands and heart and eyes toward."

Mabel gave a grave nod and leaned forward to kiss Polly's cheek. "Good-bye, Maman. Da says you will surely be back before winter ends, so I will see you in Bologna."

Bologna, Italy, where the Manzo Brothers Circus wintered. Rested. Recovered.

Polly met Bram's gaze. "I do not expect Mother will live much longer. A cough has settled in her chest, and she says the doctor doesn't have much hope for her recovery."

"I'm sorry for it."

"You don't have to accompany me out. My trunk has already been put on a wagon, and a driver has been pulled from the chaos." She waved her hand in a wide arc, encompassing all the activity around them.

He stepped near. "You will miss this?"

"I will. But it will be good to be back in New York. For a little while, at least."

"Will you visit Travis and Wells?" He tried to hide it, but distrust still lingered in those words. He knew of her *affaire de coeur* with her old circus owner's son. It was only two years after it ended that she had met Bram, so her heart had pricked when she decided to love the Scottish giant with his hearty laugh and broad shoulders. And he had seen. Had weaseled some of the story out of her. But not all of it. Most of Paul remained tucked beneath the layers of grit and agony girding her peace. Only her old friends Rowena and Robert remembered. Only they knew of the ring still hidden in the bottom of her trunk.

"I see no reason to."

"They were your family once."

"I have a family."

He swallowed, then dropped to his knees, and she went into the circle of his arms. He hadn't hugged her like this in years, always afraid it would lead to something more. Afraid the passion that had flamed between them when Travis and Wells Circus toured Europe, joining for one day with Manzo Brothers, would consume him and destroy her. And that couldn't happen. The doctor had told her after Mabel's birth that another child would kill her.

"*I have the strength of a thousand men,*" he'd told her one night when she cried for his touch, "*but I cannot resist you. It is best if I keep my distance.*"

He pressed his nose into the hollow of her clavicle and inhaled. "You should stay. I have an aching fear that you will never come back."

Polly cupped his face. "You and your Scottish superstitions. I will be back."

"And if you fall into the melancholy again? If you grow ill?"

"I am perfectly healthy. And I've not felt such things in years." She looked away, not wanting him to see the lie in her expression. *Months*, perhaps, contained more truth. But she had experience in hiding them.

She leaned into his embrace again. It was where she'd always felt safest. And it had been too long.

With a gruff clearing of his throat, Bram released her and stood. He swung Mabel into his arms. "Say good-bye to your ma. For now?" He glanced at Polly.

"For now."

"Good-bye, Maman."

Polly smiled her farewell, unable to speak past her tightening throat.

She turned to leave, but not before she saw Bram hold Mabel straight out. "High?" he asked. She giggled. "Higher?" She nodded.

He tossed her into the air, stepping back to allow her a double flip—a trick left over from those few years she'd trained in acrobatics with Polly—and a soft landing.

CHAPTER

1

INSTEAD OF LIFTING HER FATHER, Mabel MacGinnis found herself standing in the middle of the ring two months after his death, staring at a clown.

"You remember how to do this?" she asked, not quite believing it. Lorenzo, when not painted white and wearing his jester-inspired costume, typically spent his idle time flirting and writing sloppy love poems. "You must remain stiff."

"I know, *Piccolo*." He shuffled toward her, his exaggerated movements drawing laughter from the house. At the sound of her longtime nickname—never once having been little in any way—the tension drained from Mabel's shoulders. Lorenzo lifted his arms above his head, palms clapped together and his mouth and eyes making wide circles. "I can do this. *You* can do this."

Lorenzo weighed much less than Da, whom, at six feet four and 230 pounds, Mabel was able to overhead lift by the time she reached twenty-three. This was not her hardest trick. There was no reason she couldn't do it. No reason she couldn't astound the audience, who had come to watch her at Manzo Brothers Circus, by lifting a clown over her head. Only a clown.

Not a wooden dowel supporting the weight of three aerialists, which was her best-received trick three years earlier. Not standing on a towering dais and completing a 2,800-pound harness lift. Not lifting Bram MacGinnis, Giant of Scotland.

It was only Lorenzo the clown.

But when he brought his fingers to his teeth in a pantomime of fear, then crossed his arms as though shivering but really giving her a solid anchor with which to hoist him, the swirl of grief she'd been stumbling through since Da died evaporated, leaving only uncertainty. And fear. And the knowledge that the world's strongest woman was nothing without the world's strongest man by her side.

"Do it for your papa." Lorenzo's lilting Italian yanked Mabel from her thoughts. "Now. They grow weary."

Mabel glanced around the tent and saw it was true. People had begun to shift and murmur. Death for a show.

She crouched and slung Lorenzo over her shoulders like they had practiced. He allowed himself to be handled like a sack of potatoes without even a grunt. Bracing her palms against his bicep—a much smaller one than she was used to—and knee, she pushed from her middle and lifted.

For Da.

For everything they had been and done.

For the strength that was the MacGinnis heritage.

The crowd began to chant. "Bram! Bram! Bram!"

They didn't know. Mabel had asked Giuseppe to tell no one. Not until she had grieved privately and felt strong enough to face the reporters. But she saw now that had been foolish, because with every shout of his name, her resolve further weakened. Her arms began to tremble. Then her knees. Then her entire body. Shaking from the weight of carrying more than a clown on her shoulders.

Oh, Da. She couldn't do it. Not without him.

Lorenzo tumbled to the ground behind her. A solid thump. A grunt. A hiss of breath.

The entire tent went silent.

Mabel whirled and dropped into a crouch. "Oh, Lorenzo, I'm so sorry. Are you all right?"

He grinned and waved one hand at the crowd, then jumped to his feet. But she saw him wince. His lips whitened as he held his arm to his stomach.

"You're hurt," she whispered, shock making her voice a wispy thing.

"I will be fine, Piccolo." He jerked his chin toward the jumble of steel bars she was meant to bend into rings and juggle. "Finish the act."

She watched him limp away, the tip of his felt hat crushed and one arm cradled in the other. A delirious little giggle bubbled from her lips. She'd just dropped someone. Someone who weighed less than she did.

Alyona Popov, her graceful feet balanced against the back of a dun Donskaya, galloped into the ring like an avenging angel. She did a flip, swung low to grab one of the bars, and spiraled back to her feet.

With a gentle toss, the bar flew toward Mabel, and she caught it by rote.

"Finish the show," Alyona called, her words nearly lost to the pounding of hooves and buzz of spectators. "Fall apart later."

Mabel shook her head to clear the remnants of guilt and failure, then focused on one person in the audience—a child of about six, thumb stuck in his mouth. She had always before done everything for Da. Every trick, every feat, every lift. But today, she would do it for that boy.

It would have to be enough.

She twisted metal into rings, spinning them into the air and catching them, one by one, around her arm. But there was no applause when she finished her act.

Maybe because it had been Da holding *her* up all along.

———

Once Mabel was backstage and the crowd's attention had been snagged by a couple of wire dancers, she found herself surrounded not by fury but by friends.

Even Lorenzo, whose wrapped wrist attested to something a sight more serious than broken pride, offered her a sheepish smile. "It will heal, but I fear my career in strength is over."

Alyona gripped Mabel's arms, maternal despite the fact that she only came to Mabel's midsection. "You are all right?"

"I'm fine. It's Lorenzo who was hurt."

"No, no," Lorenzo said, "I can now claim to have been broken by the world's strongest woman. It is an honor I will proudly wear."

Despite herself, Mabel laughed.

It was interrupted by an incredulous shout. "Mabel!" Giuseppe Manzo, owner of Manzo Brothers Circus and the only Manzo brother who actually existed, broke up the gathering. The others, with sympathetic glances tossed her way, scattered. "What was that?"

"I told you it was too soon, Giuseppe. I need more time."

"It has been months! The show must go on. You know this. And you are our only strongperson now that your father has gone and died."

Gone and died. As though Da decided to stop his heart purely to inconvenience Giuseppe's ambitions. *"The worst sort of disservice,"* he'd said. Of course, the circus owner was prone to hyperbole. It was what made him an excellent impresario.

"I understand. I just . . . choked."

"You are not allowed to choke in the ring. You practiced this. Over and over for days."

"I know. I'm sorry." Mabel glanced Lorenzo's way, and her chest tightened. She had never before hurt anyone but herself during an act. "It won't happen again." She hoped.

"Make sure it doesn't. You have been with Manzo Brothers a long time."

"Since I was born." It was her home. A constantly shifting, moving, traveling one, but all she'd ever known.

"People come to see the strongest woman in the world. That woman does not drop skinny clowns. I don't want to lose you, but if you fail another act, I will have no choice."

Mabel went still. Even her breath paused in its journey out of her lungs. "Giuseppe, you can't mean that. What would I do? Where would I go?"

"What else can I do, Mabel?" He threw his hands up, and his drama failed to amuse her. "Six shows. Three days. That is all I can give you. Figure out a way to go on without your father, or you're done."

When he left, she found herself entirely surrounded again.

"Where is Jake?" she asked, allowing herself to be patted and hugged.

"I saw him in the backyard behind wardrobe before we went on." Lorenzo waved over his shoulder. "Practicing."

Once she ducked away from the circle of comfort, it took only minutes to find him. Most of the performers were in the ring or backstage, but Jake Cunningham never stuck around once his acrobatic act ended. Unlike the rest of them, he hated the circus. Mabel assumed he only stayed because he didn't want to return to the United States, where his wife had died in a stunt gone wrong.

She watched him for a few minutes. He was as nimble as a cheetah. As beautiful too.

He flipped into the air from standing, his gaze catching hers as he stuck the landing. "Hello." His brow furrowed. "What's wrong?"

"I dropped Lorenzo."

Jake smacked his hands against his pants and approached. "Is he all right?"

She nodded.

"Are you all right?"

She nodded. Then shook her head. Then covered her face with her hands. "I couldn't do it. I just went weak all over."

"You've been through a lot. Give yourself time."

"I don't have time, Jake. I have six shows. I can't hang around like 190 pounds of dead weight."

His hand found her shoulder and squeezed. "I know you can do this. Everyone knows you can do this." His gaze ricocheted over the dusty area, landing on the wardrobe tent, a turned-over cart, and a clutter of discarded items that would likely not make it to the next city. "Here." He darted toward the pile of junk and rolled out a wheelbarrow ringed with rusting hoops. Setting it on end, he dropped to his knees and braced his elbow against the lid. "Arm-wrestle?" He wiggled his fingers, drawing her across the packed dirt.

Pebbles bit through her tights and nicked her knees as she sank to the ground. She settled her forearm against his, noting their equal size. Flipping around a trapeze and walking on his hands had made Jake strong. But not as strong as her. "You never win."

Not from the moment they'd met—when Da had called for someone to compete in a wrestling match with his daughter. The winner would be given a hundred marks. Jake hadn't eaten in days. He'd been wandering around Germany for weeks, doing odd jobs to support himself, and only wanted a meal.

He ended up with a bruised backside and a job.

"You never know," Jake said. "You'll give me a hundred marks if I do?"

"Sure." They gripped hands, both rough and calloused from their work.

Mabel let him push back. Just a little. Just enough to release the dimples that had every woman in the circus madly in love with him.

And then she twisted her grip and slammed his arm into the wood.

"Aw, I was so close." He rubbed his wrist.

Mabel raised her brows. "You weren't."

"You feel better, though?"

"I do."

"Then I won." He grinned, and she couldn't help but answer him back in kind.

There was no one else she'd rather talk to after failure. No one else who understood the pain of smiling through loss. Jake had years of experience pretending the hurt away, and the crowds never noticed the brokenness beneath the tricks and costumes and sparkle.

"I'm grateful to you, Jake." She had been since he'd joined her on that platform, his eyes widening when he realized the strongman's daughter wasn't like any other woman he'd ever known. He'd gone on to become as close to her father as a son. As close to her as a brother.

"Good. I'm not going anywhere." His eyes danced, and he chuckled. "Except for France, Germany, Italy, Bosnia, and wherever else Giuseppe Manzo decides to take us."

He stood and bent to kiss her head, and she wished they were something less like siblings.

*　*　*

The doll looked nothing like Isabella, her childhood toy, except for having two arms and two legs. It was large, for one—at least four times the size. And it wore rough home-spun the color of October leaves instead of a fancy satin gown and leather slippers. It drew first Mabel's gaze and then her fingers.

She glanced around the performance tent, but no one was around except a handful of men preparing to break everything down before the circus headed to their next destination. Zagreb, she thought.

The doll's cotton dress was torn, its apron dirty. It only had one button eye. The other had been torn away, a few loose threads poking up from the socket like a nightmarish apparition. It had been well loved. How sad to be separated from its owner.

Mabel's thoughts shifted to Isabella, long lost to America. A pang traveled the circumference of her heart, and she wished, for only a moment, that she hadn't given the doll to her mother before she left. But that was awful. Who knew what Maman had faced in her last days? Isabella might have brought her comfort.

Be strong in all you set your hands and heart and eyes toward. Maman's constant refrain tiptoed into Mabel's spirit like the sun in May—a gentle reminder.

She tucked the doll beneath her arm and headed outside. The grass, trampled by a thousand feet, was littered with food wrappers and discarded tickets, and a few straggling towners loitered, hoping for a final glimpse of the made-up clowns or one of the scantily dressed aerialists.

Theirs was a morally sound show, though, and the moment a female performer left the ring, she slipped into a skirt and shirtwaist. Bare legs were free only to prevent tragedy. They weren't meant to titillate.

Wanting to avoid attention, Mabel ducked her head as she passed a throng of men outside the sideshow entrance. She'd learned to make herself as small as possible when not performing. Otherwise she became a target for questions and unwanted advances.

Everyone wanted to meet and touch the giantess. No one cared enough to *know* her, though.

She huffed a sigh as she slipped backyard, where spectators were barred from entering, and, after briefly ducking into one of the tents, made her way toward the line of wagons meant to transport them to the station. Trying to avoid meeting anyone's gaze after her disastrous show, she slid onto an empty bench and fixed her attention on the doll in her lap. A little girl would go to bed bereft of her companion tonight.

As the wagon bumped over the uneven ground, Mabel withdrew the sewing kit she'd pilfered from wardrobe out of her pocket and removed the scissors to trim the grisly looking threads.

"What do you have there?"

Mabel jerked and realized she wasn't alone. Giulia and Imilia, Giuseppe Manzo's daughters, sat beside her. She held up the doll. "I found it discarded in the big top. Looks like it needs a bit of tenderness and care."

"We don't think she is the only one." This from Giulia, who, a few inches taller than her twin and possessing a stronger personality, often took it upon herself to speak for both of them.

Imilia twisted her head to look at Mabel over her shoulder, a band of flesh tying her to Giulia's midsection. "That is true, though you don't have to speak of it if you don't wish."

Giulia rolled her eyes. "She must speak of it. Everyone else is."

"I bungled an act, hurt Lorenzo, and possibly lost my job. What else can be said?" Mabel replaced the scissors and withdrew a needle and card of thread. She pinched together the seam that had split on the doll's dress. "I have to pull it together before Zagreb, or I will have nowhere to go. What am I without the circus? What am I without all of you?"

Imilia forced Giulia to shift so she could reach for Mabel's hand. "You are still Mabel MacGinnis, with or without the circus."

"I have no idea who she is." Mabel brought the doll to her teeth and bit off the thread. She fluffed the skirt, her fingers snagging on the rough fabric. Then she raised her gaze and looked at her friends. "I wasn't strong today. I was weak. I disappointed the audience, Lorenzo, and your father. I disappointed myself."

"Lorenzo would forgive you of murder," Giulia said. "The audience will have already forgotten about it. And our father will be fine. He always rebounds. Like a cat." With slim fingers, she drew whiskers across her cheeks.

The wagon jolted to a stop, and Mabel disembarked. She darted across the station platform and toward the train car, knowing Giulia and Imilia proceeded at a much slower pace. Ducking her head so she didn't knock it against the door, she found herself barreling into Alyona.

"Oh!" The equestrian stumbled backward.

Mabel reached for Alyona's arm, settling her friend upright. "I'm so sorry." Her cheeks flamed, and with a spin, she darted through the car and into the next one. She entered the dining car and sank down at a table, setting the doll atop it and poking at her missing eye.

Moments later, Alyona sat beside her, and Giulia and Imilia took the bench opposite.

"I'm told you are trying to escape us." Alyona touched Mabel's arm. "I hate to tell you this, but you're on a train. There is nowhere to go."

Imilia's brows arched. "And when have you ever been able to escape the nosiness of family?"

Mabel allowed a smile, then dropped her head into her palms. "I don't know if I'm going to be able to complete my act without disaster. And then what? What will I do?" She had nowhere to go. She'd been born to the circus. Had assumed she would spend her life in the circus. It was her family. Everything she'd ever known. And the thought of leaving, of going into the world, put so many knots in her belly that not even scissors could untangle them.

There was not a soul in the world blood-related to Mabel. Not one person who would feel any obligation toward her. She was alone. And but for short excursions outside their winter quarters in Bologna and an annual shopping trip when they encamped near Paris, she never went farther than the next town over. Tents and trains had made up her world. She had no notion how to survive outside them.

With jerky movements, she opened the sewing kit and fished a glass button from it. It slid to the table with a little *clink*. She would fix this doll. Stitch it up, clean it with the sliver of Fels-Naptha soap kept in the women's toilet, and convince Karlotta, the seamstress, to spare a scrap of leather for boots.

"I have always thought I was strong. But it has become clear I'm not. I am nothing without Da."

"Mabel, no one knows what tomorrow brings." Alyona took the button and held it to the doll's face. With quick movements, she lifted the threaded needle and jabbed it into the fabric. "You have been with Manzo Brothers Circus every moment of your life. How could you ever be sure what you want?"

"I have never wanted anything else."

Alyona handed Mabel the doll and stood. "Because you've known nothing else."

"What else is there?" Giulia asked. "Stop speaking nonsense."

Alyona ignored her. "I want you to know—to really *know*—that you are more than this circus. More than your father's daughter. More than your act and strength."

"Of course she is." Imilia gave a nod. "She knows this."

Mabel smiled, but as she packed up the sewing kit, she wondered. If she found herself without an act to prop herself up on, where would she find her strength? For so long she'd leaned on Da, and without him, she felt as battered as the doll in her hands.

CHAPTER

2

JAKE COULD HEAR THE AUDIENCE before he saw it. That's how it always was—the thumping feet, people shouting to one another as they crowded onto wooden benches beneath the tent, candy butchers hawking their confections—*"Eiszapfen! Linzer Augen!"*

Not much changed—from city to city, country to country—but the language. The sweets. Sometimes the dress of the spectators. The words used to approve or not.

There would be a moment, when he pushed aside the canvas curtain separating the ring from backstage, that he forgot how much he hated the circus. How much he hated the performing and pretending and remembering.

It hadn't always been this way. Back when he first started—a horseman in his uncle's wild west show—he'd relished every moment of it. But then he'd moved to New York in search of something bigger. He'd met and married America's sweetest aerialist and joined her in an act that had less to do with horses and more to do with growing his fame . . . and his wife's.

Definitely more to do with growing Charlotte's fame.

Before she died.

Before he defected from Travis and Wells for the excessive delights of France that helped a man forget.

Before he landed in this little Italian circus, wiling away the years as an almost-famous acrobat who much preferred horses to the trapeze.

He looked past the curtain, and his gaze swept the crowd. The clowns were just stepping into the ring—only one, for Manzo Brothers was a small circus, not like the three-ring, multi-tent monstrosities that crisscrossed America's golden prairies. A collective shriek rose up when the children caught sight of the white-painted faces and exaggerated pantomime.

"I can't do this." Mabel's whisper didn't seem to be meant for anyone else's ears, but he stood near her.

He dropped the curtain and answered, "Of course you can. You are the strongest woman in Europe."

She had startled when he spoke, her clear blue eyes going wide. "Only because Giuseppe says it."

Jake dropped a wink. "You're stronger than me, and I'm not exactly a weakling."

Mabel's eyes fell to his bicep, bunching below his rolled-up shirtsleeves, and she took his measure. "I'm just a better wrestler."

"I'll tell you what—you get out there tonight, and I'll talk Giuseppe into letting us work on the trapeze before the second show."

Mabel drew her lower lip between her teeth. She glanced over her shoulder at the curtain and then back at him. She loved practicing the trapeze. She said it helped keep her flexible and graceful, but Jake thought it just made her feel closer to the mother she'd lost years earlier. According to Mabel, Polly MacGinnis had been the loveliest aerialist on the planet.

Of course, Mabel had never seen Charlotte.

"I see what you're doing. . . ."

He crossed his arms over his chest and feigned mock offense. "I'm doing nothing."

"You're trying to get me to believe I'm good enough to go out there and do *alone* the two-person act Da and I performed *together* for years. You're trying to make me forget I froze entirely during the last show and dropped Lorenzo. Jake . . . I'm strong for a woman, but strong enough to fill Da's shoes?" She shook her head and pressed her hands to her belly, fingers tangling in the tartan scarf crisscrossing her torso. Not historically or culturally accurate, but what was a Scottish maiden warrior without some plaid? "I've always struggled with nerves before a show, but they haven't been this bad since Maman left."

The music changed, gaining momentum, and the clowns stumbled through the curtain, jostling Mabel into Jake's chest.

"*Mi dispiace.*" Lorenzo touched his finger to his painted forehead in apology with his good hand. The other was still bandaged from his tumble, albeit in an ostentatious scarf.

Jake took Mabel's arm and pulled her to a quieter corner. Past the two Spanish aerialists making eyes at him—they thought he didn't notice, and that suited him fine. Past an animal handler, leaning wearily against the cage housing his dancing bear. Past Giuseppe, who sat bug-eyed in the middle of it all, calling frantic directions and adding to the chaos.

"I know this is hard. But what else can you do? You can't give up. You have the strength of a hundred warriors in your blood. Your little finger can subdue the wildest beast." He flung his hands in a wide arc. "Your shoulders have carried a dozen women from a burning building, and your thighs . . . well, it is not appropriate to mention a lady's thighs, but I've been told yours have been branded by the lightning of Zeus."

Mabel's face turned an alarming shade of carmine. "Of all the ridiculous things Giuseppe has come up with, that is the most outlandish of all."

"Giuseppe knows what you're capable of. And all that aside, you are capable of this." He nodded toward the curtain. "And you're on."

She took a deep breath and gave her sleeve a gentle pat—an odd habit he'd noticed she indulged in before every performance.

The ringmaster, Giuseppe's nephew Marco, launched into her introduction, and Mabel looked over her shoulder at Jake.

"The strength of a hundred warriors in her blood," he said, and a smile tipped her pretty lips. "Her little finger can subdue the wildest beast."

A wild look entered her eyes, and she took short, shallow breaths.

"Her shoulders once carried a dozen women . . ."

She shook her head, and her eyes filled with tears. He normally left directly after his act, desperate for space and quiet. But Mabel was the only reason he remained in Europe. He'd considered, after Bram's death, returning to his family's ranch in Kansas. But she had no one. And he remembered what that was like.

He cupped her cheek. "Her thighs—"

"I can't do this alone. I can't."

"I'm right here, friend. You are not alone." Jake wrapped his arms around her, and she sagged against him. "You can do this. And I'll be here cheering you on."

A shudder moved across her shoulders, and she inhaled before pulling away. "Trapeze after the show?"

He held up his pinky and joined it with hers. "It's a promise."

She slipped from him to take her place in the ring.

"Promise me," Bram had said, clutching Jake's arm, the words wheezing in his throat. *"She is naïve. Sheltered."*

28

Jake had glanced around their empty train car and knelt beside his friend. *"I promise."*

He would stay as long as Mabel did. He owed it to Bram, who had been somewhat of a surrogate father to him.

Watching her prepare for her first trick, Jake saw a wrinkle marring her smooth forehead when she glanced over her shoulder and searched for him. She took a deep breath at his wave and squatted before the barbell.

"You've got this, Mabel," he murmured.

And she did . . . barely. Her legs shook and her broad back hunched beneath a weight she'd lifted with ease only a few months ago. Jake took a deep breath and allowed it to settle in his lungs. Stage fright and lack of confidence had always been her Achilles' heel. He hoped it wouldn't be her downfall.

Three pretty contortionists tugged at ropes hooked around a cannon and dragged it into the ring. Jake's stomach pinched. He hated this trick, but it was a popular one. No female since the great strongwoman Minerva had been able to accomplish it—until Mabel. He watched as she drew on leather gloves to protect her hands from the impossible catch she would replicate two dozen times and forced his gaze to remain steady upon her despite the churning, shrieking memories. She would look for him, trying to find comfort in his presence.

One of the contortionists made a show of attempting to haul a twenty-pound ball into the mouth of the cannon. She wiped her brow and pressed her hands to her knees in an exaggerated huff.

The audience laughed, then grew silent when a large clown lumbered over and heaved the cannonball up and into the cannon. Another contortionist lit the fuse—false and only meant to increase the theatre—and plugged her ears. The ball shot forward, and the crowd surged to their feet.

Mabel caught it. Set it at her feet. Then she caught another. And another.

The air trapped in Jake's chest—had he been holding it since her act began?—tumbled free from his nose and lips in a hard sigh. She would be all right.

But then, on the thirteenth shot, Mabel tripped over one of the balls ringing her and landed hard on the ground. The cannonball she'd just caught flung into the air and fell. Mabel covered her face with her arms, and it slammed against her forearm before bouncing to the ground and clanging against another.

Silence fell, and the echo of it filled the tent.

Jake surged forward, but Giuseppe grabbed his shoulder and yanked him back. "Leave her. It will only make things worse if you run out there and play the hero."

He stayed put only because of the truth in Giuseppe's statement. He wouldn't bring more embarrassment on Mabel. His gaze settled on the gentle rise and fall of her chest. *One, two, three . . .*

Finally she slid her arms from her face, pushed against the ground with flat palms, and stood, her shoulders rounded.

Jake heaved a breath. "She's all right."

But when she looked at him, he could see she was not all right. An ache lodged in his throat as she trudged from the ring, exiting the far side of the tent and abandoning the rest of her act.

"She's done." Giuseppe's words dropped into the silence, heavy with resigned determination. "What use is such a weak strongwoman?"

* * *

"I have a fantastic idea." Giuseppe paced in front of Mabel, back and forth, back and forth, until she wanted to pick him up and set him in a chair. "It will give you the chance to stay with us."

"You just told me I could no longer continue my act." Mabel

could hardly wrap her mind around it. She couldn't even conceive of life outside the circus.

"You don't have"—Giuseppe offered a long-suffering sigh and turned his lips into an exaggerated frown—"dynamism alone. Your act worked because of the interaction between you and your father. Without him . . ." He held up his palms.

"I am not enough."

He gave a sad shake of his head. "And you keep making mistakes. Last time, Lorenzo was hurt. This time, you. What next?"

"I'm fine, Giuseppe."

He poked her arm, and Mabel jerked away with a hiss, the hematoma still tender. She sighed and rubbed her eyes. It had been a long day. A new city. Two shows. Being fired. Being offered a job?

"Giuseppe, please just speak plainly. No theatrics. No metaphors. Just tell me what you're thinking."

He gave her a coy smile. "Now, where is the fun in that? Come with me. Why *tell* you when I can *show* you?"

What choice did Mabel have but to humor him? Whatever it was—and she had no doubt it was something at least a little shocking—she would have to agree to it. She had no other option. Giuseppe held her future in his indefatigable hands.

Numbness stole through her body, nipping at muscle and bone. She couldn't feel her biceps tighten. Couldn't feel her calves stretch. Could hardly feel the ground beneath her feet as she followed the circus owner to the sideshow tent.

Her entire life had been built around her ability to beat her body into submission. To make it do as she willed. And now it betrayed her. Refused to respond to even the most basic commands. *Breathe. Lift. Recover.*

"Here we are." He swept aside the canvas with a flourish.

"Why are we here?" Mabel glanced around the empty tent. The show had ended an hour ago, and even now workmen were tearing down the big top. But then her gaze snagged on one display, a gaslight filling the space with its flickering yellow glow. The man sitting on a chair tipped his head toward her. "Mr. Carson?"

Giuseppe clapped his hands with barely suppressed glee and waved the man over.

"Miss MacGinnis." Lloyd Carson, the Wild Man of Buyan, had a delicious voice, low and smooth, with a tony British accent. Mabel hadn't spoken much to him—he'd only joined their circus two years earlier and mostly kept to himself—but she'd heard he was the youngest son of a gentleman and once an attorney.

She offered him a smile, careful not to spend an extra moment staring at his tattooed face and chest. She knew what it was like to be studied as though she were a slide beneath a microscope.

"Well?" Giuseppe clapped Mr. Carson on the back. "I asked Lloyd to stay and demonstrate how you can remain with Manzo Brothers Circus. It will be new. Sure to capture everyone's attention."

Mabel looked between the men and frowned. "I don't understand. Is Mr. Carson going to join my act?"

Giuseppe shook his head. "No. No, you are going to join his."

Mabel laughed, but Giuseppe's expression remained unchanged, and her heart flipped. "You're serious? You want me to become part of the sideshow?"

"Yes. You will become the Lost Princess of Amazonia. Imagine"—he swept his hands from the top of her head to her feet—"covered in artwork. Turned into a living painting. Made a—"

"You want me tattooed? That's your brilliant idea?" Mabel couldn't help but look at Mr. Carson now. She took note of the symbols scrolling his face, the portraits on his chest, the geometric shapes filling every bit of his torso and arms. And even though she'd been stared and snickered at, she recoiled from him. She knew what it was like to be different, but the thing that made her stand out wasn't something she'd chosen. It had been gifted to her.

"A single strongwoman who cannot draw a crowd does not have a future with Manzo Brothers, but a towering, tattooed beauty?" Giuseppe spread his hands, encompassing both Mr. Carson and Mabel. "Married to our very own Wild Man from Buyan?"

"Married?" Mr. Carson spun around at the word. "You didn't say—"

Giuseppe waved away his concern. "Two is always better than one. We have two female aerialists, two animal trainers, two elephants, two hairy ladies. We had two strong people, and together they entertained the crowds. Alone"—he shrugged—"it has not worked."

"I don't think I want to do this. My father wouldn't have liked it." Mabel glanced at Mr. Carson and raised her brows. "And it looks very painful."

"It is." Mr. Carson's thumb found a vibrant snake circling his wrist. "But not as painful as other types of scars."

"We would spread out the inking over a few months," Giuseppe said. "You can take your time."

"If you are willing to give me time for this, why aren't you willing to give me time to grieve my father and reinvent the act?"

"I will answer, but it's a hard thing to hear, Mabel. As a strongwoman who is no longer supernaturally strong, you have no future. Not with Manzo Brothers. Not with anyone. It is a shame. The Bridge of Zeus was going to be spectacular." He shook his head.

The reminder caused Mabel's throat to tighten painfully. She and Da had worked on the trick all winter. They were to set it up as normal, but just when the audience was expecting Bram to arrange himself on the support and allow the bridge to be settled upon his torso and knees, Mabel would take his place. And then the parade would begin, eight horsemen–strong with Bram at the helm, riding across the board held aloft by Mabel's strength.

Giuseppe gave her a paternal pat on the shoulder. "As part of the Wild Painted Couple, you could continue on in the circus. It won't matter if you are strong or young, you will have something no one else does. You will be a curiosity."

"And if I don't do this?" Mabel asked, already knowing the answer. Giuseppe Manzo knew how to run a circus and how to profit off people. He also knew she had nowhere else to go.

"That isn't an option, is it?" He said it softly, not with pity but with compassion. With a kind of aware benevolence that told Mabel he had come up with this not only for him, but for her as well. He wasn't a bad man.

Only a showman. One motivated by the spectacle. Only a man who valued pageantry would take the tragic circumstance of his daughters' condition and birth a great, traveling city that entertained the masses.

Mabel's eyes closed, but behind her lids she could still see Mr. Carson's tattoos, whirling and twisting and blurring the line between man and deviant. But Mr. Carson was well-spoken and educated. Kind. Why had he chosen to do this terrible thing to his body? Why had he chosen to erase his skin and become a circus sideshow?

She opened her eyes. "May I have a few minutes with Mr. Carson alone, please?"

Giuseppe rubbed his chin and looked between them but finally ducked from the tent.

The lamps flickered, casting writhing shadows that made the animals and figures on Mr. Carson's body dance.

"Do you ever regret it?" she asked, reaching a finger for the dragon wrapping his torso. She yanked her arm back when she realized what she was about to do.

He offered a small smile and his arm. "It doesn't change the way my skin feels." She swept her fingers over the designs and drew her brows together at the puckering. "I don't regret it because I had no choice. What you're feeling are burns, not tattoos. Over half my body was scarred when I tried to save my wife and children from a fire in our London house. They didn't survive. I did." He sighed. "Of a kind."

That Mr. Carson could smile and speak with so much kindness, even in the midst of his pain, attested to his character. Mabel hoped she could one day take all she'd lost—both her parents, so unexpectedly—and turn it into something good.

"No one could stand to look at me, you see. I'd already lost my family. I lost my job. I lost nearly all of my friends. My parents and brothers wanted to secrete me away in our Yorkshire manor. At first, I covered the worst of the scars with images of my children, Ada, Harriet, and Edmund." He pointed to each of the three children in turn. "Then my wife, Sa—" His mouth clamped down on her name as though unwilling to share it with the world. "I couldn't stand seeing my skin, so I covered it. And then I ran away to the circus." He gave her a wry smile. "I heard your father did the same."

"He did," Mabel whispered. To escape an abusive alcoholic father.

"No, I don't regret it. There are so many other things to regret. And though I will forever miss my family, I have found a home in Giuseppe's circus. He's given me a way to support myself. A way to remain my own man, not beholden to the fears of my parents and brother. He's given me friends and purpose. But I can't tell you what to do. You must make that choice yourself."

Mabel stared at the tips of her boots peeking from beneath the dark green corduroy skirt of her trotting suit. It was a fashionable ensemble ordered from her favorite dressmaker in Paris. And expensive. Giuseppe hadn't mentioned a pay cut, but there would surely be one. And the position would be permanent. There would never be an escape from it.

Mr. Carson's mellifluous voice pierced her pondering. "It isn't a bad life, Miss MacGinnis."

She gave a brief smile. "Mabel, please."

"Mabel. And Giuseppe is correct, a tattooed couple would draw much more interest than a single man."

"More than the World's Strongest Woman?" She glanced around the tent and saw the alcoves and daises and chairs meant to display human oddities. She wouldn't be known for her strength, for what she did, but for someone else's handiwork, for what she looked like. Could she find purpose in that?

A trio of workmen entered and startled at the sight of them. "Time to break it down."

Mr. Carson let her go ahead.

She nodded her thanks at the entrance. "Thank you, Mr. Carson, for your thoughts on the matter. I may well be spending a significant amount of time with you from here on out. Giuseppe says we're meant to be 'married.'" She tipped her head. "Are you all right with that?"

He shrugged, sending the leopard on his chest leaping. "I suppose it doesn't matter. It won't be real."

"No, you're right. It's the circus, after all. Nothing ever is."

CHAPTER 3

ISABELLA MOREAU bent at the waist and gently pulled her pink fleshlings up from knee to thigh. She pointed her toe, clad in a silk slipper, and stretched out the cramp in her calf.

She seemed to need longer to recover now after a show. More than the few hours between the afternoon and evening performances allowed. Her legs and arms ached, and her hot skin cried out for the cold bath she would take before the dressing tent was torn down and loaded onto the train.

Where were they today? Somewhere between Travis and Wells Circus's winter quarters in Indiana and New York City, where they would spend the month of May and part of June.

A collective gasp filled the tent, and Isabella knew to look up, toward the crisscrossing wires and ropes filling the space above the rings. She knew because in every show they'd had this season—more than a dozen of them—Annette Aubert had performed the same trick. And had gotten the same response.

Annette Aubert, their new trapeze star. Fearless and lovely

and as French as a hot dog at Coney Island. Annette was actually Mary Williams, daughter of a Kentucky butcher. Not that Isabella had an issue with taking a new name. She had too, after all. Although she actually was French.

But it wasn't the name. It was—Isabella watched Annette perfectly execute a quadruple somersault, catching the hands of one of the male performers—it was envy. Or maybe fear. Probably a mix of both.

Her career was in a downward spiral. She'd made it to the top, but age had a way of dragging everything—and everyone—down. At fifty, she'd spent nearly her entire life in the circus. She didn't know anything else. Didn't want to either. She wasn't good for much but flinging herself through the air.

From her place just inside the dressing room entrance, Isabella smiled grimly. No doubt she'd die tragically. Falling from the ceiling while attempting an iron jaw, perhaps. Or being shot not quite far enough from a cannon and missing the trapeze.

She sobered in memory of such an incident. She hadn't climbed into a cannon since that day. No one had.

"You are staring with so much intensity, I'm sure you will burn a hole in the canvas." Robert Pedersen, longtime manager of Travis and Wells Circus, came to stand beside her. "Will we have a new act?"

His question was said in jest, she could tell, but she heard the hope behind it. "If I could shoot fire from my eyes, would billposters plaster images of me across towns and cities all over the country again? Would the name Isabella Moreau be on everyone's lips once more?" Oh, she sounded bitter. She wasn't, though. Merely tired. She'd given the circus everything.

And it had exacted a high price from her. Too high, she now recognized.

"I'm sorry," Robert said. He touched her arm, but she drew away. "I will do what I can, but you must do something. Come up with something new or exciting or . . . I don't know, more than what you've been doing."

"I'm old, Robert. I can only give what my body is able to."

He was quiet, which wasn't like him. Normally he would encourage her. Say something that would send her heart back into her chest where it belonged, if not soaring. She usually didn't need soaring from him. She was perfectly capable of soaring on her own. But right now? She glanced at him, took in the jaw that used to be so strong but had softened in recent years. Hadn't they all? She watched his throat work as he tried to say words neither of them would believe.

"We are friends, aren't we?" She stepped nearer so the performers filling the hall behind them couldn't hear her words. There was so little privacy in the circus. It was, on a grander scale, like a large family. Spilling into each other's space and stealing quiet moments.

"Of course. We have been for ages."

She smiled at the memories. They had grown up together, alongside Travis and Wells. Both their families had worked for the circus. Her mother as a washerwoman after Papa's death in the war, and his parents as acrobatic clowns from Denmark. Robert had himself spent time flipping around the ring with them until he'd proven more adept at business than performance.

"Then please be honest with me," she said.

He scuffed his foot against the trampled grass, and the contours of his face seemed to sag into his neck even more. He had been a handsome man once, possibly the most handsome of her acquaintance. Now she could hardly see even a shadow of who he used to be. She pressed her fingers against the loose skin beneath her own neck. Life was cruel.

"Jerry is only keeping you because you've been with us so long. And because of your friendship with Paul." He stumbled a little on Paul's name. He knew she had been a sight more than friends with Jerry Wells's son. But Paul was long gone, and her problem was very much present.

She took a long swallow and gave a short nod. She thought she'd been prepared for it—hearing the thing she'd caught whispers of and knew was coming. But the words pummeled her. They stole her breath and stopped her heart.

"You're almost on, Isabella," Robert said.

"Don't call me that." It came out more like a reproof than a plea, but she didn't have time to fix it. To fix anything. She just knew she hated the name in that moment. It wasn't *her*. Not now. Not when she was losing everything she had been.

Isabella ran toward the center ring with light steps, a smile on her lips as bright and false as the alias she'd chosen all those years ago. Isabella was exotic. Beautiful. Strong and capable and a little mysterious. Isabella wasn't dead like Polly. Names meant something, and right now she couldn't claim Isabella.

Ahead, a trapeze waited for her. Above her, the three Danó sisters, who actually *were* Hungarian and could claim their surname, waited for the music to signal the beginning of their act from daises high in the air.

They were part of her act now that she wasn't fit to have her own. While they rehearsed over the winter, Isabella had come to enjoy their vibrant chatter and energy. They were young—younger even than the daughter she hadn't seen in almost twenty years—and slightly awed to be performing with the great Isabella Moreau.

Even if "great" was no longer used to advertise her.

She took a moment to wave at the crowd. Then she reached for the bar that would send her skyward. There would be ten minutes of unrestrained joy. The feeling of being capable. Strong. On top of the world. She would fly and remember when that had been enough. The glitter and fame from those airborne moments when the crowd adored her and no one could reach her had padded the rest of her life—all the minutes and hours and days—with layers of down. They had softened the grief and loneliness and missing. So much missing.

But it wasn't enough anymore. Now she only had the ten minutes. Once her feet touched earth, once she no longer flipped in the air and flung herself across space, she would be washed again in her failings. She would see the darkness creeping around the bright edges of her life and wonder how long it would be before she was consumed again.

The bar jerked, and her slippers left the ground. She inhaled deeply and looked up, centering herself on the tent roof. The crisscrossing wires. The next trick.

With a stiffening of her core, she flipped her legs around and around. A collective gasp swept through the tent, and her smile softened into something real.

For now, she would focus on this. These ten minutes.

❋ ❋ ❋

After the evening show, when everyone had joined in and broken down the tent city, packed it all into boxes and crates, and carted it along with the animals to the train that would race through the night toward their next stop, Isabella sat on her bunk. She stared across the small room she shared with Rowena—private, thanks to Isabella's fame and Rowena's longtime popularity as the country's only female clown—at the trunk tucked beneath the table in the corner. She thought of the box shoved into the bottom of it like a forgotten toy. Except Isabella had never forgotten. It took up more space in her thoughts than anything else ever had. Ever would.

She could normally ignore it, filling her head with bits of routine and conversations and the crowd's awe like candy floss. But facing the inevitability of loss had dissolved all the sugar and sweetness so there was nothing left but remembering.

And the little box in her trunk.

Isabella launched herself from the bunk and reached for it

before sense could stop her. She yanked it forward with more force than necessary, and it bumped into her knees. Sitting back on her heels, she stared at it, her hands caressing the worn edges like a lover after a prolonged absence. She'd carried it with her since leaving Europe. From train to train, city to city. Never opening it. Rowena had accepted its presence with only passing mentions of their "third bunkmate, quiet but a solid sort." She'd cast it sidelong glances full of curiosity, but such was the palpable anguish surrounding it that she'd kept her questions to herself.

With a girding breath, Isabella flipped open the lid.

The past unfolded before her. She dragged the trunk across the floor, bumping it over the rag rug and unsettling the wrapped package on top. Her breath caught when a little leg poked out, its black leather shoe tapping the wood, and she reached for it. The paper, brittle and yellowing, crumpled beneath her fingers and dropped flakes like kindling in a fire. With a gentle sigh, she sank to the mattress of her bunk and unwrapped her namesake.

Isabella. She ran a finger over the doll's tiny face—rosebud lips, paint-stained cheeks, and wide, staring eyes. Over the tuft of blonde hair—like straw after all these years. It had once belonged to her mother, a young child in France displaced by the chaos of the February Revolution. Isabella herself had eschewed the doll, believing it unimportant in the face of all the other things she had to accomplish—namely besting every other aerialist in training.

But Mabel's breast had contained a maternal heart. From the moment Maman had mailed it across the ocean, it became the best-loved doll in all of Europe.

Her daughter had tucked the toy into Isabella's sleeve before she left Italy. Left Manzo Brothers Circus. Left her family. Mabel had given it to her, believing she would see her doll again. See her mother again.

Grief strangled Isabella.

She set the doll aside and shoved her hand down into the trunk. When she found the enamel cigar box, she slipped her fingers beneath its lid. She could almost smell the woodsy scent of the cigars Bram had favored. For a moment her lashes settled together, and she thought she heard his boisterous laugh and felt his large hand against her back, pulling her toward him. She could almost hear him whisper, "*Ah, lass*," before taking her mouth. Her heart. Her life.

"Bram," she whispered, and directly on the heels of it, another name. Another love. Another grief. "Paul." She pressed her head against the trunk's rough edge, and her fingers searched the box, punishing her with memories. Silk and paper and a linen handkerchief hiding a ring of gold.

She jerked her hand back and withdrew, instead, another box—this one having once contained chocolates. Sweetness still clung to the cardboard. The lid didn't want to come off, but her fingers were strong after decades of gripping bars and ropes. Inside, she found a crown of flowers. They held no scent, but the tissue-thin petals slammed a memory into Isabella's thorax, and she dropped the ring of gladiolus.

She remembered that day when the sun seemed just a bit brighter than normal. Bright enough to sear through the veil. Bright enough to burn away the tendrils of melancholy that had held her captive since Mabel's birth. Bright enough to call them from the circle of tents and run, her daughter's little hand tucked into hers, down a dirt road and through a fallow field swept by wildflowers.

Behind an abandoned stone farmhouse, they had woven circlets of gladiolus and thyme, and Mabel's laughter, her shining eyes and the warmth of her sturdy body, had sent Isabella soaring.

But of course it hadn't lasted. It never did.

It was years before she finally felt free from the depressive thoughts. By then she had lost everything that would have made fighting against it worth the effort.

Isabella replaced the flower wreath—carefully, not wanting the petals to turn to dust like the paper—and reached for a stack of letters. These she didn't open. She remembered every word and knew she wasn't strong enough to experience them again. So she just counted, flipping through them as though they were a deck of cards. Thirty-seven. Eighteen from her daughter and nineteen from her husband—the final one a command.

You want America so badly, take it. But know you chose that over us. Do not write. Do not return. Mabel has not handled your abandonment well. She has become consumed by need for you and will not perform, so I've told her you died. You may as well have.

She had screamed when she read that. But in the end, he refused to come to America, and she refused to go back to the life that was only darkness pierced by pinpricks of light.

She wondered now, though, if they could have found some other place—an in-between—that would have saved them.

The door flung open, and Rowena filled their berth. She was beside Isabella in a moment. She never needed words to know. Never expected explanation or story. It seemed a compass rested within her, and she knew—always had—when she was needed.

Isabella sank against her friend, her chin tucked into the dependable folds of Rowena's neck. Her conversation with Robert brushed her conscious and then slammed against the reality of her life.

"I have lost everything—everyone—to the circus. My husband and daughter. My mother. It consumed them. It has ruined my body. And still I love it. Still I want it." She pulled back and stared, knowing Rowena would understand. Knowing Rowena's story had twisted and turned and dumped her in this place as well. The train was full of people who worked through trauma in rings and beneath tents and before hundreds of gaping spectators. "I might lose it. I might lose the only thing I have left."

Rowena took the letters from Isabella's fingers and smoothed them out before laying them back in the box. With infinite care, she began wrapping the doll back in its crumbling mantle, but Isabella made a little sound in her throat. She didn't want to hide it again. She would lose it. She lost everything.

Rowena slipped the doll into Isabella's palm and cupped her own hands around them. "Is it time to tell me about our third bunkmate? What happened, Polly?"

Hearing her real name unleashed it. Saying aloud her daughter's name made it impossible to stop. "Mabel."

"Your daughter?"

Isabella nodded. "I nearly died. More than once."

CHAPTER

4

A WEEK AFTER GIUSEPPE made his offer, Mabel wandered the circus grounds somewhere outside of Graz. The day was dreary, the clouds having mourned overnight, and the ground beneath her boots was spongy.

With every step, the slurping, sucking mud clung to her heels as though begging she reconsider. "I have no choice," she murmured. What else could she do? She'd some education. Could read and write and had a propensity for sums. But nothing had prepared her for life outside the circus. *This* circus.

Da hadn't meant to die so young. He was as strong as an ox, so who could have known a weak heart beat beneath his chest? Maybe it had been broken those years ago when he'd learned of Maman's death.

Mabel tried to remember the way her mother had looked. Smelled. Felt. But there was only an impression of gentle beauty. The fragrance of gladiolus woven into a crown. Air thrumming in her ears as she swung above the crowd, reaching for Maman's hands as their trapeze bars drew close.

Her mother had been gone for two years when she died. Long enough for Mabel to have mostly forgotten what it was like to have one. Not long enough to forget that Maman had chosen to stay in New York even after Grandmother's health improved. Had chosen not to return as she'd promised.

When Mabel arrived at the women's dressing tent, Karlotta was seated at a stool, deftly stitching the seam of a costume. "You're here early. I'm nearly finished."

"Giuseppe says I'm to wear this while . . . going through the procedure?"

"That way the tattooist knows the areas to begin working on." The needle froze, and Karlotta squinted up at her. "Your father would not be happy about this. Are you sure you want to do it?"

"I have no other choice."

"Have you spoken to anyone about it? Alyona? Giulia? Imilia? That handsome acrobat you hang around?"

Mabel's cheeks flushed. "I don't 'hang around' Jake all that often."

Karlotta snorted, set down her needle, and snapped the fabric out of its folds. "Well, I suppose you know what you're doing." She stood and held up the costume. "Truth be told, I'm glad your father can't see this bit of madness Giuseppe wants you clothed in."

Her stomach twisting in knots, Mabel crossed the tent and reached for the fringe dangling from a circle of pale green satin. "You can't be serious. Where is the rest of it?"

"For your breasts," Karlotta said, lifting something that looked as though it had been cut from the top of a corset. She thrust the bit of fringed nothingness toward Mabel. "And bottom."

Mabel swallowed and held the piece against her skirt. It

wasn't much more revealing than what the aerialists wore—except the entire costume was missing a middle—but it was so much *less* than she was used to wearing. Of course, as a strongwoman, she was meant to show her muscles. Her calves and arms and shoulders. But this would show nearly everything.

Karlotta gave a long sigh and shook her head. "You're to be entirely tattooed except your feet, hands, face, and anywhere this covers. Get dressed. The tattooist is waiting."

Giuseppe hadn't spared any expense. Mr. Szabó, having spent a year working beneath the famed American tattooist Samuel O'Reilly, commanded a tidy sum. It would take months and months of work for her skin to become covered enough that she could begin her life as a sideshow oddity. Mr. Szabó's train tickets alone, back and forth between his home in Debrecen and wherever Manzo Brothers set their tent, would indebt Mabel for a year.

She had to do this. If she didn't, not only would she have no way to support herself, but Giuseppe would lose an immense amount of money.

So, with cold fingers, Mabel undid the buttons of her jacket. She forced down the nausea threatening to spill into her throat and stepped out of her skirt. So many layers, meant to safeguard her from lewd stares and accusations of immorality. Did the shedding of them mean she could no longer claim that protection? So much of a person was wrapped up in what they wore. What if someone wore not much at all?

Karlotta helped her into the costume, and Mabel forced her arms down to her sides when she wanted to cross them over her stomach. Tears pricked her eyes when a cloak was laid over her, and she wrapped it around herself, fingers knotting in the wool.

"For your walk to the tent Mr. Szabó has been furnished."

Karlotta's hands were warm on Mabel's shoulders, and she resisted the urge—the need—to sink against them. Despite

48

having spent most of her life motherless, Mabel could recognize when one was required. But this was her choice. Her life. Comfort was a fruitless thing.

She left her clothing in a heap on Karlotta's table and walked to the tent, eyes straight ahead. All around her, the sounds of a circus being built up from the ground clanged, and she let it crowd out the doubts and fear and fill her mind until she knew there was nothing else she could do if she wanted to remain a part of it all.

Mr. Szabó was not what she expected. When she ducked into the tent, she stopped short, thinking the man before her was an assistant of some sort. But he rushed forward with an energy bordering on manic, his black hair puffing about his head like an overexcited raven, and pumped her hand.

"Hello. Hello. I am Endre Szabó."

He was a small man. Wiry everywhere, from his limbs to his hair. Even the eyebrows leaping about his face like twin trapeze artists. And young. Not any older than Mabel's twenty-eight years.

The only furniture in the tent were two ladder-back chairs and a table set with a black case. This Mr. Szabó scurried toward and opened with a flourish. "It's Charlie Wagner's tattoo machine. He trained with Samuel O'Reilly before I did." He looked at her, an oddly sincere expression on his face. "O'Reilly worked on twelve—*twelve!*—tattooed ladies, including Mrs. Emma DeBurgh."

Mabel made an appreciative sound in her throat. He smiled and lifted the device, and she swallowed at the sight of its long needle.

"Emma DeBurgh was covered everywhere but her face," Mr. Szabó said, his animated brows jumping. "I don't believe she was anywhere near as strong as you."

Mabel tore her gaze from the machine and set her jaw. She knew pain. She'd pushed her body past what most would say were the limits of endurance. She'd pulled muscles, twisted limbs, bruised skin. She'd broken a few ribs. Tattoos were only skin-deep. And, besides, nothing could ever be as painful as losing her parents.

Mr. Szabó motioned her toward him with a wave. "Take off your cloak, please, and let me see what I have to work with."

Mabel's chest tightened, and her ears burned. Da had always laughed when she grew embarrassed, her face turning as red as an apple. But it couldn't be helped. She'd never felt so exposed in her entire life, and she'd spent a lifetime wearing revealing clothing. But always with a purpose—to keep from tangling in weights and hurting herself—and always with her torso covered and fleshlings keeping the skin of her legs from view.

She blew all the air trapped in her lungs from her lips with a great puff, then relaxed her stiff fingers. Mr. Szabó caught the cloak, and his gaze swept her from head to toe. She squeezed her eyes shut.

"Magnificent," he said. "This is a grand canvas for my art."

Oh, she would die. Could one die from mortification? Surely she was near it. The pulse at her temples throbbed, sending blood rushing to her face. She opened her eyes. "Where will you start?"

"I think the outer thighs. It is one of the least painful places, and the area is large enough for my initial designs. I had thought to use your abdomen, but I like the idea of saving that space for something a bit grander."

Mabel glanced down and flexed her quadriceps. They bunched beneath the fringed skirt, and she hated them. She wanted leaner limbs—shorter ones, too—so that she could have continued training with her mother and become an aerialist. They were interesting enough by themselves.

"All right." She sat in the chair. There was no use wishing for something that could never happen. She'd learned that long ago.

Mr. Szabó took the other seat and filled the hollow needle with ink from a pot. He flipped the switch, and it came to life with a whir. Mabel braced herself against the seat back and clenched her hands together in her lap. She was so stiff, she didn't even jump when Mr. Szabó placed his palm against her thigh, his fingers making chilly imprints on her skin. No one had ever touched her in such a softly intimate way, though, and her eyes filled.

She blinked the tears away. There was no room for sentimentality now.

"I will do earth on this limb and sea on the other." Mr. Szabó tapped her leg with his pointer finger. "What is your favorite flower?"

Mabel answered immediately, without forethought. "Gladiolus. The Italian variety. They are delicate and vibrant pink." Maman, between her spells of melancholy, had taken Mabel hiking one day when she was six. There weren't many moments Mabel had felt her mother was entirely present, but that was one of them. Maman had met her eyes and laughed and told her stories of growing up in the American circus. And she'd woven wildflowers in Mabel's hair, the gladiolus dancing around her head like a coronet come to life.

The needle bobbed like the one on Karlotta's sewing machine, and Mabel watched, entranced, even as pain scratched itself over her skin. She drew a whistle of air through her teeth. But then the ink began to deposit, and her floral memory took shape. "Oh. How lovely it is."

Mr. Szabó smiled up at her. "I will do a cluster here, you see." He traced his finger down her leg. "And then—"

Mr. Szabó was tossed from the chair, his tattoo machine clattering to the floor.

❊ ❊ ❊

The moment Mabel jumped to her feet, his name spitting from her lips like a curse, Jake realized the state of her dress. Or, rather, undress.

51

"What are you doing?" he asked, his gaze bouncing over her shoulder. Bram would be enraged at his daughter sitting there with a strange little man's hands all over her.

"I could ask you the same thing." She glared at him, then hurried over the flattened grass floor, hand outstretched. "Mr. Szabó, are you all right?"

"Yes. Fine." The man sat on his rear, knees poking toward the ceiling, and scratched the back of his neck. "Believe it or not, this isn't the first time I've found myself tossed so unceremoniously to the ground."

Heat swept Jake's face, and he cleared his throat as he met the man's eyes. "I'm very sorry. That was uncalled for."

Mr. Szabó, on his feet now, lifted his machine from the floor and set it on a small table. "Miss MacGinnis, should I return in a few moments after you've had an opportunity to speak with the gentleman?"

Mabel returned to her seat. "No. Please continue your work."

"What are you doing?" Jake repeated.

"I'm ensuring my future." Mabel fixed her attention straight ahead.

Mr. Szabó approached cautiously, his soft steps and darting eyes grating Jake's nerves. This was his nearest friend's daughter. He'd watched her grow from an unsure, awkward girl into a lovely woman, and he'd been tasked to protect her. What had Bram been thinking? Jake could hardly care for himself, and without the structure of the circus—awaken, eat, perform, eat, perform, eat, sleep, repeat—he would likely be sitting in some decaying Greek tavern. That was where he'd been heading before Bram and Mabel had stepped in and became family.

Jake stepped to the side as Mr. Szabó flipped a switch and his machine whirred to life. But when the tattooist's palm gently slid atop Mabel's thigh, Jake growled.

"Enough, Jake. If you cannot handle watching, you should

leave." There was a warning in Mabel's tone. But also a whisper of . . . doubt?

"Your father wouldn't like this."

"He isn't here, though, so whether or not he would approve is irrelevant."

Mr. Szabó put the pen-like apparatus to Mabel's skin, so pale and unblemished that the blue-green of her veins made a map upon her thighs, and bent over it. A flower. It was small and innocent—even a bit pretty—but Jake had seen Mr. Carson. The man was covered neck to ankle in ink, and he couldn't imagine such a thing for Mabel, who radiated wholesome beauty and who could only tolerate the stares of others when she was demonstrating her strength in the ring.

Jake knelt beside her. "You didn't even tell me about this." She told him everything. They'd been as close as siblings for years. Closer, if one was comparing their relationship to Jake and his brother's.

"It's my choice to make."

"I know. I know. But have you thought it through?"

"Yes." She turned to him, and her eyes were wet, her lashes clumped into spikes. "I have no other choice. Giuseppe made that clear. My single strongperson act isn't enough."

"It doesn't sound as though you *want* to do this."

"Of course I don't want to." She shrugged. "There have been many things I've had to do despite not wanting to."

"There has to be another way, Mabel. Just think on it. Please."

"To what purpose? I have no other choice. Nowhere else to go. And it won't be a bad life. It will be familiar, at least." She leaned back in the chair and let her head fall so that she stared up at the ceiling. "Giuseppe has offered me a solution."

Jake gripped the chair's arm as Mr. Szabó refilled the machine with ink, then patted at the pinpricks of blood seeping around the edges of the flower with a snowy white handkerchief. Bram's memory goaded him onward. "It's such a permanent solution, though. Can you not give it a day or two? Give me time to think of something else."

"It won't change anything. A woman without a choice is at the mercy of the opportunities offered her. I have no other."

"Please." There was a note of desperation in his voice. He couldn't hide it. But Bram had done so much for him. Had saved him, really. Jake would honor his friend in protecting his daughter. Even if she didn't think she needed it.

Mr. Szabó tipped his head and stared at Jake for a moment, then cleared his throat and set the machine aside. "There is no hurry. I'm here all week. And I would never want to tattoo someone who wasn't absolutely certain." He gave Mabel a gentle look. "It *is* very permanent. Maybe you should think about it some more?"

With a sigh, Mabel straightened and looked between the two of them. "Fine. One day." There was a flicker in her gaze, a gentle release of breath, that suggested she was not as put out as she pretended to be.

Jake would do anything to make sure she didn't feel bullied into something that wasn't entirely her choice, for a career in the circus wasn't worth such a sacrifice.

※ ※ ※

Mabel awoke to the sound of a dull thump and a muttered curse.

"This can't stay in here, Mabel. Mabel? Are you awake?" A huff, and then the woman stomped from the virgin car.

Mabel turned over on her bunk. She'd slept late—not only because she'd no show to work, but because she'd spent half the night staring at the underside of the bunk above her, tracing the scabbing gladiolus round and round. She was alone now. No snuffling or snoring or performers dressing in haste as they rushed to make breakfast.

The trunk that filled the narrow space between the car's

two rows of bunks drew her attention. She would have to go through it, if only to prevent another stubbed toe and bruised shin. With a groan, she flopped to her back.

She could do it now. Should do it now.

There was nothing waiting for her but Mr. Szabó and his spirited machine. Despite Jake's insistence that he could conjure up some realistic way for her to stay with the circus without making her a tattooed lady.

She swept her legs from the mattress and sank to the floor. With tentative fingers, she reached for the flat lid of her father's trunk and tried to feel his touch. To sense his presence. She was so very lonely. So very *alone*.

"I'm sorry, Da," she murmured as she lifted the lid. "I'm sorry I couldn't do it."

She had ruined their act. Failure was her legacy.

Inside the trunk, she found a compartmented tray. Two spaces held shoes, and the others were filled with his pocket watch, wallet, and clutch of receipts. Inside the wallet, she found two months' worth of pay.

Mabel removed the tray to reveal her father's belongings— a few sets of clothing, a clumsy painting she'd made of their winter quarters in Bologna the year she turned ten, and his family Bible, which had been tucked into his rucksack by his mother when she discovered him sneaking from their home the year he turned fourteen. He'd run away to the circus, run away *from* a father who let alcohol turn him mean.

Beneath it all, a pasteboard box full of yellowing letters.

Mabel pulled these out, expecting bits of longing between her parents and exhortations to return home to Europe.

Instead she found something that stole the breath from her lungs and muffled the sounds outside the train—the trumpeting elephants and shouts and the tinny strains of a violin.

Bram—

I should not allow it—she is my own dear daughter—but I've no wish to continue causing her harm. And perhaps you are right ... Mabel will find a better life if she supposes I am dead.

Always yours. Always hers.

—P

Mabel dressed quickly, then caught up the letter as she left the coach. She'd never had cause for anger. Her life had been ordered by someone else, protected by someone else, arranged by someone else. Always others had made sure there was little she had to concern herself with.

Be strong.

The only thing expected of her.

Perform well.

And she had. She'd done everything others wanted from her until life—and death—had given a vicious shove and she stood in the middle of the shambles, staring around like Lorenzo feigning at dropping his balls.

A pair of zebras that made about as much sense in Hungary as the lacerating words printed in her mother's handwriting trotted by, and Mabel's march to nowhere in particular halted. She stared at them. Glared at their handler when he tipped his hat, then scuttled away. Her gaze stabbed at the tents that stood like gleaming white sentinels breaking up the expanse of brown scrub and grey sky. At Lorenzo, who strolled aimlessly, lost in a poem or love song or memory of a particularly pretty woman. At the twins, joined in everything but personality, stepping from the administrative tent, having likely had another conversation with their father about the possibility of retirement. Theirs, not his. Giuseppe's business aspirations were entwined with his daughters much the way their limbs were. Imilia and Giulia, though, had wanted to settle in the Italian countryside for as long as Mabel had known them.

She'd known them a long time. She'd known Lorenzo the same. And they'd all known her mother and father even longer.

Before she'd even consciously decided to move toward them, her legs were eating up the distance. She grabbed for Lorenzo's arm, pulling him along as he yelped and stumbled after her. Then she stood silent, unable to speak for the chattering of her teeth.

"Yes, Mabel?" Imilia scratched her chin, her fingers brushing the beauty spot gracing the very corner of her lips. She was the prettier of the sisters, though they both laid claim to an uncommon beauty. Part of the appeal, Giuseppe said. The world expected ugliness in the different. In the other.

The Manzo sisters were lovely in so many ways, though. Dainty and accomplished. Undeserving of the anger simmering Mabel's blood. She knew if she opened her mouth, it would spew out and burn them, so she just thrust out the note, waving it until Giulia raised her brows and took it.

Their eyes scanned the letter in a synchronized choreography that danced matching emotions across their faces—shock, horror, realization.

Imilia made a sound in her throat, and her lips parted, but Giulia's elbow met her rib, and she swallowed whatever words would bring Mabel clarity and understanding.

"We don't know what this is," Giulia said, her voice cloaked in compassion and girded with obstinacy. She took Mabel's arm and placed the letter back into her hand, curling her fingers so that none of them could see the words pointing toward deception.

"You know something," Mabel insisted.

"We know nothing."

Imilia cast a desperate glance at her sister, but she pinched her lips tight.

"*You* know something." Mabel's voice trembled, and she pinned her eyes on the gentler twin. "You must tell me. What does this mean?" Why had Da told her Maman had died when she hadn't? A thought so incredible, so fraught with desperate possibility spiraled into her conscious. "Is she still alive?"

So many more things were caught up in her question.

Had Maman truly abandoned them?

Why had she never returned?

Where was she?

"We know nothing." Giulia glanced at Lorenzo, who stared at the paper dangling from Mabel's fingers with drawn brows.

"Piccolo . . ." He reached for her arm. His hand was large and warm, but she drew away and rubbed her skin as though his touch had branded betrayal upon it.

"Did you know?" she asked. Something shifted in his gaze, and she knew—she *knew*—that she had been purposely deceived not only by her father, but by everyone. Her eyes burned, and she bit down hard on her cheeks. She waved the letter at him. "Did you?"

He held up his hands and took a step back as though she'd lifted a sword.

"Tell me the truth, Lorenzo. I can see you know something."

"Piccolo—"

"I want the truth!"

"I cannot tell you. I promised your father."

Mabel glanced between him and the twins. "Then I will find someone else who will." She turned, but his soft words stopped her.

"They won't tell either."

"Who?"

"Everyone. They have all promised him. And we loved him. Love him still."

"You would honor your love for a dead man over your love

for me, someone very much alive. Someone standing before you. Begging you . . ."

He shrugged, and his chin fell against his chest.

"What's going on?" Jake slid beside her, the scent of coffee, leather, and horses an embrace.

"My mother might very well be alive," Mabel said, the words scraping from her throat and sounding of accusation. "My father lied to me. Everyone lied to me. I found her letters. She didn't die. She left. And he decided . . ." She looked up at the sky. At a faraway V of birds. At the watery sun tiptoeing around the clouds. It didn't help. Tears still pricked her eyes. "He decided it would be better for me if she were dead."

His eyes went wide, and his brows disappeared beneath the fall of his hair, but he said nothing, and she was grateful. She couldn't bear questions that she couldn't answer right now.

"We must tell her," Imilia said, and Mabel jerked her head around.

"No, sister. It will be too hard for her."

"She is stronger than you think."

Giulia heaved a sigh, her full lips flaring beneath it. She glanced at Lorenzo, who dropped his head into his hands. "I cannot bear to see your heart broken, Piccolo." Then he stumbled away and disappeared into the backyard.

They watched him, Giulia looking as though she wanted to follow, but she straightened her shoulders, and her gaze pinned Mabel. "You will need to be very strong."

Jake stepped nearer Mabel, his shoulder bumping hers, and he gave her fingers a comforting squeeze. "She is. The strongest anywhere."

Mabel wished more than anything that she could be.

Giulia smiled. "Yes. But, you see, your mother was not. She went to America to care for her own sick mother. But when your grandmother didn't die, and your mother stayed, you grew despondent."

"Melancholy." Imilia pressed her hands against her stomach. "You wouldn't eat and lost so much weight. You became pale and rarely smiled. You turned into someone wholly unlike yourself."

"And you began having terrible stage fright. You would freeze, and nothing could induce you to get in the ring. Mabel, do you remember any of this?" Giulia asked.

"Vaguely." She remembered the ice. The cold sweeping her body before each performance. Her father's cajoling voice. The falling silence after the ringmaster called their act and the crowd waited. And waited. Giuseppe's frantic shouts. And her own childish voice filling the stillness. *"I cannot do it. I cannot do it without Maman."*

Father's wild stare. His hushed conversations with Lorenzo. Her narrow cot on the train and a short trip to the ocean, where Da told her Maman had died. She had died and wasn't coming back.

"He told me so that I would get back on stage." Mabel could hear the incredulity in her voice. It pitched steeply—foreign and dreadful.

"No, no." Giulia stepped closer, bringing her sister along. She nudged Jake away and took both of Mabel's hands in her own. "He told you so you would live again. You were wasting away. He couldn't bear it. None of us could bear it. And your mother . . . she was never coming home. She didn't want to."

Imilia shook her head. "That isn't entirely true. She would have wanted to, but your mama was beset by black moods. And sometimes they consumed her."

"She was weak," Giulia said flatly.

The sisters drew their brows together and tipped their heads. But Mabel remembered that too. She remembered a heated argument between her parents before Maman left for America.

"You cannot go, Polly," Father had said, trying to muffle his voice beneath the scratchy blanket. *"You are too weak."*

"*I'm not. I won't be! I'm completely recovered. I have returned to work.*" Maman's voice was harsh, and it was never harsh. Usually she sounded as though it took too much effort to breathe, let alone speak.

"*You are. Maybe not physically anymore, but your mind . . .*"

Mabel had fallen asleep that night to the sound of her mother's weeping.

She pulled back from Giulia. She couldn't think. It was too much to process. Too much to understand.

But one thing was certain. One thing she knew.

"I'm going to New York. I'm going to find my mother."

Imilia gasped. "What? You will leave us?"

"I can't stay here anymore. How could I? You—all of you— kept this from me. Every moment I cried myself to sleep wishing for my mother. Every time I watched the other children find comfort in a soft embrace. And I thought she was dead. You allowed me to think that."

"Your father—"

"He was wrong, Imilia. So wrong. A girl needs her mother."

"She chose to stay away, though." Giulia's words were spoken softly, with kindness, but they were razor-sharp in their aim. "She didn't want to come back."

"I need to make sure of it myself." Mabel squeezed Jake's arm. "Do you think I should stay?"

Jake stared up at the peak of the tent, his tongue making a nervous swipe of his lips. Then he looked at her again, and a muscle in his jaw twitched. "No. And I don't think I shall either."

CHAPTER 5

JAKE STEPPED OUT OF THE RING two days later and realized, as his heel struck the ground, that he'd performed for the last time. A chill swept through him, prickling the hair at the back of his neck and stiffening his lungs around a cold inhale.

He somehow managed to push through a crowd of performers and make his way to the men's dressing tent without releasing the breath. Without taking another.

This was it. He was done.

He thought he'd feel differently about it. Free? Happy? At least a little bit. But he felt nothing. As though this decision had nothing at all to do with the one he'd made nine years earlier when Charlotte died and he left Travis and Wells, thinking *that* was the end of his career.

In a few minutes, he'd changed, the flickering lamps casting writhing shadows. Tossing his costume onto a stool, he left the dressing tent without a backward glance.

He would see Mabel settled and then head to Kansas. To

the ranch he'd escaped years ago. To Will, the brother who still kept track of all the things Jake had selfishly pursued. All the things he himself had sacrificed to remain.

Jake's pulse throbbed almost painfully in his neck, and he shoved into the backyard. Much like Mabel, he had no other options. Where else could he go? Kansas it had to be. Will had written, saying the same thing he did in each of his annual letters.

I know Pa said to never come back. But he's no longer here. I will allow you to return. I don't expect you want to.

And Jake never had. Return to the drudgery? The guilt? The silent judgment?

But without Bram and Mabel, what purpose was there in staying with Manzo Brothers? He hadn't enjoyed performing since Charlotte's death, and he certainly didn't want to return to bumming around Europe.

Laborers scurried in and out of the pad room where the ring stock supplies were kept, and horses were being hustled across the lot. The train had to push off as soon as possible to make the next jump, so the circus would begin to break down the moment the big top erupted with applause. First the dining tent and sideshow, then the animal menagerie and all the rest. By the time the audience poured from the grounds, the main tent was the only thing left standing.

"Let me help with the haul," he called to the lot manager. The man gave a short nod, and Jake was handed the lead of a liberty horse—a startling white Lipizzan—and he stroked the animal's muzzle. "Another town, another show. For you. I'm leaving tomorrow."

The horse nickered, and the sound loosened the tight band around Jake's chest. He didn't want to go home, not really, but there he could at least work with the horses again. Of course, they would mostly be draft horses. Nothing like this trained beauty.

Nothing like the ones he'd performed with in his uncle's wild west show. He'd thought they were his future until he met Charlotte and she convinced him to join her in the air. She had been so beautiful—so dazzling—that he couldn't deny her.

When he landed at Manzo Brothers, he'd asked Giuseppe if he could work with the horses, but there hadn't been room in the show for another equestrian—there was an entire family of Russians already. And Jake was a flyer without equal.

But he missed it. Missed the power beneath his feet. The relationship forged between man and animal. The intimacy that came from relying on a living thing instead of a manufactured object.

Stroking the Lipizzan's mane, Jake watched for Stella— the chestnut Arabian with the star marking he'd grown to love over the seven years he'd been with Manzo Brothers. He hadn't been permitted to perform with her in the ring, but he'd worked with her every chance he had. Giuseppe hadn't liked it, but he allowed it in order to keep Jake happy.

Stella's handler led her from the ring stock tent, and Jake handed off the Lipizzan's lead in exchange. He pressed his cheek against Stella's muzzle and inhaled her earthy scent. "I'm going to miss you."

In that moment, the shouts and claps creeping beneath the tent, the laborers calling out directions, the elephants trumpeting, and the excited shrieks of children conspired to overwhelm Jake's decision and pull him back into it all.

But then Mabel peeked out from the women's dressing tent, having wanted to watch the show one final time. Her eyes searched the backyard until they found him. She smiled and waved, her expression cautious, full lower lip sucked between her teeth. She was scared, though she'd never say so. And he couldn't send her off by herself.

Some people ran away to the circus, intent on seeing the world. Mabel MacGinnis had been sheltered beneath its flapping canvas. She had no idea what awaited her. No idea how to navigate a city like New York.

"Take care of my daughter," Bram had told him. And Jake wouldn't go back on his word.

"I'm going to help bring the stock to the rail yard," he called. "I'll meet you at the station."

Then he vaulted onto Stella's back and rode away from Manzo Brothers Circus for the last time.

❊ ❊ ❊

Isabella couldn't begin to unravel what had happened on that rope. She'd done the routine hundreds of times. Grab ahold and climb, stopping every few moments to do a rotation or pose, extending herself as though held up by an invisible hand—it was only sheer strength, but it looked like magic to the audience—scurry a little higher, wave, smile. Smile. Smile.

But this time, between a trick and a smile, Isabella's arm went weak. Her body crumpled. And she fell.

A roar swept through the crowd, but Isabella's foot became tangled, offering her a second where she hung between shock and impact, and she grabbed for the rope. After letting herself down, she walked woodenly from the tent and through the dressing room hall.

Then she collapsed behind the screen and wept.

Now, an hour later, she shifted in the medical tent chair and stared out at the fallow Ohio farmland Travis and Wells had trampled flat in an effort to capture Cincinnati's imagination.

The ice, wrapped in a scrap of flannel, nearly fell from her ankle, and she leaned forward to adjust it. She poked her finger beneath the pack and prodded at the swelling. It wasn't bad. Not bad enough to warrant missing even one performance.

Dr. Covert, his kind blue eyes watery and nearly obscured

by a set of bushy brows, leaned close to inspect a laceration on her arm. "You don't need stitches. I'll just clean and bandage it. You're lucky, Isabella. This could have ended much worse. Why you refuse to use a net is beyond me."

"It's what sets me apart."

"You don't need dangerous stunts to set you apart." He applied a foul-smelling ointment to the wound, and she hissed through her teeth at the burning. But she leaned into it, wanting it to consume all her skin. Her bone and muscle and memories. Her very soul. Until she was nothing upon nothing. Forgotten and erased.

What would happen then? Would she find peace, finally, in the nothingness of the after? Or had Maman been right to promise golden streets and mansions?

Not for Isabella, though. Even if it were true. She'd been plagued too long by chasing darkness. She'd even once given in to the plaguing thoughts. There would be no forgiveness, no castles in the clouds, for her.

"Isabella!" Robert hurried inside. Tossing a newspaper onto the table, he strode toward her. "Are you all right?"

"I'm fine. It was nothing. Nothing at all."

"You nearly fell to the floor. What happened?"

"It was just a miscalculation." She'd miscalculated how quickly age would creep up on her. Miscalculated how hard it would be to let go of the circus. Of the only thing she had and did that gave life any meaning at all. She swept her fingers over the top of her bodice, finding reassurance in the miniature doll tucked there. At least she had done something worth doing. Once.

"I'm about done here. She'll be fine," Dr. Covert soothed, "but she should take the remainder of the week off. Rest and ice."

"No, I can continue working." Isabella lifted the ice and placed it on the table. She stood and smiled, clenching her teeth to keep from releasing an involuntary gasp. "We have another show tonight. There isn't enough time to shift things."

Dr. Covert merely stroked his short beard. "I suggest you don't do that. Your ankle is badly twisted. You should stay off it."

Isabella gave a light laugh. "Really, Charlie, you've known me nearly my entire life. Do you think I will? Besides, what's the worst that can happen? It will pain me a bit, but pain is a part of this job. I will push through."

The doctor twisted the caps of a few bottles, ensuring they were tight, and placed them carefully in a padded case. "The worst is that you can prolong its healing and possibly cause further harm to your ankle. You must know when to listen to your body, Isabella. It is time for a rest."

"Rest in the circus is a career death sentence."

He looked at her as though that wasn't the worst thing in the world, but she'd already faced too much loss. She would not lose this as well.

"I'll leave you to it," Dr. Covert told Robert. "I won't compromise my recommendation. She should definitely stay off that foot for at least a week." He shook his head as though he knew making demands of Isabella Moreau was a hopeless cause. "I have another patient to check in on. I hope not to see you in the near future." He slapped his hat onto his head, shoved the case beneath his arm, and left.

"You should rest," Robert said. He motioned her back into the seat and crouched. With gentle fingers, he pressed against her foot and ankle, pausing when she drew it back with a little growl. He held up his hands and stood.

"I'm not resting. I don't have that luxury. You know as well as I do that I'm standing on shaky ground."

"It will be a good time to prepare yourself, Isabella. Time to reflect and figure out what you really want."

"What on earth are you talking about? I want to continue doing what I've always done."

"That isn't possible."

The pain in her ankle faded, and she stared up at him. "Why?"

His entire being seemed to crumple—his already sagging face, his shoulders, his once impressive chest. Even his hair, unable to be forced into submission by pomade, fell into a sorry droop. He reached for the chair on the other side of the table and set it before her. When he sat, his knees bumped hers.

"I was watching from a seat in the bleachers. I saw everything. You can't pretend you miscalculated anything." He swallowed and stared somewhere over her shoulder, parroting words he surely hadn't strung together on his own, for Robert Pedersen had never said or done a thing to make Isabella regret her association with him. "You've become a liability. You don't draw the crowds you used to. You aren't able to do the types of things you used to."

"Where is this coming from? Has Jerry said these things?"

Robert reached for her hand, and she let him take it. Allowed it to settle like a glove, limp and devoid of anything sparking life. Empty. Used and tossed away. "The truth is, we already have three other female aerialists and Annette on the trapeze. You've become redundant. Jerry isn't even sure he wants you to finish the year. He told me so before he left the winter grounds. He's kept you this long because of Paul, but once he hears of this . . ."

"Well, why would he?"

"You nearly fell sixty feet to your death, Isabella. Do you think there were no reporters in the audience? This is Cincinnati, not some rural town. He will find out."

She could hear her own breathing in that quiet tent and recognized that it came in tandem with the rising of her chest. But inside, her thoughts buzzed and raced. This could not be how things ended. This was not her story.

"That's why you brought on the Danó sisters? I wasn't

merely training a new act. I was preparing my replacement."
She silently urged him to refute the accusation. To dismiss
her concerns with a laugh. But he didn't.

"I didn't realize it until recently." He squeezed her hand
between both of his, pressing until her fingers began to tingle
with warmth again. Pinpricks reminding her she was made
of flesh and blood. Weakness and failure.

"But no one else has the range I do. They are—all of them—
one trick ponies. I can do so much—trapeze, ropes, rings, cannon. Would he want me to do a human cannonball act again?
I know it's been a long time, but I remember. We haven't had
one since Char—"

"No. You were the best. Everyone knows it. Jerry knows it.
But that was before. You have to think rationally."

Isabella pulled away and, elbows biting into her knees,
gripped her head in her hands. "What will I do? What can
I do? Robert, there is nothing else for me. How mortifying.
To walk around so diminished." Soon the Danó sisters would
begin to look at her the way Annette Aubert already did.

Robert was on the ground before her now, his fingers firm
on either side of her knees. "Polly, look at me."

She did, and the expression on his face—the naked wanting—
sent her spiraling toward the nothing days that had precipi-
tated losing all she'd had. She sat up straight and pushed
herself against the seatback as though it would grow itself
around her. Cushion her from what he was about to say.

"No, Robert."

"Yes. You must know I love you. Must know I've always
loved you. Before Bram. Before even Paul."

She shook her head. The chair scraped as she pushed at it
in an attempt to escape. "Don't say such things."

He scrambled to his feet and followed her to the back of
the tent where she paced, gripping the sequined skirt of her
costume. A sharp pain shot from her ankle and down her foot

with every step, but she welcomed it. Courted it. Anything to keep her grounded. To keep her here.

"There is no reason I should not."

She halted her march. "No reason . . . Robert, I'm still married. You know that."

"You aren't." His voice had dropped to a whisper. "Have you not seen the paper this morning?"

Her skin—every bit of it—went clammy, and she swayed as black spots danced before her. "What has happened?"

He slogged back to the table and picked up the newspaper. Peeling back its thin pages, he returned to her and handed it over.

The first thing she noticed was Bram's smile, and her own responded in kind, for she'd loved him from the moment they'd met—she'd been so surprised by that, after Paul—and not even twenty years of separation and hurt could dissolve it. He looked older, with deep crevices crawling from his lips to his chin, and Isabella stroked her thumb over them, wishing she could erase them. Wishing she could erase the years and miles between them. He was still so handsome.

Then she read the headline. She recognized that Robert spoke, fuzzy and distant, about the event that had taken Bram MacGinnis's life. Impossible. He looked strong still. He'd always been as healthy as an ox. He hadn't aged in her thoughts, not the way her own body had.

World's Strongest Man Dies of a Weak Heart, the printed words fairly shouted.

She pressed her husband's face to her chest and left.

✻ ✻ ✻

"Is your ankle bothering you? You're quiet today." Rowena tucked her hand into Isabella's elbow, and they stepped off one of the many bridges crossing the lagoons at Millbrook Park. "Was coming here too much? You're back to your schedule tomorrow, and you might have rested instead of tromping all over."

"No, it's not that. Honestly, my ankle is completely healed." Isabella forced a smile. She hated to ruin this outing. Every year, Robert made sure to include a stop in New Boston, Ohio, to coincide with a Saturday so that the circus workers could enjoy a Sunday at the park. With a lakeshore and skating, dancing and a roller coaster, everyone looked forward to it. She normally did too. "I'm only distracted by the possibility of losing my position. And I'm sorry for it. This is not the time to cast a shadow over things."

Despite her declarations to the contrary, Isabella had found she could not, in fact, work the week Dr. Covert had suggested she rest. After walking from the medical tent to the rail yard, she'd crawled into her berth and cried through gritted teeth at the pain. Then she cried some more, thinking about Bram.

And Mabel.

What had become of her daughter? The article made no mention of her, but she and Bram had been part of an act since Mabel was eight. Had the loss left her adrift? Would she be able to transition to working alone?

Was she sad? Lost? Lonely?

Isabella was certain Bram had cut her loose with every intention of living forever. His people seemed to, tucked away in the highlands, as strong as the shaggy cattle that roamed those parts. If he'd known he would leave their daughter so soon, would he have suggested such a thing?

When they reached the pavilion's covered walkway, Rowena pulled Isabella into a shadowy corner. "If you need to talk or worry about this right now, there is nothing else I would rather do. You will not ruin my day."

Isabella's shoulders dropped, and she tucked her chin into her chest as every bit of pretense fell away. "Thank you," she whispered. "This has weighed heavily since Robert spoke with me about it."

"Of course it has. I can see no alternative. With those few words, he turned your entire world upside down."

She looked up at Rowena, blinked back tears, and gave a shaky nod. "I have no idea what I'm going to do. Jerry Wells isn't a bad man, but he is a businessman, and I am no longer making him money."

"Can you not retire? Surely you have some money set by. You were their most popular act for years, and everyone whispers about the exorbitant salary top billing gets."

"No. My mother was so sick, and after Bram sent that letter, she was all I had. I spent most of my money sending her to sanatoriums. I have nothing." From underneath the porch roof, Isabella watched as an old lady dressed in a serviceable, well-mended gown leaned heavily on the arm of the young man beside her. She walked with slow, unsure steps, her cane clicking on the asphalt. "I'm so afraid I will become like Maman, my body broken from hard work. Sick and exhausted. Those years in the laundry killed her. And what if I end up there? I'm not strong."

Bram's condemnation after Mabel's birth—unsaid but felt with every fiber of her being—haunted her. What type of mother nearly killed her baby during delivery? What kind of mother simply gave up pushing and told the doctor to tear the child from her womb? What mother was brought so low during childbirth that she didn't have the strength to nourish the babe at her breast?

What kind of mother?

A weak one.

"I'm not strong enough for the laundry," she repeated.

"I'm sure it won't come to that. There are always jobs to be done in the circus. I'm positive they will find a place for you." Rowena tipped her head and made a show of studying Isabella from head to toe. "Maybe you can become a clown."

Isabella laughed. "If only I had. Then my job wouldn't be so dependent on the impossibility of eternal youth."

"They would have never let you anyway. You're too beautiful to be covered in paint." Rowena glanced up the stairs that led to the second-floor skating rink. "Why don't we have some fun? A bit of physical exertion might help us think of some way to resolve this."

Isabella allowed herself a spark of hope as she and Rowena climbed the stairs and rented skates. She stood in them, testing the strength of her ankle, and they circled the rink a few times, turning circles and weaving between couples holding hands and children feeling out the wheels.

Through the canvas awnings rolled up and affixed to poles holding up the roof, sunlight spilled a pattern of boxes onto the polished wooden floor, and Isabella turned it into a game, going around them, the wheels of her skates just skimming the sides.

She made little, futile vows. Bargains with the God Maman had loved—the God who had spared little love for the poor war widow—that if she stopped midway through a box of light, Jerry would give her another chance to prove herself. If she made a rotation of six at the corner of one, her shows tomorrow would go perfectly. If she skated the entire length of the rink on her right foot, Mabel would . . .

No. Thoughts of her daughter would only lead to more pain.

It would be enough to save her career. She couldn't wish for more than that.

With each vow, with every accomplishment, her heart grew lighter. Optimism bloomed brighter.

And then Robert slid into the rink and caught her eye, his mouth a firm line and his gaze steady upon her. She skidded to a stop, the person behind them bumping into Rowena with a muttered curse.

"So sorry," Isabella said. She found a bench and undid the skate buckles with fumbling fingers.

She'd managed to avoid him all week, ignoring the notes delivered by the porter asking her to speak with him. She stayed in her room aboard the train and had food delivered, not because she couldn't walk to the meal tent, but because she wanted to ignore the fact that Robert had made a declaration, and she had run away from it. She hated hurting him, but there was no way around it.

"Are we done?" Rowena asked, sitting beside her with an inelegant grunt. She bent to remove her own skates.

Isabella glanced up and saw Robert moving across the rink toward them. She yanked Rowena's remaining skate from her foot and dropped it on the floor alongside her own. Then she shoveled up their shoes and hustled from the building.

"What's going on?" Rowena asked as they skirted the retaining wall below the pavilion.

Isabella eyed the rowboats pulled up on the grass, their bottoms lying heavy in the lake's placid water. She decided against rowing. Hiding seemed a better option, so she pressed her back against the wall and handed over her friend's shoes, then bent to slip on her own. "Robert told me he loves me. I believe he wants to marry."

Rowena gave a shaky laugh. "I mean, it's not unexpected now that Bram has died."

Isabella gave her a sharp look. "Isn't it?"

"He has been in love with you forever. I never understood how you couldn't see it."

"I just . . . I never thought of anyone else like that. I was still married. Still . . ." She looked at the lake, placid waves lapping at the rocky shoreline. "I still loved Bram. Is that foolish? It must be. He certainly didn't feel the same. His heart failed me long before it failed his body."

Rowena pushed away from the wall and pulled Isabella along with her to the shoreline. "What will you do about Robert?"

"Not marry him. I cannot. I never will. My last marriage was a disaster, and it feels like giving up on myself. My only family is the circus, and I want to hold on to it. I must, Rowena. It is everything to me."

The stirrings of an idea flamed to life in her thoughts. At first, she ducked from it. Afraid to be burned. But it was a simple solution. One she'd not been free to pursue before. But with Bram gone . . .

A fire spread. She wouldn't marry Robert, but he still had the power to save her career. She only needed to be willing to compromise her integrity a very little bit.

And that seemed like such a small thing after everything else she had lost.

CHAPTER
6

MABEL LEFT MANZO BROTHERS CIRCUS without much fanfare. Giuseppe was angry to have lost his tattooed woman, but angrier still to have lost his favorite acrobat and trapeze artist. He tried to milk as much profit from the event as possible, sending out advance men to plaster the villages they passed through those final few days with bills proclaiming Jake Cunningham's retirement.

Final opportunity!

Last show ever!

Don't miss your chance!

The crowds were large that last day. Mabel had watched Jake perform for the final time from the side of the tent, surreptitiously rubbing her thumb over the interrupted flower on her thigh. Trying hard to pretend she wasn't responsible for robbing the world of his talent. As he flung himself through the air, the muscles in his shoulders and back and arms visible even from that height, Mabel allowed herself a moment to admire him.

She rarely indulged.

Now, a day later, she sat across from him on the train and tamed her heart. She couldn't very well stare at him the entire way to Genoa.

"Are you sure you want to do this?" she asked. "I just don't understand why. Your place in the circus is secure. Everyone adores you."

He glanced up from the book upon which he had been scratching away for an hour. "I'm done, Mabel."

She tipped her head. It made no sense. He was the best acrobat she'd ever seen. And she knew he would have become the best the world had ever seen if he'd stayed in the United States.

"I can feel you looking at me." He used his pencil to scratch the back of his neck. "I loved your father. I feel responsible for you." He glanced up. "He's gone and you're leaving, so why should I stay?"

"What will you do, though?"

He scribbled something, then stuck the pencil in his book and closed it. "I think I'll return to the family ranch in Kansas. My father is dead now, and with him, the forbiddance that I ever return. My oldest brother is the only one remaining. I think he would welcome the help."

Mabel nodded and tried to envision Jake steering cattle. She could, which made the daydream a bit frightening. She could absolutely see him atop a sleek horse, his face shadowed by a hat. She could hear his steady voice as he called out over the prairie. "Will you leave for it as soon as we arrive?"

He glanced down at the book, his face pulled into long lines. "No. I can't just leave you there. Your father's ghost would haunt me. You have no idea what life is like outside the circus."

She bristled and drew herself more tightly into the corner, her gaze pinned on the dilapidated farmhouse they chugged by.

"I'm sure I would be fine. I'm not nearly as weak as everyone makes me out to be."

"You aren't weak at all. But it's *different*. The rules and expectations. What type of friend would I be if I just abandoned you?"

The word lodged between her heart and ribs, a tough little stone of confusion and generational betrayal. Who had abandoned whom? Her father. Her mother. Herself?

Of course, she knew it hadn't been her fault. She'd been a child and couldn't have changed anything even had she known. But her earliest memories were of Maman weeping and handing her off to someone else. Of Mabel knowing she was too much, too heavy a burden. She'd tried so hard to be good. To be quiet and obedient and not a nuisance. But her trying never seemed to accomplish much of anything.

Her tense muscles relaxed, and she scooted toward the middle of the bench so that only a handbreadth of carpet separated her from Jake. He didn't know how much it meant to her that he was willing to stay. "Can I see your figures?"

He rubbed his brow and handed over the book. "Maybe you can make sense of how this will all work out."

She flipped to the pages where he had been tallying their funds and making projections as to their costs. Her gaze skimmed the numbers, and she sighed. "I cannot believe this is all Da had after dedicating so many years to Manzo Brothers. It seems criminal."

"Your father lived a lot of life in every moment. Also, you paid Giuseppe back for Mr. Szabó's initial fees."

"And I just replaced my wardrobe when we passed through Paris at the end of the season." She ran her finger down a column of figures and tapped a number. "I can't allow you to contribute so much when I have very little to offer."

"We don't have much of a choice. In fact, even combined, there isn't enough to see us very long in New York. You will have to find your mother quickly, or we will need to secure work in order not to end up destitute."

"Work?" Mabel turned to stare out the window. But of course she must find work. She couldn't expect to find her mother right away. And even if she did, she couldn't—wouldn't—waltz back into Maman's life and demand she care for her lost daughter.

Outside, the Italian countryside slid by, the train's speed turning it into an Impressionist masterpiece, blurred and dappled by light and shadow. *Good-bye, Italy.* Nausea threatened, and she pressed her fingers to her lips. Everything was changing. Too quickly. Too much.

"There are circuses in America," Jake said, his words gentle but not at all reassuring. "Bigger ones than Manzo Brothers. You could become a star, Mabel."

She shook her head. "Who would have me? I cannot perform on my own. It would only be made worse by bigger crowds." She glanced at the book. "We can travel steerage."

His brows lifted. "Second class, I suppose, would be a good compromise."

"But not enough of one. Two cabins on the ship, even second class, will cost the same as a room at a modest boardinghouse in New York for a month." She pressed her fingers to her forehead, kneading away the tension. "And what are we going to do when we arrive? We only have enough to support one household for a couple of weeks. This is madness. I see that now. I'm so sorry I've drawn you into it."

The train shuddered to a stop outside a small stone station nearly consumed by wisteria. As people began to exit, Jake slipped onto the bench beside her and took the notebook. He tossed it onto his own seat and held out his palm. Mabel stared at it until he waggled his fingers. His hand was smaller than hers—which wasn't out of the ordinary—but when he placed his other one atop hers, she felt for all the world as though he were embracing her.

"I was under no illusion that we would be traveling in luxury. I have been in worse places, Mabel. Accompanying you to New York is no hardship. But we do need to make some pragmatic decisions. Namely, what can we do to ensure we have enough to live off of until you find your mother and are able to support yourself?"

"Excuse me, sir." A young girl stopped beside them, her voice draped in the poetry of Italy. She held out a basket piled with mottled green and brown pears. "Would you or your wife enjoy some fruit?"

Mabel blinked up at the girl as Jake pulled out his wallet and paid for two, then handed her one. He stretched out his legs, the hem of his pants slipping past her ankle.

Her body responded—a delicious twisting sensation in her stomach. The hairs on her arms stood at attention.

She could only think of one solution to their problem, and given how she reacted to his nearness, it was a very ill-advised one. But one she might have to live with. "We could . . ." She glanced around and, satisfied no one was within hearing, leaned nearer him. "We could stay in one room aboard the ship and when we reach New York."

Jake drew back sharply, his eyes darting like a frightened rabbit's. "Mabel. That would ruin your reputation."

"No one need know. It's only meant to save on expenses. It solves everything." She turned the pear in her palm, examining the brown patches and perky stem, and pretended to be completely unruffled. Oh, but it was hard with her heart tripping and her lungs compressing. Her cheeks burned, and she cursed her father's Scottish blood that so easily revealed discomfort.

With a sidelong glance at Jake, though, she felt assured he hadn't noticed. He stared straight ahead, his profile engraved in granite. His expression unreadable. She pretended interest in the pear's markings.

Finally, just as she'd bitten into the fruit and was wiping juice from her chin, he shifted and turned toward her.

"Fine. But we must act above reproach."

The pear stuck in her throat, and she gave a violent enough cough that it hurtled into her gloved hand. She closed her fingers around it and blinked watering eyes. "Of course, Jake. I'm not . . . I wouldn't . . ."

He gave a short nod but didn't look at her as the train began to pull away from the station.

❄ ❄ ❄

The *Principe di Treviso* cared little about Jake and Mabel's good intentions. Mabel blinked at the ticketing official and translated the Italian into English. She spoke it fluently, without an accent, but Jake had come to Manzo Brothers as an adult and could only pick out a few phrases and words.

"He says the ship has been delayed two days, and he's sorry, but there's nothing that can be done about it. We will need to find lodging."

"How much will that be?" Jake's expression was tight.

Mabel asked the man approximate rates, and when she told Jake the cost, his jaw flexed and her stomach rolled around the pear she'd eaten earlier. "It is not ideal, spending so much before we even leave Genoa," she said.

"It's not." He slipped his hand into his pocket, and Mabel knew he was clutching the notebook.

"I will pay you back, Jake. Every penny. I promise."

He blew out his cheeks with a harsh puff of air, then offered her a crooked smile that flashed a dimple. "No, I'm sorry. Of course you don't have to pay anything back. We'll be fine. I'm sure there are plenty of rooms to let for a night."

But there weren't. After they purchased tickets for a second-class suite, they paid to store their trunks in the building behind the ticket office and trudged from *albergo* to *pensione*.

For hours, they crisscrossed winding cobble streets where narrow homes painted the colors of sunset huddled together. Jake took her carpetbag and slung it over his arm, where it settled in the bend of his elbow.

"Don't worry. I'm sure we'll find something soon. There has to be a free room somewhere in this city." Jake squeezed her hand as he guided her around a suspect puddle.

Mabel's stomach rumbled in pessimistic protest. She'd long since digested her paltry pear lunch. As they passed a slate building, its exterior broken up by large paned windows, her gaze snagged on a display of pretty fondants and crystallized fruit arranged in open boxes and on porcelain platters.

"Oh."

Her sigh must have traveled on the salt-laced breeze, because Jake's steps paused and he looked at her, his brow wrinkled with leftover worry. "Yes?"

"Only . . . aren't you hungry?"

As if on cue, her stomach grumbled—a very put out grumble— and he laughed. "I think I am."

The scent of sugar and rose syrup nearly made Mabel lightheaded as they entered the sweet shop. She poked around dark cabinets and glass-topped counters, everything shining and smelling of orange oil, and finally settled at a display of conical glass jars, each one filled with a mound of pastel *dragées*. Aniseed, pistachio, cinnamon, and orange. Her mouth watered. And then her thoughts sprouted a memory—long buried and lost to sugar-scented daydreams.

"How about a sweet for my sweetheart of a girl?" Maman had hardly said a word to her for weeks, Mabel recalled. Each show, she had walked into the tent as though in a trance, flipped and sailed through the air—as graceful as one of the bee-eaters they had seen dancing above the hills in Greece—then left just as quietly. Just as alone.

And then one day, Maman had grabbed Mabel around the

waist and swung her round and round, laughter and pine nut *dragées* spilling over her head in benediction.

Mabel pointed at the sweet when a man appeared behind the counter. He filled a paper cone with a shower of them and handed it over. "Thank you," she whispered, her thoughts firmly lodged in childhood.

She had always known something wasn't right. Sitting on Maman's lap, singing silly songs, the vacant look in her mother's eyes had frightened her. But still . . . a girl's heart longed for mother-love. It never grew out of the need for it.

"Ready to begin our search again?" Jake approached, a box in his hand and swipe of chocolate at the corner of his lips.

She pointed to her own, and his tongue flicked the offender into the sweetness of his mouth. Her face burned, and she ducked from the shop.

"It's nearly dark," she said, stopping just outside the door. "I hope we find something soon, or we'll have to sleep on the street."

"You are looking for a room?" A man wearing a floppy hat and water-stained pants stopped his march down the street and turned to face them. He balanced a basket against his hip, and the scent of fish enveloped him. Mabel discreetly pressed the cone of candies to her cheek and sniffed.

"We are," Jake answered, drawing her nearer the fisherman.

"You are lucky today. My mother has one room open in her inn." He waved behind his head. "Come. Come with Carlo. I will take care of you. We will have fish, wine, and conversation. It will be a good night."

Jake glanced at Mabel. "What is he saying? He is speaking so quickly, I can't follow."

"We have somewhere to sleep tonight." Mabel smiled at Carlo and nodded. "Yes, please. We are grateful."

They followed him down increasingly narrow lanes until,

had someone asked Mabel directions to the port, she would have been hard-pressed to answer. In this part of Genoa, stones echoed the past—stories in the clicking of their heels and shadowy corners. Carlo kept a running dialogue, filling the silence that would have been eerie without his chatter.

He insisted on practicing his English with Jake, asking questions like, "Where do I go for prawns?" and "How do you know my sister?"

Jake answered with equally nonsensical responses. "You must get them after the full moon in Manhattan" and "Your sister stole my heart and buried it beneath a mountain."

By the time they reached the three-story building wrapped round on the top two levels by rusty iron balconies, the three of them had become good friends.

"Mamma," Carlo called as they ducked beneath the doorway. Inside smelled of roasting meat, and the paper-wrapped sweets' appeal dimmed. "I've brought friends."

A woman bustled through a low door on the other side of the room, wiping her hands on the rumpled apron tied around her waist. She was as solid and affable as her son.

Scarred walnut tables crowded the room, four stools pushed beneath each. There were no cloths or vases of flowers. No chandeliers or white-coated waiters. But what the space lacked in refinement, it made up in warmth and welcome.

"I found them wandering the streets looking for a place to stay until Wednesday." Carlo placed a loud kiss on his mother's cheek. "Mr. Cunningham and his wife."

Jake stepped forward. "We are not mar—"

Mabel jabbed her elbow into his ribs and smiled. "Very nice to meet you. We're so grateful you have room for us."

Carlo's mother smiled and waved them toward a table, then hustled back into the kitchen, calling for Carlo to take their bags up to the room.

Jake rubbed his side after they had settled into their seats. "That wasn't very nice of you."

"They have one room. One. Enough for a *couple*. And we're planning on posing as married the rest of the trip anyway."

He rubbed his forehead, smoothing the lines that had appeared as he read his accounts book on the train. They reappeared the moment he dropped his hand. "I fear we will regret this."

"Do we have another option?" When he said nothing and only set his gaze on the crucifix hanging above the door's lintel, she gave his hand a light touch. "We are doing nothing wrong. You are like my brother." Not entirely true. Not at all true. Mabel knew it was for him, though. She'd always known it. He only needed a reminder.

Jake's eyes slid closed, and he inhaled, then nodded. "You are right, of course." His lashes lifted, and she could have filled every hunger in her body and soul with the beauty of his gaze. "Having had only brothers, it is nice to have a sister."

He smiled, and Mabel was saved from too close an inspection by Carlo's arrival.

"Wine!" He poured three glasses and sat on a free stool. "Say you are hungry. Mamma makes the very best anchovies."

"I am hungry," Mabel said.

Carlo's eyes danced with pleasure at her Italian. "You sound as though you grew up in Italy." He tipped his wine glass toward her.

"I did." She tapped her own glass against his, and a pleasant *clink* sounded between them. "I've spent every winter of my life in Bologna."

"And you?" Carlo turned toward Jake. "Have you lived in Italy long?"

"No. I came seven years ago," Jake said, his pronunciation adequate but accented. "My Italian is not as good as Mabel's."

"She is more than good. She speaks as well as anyone here." Carlo watched her over the rim of his glass, his gaze full of admiration. "Why only winter in Bologna?"

"We're with the circus and travel the rest of the year."

Carlo's mother approached the table carrying a platter stacked with thick porcelain plates and an earthen dish emitting the most delicious scents. Mabel nodded her thanks when the woman served her a hearty portion of baked fish sandwiching a fragrant stuffing.

"The circus?" Carlo turned toward his mother. "You should tell Maria to come." When she returned to the kitchen, the tray tucked beneath her arm, Carlo waved his hands. "My sister, Maria, has a great love for the circus. She saved for four months to see the Manzo Brothers show last year—do you know it? She receives magazines about the performers."

Jake shook his head, unable to follow Carlo's rapid speech, but he nodded at the mention of their circus. "Yes, Manzo Brothers," he said, but his smile dropped when he caught Mabel giving a frantic shake of her head.

Maybe Maria wouldn't recognize them.

But Maria, a young woman of about twenty with a wild mane of dark curls and a smile as wide as her hips, stopped short of reaching their table, her eyes as wide as moons.

Carlo waved her forward. "Meet my new friends, Mr. Cunningham and his wife."

"Married? You've married!" Maria darted toward them, clapping. "I knew that couldn't be the end of it. When the magazine said you had retired, I knew there was a story behind it. And there is!" She gave a little hop and pressed her fingers to her lips.

Jake shook his head and looked at Mabel in bewilderment, but she couldn't explain. Couldn't translate. Oh, this was bad.

Maria stole her brother's glass and raised it above her head, a bit of wine sloshing out and spilling into her hair. "To Jake

Cunningham and Mabel MacGin—no, Cunningham. May your life together be like good wine." She took a gulp and set down the glass, then looked between them. "Married!" She whirled and clattered back into the kitchen. "Mamma! I must tell the girls. I will be back shortly."

CHAPTER
7

THAT NIGHT, Mabel lay on a bed hardly big enough for her. She wasn't sure how Carlo expected two of them to fit. Though, if she really were married to Jake, she imagined she wouldn't want to be very far from him and would welcome the forced closeness. Wrapped in his arms, legs thrown around each other, his hands on her back . . . her shoulders . . . her—

Mabel's eyes flicked open, and she forced her gaze onto the ceiling. From the floor beside the bed, she heard Jake stir. After a tense hour where they ate and talked and Mabel pretended nothing unwonted had happened, Carlo finally took his leave to visit with a group of arguing men, and she told Jake what had occurred with his sister. They hadn't been alone more than five minutes before Carlo returned—long enough to see the horror pass over Jake's face. To be reminded that if anyone discovered the truth, her reputation would be ruined.

Their room was small, uncomfortably so, with no screen to provide privacy for changing. So they decided, wordlessly and with much glancing around, to sleep in their clothing. Jake had tugged the counterpane and one of the pillows from the bed and settled himself between its rickety metal frame and the diminutive washstand.

Mabel turned onto her side, pulling her knees up and drawing her feet beneath the covers, and looked at the stand. The moonlight filtering past the linen curtains outlined its turned legs and the chipped pitcher and bowl. Jake would knock into it if he moved so much as an inch during the night, and it would fall atop him. Maybe he stayed still as he slept, his legs straight and his hands folded over his stomach.

She could hear him breathing and matched her own to the rhythm of it. Then, as quietly as she could while lying on the loudest bedstead in all of Europe, she inched her shoulders and head toward the side and peered over the mattress.

She blinked three times to adjust her eyes to the murky darkness and found herself staring directly into his. "Oh."

"What is it, Mabel?"

"I only wondered if you might not be more comfortable on the other side. There's not more room, but it is between the bed and the wall, so you are less likely to give yourself a concussion in the middle of the night."

"I'm fine." He sighed and scrubbed his hands over his eyes. "It's unlikely I'll sleep much anyway."

"Are you worried about Maria's recognition of us?"

"Aren't you?" He sat up and scooted against the wall, draping his arms over his bent knees. His head was beside hers now, and if she reached her fingers nearer the edge of the bed, she could touch him. "I feel a responsibility to you. To protect you. To honor your father in that."

"You don't owe me or him anything."

"But I do. I was in a dark place when we met. So broken after losing Charlotte the way I had. I watched her die and was unable to do anything about it. It felt as though I'd lost the very best part of me and there was no use pretending to exist anymore. Your father brought me out of that. His friendship saw me through it."

Mabel's breath caught in her throat as the words tumbled from Jake's lips. He'd never before spoken with her about his wife's accident. They all knew, of course. Within days, the entire circus—the large ones in America, as well as the smaller ones that canvassed Europe and Asia—had heard about the death of beautiful, charismatic, supremely talented Charlotte Cunningham. She'd been shot too high from a cannon. Had hit her head on a support beam and fallen to the ground like a felled bird. Her broken body, swanlike in a gleaming white leotard, had been photographed and printed around the world.

And Jake had been present for the tragedy, watching helplessly from the platform above.

He turned to face her, his hair scratching against the faded wallpaper. Mabel saw the grief still shadowing his eyes and drew her creeping hand beneath her cheek. Everyone knew of Jake and Charlotte. Their romance had been the kind fairy tales were made of. Charlotte was nearly idolized by the public, and he had never hidden his admiration for his wife. Young women sat in the seats beneath the big top and sighed, wishing for a love like theirs.

Mabel had heard the stories and wondered what it was like to be so fiercely adored.

"I'm sure it will be fine," she said. "This is only a few people in a small Italian city. How would anyone else find out?"

"I don't know, but is it worth the risk? If word does get out that we posed as a married couple, slept in the same room, boarded a ship together . . ." He reached for her cheek, and it was every bit the gesture of a big brother and his young, callow sister. "You would never find work again."

"There's nothing we can do about it." She flipped onto her

back, jealous for his fingers against her skin again. Furious at herself for it.

"There is. I've been thinking on it. I fear we have only one choice. It's a hard thing, what I'm about to ask you, but I believe your father would expect me to do it. For you."

She pinched the bridge of her nose and squeezed her eyes shut. Why must he always bring up her father? As though Da had any right to demand anything of anyone after the dreadful way he'd treated Maman.

She dropped her arm back to the bed and offered up a silent *Sorry, Da*. She had nothing but a clutch of letters to go on. No real information. She shouldn't—wouldn't—dismiss all the years he had loved and tended to her because of a few lines scribbled on a crumbled bit of paper by a woman who had, from all appearances, abandoned her family.

Mabel turned her head to look at Jake. "What do you think we should do?"

"We must marry for real."

She bolted upright and stared at the far wall. Frozen. If she stayed extremely still, she might not waken from this dream. But the mattress sank beneath his weight when he sat beside her, and her shoulder fell into his. She chanced a glance at him.

"I know this is a shocking suggestion, but it really is the only way to protect you from gossip. Once we arrive in America, we can live together and not have to worry so much about our funds. You will have time to find a job with the circus. To find your mother too. Your reputation will not be at risk. And then, once everything has settled and you're reunited with her, I can move back to Kansas, and you can file for an annulment on grounds of abandonment."

Mabel's shoulders—her heart and stomach too—sank. "But then *your* reputation would be ruined. Do you really want people to think that of you? You are so loved."

He shrugged, his arm brushing hers and sending shivers

up her spine. A marriage of convenience in every sense of the word. Could she settle for such a thing? With Jake? Knowing he would disappear. Knowing her heart would likely become more entangled with his as the days passed. Knowing he would spend the next however many nights sleeping on the floor inches from her.

"I don't care what people think of me," he said. "I'm done with all of this. I only want to go home."

"But you would likely never be able to marry again, Jake. No one respectable would join her life to someone who left his wife."

"I never planned on marrying again anyway. That matters little to me. But it would protect you from such a fate. You might have to deal with a little pity, but after a while, you could remarry. For real."

"What if I don't want to marry anyone else after all of this?"

"Well, in that case, I guess neither of us would be any worse off for the deception. I will leave, and you will be able to live your life free of a husband again."

That was not what she meant, of course, but she remained silent.

He slipped back to the floor, and Mabel lay down again.

"What do you think? Will the scheme work for you?" There was a heaviness in Jake's voice she thought wholly unsuited to a proposal, whether or not it was real.

"Yes, I believe it will suit. There is much logic about it." That was what every girl wanted from the man she loved. Logic and falsity.

"We will see about arranging it tomorrow morning."

That was the last he said, and quite soon, his light snores filled the room, as though he only needed to unburden himself of the terrible revelation in order to find enough peace to sleep. Mabel drew the covers around her shoulders, and as slumber stole over her, she might have, in her most honest moment, admitted that she imagined the hand she'd wrapped around her waist belonged to him.

* * *

Weddings were supposed to include flowers and family. Friends and food. A fancy new dress that—Mabel tipped her head and stared at the sky—boasted frills.

As she and Jake were ushered up the swaying metal staircase that spilled people into the *Principe di Treviso*'s belly, Mabel cast around for other *F* words that would describe a wedding.

Words that couldn't describe hers.

Fairy-tale. Flirtatious. Festive.

Jake bumped her shoulder. "They're moving forward."

Mabel shuffled a few more steps. Their second-class tickets had afforded them a porter, at least, and they weren't responsible for seeing to their own luggage. It had been a costly decision, though, and she knew they might come to regret it when they landed in New York.

But her sham wedding . . . would she regret that? As false as his promises, uttered in stumbling Italian, were, Mabel could never begrudge her heart these few moments of pretense. It might be the best she would ever receive.

And if their marriage became a true one, a lasting one, she might one day come to cherish the memories of the early-morning ceremony in a crumbling chapel. The whispered vows, Jake's shy smile despite the situation, and the dust motes dancing before stained-glass windows.

She could live with the simplicity and homeliness of it. If there had been an assurance of love. Of security. Of belonging.

Without that, though, all Mabel *had* was the ceremony.

The line continued to inch forward, and finally they broke free and found themselves walking down a black-and-white rubber-tiled hall alongside another couple.

"This is your first ocean crossing, isn't it?" the woman said. She was small and pert and cast adoring glances at their surroundings, the little dog in her arms, her husband . . . even Mabel.

"It is for my . . . wife. How did you know?" Jake asked, scanning the gold numbers on each door.

"She has the look about her. We are returning from our honeymoon. Two months in France, Italy, and Spain, and now we are headed to New York to visit Morty's family before returning to Boston. And you? I can tell you have been married much longer than us. Don't you think, darling?" She released one hand from around the dog and wove it beneath her husband's elbow.

He gave a noncommittal grunt.

"You have a settled look about you," she continued in a mock-whisper. "As though you have run through all the early passion that makes one want to just scream from the sheer joy of it."

"We actually married just yesterday morning," Jake said, and Mabel glared at him. He shrugged and stopped in front of a door.

"Well, you are self-contained, aren't you?" The woman sent Mabel a grin she was sure meant something more than it seemed on the surface, then released both her husband and the dog to give a joyful clap. "You're our neighbors! How fun. We must meet before luncheon and sit together. Promise we can." The dog began to yap and nip at his mistress's ankles. She stooped to swing him back into her arms.

Jake pushed the door to their room open, grabbed Mabel's arm, and tugged her toward him. "We'll let you know."

The door shut with a nudge of his boot.

"That was rather rude," Mabel said.

"She's irritating."

"I think she's very friendly." Mabel turned to scan the space they would call home for the next two weeks. "This is suitable enough."

Jake took a stroll around their stateroom: three steps past the compact lavatory that featured a white porcelain sink and a mirror set into a teakwood cabinet, three steps past the built-in wardrobe, and another two steps to the berths—two, one set on top of the other and draped with blue challis curtains.

"I'll take the top." He tossed his hat onto the upper bunk but threw himself onto the lower one. "I hope I don't feel too trapped before the trip is over." His face drained of color, and he tossed his arm over his eyes with a groan.

"You've already experienced this once, Jake. How did you manage the first time?" She crossed the crimson carpet, a nice contrast with the blue of the bed curtains and the small window set across from it, and sat beside him. She nudged at his leg with her hip until he allowed space for her.

"I hardly remember a thing. That entire crossing is a haze. I took meals in my room, and don't think I left it more than a handful of times." He removed his arm and looked at her. She saw in his eyes everything he seemed afraid to say. He couldn't hide it.

Pain was like an infection. It had to come out somewhere, or it would fester. Grow and spread and fill every bit of space until one was consumed by it.

"Do you want to talk about her?" It would kill her to hear it, but she would do it for him.

He shook his head, and then she wanted nothing more than for him to tell her. If he did, might he release his wife? Maybe he would find space in his heart for *her*.

He knocked against her back with his knee, and she looked at him again. "She reminds me of Charlotte."

"Who?"

"That chatty woman in the hall. In looks and mannerisms

and . . ."—the arm was tossed back over his face—"and every-thing."

"Then we shouldn't have dinner with them. I've no desire to see your grief increased." She went to the lavatory and removed her hat. The pins were next, and she rubbed at the raw spots where they had dug into her scalp. "We should hurry. The ship will push off soon, and I don't want to miss my last chance to see Italy." Using her fingers as a comb, she smoothed her low pompadour back over the rat and twisted her hair into a French bun. "I think I might cut a fringe. It seems a good—"

She had seen Jake approach in the mirror, but even so, when his fingers curled over her shoulders and he reached to press his lips to her cheek, she yelped.

"I'm grateful to you, Mabel. You're a very good friend and the most selfless person I've ever known."

She looked at their reflection, her eyes wide. He lifted her hat and handed it over, giving her something to do to mask the effect of his kiss. She didn't touch her face, but it took considerable effort to resist.

"I would never ask you to forgo an enjoyable dinner just to prevent me a small bit of discomfort. Don't even think about it."

He replaced his own hat on his head, so she followed suit, and they left the stateroom that suddenly felt too small. Too close. Too hot.

They strolled down the hall, arm in arm, and took the hand-some staircase to the deck. Jake seemed completely unaffected by that kiss. How could it be so? She lifted her fingers to her cheek with a surreptitious movement, but her gloves were a frustrating barrier. And she couldn't risk removing them merely to touch the spot where his lips—oh goodness, his lips—had landed. How would she explain it?

She satisfied herself by looking at him and recognizing that she loved Jake Cunningham. She always had, so that wasn't a particularly startling revelation.

But for the first time, she no longer found herself satisfied with friendship.

She stood beside the rail with hundreds of others—caring only about the man at her side—and watched Italy, her childhood, and Manzo Brothers Circus slip away.

It was time to move on. Time to grow up. And maybe time for Jake to recognize that the woman beside him was more than brawn and kindness.

"Good-bye, Italy. You have been good to me." Jake's words skipped with the breeze over the gentle curls of the Ligurian Sea, and he swung his arm around her waist. "Who knows, Mabel, what America has for us."

"Yes. Precisely."

It was a start.

CHAPTER

THE LAUNDRESSES SCRAPED the bottom of circus hierarchy. Unseen, doing what no one thought of, hidden from the eyes of everyone who mattered.

Isabella hadn't had occasion to speak with them since her mother retired, broken and spending nearly every moment gasping for a full breath. She'd left the circus just as Isabella literally climbed into stardom.

Isabella had been so full of hope then. Of dreams and plans and romance with the son of Travis and Wells's prominent owner. She could take care of Maman and handed over most of her pay—enough for a room in a safe boardinghouse. Clean. Simple. Better than anything Maman had had since they lost the farm.

From the very top of the tent that first show on the road—her first time ever without Maman—Isabella had seen the awe written on the spectators' faces. She could hear their collective breath. She had grabbed a rope, been hoisted upward, and flipped again and again, dislocating her shoulder so that she could make a full rotation with each turn. How many flanges had she done? She'd stopped counting when her entire being filled with the buzz of admiration. And then, throwing herself off the platform and grabbing ahold of the bar tossed her way, she knew she could give her mother a better life. She was lucky enough to have been born with all the charm and beauty of her Gallic ancestors, crowned with her father's black curls. In the circus, you had to be either extremely different or extremely beautiful. Polly Grant was both.

Isabella watched the laundresses now, bent over steaming tubs, their hands permanently red and raw from the lye they used. She ran her palms over her cheeks, pulling the skin taut so that, she imagined, she looked the way she had years ago when she'd caught the public's imagination. These women, she knew, were her age or younger.

They didn't look it.

It was hard work. Tireless and punishing and never ending. Many circuses expected performers to do their own laundry on Sundays, but Jerry Wells was a stickler for observing the Sabbath and wouldn't allow any of his employees to work it. Not even the laundresses.

Isabella had just finished her first show since injuring her foot. Only one day short of Dr. Covert's seven-day recommendation. It had sucked every bit of stamina from her, and she knew it wasn't a performance that would win her security. When her feet had hit the floor, she hadn't even bothered to smile at the audience. She shuffled out of the way as the Danó sisters bounded past, their hands waving and steps light.

They had done well.

She was the weak link. She could see that. So she'd wrapped a shawl around her shoulders, slid past the other ladies peeling off layers of costume to change into respectable clothing, and escaped.

"Do you need something, ma'am?" one of the laundresses called, and Isabella jerked her gaze up. She remembered that she stood in the backyard, half hidden by taut canvas spiked into the ground.

"No. No, I'm just thinking." She smiled. Not genuine. Not the one she'd been tossing to strangers all these years.

The woman shrugged and went back to her work. She was pregnant, and a toddler played near her feet, his skinny legs sticking out of too-short pants. Jerry had hired many widowed women over the years—his own mother had been forced into menial labor when his father died—and they were grateful for the job. Her mother had been. It kept them fed. Offered a family of sorts. Provided protection from the things that threatened women alone in the world.

And it hadn't been a bad way to grow up. Isabella had made lifelong friends and been taught a skill that would have made her very wealthy had she not tried to prolong her mother's life day by day, hour by hour. And in the end, minute by minute.

So much joy and grief was wrapped around the issue of the laundry. But Maman had come from nothing and received everything. If Isabella ended up there, she would be leaving everything and receiving only a more broken body. She'd wind up ill and shriveled and unable to care for herself. Like Maman.

Just as broken and weak as Bram had always accused her of being.

Isabella stiffened her shoulders and clutched the fringed ends of her shawl over her embroidered bodice. The back of it fell to her knees, not quite providing the modesty Jerry required of his female employees. She wasn't supposed to go out onto the grounds in costume while the public was here. She should go back into the dressing tent and don the cream-and-black-striped walking suit she'd worn that morning.

But she could hear Annette's voice, and it dug deeply into the wounds that had opened when she'd given her best for the show today and had known it wasn't enough. Annette's laughter scraped her nerves, and Isabella couldn't face it.

She'd heard, along with the Danó sisters and Annette, that Jerry was disappointed in her. And *everyone* knew what that meant. He was a fair man but wouldn't hesitate to release dead weight.

Isabella stepped over the tent peg, and her satin slippers sank into the soft earth. She kicked off a clod of dirt and took another step. And another. With the shawl wrapped tightly around her and her head down, she hurried across the circus grounds. By the time she passed the big top entrance, the sideshow barker where a cluster of titillated society ladies giggled, and a pair of candy butchers taking a break, she was practically running.

Every step brought her toward the decision she'd made. The one that would keep her from Maman's future.

Her body had failed her too many times—in pregnancy, in motherhood, in marriage, and in work. She would not allow it to fail her again. And what was the point of it all, of the sacrifice and soreness and abuse, if she couldn't use it to save herself now?

"Polly?" Robert stood at his desk when she slid past the open tent flap of his mobile office.

"Are you expecting anyone?" Now that she had arrived, her stomach began to roil like a boat tossed at sea, and she cast a glance over her shoulder.

But she had no reason to feel guilty. Bram was dead.

"No. Everyone is about their work. What's wrong?" Robert rounded the table and ducked his head to see her face, which she'd turned toward the floor.

"I need to speak with you." She met his eyes, saying everything with them she could think to say, knowing he wouldn't hear a word. "Privately. No one must interrupt. Can we go to your coach?"

He drew back. "You know that isn't allowed."

"You're the manager. Make it allowable." Her teeth began to click against one another, and she clenched her jaw.

He stared at her a moment, his brow furrowed and his fingers rolling a pen back and forth. "All right."

Isabella allowed him to dictate the pace. Slower than her mad race to him. She welcomed it, because she knew every one of these steps would stab Maman's heart if she were still breathing. Would slap Bram's face, though Isabella didn't know if he'd remained faithful to her.

Robert gave a cursory glance when they reached the rail yard, but no one was around. Every person in the circus played a part on show days. Every hand was needed.

His was a private stateroom, fit into half a coach, and well furnished—the benefit of being the most trusted and well-paid employee with Travis and Wells Circus. He urged her toward the tufted sofa that dominated the room beneath a mirrored wall flanked by sconces, but Isabella didn't sit. She stood off to the side and looked through the doorway that led to the bedroom. Her heart sounded like the drums used in the parade, but Bram was dead, and she was facing a bleak future.

She swung around to face her oldest friend and forced courage into her spine and arms and every empty part of her.

"Are you going to tell me what's going on now?" he asked.

"Will you convince Jerry to at least allow me to finish the year? To complete this show?" If she had a year, she might be able to come up with a plan. She might be able to find a place to land that wouldn't require a strong back and every shred of beauty she still retained. Or maybe she could regain her strength and flexibility somehow. Recapture what she'd lost.

"I don't know if I can. He's adamant your best days are behind you." He reached for her shoulder, and his hand was warm. Kind. "I'm sure he will offer you another job. A way to make a living and continue on with us."

The laundry? "Please, talk to him."

"What use would it be? You know how he is when he makes up his mind."

She pressed her fingers over his hand and let the shawl fall around her feet. "You must convince him to let me continue performing. For the year, at least." She stepped close—slippers touching his polished shoes, breasts brushing his stomach—and tilted her head to look up at him. He was taller than her but not nearly as tall as Bram. He wouldn't make her feel safe the way her husband always had, but he wouldn't frighten her either.

Robert went still, but she could feel his heart beating beneath her palm when she slipped it between their bodies. Even through his coat, it battered her hand.

"What are you doing?" His words were mangled. Pinched together and reaching for clarity in that mahogany-encrusted train car.

"I will never marry you, Robert. I won't ever give anyone a chance to destroy me again. But I can give you this."

"No." He stepped away, and her hands fell from him. "I don't want *this*, Polly. I want a marriage."

"Will you speak with Jerry? Please."

He took a few stumbling steps backward, then turned and crossed his arms. "There is no point. He's decided. He doesn't think it's safe for you anymore, and Travis and Wells cannot handle another disaster. Another performer's death. I'm waiting to hear from him, but likely you only have a few weeks left."

Her slippers were silent against the carpet, and when she slid her hand under his jacket and touched his back, he jerked. Spinning around, he caught her gaze, and she saw he was stuck between his conscience and his love.

"Talk to him." She reached for his arm and pulled him toward the bedroom. And because he had always wanted her, she was able to disabuse him of his objections.

She hadn't been with a man since Mabel had been torn from her womb. Bram hadn't so much as pressed his lips to hers, fear of losing himself to lust and getting her with child again keeping him as cold as an iceberg.

A part of her wanted this for more than practical matters.

But when it was over, Isabella pressed her face into the pillow and let it catch her tears. She had never fully embraced the faith of her mother, but she'd paid it lip-service, at least, and kept herself apart. She'd never taken any issue with the strict rules of the circus.

She'd done that for Bram's sake, though. For their sham of a marriage. But now her husband was dead.

She forced herself up and sat on the edge of the bed, letting her gaze sweep over the sheets twisted around Robert's legs.

She was wholly alone, and there was no one but herself to see that hard work didn't kill her the way it had her mother.

❃   ❃   ❃

Jake had forgotten how big New York was. They had been searching for lodging for half the day—since leaving the ship late that morning. Plodding up one street and down another without any luck. He knew the areas to avoid and a general idea of where to find suitable housing, but as of yet, they'd had no luck.

Beside him, Mabel took in the chaos with round eyes and seemed unaware how much interest others were taking in her. She was rumpled after their long journey, her travel coat creased and dingy, but she observed everything with such a delicious air of awe, cheeks pink with pleasure, that it would be impossible for even the most jaded New Yorker to resist finding her completely delightful.

Besides that, her height, breadth, and handsomeness demanded notice.

Jake grabbed her arm before she could step out in front of a hurtling automobile.

"Oh," she said and offered him a sheepish smile. "I should pay better attention. There's so much to see here, though, isn't there?"

"I suppose." He'd dreaded their arrival in this city, wondering if he was opening himself up to the devastating pain that had consumed him after Charlotte's death. It was in this city, after all, that she'd fallen. This city where they'd last spoken and worked and loved. But in the end, he had been too busy seeing to the storage of their luggage and finding the streetcar that would take them to the most promising location for their search that he felt very little at all.

And then he found himself entirely entertained by Mabel's response to America. Youthful, he would have called it, if she hadn't been so near his own age. Innocent. Delighted.

"I don't think I've ever seen such a crush of people. Even in Paris." She snugged her arm more tightly around his and grinned.

"You went shopping in Paris, though, so you missed the truly crushing parts."

"I think that was a mistake, then, for this is"—she flung her free arm wide, as though trying to draw him into embracing it all—"captivating."

A small girl in front of them turned at Mabel's words. Her gaze grew still as it traced Mabel upward. "You sure are tall."

Mabel laughed. "Yes, I know."

"You're pretty, though. I didn't realize a lady could be pretty and still be as big as a man." The girl, not at all tall, wrinkled her nose. "The only other tall lady I know is ugly as a potato. That's Mrs. Cartwright, the grocer's wife. The grocer died two years ago. I think she killed him."

Jake shot the child a sharp look. "Because she was ugly?"

"Oh no. I don't think that kills people. I think it was her un-charible-mess." She gave a sad shake of her head. "She once smacked my hand just for *touching* the candy jar."

Mabel pressed her hand to her mouth, and Jake shot her a wink. "I'm Miss . . . um, *Mrs.* Cunningham, and this is my husband, Mr. Cunningham." Even after twelve days crossing the Atlantic, Jake hadn't quite gotten used to hearing her new name, and because she stumbled every time she said it, he imagined she hadn't either. "What is your name?"

"Katie Grace. Mam said I got two names because one wasn't enough to handle all my personality."

Mabel laughed again, which seemed to reinforce Katie Grace's outlandish extroversion, for she began to dance around them, nearly stepping into a pile of horse excrement and falling onto the cobblestones. Jake lifted her and swung her back onto the sidewalk just before a streetcar turned her into pancake.

Mabel shifted her carpetbag to her other hand and took hold of the child's arm. "Where do you live, Katie Grace? We can walk you home."

"I can't go home yet because I'm s'posed to be at school. It isn't over until two." She gave a little shriek and darted toward a pile of broken-down boxes prickled with rusty nails. "Look!" She emerged from the mess with a ragged kitten in her arms. The poor thing was missing half its ear and looked as though it had never eaten in its life. It was mottled grey, though that might have mostly been dirt. "Mam won't let me keep it. She never does. Says strays eat more than I do, and I eat an awful lot. And Mrs. Luvotti would likely raise our rent." She tucked the cat into her sweater and cradled her arm around it. "I might try to hide it in my room, though. Last time, Mam didn't notice for days. She's pretty 'stracted."

"Why aren't you at school if you're supposed to be?" Jake watched as Mabel poked her finger into Katie Grace's sweater to scratch the cat's head and then pulled back quickly to wipe her hand against her skirt.

"You should put the animal down. It's covered in fleas," Mabel said.

Katie Grace gave a sage nod but ignored her. "I hate school." She looped around Mabel and inserted herself between her and Jake before beginning to skip beside them, the cat giving a terrified little *mew* every time its head jostled.

"Why is that?" Jake asked, setting his hand against the child's shoulder in an attempt to save the kitten's life.

"'Do hush, Katie Grace,'" Katie Grace mimicked with pursed lips and her round eyes scrunched. "'Come here and receive a strike. You will be the dunce for today. Why must you try me at every turn? I have told you once if I've told you a hundred times, it's twenty-four, not forty-two. Heed the lesson. Pay attention. Attend to this, Katie Grace!'" She sighed and gave a great heave of her narrow shoulders. "School just isn't for me, I've decided. All the numbers just get mixed up, and I can't see the reason behind them."

Jake met Mabel's eyes over Katie Grace's head and pressed his lips together to stem a smile. He'd always liked children, and this one was particularly charming, if a little mutinous. His insides gave a twist, and for the first time in years, he regretted having not had any with Charlotte. It wouldn't have been possible, of course, for Charlotte had been adamant they not have any. And until she was no longer with him, he'd been all right with it.

"And anyway," Katie Grace said, pointing toward a crowd at the top of the street, "the circus is coming in today."

"What circus?" Mabel's steps hastened, and Jake knew she hoped to see her mother. Though how she would recognize her, he didn't know. Bram had told him years ago that he'd destroyed every photograph of her. It seemed odd and, in the end, inconvenient for Mabel as she searched for a woman she didn't know.

"Travis and Wells." Katie Grace heaved a great sigh of longing.

Jake swallowed hard and tried to untangle the churning

in his stomach. Disappointment for Mabel that she wouldn't find her mother so easily—unless the woman had joined his old circus after he'd left—or maybe just knowing he was so close to them. To the people who knew Jake when he was Jake and Charlotte.

"It's one of the biggest, you know," Katie Grace continued. "Daddy was going to take me this year before he got his head smashed in by that no-good thief. That man was not—"

"What did you say?" Jake held up the girl's hand, trying to catch the words Katie Grace was spitting.

"Daddy was attacked by a man on his way home from work one day last summer. He stole his wallet and pocket watch, even though that was very old and not worth very much."

"And he is not well because of it?" Jake steered them through the jostling crowd.

"He's dead." Katie Grace blinked as though not quite believing she'd said such a terrible thing, then lifted onto her toes and craned her neck. "I can't see anything." She grabbed the coat of the man in front of her, earning a smack.

"I have an idea." Jake crouched in front of the child. "Give Mrs. Cunningham your kitten."

Katie Grace tightened her grip around the cat and eyed Mabel with a look of distrust. "You will take care of her?"

"Of course," Mabel replied.

Katie Grace deliberated a moment before withdrawing the animal, which stiffened and reached its claws for the nubby knit of her sweater. "It will be okay," she soothed and pressed the kitten to her face. With a hasty thrust, the cat was in Mabel's hands, and Jake swung Katie Grace up onto his shoulders.

"I should sit atop her, don't you think?" Katie Grace patted Jake's shoulder. "She is taller than you by a head."

"But she has other talents." Jake grinned and gave Mabel a nod.

"And one of them is moving a crowd." Mabel tucked the kitten against her breast.

It didn't take long to convince the crowd to part for them. A nudge here and a cleared throat there. Mabel could have employed a more aggressive approach, but in truth, most people stood aside, their mouths hanging open in shock as she passed.

"She's impressive, isn't she?" Jake whispered to Katie Grace.

"Yes. Is that why you married her?" Katie Grace did not bother to whisper.

"Well, when you have the chance to marry the strongest woman in the world, you take it. Don't you think your heart would be safe with someone like that managing things?" Safe because she would never knowingly harm a flea. Safe because she hadn't the ability to hurt him the way Charlotte had. Safe because there was nothing real about their marriage.

"We're all the way at the front," Katie Grace exclaimed. "I never thought I'd be so close!"

Jake set her down, and the circus paraded itself before them—elephants in their finery, acrobats and jugglers, camels, and brightly painted carts that proclaimed exotic animals.

"Travis and Wells winters in Indiana," Jake said as they watched a troupe of ballet girls wearing gauzy green pants and long, tasseled veils. "They perform in different cities as they travel east across Ohio and Pennsylvania, but they consider New York their season opening. They spend six weeks here in the spring."

Mabel touched his arm. "Are you all right watching them? Is this painful?"

"I'm fine." Katie Grace laughed at the antics of a clown, and he couldn't help but smile. "It's worth it to see this poor child happy."

Mabel didn't answer. She lifted the kitten, its head nestling at the base of her throat, and gave Jake a strange look. "You're a very good man."

He snorted, because nothing could be further from the truth. In that moment, though, as she looked at him with eyes that shimmered like the Aegean, he wished to be one. He wished he could give her everything she wanted—courage, her mother, the family she'd had to leave behind. But all he had was a faded memory of New York City neighborhoods and maybe enough charm to convince someone to give them a room.

He pushed his hat back and scratched his forehead. "We should go. If we don't find lodging this afternoon, we'll have to find a hotel tonight and try again in the morning."

Katie Grace glanced up and looked from Mabel to Jake and back again. "If you need a room, there's an empty one at our boardinghouse. Mam says it's nothing fancy but better than the 'ternative. What does 'ternative mean?"

Jake grinned. "It means it's better than spending money we don't have on a hotel. I think that sounds fortuitous."

Katie Grace wrinkled her nose. "I don't know what that means either, but I don't care. This is starting to feel like school." She turned her attention back to the parade, and Jake felt the tentative brush of Mabel's hand as she reached for his.

He shouldn't allow it, but there was such solace in her touch. It was familiar and comforting and safe.

But when she wove her fingers between his, his heart gave a small leap—nothing grand, more the cautious attempt of a beginner acrobat—and he wondered if she wasn't as safe as he'd assumed.

CHAPTER
9

THE MOMENT ISABELLA entered the women's dressing room at Madison Square Garden, she tore the veil from her face. Bunching it into a ball, she flung it against the wall, but it simply unfurled and fluttered to the floor like a dying butterfly.

An apt metaphor.

Down the hall, she could hear the stampede of ballet girls, performers, and animal handlers sounding like a gaggle of geese screeching over a winter lake. She'd slipped from the parade as soon as her section of dancers had crossed Broadway. She'd cut through Madison Square Park, ignoring the trails, instead darting across green spaces and around trees and statues, until she reached the arena that would be her home for the next six weeks while Travis and Wells entertained New York's masses.

Normally she enjoyed settling into the city for an extended time.

Normally she wasn't forced to hide her face.

The clatter of footsteps grew louder as the mob approached. Isabella unwound the gauzy yellow fabric from around her body as she made her way toward the alcoves against the far end of the room. Piece by piece, she dropped her costume onto a bench—first the scarf, then the satin slippers, the bodice rimmed in tassels and bells, and finally the pants that were delicious to slide into but required exacting movements to unbutton the snaps that kept them tight around her ankles. The fleshlings she left on the floor—narrow, limp skins twisting into a heap of silk and sweat.

"Do you need help, Isabella?" a ballet girl asked as the group of them clattered into the room.

She continued working out the laces of her corset and shook her head. She was young enough, at least, to undress herself. She sniffed and dropped her undergarment onto the bench, where it nestled into the deflated puff of her costuming. The air nipped her skin as she reached for the clothing hanging on a nail inside the alcove, and she crossed an arm over her breasts. April in New York was a temperamental beast. One never knew what you were going to get. This year, it seemed uneager to release winter.

Behind her, the other women whispered furiously. Not a low whisper that would only tickle Isabella's ears with random words that, strung together, made no sense. But in a whisper that wasn't really a whisper. Perhaps they thought she'd gone deaf in her old age?

"What's wrong with her today?"

"Mr. Pedersen told her she needed to wear a veil."

A titter of giggles erupted.

"I mean, she has to be over fifty. It's time."

Isabella snapped the wrinkles out of her skirt. She was exactly fifty years old, thank you very much.

"I heard she's on her way out. It does seem desperate that someone her age is still aiming for center ring."

Isabella whirled, the skirt pressed against her stomach. "I can hear you, if you don't mind."

The women—girls?—froze in their cluster of youthful stupidity. Long arms reaching for clothing. Perky breasts, not a silvery stretch mark in sight, demanding an artist's sketchbook. Leanly muscled legs with pointed feet stretching out kinks. Taut bellies that had never heaved life into the world. Open mouths and wide eyes and pink cheeks.

Everything about them was a blazing poker burning away the hazy mist of the circus's magic. Like a magician who had been exposed. One minute, caught up in the illusion—glitter and lights and sleight of hand. The next, realizing that everything you thought you knew was only a trick. A mirage.

Isabella caught her reflection in the long, narrow mirror behind the dancers. She could see their tight, round rears and smooth backs, and behind them, herself. Breasts hanging over her fisted skirt. Ankles that had long since given up any pretense of daintiness poking beneath the draped material. The pockets and folds of flesh that seemed to be everywhere.

And a face that had, only minutes ago, been covered so the spectators wouldn't be offended by the old aerialist who had come to the end of her career.

Isabella turned and dressed. The dancers had fallen silent, and not a word was spoken until she left the room and shut the door behind her. Pressing her hands over her ears to block out the mocking laughter and insults sliding into the hall, she ran through the building's twisting back corridors and stumbled outside beneath the portico. In a few steps, she stood on the street, looking over the building's arches and minarets and the tower—said to be the second-tallest structure in the city.

"Lady, out of the way." The shouting driver, clatter of hooves, and crunching wheels sent Isabella back to the sidewalk, where Robert stood, leaning against one of the pillars, arms crossed over his chest.

"Are you all right?" he asked.

"I'm fine." She began walking down the street and only rolled her eyes a little when he caught up with her.

"You don't seem fine."

She skirted a large barrel of onions outside a grocer's and stopped to look at a milliner's window display. The green-striped awning cast the hats stacked atop tiered stands like wedding cakes in shadow, so she pressed her face close to the glass and peered inside. She didn't need a new hat. She needed Robert to leave her alone. If he didn't, she would likely spew every ugly word crowding out her thoughts all over him.

He stood at her elbow, waiting as patiently as a saint.

"What do you expect me to say, Robert?" She took a step back and continued her march toward the hotel Travis and Wells provided for circus workers while in New York.

"I just want you to tell me what's wrong." He walked beside her, his hands in his pockets, looking very much put out, which set her teeth on edge.

"Would you have complete access to my thoughts as well as my body?" She stomped around the corner, her face flushing at having said such a thing aloud. As though the speaking of it was almost worse than the *doing* of it.

"That's not at all what I meant." His words were cloaked in softness and maybe a little hurt. "I hope you know me better than that by now."

She deflated and turned to face Hotel Veronica with slumped shoulders. How heavy they felt. How tired she was. Their heels clicked a staccato against the tiles as they crossed the lobby.

"I'm sorry," she said as they waited for the elevator to descend. "I know that isn't what you meant."

A red-coated employee opened the gate, and their ride was quiet but for the grinding gears and gentle creaking of the cage. At the third floor, Isabella stepped into the carpeted hall and waited while Robert slipped a coin into the attendant's gloved hand. The elevator lumbered back down its chute, but they stood there, still and staring at one another.

"Very well," Isabella finally gave a nod. "If you really wish to know what is bothering me. This morning, in one breath, you told me not only that I had lost my position with the other aerialists in the parade and would be relegated to the ballet troupe, but that I was also required to veil my face."

He stared at her before comprehension finally slackened his mouth and unknit his brows. "But, Polly . . . it's only business. You must know that. Most performers are veiled once they hit a certain age, and it's usually younger than the one you've reached."

"That doesn't make it any easier."

"It doesn't mean anything, though."

An incredulous puff of laughter escaped her lips, and her stomach pulled into itself, turning hard and heavy. "It means everything." She waved her hands from her head down the lines of her body. "It means this is no longer enough."

It had never been enough. Not really. Not for Bram or Mabel. But at least it had been enough for the circus.

A door opened down the hall, and Isabella hastened toward her room. Robert followed. When he stopped at the door one over from hers, she shook her head and pretended not to notice. Of course he had arranged that. She'd only been with him twice more since that day in his coach.

Three times she had ignored her conscience. Three times she allowed a man not her husband to use her body—all she had left of it—to satisfy years of need. Three times for what? A demotion and a veil.

"I should let you know that I talked Jerry into allowing you to stay until the end of the New York season. It's all I could do, Polly." Robert jiggled his key in the knob and pushed open the door. "And also . . . you've always been enough for me. Every bit of you."

She stared at the wall between their rooms for a moment, registering the click of the lock as he gently shut the door and the *hush sweep hush* of the elevator bringing up another few guests.

Her eyes slid shut, and she bumped her forehead against her cupped palms. She'd hurt him. It seemed she always did. But he wanted too much of her, and she couldn't give it. Her heart had nearly been destroyed by marriage once before. It might be the only piece of her still worth preserving.

All she had was her failing, aging body and a face Jeremiah Wells insisted she cover. It was beyond her why Robert wanted even that.

She shifted a few steps and knocked. When Robert opened the door, his jacket off and shirtsleeves rolled above his elbows, Isabella pushed past him into his room. She'd give herself to him once more. This time as a thank you instead of a bribe.

❊ ❊ ❊

Katie Grace honored her word and, after the parade, led Jake and Mabel to a respectably shabby boardinghouse in the southern part of Greenwich Village on Minetta Lane. Cuddled between a bakery and a plumber, the building had the look of an aged gentleman. Once sharp and hopeful, now settling into rumpled obscurity.

But it was clean, and because the area had been settled by Italian immigrants, it seemed to welcome Mabel with open arms and a generous *benvenuta*. She hoped they might claim a front-facing apartment, for the street teemed with life. Wagons and taxis rumbled over the iron tracks embedded into New York's crisscrossing streets, and pedestrians darted between electric streetcars. It was a consuming chaos. One that brushed Mabel's skin and sent thrills along her spine.

"Mrs. Luvotti isn't very friendly," Katie Grace said as she gave a furtive look around and stashed the kitten in a box beside a small outbuilding. She led them through the front door and into a dim foyer empty of furnishings and any speck of dust that might have wished to settle on them. "But she keeps a clean house and makes very good biscotti."

"It's good to focus on the important things." Jake's words bounced around a laugh.

Katie Grace slanted a look at him. "Are you being patron-izin'?"

His face fell into grave lines, and he shook his head. "Not at all. That's a very big word for a small child. Did you learn it in school?"

"Does anyone learn anything in school? It's a waste of time, if you ask me. Just a bunch of senseless rules and dull, tired teachers droning on and on about things that don't much matter." Katie Grace gave a resolute nod and stepped through a door at the back of the hall past the gleaming oak staircase. "No, I have learned less than nothing at school. My father used to say, 'Kitty'—that was his nickname for me—'Kitty, never allow anyone to patronize you.' He spoke to me like I was all growed up. No one, not even Mam, does that anymore."

Nothing else could be said, because Katie Grace pushed open a door and led them into a kitchen so full of delicious scents that Mabel's stomach released a demanding growl.

"Mrs. Luvotti, I've brought new boarders. They can have Miss Meyer's old room." Katie Grace hopped onto a stool tucked beneath the long, battered table taking up the middle of the kitchen and glanced over her shoulder at them. "Miss Meyer up and married some no-good Bohemian, isn't that right?" She shrugged when Mrs. Luvotti only glared at her. "I thought he was a writer. What's a Bohemian?"

Jake coughed and stepped up to the table to introduced himself and Mabel to the woman standing on the other side, chopping cabbage. Her face had the look of a sparrow—closely set eyes, a beakish nose, and a chin that sank into her neck like an apology.

"What do you do?" Mrs. Luvotti asked. "I run a respectable place."

"Right now, we don't do anything. We've recently come from Italy, though we are not Italian, and will be looking for work." Jake reached back and took Mabel's hand, tugging her forward. "But I assure you, we are respectable."

Her gaze darted between the two of them. "Work doing what?"

"They're from the circus!" Katie Grace exclaimed.

Mrs. Luvotti's knife clattered to the counter, and she stared at them, her throat working around, Mabel was sure, all the names she could think to ascribe to them.

"We were performers, it's true, but very respectable ones." Jake's dimple peeked at the proprietress, and she blinked.

Mrs. Luvotti raised her hand to her throat as a flush crept above the high collar of her serviceable shirtwaist. "Well . . . yes." She glanced at Mabel, and the steely glint reappeared in her eyes. "Three weeks' payment ahead of time."

She named a price that had Mabel mentally counting wildly disappearing coins. It would leave them with very little until they secured work. But at least they would have a roof and food. And though it seemed Mrs. Luvotti could claim not a morsel of sweetness, the smell wafting from the oven across the room promised she knew a thing or two about baking.

"Is that pie in the oven, Mrs. Luvotti?" Mabel asked.

"Dried apple." The woman smacked Katie Grace's wrist, and a clutch of raisins fell to the table. "Enough of that. Go to your mother, or I'll tell her you skipped out on school again today."

Katie Grace snatched her hand back, and her eyes went wide. "Yes, ma'am." She scrambled from the stool and disappeared up a narrow staircase tucked into the corner.

Mrs. Luvotti pulled off her apron and hung it on a hook. "Come and I'll show you the room."

They followed her into the main hall and up the stairs. "It's the third floor. There are four rooms and a bathroom on each." She declared this with no small amount of pride. "My husband ran the plumbing shop next door. Now it belongs to our sons. You won't find many boardinghouses in this area with such a feature."

Mabel made an appropriate sound that seemed to assure Mrs. Luvotti of her pleasure. She followed the woman into the room, no larger than the one in Genoa but less full of hospitality and laughter and argument.

It had a front-facing window, though, and Mabel took four steps across the bare wooden floors that would likely prick her feet with splinters come nighttime and pushed aside the checked curtain. On the street below, she found her peace. Her center.

The buildings all around looked about as solid as matchstick houses. They declared neither history nor importance. This was not Bologna, with its sunset-colored brick and stucco buildings. It wasn't any of the European cities the circus skirted, nor the rural villages hewn from the rocky ground that had been there so long no could remember what came before.

New York was young. Vibrant and brash and absolutely pulsing with excitement. She could see a future here. More than the next show, the next town, the next act. She could sense it in the blood moving through her veins. This was a place one could settle. Sink roots and grow tall alongside the city around it. It might make up for being forced out of the circus.

She dragged her fingers across the wavy glass and turned to look at Jake. "This will do, I think."

Mrs. Luvotti raised her brows as though thinking, *Of course, it will more than do,* and stepped toward the door. "Dinner is at six. I won't tolerate tardiness."

Mabel resisted the urge to salute. "We will need to hire a cart to retrieve our baggage. We left it at the dock." She set her carpetbag on the bed and pressed against the mattress with firm palms.

"I will send someone." The landlady left, and the moment her shoes clattered against the stairs, Katie Grace poked her head inside their new home.

"You're staying?" Her eyes were bright, and she pressed her hands together. "Truly? I'm so glad." She darted into the room and threw her arms around Mabel's midsection. "I feel we will be great friends."

Mabel patted the girl's head and resisted the urge to chastise her for her obvious distaste for comb and braids. Katie Grace had a mother already. But she obviously needed a sister, and Mabel had always wanted one. "Since we are friends, I want to give you something."

Katie Grace stepped away and watched with no small amount of restraint. Her skinny legs, poking beneath the hem of her skirt, fairly trembled as she bounced on her toes. "Oh, oh!"

Mabel smiled as she pulled the doll from her bag. She hadn't known why she kept it and only thought to see it mended and cleaned. But something about it touched her heart and nudged aside her preoccupation with her father's passing. Now she would give it a home the way Katie Grace had given one to them.

"You must name her," Mabel said, handing it over.

Katie Grace clutched the doll to her chest and screwed her eyes shut. "I think I will call her . . . Patricia Millicent Elizabeth. Because two names are not enough for her." A sound in the hall made her eyes pop open, and she grabbed Mabel's hand. "I nearly forgot. Mam asked that I invite you into our rooms for tea. Will you come?"

"Of course."

They followed Katie Grace down the stairs and to the end of the second-floor hall where a door stood propped open against a large, polished rock.

"Mam!" Katie Grace darted inside, stopping midway into the room and motioning them forward.

A small woman with a pile of blonde curls and Katie Grace's impertinently tipped nose swept into the room through a door. Dark circles rimmed her eyes, and the deep lines bracketing her mouth made clear her recent grief, but Mabel thought she looked like spring—all dappled sunshine and gentle breeze.

Her eyes went a little wide when she saw Mabel, but she quickly schooled her features. "Katie Grace has told me that I must make your acquaintance." She offered the type of smile that slowed one's heartbeat. Everything about her exuded warmth and calm. Very different from her chaotic and lively daughter.

"It's very nice to meet you," Jake said, making introductions. "Do you have two rooms, Mrs. Russo?"

"Please, my name is Alice. And yes, there is one suite, as Mrs. Luvotti calls them, on each floor. My husband secured it just before we married. They aren't easy to come by in this part of the city."

"We're moving into one room at the end of the week," Katie Grace said, hopping from foot to foot, "'cause Mam doesn't make much with her sewing. At least not as much as my father did when he worked at the bank."

"Katie Grace, hush." Mrs. Russo led them through the room—the same layout as Mabel and Jake's but boasting a little trundle bed tucked beneath the larger one and crocheted lace curtains at the window—into another that was smaller and cozier. A small round table topped by a painted tea service was hemmed in by a settee and a matching chair.

"What type of sewing do you do?" Jake asked after he and

Mabel had settled onto the settee, Mrs. Russo in the chair, and Katie Grace on the floor, her legs extended and crossed at the ankles.

Mrs. Russo poured tea and handed a cup to Jake. "All sorts of needlework. I learned at my grandmother's knee. I can make lace, as well. It's a family tradition going back to Ireland."

"Mam sews everything." Katie Grace leapt to her feet. "She made this."

"It's very pretty." Mabel admired Katie Grace's dress—the pintucks and ruffles and neat darts.

"But sewing doesn't pay the bills. Not all of them, at least." Katie Grace dropped back to the floor with a sigh. "I keep telling Mam that she can save the money she spends on my schooling, but for some reason, she seems to think it is necessary."

Mrs. Russo laughed and reached forward to give Katie Grace a little tickle. "Someone needs to civilize you." She sat back. "And you, Mrs. Cunningham, are you a fan of traditional schooling? If it were up to Katie Grace, she would learn all of her lessons on the streets of New York."

Mabel took a sip of tea and smiled over the rim of her cup. "I'm sure my education was quite . . . peculiar. For one, I've never set foot inside a school. And my lessons consisted of acts you might consider much more dangerous than running the streets of any city. I'm a circus performer. Or rather, I was."

Mrs. Russo made a little squeak as her cup clattered to its saucer and tea sloshed over the edge, leaving a spreading stain upon her skirt. "A . . . circus performer?"

"She's a strongwoman, Mam," Katie Grace said with measurable glee. Her gaze swept Jake. "But you don't *look* like any of the strongmen I've seen on the posters. And I've seen most of them. They've been pasted all over the city."

Mrs. Russo paused in her effort to blot at the tea stain with a handkerchief. "I should hope you've not managed to see every poster, darling, for that would mean you've not spent one moment at school."

Katie Grace swallowed and ducked her head.

Mrs. Russo sighed and dropped the handkerchief onto her lap. "What is it you do, Mr. Cunningham?"

"Mainly trapeze. Acrobatics too. I started as an equestrian."

Mabel admired the woman's ability to pull in her emotions. Her expression, after the initial shock, was now one of relaxed curiosity. Only her eyes revealed her tumbling thoughts. "Are you done with that life, then?"

"I have been done for a long while now," Jake said, and Mrs. Russo's questioning gaze settled upon Mabel.

"I wouldn't like to be, though it seems it might be done with me."

Mrs. Russo inhaled deeply, and her hand found the top of Katie Grace's head. "You don't strike me as a person easily manhandled, Mrs. Cunningham, if you'll forgive me for saying so. In fact, I do believe you are capable of most things."

Mabel dipped her head in the face of such praise. As she stared at her lap, running her fingertip over the velvet piping of her skirt, she considered the fear that had overcome her each time she'd stepped into the ring since her father died. The panic that choked her and filled her chest with the numbing knowledge that with Da, she'd been the strongest woman on Earth, but alone . . . she was just a singularly tall woman.

And then, just as she thought she might be able to conjure up that paralyzing terror by the sheer intensity of her thoughts, Jake's hand slipped beneath her elbow, and the weight of it settled atop her roaming fingers.

His voice echoed in the room. So solid. So sincere. So

confident. "Mrs. Russo, you're correct. Mabel Cunningham is the strongest woman this world has ever seen, and she can capture anything she sets her mind to."

Mabel squeezed his fingers and wondered if she should say she'd determined to capture him.

CHAPTER

10

HIS ARM HAD WOKEN her up. It was corded with muscle, even in sleep, and when he tossed it over her before the sun tripped into the sky, Mabel had found herself in the peculiar position of holding her breath so her husband wouldn't be startled out of touching her.

It had been happening with increasing regularity since they'd spoken hurried vows beneath a mural of clouds and cherubim. The breath-holding and the touching.

Her arm, cradling the pillow beneath her head, began to tingle. She had hardly allowed herself to blink in the hours since Jake had rolled over and she found herself tucked into his accidental embrace. She ignored the sensation. Just another few minutes. She could handle the physical pain necessary to extend Jake's affection, unconscious though it was.

She glanced at the spot on the floor where Jake had settled the night before. Until he heard her shivering for want of a warm nightgown—their trunk would not be delivered until morning—and the blanket he had wrapped around himself. For want of flames in the fireplace Mrs. Luvotti said would not be lit again until mid-October.

She had tried to make do with the thin quilt that had been folded at the foot of the bed, but the room was so very cold. And the blanket so very insufficient.

"This is foolish," Jake had said. *"I will not listen to you freeze all night. Not when there is no reason for it."* So he climbed into bed beside her and tried unsuccessfully to maintain a sliver of space between their bodies. It was a very small bed. Finally he muttered, *"We are doing nothing wrong"* before turning onto his side and falling promptly to sleep.

Mabel had lain awake long after and then slept only fitfully until Jake's arm had slapped over her torso.

The prickling in Mabel's arm grew too dreadful to ignore. She sucked a bit of air through her lips, let the breath swirl around her lungs, and as carefully as possible, rearranged her body so that she could rescue her offended limb. Rolling onto her back, as near the edge of the mattress as possible, Mabel exhaled gently.

Jake's arm had shifted, and now his hand lay over her middle. Glaring at the blanket twisted beneath his fingers, she stretched her arm into the air and gave it a little shake before bending her elbow and settling her hand above his. Between her pounding heart and his skin. If she were to *accidently* brush his hand in her sleep, well, she couldn't be held responsible for that when he was the one who had crawled into bed with her.

She closed her eyes and let her pinky bump against his thumb. He snuffled, and she pinched her teeth together. No. It wasn't enough. And when he awakened, she would have little to show for their night together but the knowledge that their hands had touched.

"Good morning," Jake whispered.

Mabel startled and nearly threw herself out of the bed.

"Sorry. Did I wake you?" He blinked, his eyes misted with hazy sleep.

"Yes," she answered truthfully. "But I don't mind." Also truthful.

"I'm leaving directly after breakfast. One of the boarders here told me there's a steeplejack position open with the construction company he works for."

"Steeplejack?"

"Those are the people who climb buildings to make repairs." He chuckled. "Don't look so grave. I'm uniquely qualified for such a thing."

"It sounds dangerous."

He grinned and lifted his hand to brush the hair from her eyes. She missed the weight of him against her but didn't mind the tender gesture. "I have solid nerves and a good grip. All will be well. And, after paying Mrs. Luvotti, we have nothing left. I must work."

She turned onto her side to look at him and tucked her hands beneath her cheek. Their faces were close now. So close she could feel his breath sweep across her lips. Could pretend that he kissed her instead. "I will find a job too. And you will soon be free to go to Kansas."

"Make sure you take some time to find your mother, as well."

"I'm sure I will promptly. She never did blend in, and how many aerialists named Polly could there be?"

Before Mabel was ready, the mattress shifted, and Jake was striding across the room and reaching for the shirt he'd hung on a peg.

"Don't," she whispered.

He turned. "What was that?"

"Nothing." She clenched the quilt in her fists at her chin and watched from beneath lowered lashes as he pulled his shirt over his head.

* * *

After breakfast, Mabel happily dug into the trunk. It had been delivered to her room by a wiry Italian whose eyes widened with delight when she greeted him in the language she hoped wouldn't grow too rusty from disuse. She dressed in a blue-and-white striped suit with a snowy frilled shirtwaist and practically danced down the stairs and through the front door, so thrilled to have her wardrobe again that she cared little that the wrinkles hadn't had time to fall out.

"Where are you going?" Katie Grace peeled herself from the wall of a not-very-reputable-looking building with boarded windows as Mabel passed on her way to the streetcar stop.

"Shouldn't you be at school?"

Katie Grace merely rolled her eyes and fell into step beside Mabel.

"I'm seeking a job."

"You're lucky, then, because Travis and Wells camps out at Madison Square Garden the entire month of May and part of June too." Katie Grace heaved a sigh. "I wish I could see the circus. It's so exciting. I might run away and join it someday."

"My father did. But he was escaping a very challenging situation at home, and you have a mother who loves you. That is something to treasure, not run from." Mabel took Katie Grace's hand, and they crossed the street, weaving between chugging automobiles and wagons carrying haphazardly stacked crates of produce. Mabel's heart nearly stopped more than once as she navigated the traffic, and she gave a relieved laugh when they reached the other side. "I'm not seeking a position at Travis and Wells anyway."

"Why? Aren't you the world's strongest woman? That's what Jake said. Don't you think they'd want you?"

"Probably not." Unfortunately, not many people did. Katie Grace would likely be disappointed if Mabel told her she was only looking for someone who might work for the great circus. Or at least someone who once did a long time ago.

Mabel waved her hand as a streetcar approached. "You should go to school, Katie Grace. Or go home."

"I won't." She crossed her arms. "Mam saw me bring the kitten inside yesterday and told me to take her back out, and now she's gone. I'm gonna look for her, and school can wait."

"What will you do when you find her if your mother won't allow you to keep a cat?" The streetcar creaked over the tracks before rumbling to a stop.

Katie Grace blinked. "I don't know."

Mabel climbed the steps, but before the driver could pull away, she turned and reached for Katie Grace. "Come with me, and when I've completed my errand, I will help you look for her. Maybe we can devise a way to keep her in the courtyard."

Something about the child's quest felt linked to her own. If she could help Katie Grace find the kitten, maybe she would find her mother too.

After twenty minutes sitting beside the girl in a crowded streetcar, though, Mabel seriously questioned her plan. "Why don't we play a game? A game of quiet. If you can make it the rest of the ride without speaking, there will be a surprise for you at the end of our trip."

Katie Grace gave her a look of distrust but clamped her mouth shut.

It opened the moment they disembarked outside Madison Square Garden.

"Are we going to see the circus? Have you brought me?" Katie Grace stared at the building and squealed.

"Well, we haven't come to watch a show, but I need to speak with someone here, and I'm sure we will be able to get a peek at their practice. Maybe even see an animal or two."

"Who do you need to speak to?"

"I'm not entirely sure yet." Mabel tugged at the hem of

her jacket and straightened her hat, then held out her hand. "Come along."

They passed between polished granite pillars and swept into the building. Inside, there were more squeals. More questions. They entered the amphitheater, where a few clowns were practicing beneath thousands of electric lights for the show that would begin in a week, and Katie Grace watched them, still and quiet for the first time since Mabel had met her.

Mabel laughed along with the girl as the clowns tumbled and flipped, their exaggerated movements and comical mannerisms belying the effort that went into their routine. The athleticism and strength.

"I want to be a clown," Katie Grace whispered.

"A clown? Not an aerialist or rope dancer?" Those were the romantic acts. The ones little girls imagined being part of. Mabel had experienced the magic of performing to awed crowds for a few years until she disappointed everyone by growing entirely too tall. *She is too big. She was always too big.*

Maman couldn't know Mabel had heard those words. And certainly couldn't know how much they had pierced her fragile child's heart. How they had found a home in her spirit and made her so very conscious of a thing she had no control over. Too big for what? Not only a circus act, Mabel knew.

"Why do you want to be a clown?" she asked.

"They make people happy, don't they? I'd like to make people happy for a change."

How well Mabel understood that. "Come. Let's see about my errand."

They walked down to the floor and around the ring, and Katie Grace nearly lost all sense when one of the clowns waved at her. Near what looked to be the corridor to the dressing rooms, they came upon a cluster of women wearing fleshlings and fringed costumes. They were all very pretty and very small and, judging from the looks they cast over Mabel, very unimpressed with her.

"Would you be able to tell me if Polly MacGinnis works with this circus?" Mabel stopped a few feet away. "She is an aerialist and does trapeze as well." Maman had been adept at everything she set her hand to.

"No," one replied.

"Are you certain? Could she have performed with Travis and Wells before you came? Have you heard anything about her?"

"Nothing. And we would know. We're aerialists."

"I do trapeze," another said, one haughty brow arching. "You really shouldn't be here. The show is for those who have purchased tickets."

"Who can I speak with about auditioning?"

"That would be me."

Mabel turned and saw a man, of average height and middle gone soft, but who walked with an agility that promised an athletic past. He smiled at her, his somewhat jowly face transforming with kindness. "What is your act?"

"Strongwoman."

A collective laugh rose from the aerialists, but the man ignored them. "We already have a strongman, but I'm curious to see what a woman can do."

In less than ten minutes, Mabel found herself in the ring, a set of weights before her. She handed her jacket to Katie Grace, whose toes tapped with excitement.

Wiping her sweating palms against her skirt, Mabel approached a barbell and hunkered into a squat. She rounded the bar with her fingers, settling into the familiarity of it. Pitted iron rubbed against calluses that had smoothed since her last show.

Her skirt strained against her knees, and she drove her heels into the ground as she lifted and pushed. Sweat trickled down her temple and spine, not justified by the weight she held aloft. Her hands began to tremble, and her cheek twitched.

No. No, no, no. Could she not even do one simple act?

"Remember who you are, Mabel MacGinnis." She relaxed into Jake's reassurance.

"Whose girl are you?" Da had been inordinately proud of her. Of her strength and achievements. Of the title bestowed upon her by a German newspaper—World's Strongest Woman. It might well be the only one Giuseppe could claim contained a nugget of truth.

"I am Bram MacGinnis's daughter," she pushed through gritting teeth.

But it was a worthless talisman. The bar shifted a little over the slick of her hands. Her arms began to shake, muscles bunching with tension that had little to do with the weight.

She leapt back as the bar slid from her grasp. Falling to her bottom, she slammed her hands over her ears to drown out the clanging metal and laughter rising up around it.

Mabel scrambled to her feet and swung around. Her arms fell limply to her sides, and the inky blackness that had consumed her when her father died dropped like a curtain now. With the dimming of the aerialists' faces, with their laughter echoing, she plunged like Alice through the looking glass.

"Och, my girl, root out any weakness. You are a MacGinnis. Your father is the strongest man on Earth. And you will be its strongest woman. Do not cower. Do not fear. Do not fail."

How very grandly she had failed.

❊ ❊ ❊

Isabella had been sliding in and out of the shadows for a few days—ever since she discovered New York might be the end of her career. Everyone knew, and she couldn't stand the looks of pity. The snide comments. The sidelong glances.

For all its billing as a place of joy, the circus could be painfully cruel.

She practiced only. Otherwise, she avoided talking with the others. She didn't take meals in the Madison Square Garden dining room but instead grabbed a sandwich at the delicatessen down the street and ate alone on a bench at Madison Square Park.

She'd even been dodging Rowena. Not because of anything her friend had said or done, but because Isabella couldn't stand the prickling shame that swept over her for keeping her relationship with Robert a secret. For even having such a relationship in the first place.

Her steps were quiet as she made her way down the dressing room corridor. The other performers didn't notice her approach. They were consumed instead with the retreating figure of a handsomely dressed woman.

Annette's ugly words challenged her lovely voice. "What a monstrosity she is."

The Danó sisters laughed, but Edlyn, the eldest, glanced over her shoulder and, meeting Isabella's gaze, cringed and shuffled a step away from Annette. "I didn't think you would make it."

The other three turned, and Isabella shrugged. "Sorry I'm late, but it looks like the clowns took some extra time." She watched the tall woman the others had been mocking duck out of the amphitheater, her hand tight around a little girl's. "Who was that?"

"No one of importance," Annette said.

"She's striking." Isabella could only see a shadow of the woman now.

Annette gave a snort. "If by striking you mean lumbering, I agree."

Clowns filled the narrow hall, and one of them—the only female—reached for Isabella's arm. "We need to talk."

Even painted, Rowena's expression was soft, the corners of

her eyes creasing and her smile spilling benevolence. Isabella couldn't bring herself to look at it.

"Not now," she said with a light laugh and a wave toward the aerialists running with graceful steps into the ring. "I must practice."

"After?"

Isabella chanced a look at her always-too-perceptive friend's eyes and immediately regretted it, for her throat began to tighten, and her arms began to quiver. She gave her friend a tight smile but didn't commit.

All she had left was Rowena's good opinion of her. She certainly couldn't claim one for herself.

It took every one of the twenty steps to the ring to calm her frazzled nerves and stave off the trembling. She motioned for a rigger to lower her rope, then grabbed it and pulled herself off the ground.

Standing nearby, Annette rolled her eyes. "I don't see why I should have to put up with your airs. As though you're anyone anymore."

The rope bit into Isabella's skin, and she wrapped it around her foot and began to climb, pretending Annette's words meant nothing.

Annette stomped toward the platform ladder, and the other three women scrambled after her.

Isabella paused in her ascent and watched the Danó sisters. They worked together, a well-rehearsed trio that perfectly complemented one another. They were beautiful. Attuned to one another. Almost clairvoyant. And the counterfeit French woman above them spun the flying ladies of Travis and Wells Circus into something enchanting.

There was no room for Isabella. She was a perfunctory sideshow. She knew it. They knew it.

She began her routine. Flipping, twisting, climbing. It was the same one she'd been performing for the last five years.

Nothing new. Nothing added. Nothing exciting. But it no longer seemed rote. It took every bit of focus and effort to complete.

When had that happened? When had she become too old to do what had always seemed easy before?

She began her trademark move, thankful her shoulder still easily slid into and out of place. But there was a twinge. A new ache. Her heart fluttered and fell to her stomach. She wished she could scream at the betrayal of it all. The failure of her body. The years callously marching on. But she was meant to accept it. Retire and throw herself into . . . what, elegant invisibility? *Genteel* poverty?

How could she do that when everything she'd always been was riddled with fractures? Waiting to shatter and spill her out over the ring below.

Maybe she could convince Jerry to allow her to stay, but how long before it became impossible? How long before her joints splintered beneath the stress of constant abuse?

She might not even *have* a year.

The sounds of a body whishing by, feet landing with a dull thump against the platform, and feminine grunts of effort drew Isabella back to the rope where she hung. She glanced over at the Danó sisters, who were swinging between one another from Roman rings. How strong and beautiful they were.

Isabella set her jaw. "I will not go out quietly." She had given up too easily in the past. She'd lost too much—allowed circumstances to dictate her choices.

She climbed higher, determination and maybe a little fear pushing her upward. She'd tried this trick once, low on the rope before she'd left Manzo Brothers Circus. She'd fallen, her face scraping the floor and her husband demanding she stop attempting things that were too hard. Too dangerous. Too much for a woman like her.

"You're just not strong enough, Polly."

Even now, years later, Isabella's throat burned with all the things she wished she could say to him.

She would. She would scream them, and maybe the heavens would open just long enough that he would be knocked over by the strength of her anger.

Holding herself aloft, she brought the dangling rope to the front and swung her leg until it wrapped around her thigh, just above her knee, and her calf. Reaching her arms straight out, fingers pointed like a ballet dancer, she released her tense muscles and allowed her body to roll out of its binding.

Her shout reached for Bram's ears but was swallowed by another. She flipped, as planned and as she should have all those years ago, and caught the rope behind her knee, gripping it with her toes.

She pulled herself up and glanced around. The other aerialists stood clustered together on a platform, watching her with wide eyes. Edlyn looked pale even from this distance. But it was below her that she discovered the person who had sounded a cry of alarm so loud, it had stolen her moment of recompense.

"Robert?"

He stood outside the ring, two circles of color high on his cheeks and his hat crumpled between his hands. "Isabella, what was that? What were you thinking?" His voice was tight and controlled. His movements not so much.

"You're going to destroy your hat," she called as she let herself off the rope.

He met her in the ring. "What were you thinking? I thought you'd fallen again."

"I wanted to try a new trick. It worked."

He slammed his hat onto his head and gripped her arms. "You could have killed yourself."

"But I didn't. And now that I know I can do it, and do it well, I will add it to my act. It nearly stole your breath, did it not? Imagine how the audience will feel."

"No."

"No? What do you mean 'no'? Jerry will love it."

His hands softened, and they were warm as he dropped them and wove his fingers through her own.

"This could save me, Robert." Her words hooked on all the desperation that had gathered within her and provoked her toward danger. "I could develop a new routine."

"You limped."

The other girls gathered behind him, hands pressed to their lips, but he seemed not to notice.

Isabella's brows pinched. "What?"

"You limped when you walked toward me. You've hurt yourself." And then what could have been construed as a gesture of friendship, decades old, turned into something no one could imagine meant anything other than intimacy. He pressed his palm against her hip.

"Robert," she hissed, her gaze darting to the other women. While the Danós seemed not to notice, Annette's eyes narrowed. "We have an audience."

He dropped his hand and turned. "Isabella has injured herself. I will accompany her to the doctor."

He offered Isabella his arm, but she ignored it and made her way out of the ring. She also ignored the clicking sound in her hip.

"Isabella!" Rowena appeared at the dressing room corridor entrance.

"So sorry, Ro, but I've got to see the doctor." Isabella waved over her shoulder toward Robert, who trailed her. "Boss's orders."

"But . . ." Rowena crossed her arms as they passed, but Isabella patted her hip and ignored the stabbing guilt.

She might be losing her strength, but she was definitely getting better at pretending everything was okay when it clearly was not.

* * *

"Have you any useful skills you haven't considered?" Alice Russo sat in a rickety chair, a length of fabric over her lap. She looked up from her stitching and tilted her head as though an idea was just waiting to be knocked loose. "You must be able to do something."

Mabel laughed. "I can lift. I can pull and press and bear the weight of a hundred bricks. But I spent my entire life training to be strong, not useful. I can do nothing else."

God knew she'd tried. It had been four days since Jake began working as a steeplejack for the city's largest and busiest builder. She'd hoped to have work by now so she could contribute toward the next month's rent, but she had spent hours each day looking with nothing to show for it but gaping mouths and flapping hands.

It seemed no one wanted to hire a distinctively tall, retired strongwoman who couldn't stitch, clean, or cook. And given her overwhelming stage fright, it was unlikely she would secure a position with any circus.

She sighed and set her teacup onto the saucer. She missed it. Missed the performing and the crowds and the *family* of the circus. Jake left most mornings after gulping down a quick breakfast of ham shoved into a stale leftover biscuit and didn't return until they were sitting down to dinner.

She enjoyed her afternoon tea with Alice and appreciated the friendship that was growing between them, but Alice worked almost constantly to provide for herself and Katie Grace. With the money her husband had saved before his death dwindling and a room in a tenement closing in on her, she didn't have much more than a few stolen moments to give.

And Mabel was lonely. She'd never experienced such a thing before.

"What about becoming a shopgirl?"

"I don't think they pay very much at all." Mabel lifted the teacup to her lips and averted her eyes.

She didn't tell Alice that she'd taken the streetcar two days ago to 59th Street and walked across Bloomingdale's checkered black-and-white floor with high hopes. She could sell things. That required a general ability to speak, which Mabel claimed. Basic skills with sums, which Mabel more than claimed.

And . . . a foot and fifty pounds too much, it seemed.

"I couldn't hire you," the manager had told her. "What woman wishes to be served by someone who could outwrestle her husband?"

Mabel hadn't said she could, quite literally, wrestle any woman's husband. She also hadn't said she possessed a keen eye for fashion and could, without fail, determine with a glance the proper color, fit, and style that would most flatter any person.

Because it didn't matter. They didn't see her smart walking dress. Didn't see her Parisian hat. Didn't see a woman worth a chance. They only saw what set her apart. What made her different.

The world wasn't kind to the peculiar. The atypical. Her.

Alice stabbed the needle through the gown she was trimming with jet beads. "There has to be something," she muttered. She paused, midair, and looked up at Mabel. "I could teach you to sew."

"You don't have time for that, Alice."

"No, you're right. I really don't. I wish I did, though. You have been so good to Katie Grace. I believe you've convinced her of the importance of school."

"I'm not sure that's true." In fact, Mabel was quite sure it *wasn't* true. She'd seen the child darting down alleys and hiding in doorways in order to avoid detection as Mabel went about canvassing New York in her attempts to find work. What she'd convinced Katie Grace of was the need to impress the circus entertainer who might hold the key to unlocking her dreams.

Though what a bungling *former* circus performer could offer, Mabel didn't know.

"I will leave you to your work," she said. "I want to ask Mrs. Luvotti to save a plate for Jake. He will be home late tonight."

The landlady begrudged every disruption to her schedule and reminded Mabel of the previous two times she's asked for such leniency, but she always gave in. Jake worked hard—everyone could see that—and he was the most charming man on the planet. Not even their surly landlady could resist his dimples and sincere compliments.

"I'll just put an extra bit of cherry cobbler on his plate," Mrs. Luvotti said when Mabel made her request. "He works so hard, poor boy." She slanted a glare over the table, as though Mabel was solely responsible for the state of Jake's grueling schedule. "I'll keep it warm in the oven. Just tell him to take all he needs."

After dinner and only one small serving of cobbler, Mabel sat on her knees in front of their bureau and pulled out the bottom drawer. There, beneath her silk hose, corset covers, and petticoats, she found the clutch of letters. She did this occasionally. Sat in her empty boardinghouse room and pulled out the proof of her father's cruelty. Her mother's abandonment.

She never read them, though. Not since that night in the train when she'd gone through Da's things. The words were still plastered across her mind like the circus bills that covered the buildings of Longacre Square.

She could remember those, too, because she roamed the streets after her rejections and stared at every face in an effort to find her mother. Mabel clutched only hazy memories of Maman's dark eyes and hair. Her sad smile and quick movements. She wasn't certain she'd recognize her if she saw her. But maybe her name emblazoned in ink would catch Mabel's attention.

She had to find her mother. Not only because she wanted answers and perhaps a relationship, but because Jake was working himself to death to support her, and she'd seen an envelope sporting a Kansas address atop the dresser and knew he must be anxious to return home.

She pressed Maman's letters to her chest, grateful, at least, that the love she'd received at her father's knee was beginning to conquer the anger she'd harbored since discovering he'd lied to her. He must have had his reasons. She couldn't let that one decision destroy all the good he'd been and done.

She slipped the letters back into her drawer and went to wait for Jake on the bed. A thrill swept over her, and she shivered with the anticipation of another night beside him. They'd grown comfortable in the weeks since leaving Italy, and he no longer slept facing away, his body hugging the edge of the mattress. He no longer held his limbs stiff so that no part of her skin touched hers.

It wasn't everything she wanted from him, but it was enough. For now.

After an hour, she changed into her nightclothes and tucked herself beneath the covers with a book—*A Girl of the Limberlost*—that Alice had lent her.

An hour after that, she got out of bed and stood at the window, looking over the street, quiet now that the streetcars had stopped running for the night, and watched for her husband.

Twenty minutes later she sat on the edge of the bed and pinched the quilt between her fingers until she nearly wore a hole through the fabric.

He came in after ten, right as Mabel determined to awaken Mrs. Luvotti and call for a police officer. Even had Mabel still been watching the street, she wouldn't have recognized him.

His shirt sleeve hung in tatters around his right arm, its cuff torn clear off. Mabel couldn't begin to make sense of what had happened to his hair. Normally so neat and brushed back, it hung limply over his forehead as though having given up all attempts at life. Blood streaked his face.

"What happened?" She jumped to her feet and reached for him.

He held up his hands. "I'm a mess." He sank onto the bed with a grunt. "I fell."

"You . . . fell?" What an odd statement. She didn't think she'd ever seen Jake take one misstep, one tumble, in all the years she watched him jump from horses, walk across wires, and flip through rings. She saw the abrasions on his arm, and her knees went soft as pudding. "You fell off a *building?*"

"Only one story." He gave her an exhausted, crooked smile. "And it was more like sliding anyway."

"Jake!"

"I know. I'm sorry if I worried you. I did see a doctor—that's why I'm so late—and by the time I left, I had a bear of a time finding a streetcar. I didn't want to spend the money on a taxicab. Those things are appallingly expensive." He bent to remove his shoe and groaned.

Mabel sank to the floor and reached for his shoe. "Here, let me help. Mrs. Luvotti set a plate in the warmer for you. Would you like me to bring it up?"

"No. All I want is a bath. And barring that, a bowl of water and a rag."

She slipped the boot from his foot and started on the other before standing. "I'll go fetch them."

She warmed the water on the stove while discarding Jake's untouched dinner and stopped in the bathroom for a sliver of Ivory soap upon reaching their floor. When she returned to the room, she saw Jake had removed his torn shirt and undershirt, stained with blood, and tossed them into a heap against the wall. He lay flat on his back, the bib and suspenders of his overalls twisted around his back, and stared at the ceiling.

"I can't move, Mabel."

She huffed a little laugh. "Don't, then." After placing the bowl on the table, she dipped the cloth into the water and set about dabbing the blood from his face. "I'm very glad you're okay."

His dimple flashed. "Worried about me?"

"Always." She moved to his shoulders and arms, wiping away the grime. Trying not to notice how broad they were. How strong. She shifted, moving closer as she reached over him to take care of a scrape on his far arm. When she pulled back, she saw him watching her. His breath seemed to have become trapped beneath the palm she had rested on his chest.

"What is it?"

He blinked and shook his head. "Nothing. I'm very tired. And you are very wonderful."

"Not so wonderful that I'm going to let you sleep in those filthy clothes. Come on. Up."

"What a brute you are." He stood with a groan, and she took the dirty water down to dump outside the kitchen door while he changed. When she returned to the room, Jake was already beneath the covers, his breathing even and soft in sleep.

She lay beside him, turning so that her body curved around his. Not touching . . . at least, not touching very much. But she did lift onto her elbow and place her fingertips lightly against the spot on his arm where he had sustained the deepest scratch. Without allowing herself to consider it, she pressed a gentle kiss against the sleeve of his nightshirt.

He shifted, turning toward her, and a name left his lips on a sigh.

"Charlotte."

CHAPTER 11

"WE'RE GOING to have to divorce."

Mabel's fingers stilled on her hair, and she turned from the little mirror on the wall to face her unhappy husband. "What was that?" she said around the pins between her teeth. She forced her hands into compliance and took one to stab into the knot she held at the back of her head. It grazed her scalp.

"I consulted with a lawyer a couple of days ago."

Her stomach sank to her toes. "Already?"

Jake gave her a curious look. "We've been here nearly a week. You'll find work shortly, and I thought it best to understand our options. Anyway, he told me abandonment isn't, as a rule, grounds to secure an annulment. You would have to file for divorce." He sat on the edge of the bed and rubbed his forehead. "I had no idea, Mabel. I really didn't. I would have never suggested this if I'd known."

She blinked at him and poked the rest of the pins into her hair. "I'm not sure I want to move through life as a divorcee."

"You will never be able to remarry if you don't. Not unless you want to commit bigamy." He offered her a crooked smile. "Which, incidentally, *is* grounds for annulment."

"Well, who would want me anyway?" She lifted her stylish, fur trimmed bonnet from beside Jake and smiled at him.

"My brother has written of half a dozen women in his church eager to meet me." He waggled his brows. He teased. She could see it in his brilliant eyes and flashing dimple.

But his words pulled a painful gasp from her throat anyway, and she stiffened her legs against the weakness in her knees. He didn't know. He couldn't know how much that hurt her.

She settled the hat on her head. "We'll worry about it later." She could not think about this now.

He nodded and pulled on his shirt, hissing as it snagged on the bandage wrapping his arm. His wounds had been healing nicely since his fall two days earlier, but the one on his bicep had turned an alarming shade of red, and Mabel worried it might be infected.

She went to the dresser and pulled a few coins from the box atop it. What remained after Jake had paid Mrs. Luvotti wasn't even enough to hide the pasteboard bottom. "I'll stop at the drugstore on the way home and pick you up another tin of salve." She dropped the money into her beaded reticule.

"Will you bring me back a Pepsi-Cola? I've had a headache since my tumble."

"It's no wonder."

Mabel left the room and congratulated herself on holding her emotions tightly. After all these weeks together, she'd hoped Jake would have softened toward her a bit. She caught him watching her sometimes. Especially at night after she'd changed into her nightgown and was approaching the bed, the moonlight spilling through the window and, she knew, tracing her shape through the thin cotton.

But then, Jake was a man. And Mabel had heard enough

about her comely legs to recognize his attention might not have much to do with her personally. Disappointing in the extreme. But she bolstered herself with the knowledge that at least he might find her somewhat attractive. And many happy marriages had started with much less.

Mabel's walk from their Greenwich Village boardinghouse to her next job possibility left her with a settled, comfortable sense of homecoming.

For Manhattan was a circus.

Cutting through Washington Square Park, Mabel saw a collection of people outside the norm of polite society. Suffragists holding painted signs and shouting for the vote clustered together beneath a marble arch. Women wearing knickerbockers, their long hair caught beneath short-billed caps, bounced on their bicycles over the paved paths. Artists sitting on stools in front of easels and smoking long cigarettes had deep conversations with their companions about light and theme and things Mabel had never considered.

The streets were crisscrossed overhead with telephone wires that begged for a particularly handsome acrobat to spring between them. There were old buildings, stone and brick exteriors melding into newer ones that sported terra-cotta façades and iron stairs climbing to roofs that kissed the clouds. Not unlike the lithographs pasted over every wall, New York City promised novelty and excitement. An easy distraction. A way to lose oneself.

There was something at once devastating and optimistic about it all.

Mabel chose to latch on to the optimism. She ran her hands over the jacket of her smart, pinstripe walking suit of brown and cream wool. Its wide cuffs, velvet piping, and spill of white lace kept it from being too staid. It branded her a fashion enthusiast. Someone women could trust with their wardrobe. Hopefully, the women's wear manager at Wanamaker's would agree. She'd not given up entirely on becoming a shopgirl. It was one of the few respectable options open to her, an uneducated immigrant—she wasn't certain her half-American parentage would help her much—whose only experience mocked practicality.

"They will hire me," she muttered as she left the park and turned up Broadway. Ahead, the department store took up two city blocks, connected by an arched skywalk.

She stared up at it, acknowledging the catch in her chest. Everything about this country seemed big. Over the top. It was a loud exhibition and, for a woman raised within the homey embrace of canvas, sometimes overwhelmed her. There were a thousand women just like her looking for work. A thousand women familiar with this country and its people. Mabel knew the only thing that set her apart also branded her unsuitable for most things.

A provincial misfit.

"Stand tall, my girl. Don't hunch as though your size is a hindrance." Even now, Mabel snapped to obey her father. Would that she could wrap his confidence around herself as easily as she straightened her spine.

"I will get a job."

She needed to. For all her airs this morning, she didn't want to trap Jake in a loveless future. He was meant for passion. It spilled out into everything he did. Except his marriage. The second one.

Mabel knew the first had been feverish and intense. Everyone knew about the great love affair catapulting Jake and Charlotte into stardom. And the devastating tragedy that hadn't only stolen from the world its most talented aerialist, but also plundered Jake of his purpose.

Mabel had no doubt he would love again one day, though. Maybe a red-cheeked farmer's daughter? She would be young and lovely and small enough for him to tuck beneath his chin. He deserved such happiness.

And she didn't want to be the one to keep him from it. She only wanted a bit more time to see if he could ever love *her*.

Something dashed past Mabel, snagging her attention, and she saw a ragged cloud of grey fur throw itself off the sidewalk and slide beneath a cart of lumber. It stopped and scratched its back against the wheel, giving her the opportunity to recognize its mangled ear.

The kitten Katie Grace had been looking for all week, ignoring her education in favor of scouring wharves and alleys and places better left unvisited by a small child with a big mouth.

Mabel approached the cart and crouched. "Come here, little one." She held out her palm, but the cat skittered back. She removed her hat and laid it aside with her reticule before lowering to her stomach and peering into the murky darkness.

"What are you doing, lady?" a man called.

"Leave her be, Fred. I quite like the view."

Mabel wiggled farther beneath the cart, engendering a few whistles and salacious laughs. She ignored them and snagged the cat by its scruff. It batted at her hand, its tiny claws pricking her skin, but she managed to pull it out and get to her feet. Brushing at the dirt streaking her jacket, she gave a triumphant smile.

"Whaddaya want it for?" Fred, Mabel presumed, and a butcher by his blood-stained apron, squinted at her prize.

"It belongs to a young friend. She will be—"

"Hey!" Fred started forward. "He just stole your purse."

Mabel spun and saw a man darting through the crowd, her reticule flinging around his arm. She took a few running steps before shoving the kitten into Fred's arms. "Watch her," she called as she took off after the thief.

The man wasn't very fast, and Mabel's anger dissolved as her long strides ate the distance between them. It spilled thin and filled her veins with a popping energy. It had been a long time since she had exerted herself. Had pushed and moved her body and found her chest heaving beneath the effort to catch a full breath.

The thief glanced over his shoulder, and his eyes went wide. He pumped his arms and picked up his pace, and Mabel laughed.

A moment later, she passed him and threw her arm out, catching him just below the chin. His feet flung out from beneath him, and he stared up at her as she drew over him.

"My reticule, if you will." She held out her hand.

He scrambled to his feet, tucked the purse into the drooping waistband of his pants, and took a boxer's stance.

Mabel's brows rose, and she pushed her hair, which had fallen from its tidy knot during the chase, back from her face. "You don't want to do that."

His lips twisted, and he shuffled toward her.

It wasn't a very fair fight. But he *had* stolen her bag, so Mabel had little motivation to show mercy. She blocked his punch—what kind of man struck out at a woman?—wrapped her arm around his neck, swept his feet from under him, and, when he was on his back once more, pressed her knee into his abdomen.

"My reticule. I prefer not to reach for it."

His eyes bulged, and his face began to turn purple. Mabel eased up on his windpipe. He patted until his fingers found the strap to her bag, and he yanked it from his pants and tossed it toward her.

When she stood, she found herself facing a clapping audience. A trio of burly men cornered the would-be thief, and Fred held the kitten toward her. Mabel slipped her reticule back over her wrist and pressed the cat to her chest.

A very tall man wearing a vibrant suit and beaver top hat separated himself from the crowd. "Fine show," he said, studying her with an air of fascination. "You are a natural performer, I can tell."

Mabel bit back a laugh. There had been nothing natural about any of the hundreds of times she swallowed pulsing fear and stepped into the ring. She wasn't sure what most proved her strength—the stamina it took to lift more weight than any woman ever had, or the courage it required to do so in front of people.

The man's smile spread, and he bowed with a flourish before spinning and sweeping his hand in an arc through the air. Mabel looked at the building he motioned toward, and her gaze snagged on the large letters painted over the white-washed bricks.

Flok's Midtown Museum
The best in the city! For men, women, and children! Wonders of the world!

The theatrical man with his fancy clothing and—Mabel leaned toward him and squinted—rouged cheeks tapped his copper-tipped cane against the street and swung his gaze toward her. "Well, my dear . . . would you like to join the show?"

❊ ❊ ❊

Isabella took the paper cone of peanuts and handed a nickel to the vendor. "Thank you." She held the treat to her nose and inhaled, then turned to Rowena. "I've not been to Coney Island in years, Rowena. This was an excellent idea."

"I knew you would have wasted our last day of freedom before the show starts rehearsing if I didn't get you away from Hotel Veronica and Madison Square Garden."

Isabella poked her nail through a peanut shell and split it open. "Rehearsing is never wasted."

Rowena rolled her eyes. "Honestly, Isabella, you're the best aerialist Travis and Wells has ever seen. Maybe relax a bit."

"I can't. I need to prove myself capable. If I don't impress Jerry over the next six weeks, I'll be forced to become a grunt."

"You will never be a grunt." Rowena swiped one of Isabella's peanuts and popped it open.

"How do you know? There's nothing else I'm good for. And I'll never leave the circus. Whether I'm center ring or washing costumes, I have no idea what life is like outside it." Isabella stopped to stare up at the entrance to Luna Park. Done in primary colors and boasting minarets and domes, it promised excitement. She'd heard of the Witching Waves ride and was desperate to experience it. "We'll have to come back on a Sunday after the parks have fully opened. Or maybe we should go swimming in the ocean." She could hear waves crashing against the beach just over the line of buildings heavy with signage that called out attractions and ten-cent ride admissions.

"If you can bring yourself to relax on your day off, I'll treat you." Rowena took Isabella's hand. "But for now, let's have some fun." She clamped her hat to her head and pulled Isabella into a jog as they crossed the street and approached a line of white-shingled shops.

"A dime all day," said the man behind the window Rowena had dragged her toward.

Isabella craned her neck and spied the bicycle rental sign hanging crookedly above the sill. "We're hardly dressed for riding."

Rowena snorted. "As though there is anyone left in the country who has yet to see your legs." She paid, and they chose their bicycles. "Do you remember the year we did the History of Transportation Spectacle?"

Isabella squinted at the bike and looked down at her skirt. "Yes. It was an odd choice."

"But we had fun."

"We did." It was the only time in their years with Travis and Wells that Isabella and Rowena had actually worked together in an act. Jerry had told them to study a book published by a cycling enthusiast named Isabel Marks called *Fancy Cycling*.

They'd had only a few months to learn not only how to ride the contraption—Isabella had never even been on one before—but how to do tricks that would turn a normal rider's stomach.

Rowena gave Isabella an expectant look.

"What?"

Her friend's gaze swung to the bike and back again. "What do you say? There's a crowd. Want to put on a show?"

At those words, a thrill shot through Isabella, and she shivered with anticipation. She reached into the waistband of her skirt, pulled the fabric through so that it ballooned around her middle and left her calves unencumbered, and threw the man behind the counter a wink. Then she took one of the bicycles leaning against the wall and tossed her leg over it. Walking the bike into the street, she waited until Rowena joined her with a laugh. Then they took off.

With deft movements, she avoided pedestrians and carts, not allowing any obstacle to slow her. Speed. Her heart flying. The salt-scented air tearing at her.

Seeing a clear path ahead, Isabella glanced over her shoulder and called, "One foot coast."

That had been the start of their act, and Rowena remembered, for she grinned and brought first her left foot, then her right foot onto the saddle. Isabella pedaled, gaining momentum, then followed suit.

"Now," Rowena called, and Isabella lifted a leg behind her, knowing Rowena did, as well.

A couple walking with a child paused to stare as they swept by.

"Come see the great Isabella Moreau at Travis and Wells Circus," Rowena called out.

Isabella laughed and brought her leg down. She took a deep breath and let the brine and joy swirl into her lungs. With an exhale, her worries swept between her lips and were flung toward the ocean.

"Hop!" she cried out. Bringing both feet to the pedals, she

bounced the bike down the road, rubber tires making a distinctly satisfying *bump, bump, bump* against the brick.

They did tricks the entire length of Surf Avenue, drawing a shouting, cheering crowd for their ride back up.

Rowena pedaled beside her. "Do your trick."

"Which one?" Isabella had lost her hat at some point, and her nose had begun to tingle from the sun. It would be pink in the morning.

"The *one*."

Isabella's heart became a drum beneath her ribs. "I haven't done that in years." She'd risked a broken nose every show to complete it. To please Jerry. To please the audience.

There was a challenge in Rowena's gaze, and she lifted her hands from the handlebar and held her arms wide as though hugging the people who lined the street ahead. "You're practically on the ground."

Isabella laughed, and her pulse sped. Her feet sped. The bike sped. She looked down at the street whizzing beneath the cycle's wheels. She'd plunged farther. Many times.

And besides, she wouldn't fall.

Rowena braked, but Isabella kept going. She lifted her right leg over the saddle and, bracing her foot against the crook between the bars, lifted her left leg beside it. Hands secure against the handlebar and seat, she pulled the bicycle in a little so that it began to turn before she reached the intersection. Parallel with a man who had parked his gumdrop cart in the middle of the street, his mouth wide as he watched her, Isabella pushed into a handstand, slowly raising both legs behind her in a wide V, then drawing them together. Her skirt nearly flipped over her head, exposing her drawers, but the fabric couldn't drown out the applause and shouting.

Bending her elbows, she lowered her chest to the saddle, brought her legs together, and slid her feet back to the pedals. She came to a stop a foot from her friend.

"The great Isabella Moreau, ladies and gentlemen," Rowena whispered. She pressed her fingers to her lips and blew Isabella a kiss. "You are amazing."

They returned the bicycles, and Rowena looped her arm through Isabella's as they started down the street.

"That was fun." Isabella sighed.

"It's been a long time, hasn't it?"

"A long time?"

"Since you've had fun. I thought you needed a reminder of what it feels like to do something for the sheer joy of it."

"I do that every day, Rowena. With every show."

"I don't think that's true. You do a lot of things because of expectation. Desperation. Fear." She gave Isabella a pointed look, but then her eyes brightened with tears, and she glanced away. "I feel as though I'm watching you plummet to Earth. You're on fire, and I don't know how to put it out."

"What are you going on about? I'm fine." Isabella extracted her arm and clenched both over her stomach. She withdrew from her friend and made herself small. As weak and fragile as Bram always accused her of being.

"So you haven't . . ." Rowena pressed her knuckles against her cheek yet barreled on "entered into an agreement with Robert?"

Isabella's mouth turned arid. "Why do you think that?"

"*Everyone* thinks that, Polly."

Isabella jerked her head around, eyes wide. "What?"

"I thought it was only rumor and jealousy. You know how it can be. But I've been watching the two of you together, and something has changed. There's a strain between you that's never been there before. You and Robert have been friends a very long time, and I've known forever that he loves you, but he no longer looks at you with longing, and that leaves me wondering if it's because he's finally gotten you."

Isabella's stomach turned into a hard little rock. She reached for her hat to pull it lower over her ears but remembered when her hand found only hair that she'd lost it during her wild bicycle ride. "I don't see how this is any of your business."

"Oh, Isabella . . . you know if Jerry discovers this, he might well kick you both out. You are not in a secure position right now." Rowena touched Isabella's arm, and she jerked. "Why won't you just marry him?"

"I don't love him. Bram destroyed that for me."

"Then why are you doing this?" Rowena tugged Isabella's arm nearer despite the icy wall between them. "Why have you let him use you so poorly?"

Isabella laughed, and she hardly recognized the sound. Hardly recognized the bitter words that came to her lips. "It's quite the opposite. I am using him."

Their feet ate up the distance, and Isabella wished for the bicycle. Wished for a cart or horse or any mode of escape. She couldn't stand the confusion and embarrassment in Rowena's eyes. "I don't see how it's any different than what I've been doing my entire life. What every woman in the circus does twice a day beneath the big top or in the sideshow tent. We all use our bodies in one way or another to entertain. I thought"— she took a hitching breath—"if I gave Robert what he'd always wanted, he would work harder to save me."

Rowena pulled her into an embrace and squeezed. Squeezed and squeezed until Isabella felt as though her friend held her together and perhaps she wouldn't shatter if she admitted the truth.

But she never would. Because she'd rather Rowena think her licentious and wicked than know that Isabella was falling. Tumbling into the darkness she thought she'd left in Europe but which had decided once again to give her chase.

CHAPTER 12

JAKE'S EXPRESSION was thunderous. "When you said you had secured a position, I didn't realize it would be at a place like this."

Mabel looked up at the façade and tried to view it through the lens of Jake's experiences. Flok's Museum looked perfectly respectable. Even a bit affluent, with its Greek Revival columns and symmetry. "I don't see anything wrong with it."

"It's a dime museum, Mabel. It's so far beneath you that you have to lie down to reach it. I don't understand. You were a sensation. The most popular act in one of Europe's most respected circuses. You are better than this."

With every charge, Mabel's shoulders sank lower. She hated to be made smaller in his eyes, but she couldn't allow him to maintain such delusions. "Not anymore."

His head jerked toward her, and she was almost undone by the compassion shining in his beautiful grey eyes. She offered him a tremulous smile and held out her hand. "I know you aren't happy to see me here, Jake, but I'm glad for the work. Will you come in with me?"

His chest lifted in a heavy sigh, but he reached for her. "Of course. I'm glad my half day fell on your first so I could."

Mabel grinned and started across the sidewalk, her hand warm in his. "If my show proves popular, Mr. Flok says he will put up bills."

"The Strongest Woman in the World takes on New York City."

"Hopefully." She held up her crossed fingers, but her steps faltered just inside the building. "What if I get stage fright again?"

Mabel had ignored the possibility. After her conversation with Mr. Flok, the museum's proprietor, a day earlier, she'd nearly floated home on a cloud of satisfaction. Then she spent the rest of the night lying wide awake beside her husband, realizing her accomplishment was inexorably entwined with his leaving.

But she could give him that. Freedom. Escape from this burden of a marriage. This burden of a wife.

Jake opened the front door, and they stepped into the hall, but he stopped her progress with a gentle tug of his hand. She turned toward him, and he ran his thumb over the scratch beneath her jaw—courtesy of her scuffle with the thief. His fingers slipped to her shoulders, then down her arms. He gave her biceps a squeeze, and Mabel found herself as frozen as she ever had been facing an audience, her breath caught somewhere between her lungs and her throat.

"If you find yourself with stage fright again, you just need to remember one thing," he said.

"And what's that?" Surprised she was able to form a coherent sentence with her tongue pasted to the roof of her mouth, Mabel managed to tear her attention from his thumbs, which were rubbing circles on her arms. Why couldn't he show such affection at night, when she was in her cotton nightgown and not wearing four thousand layers of clothing?

"Remember who you are." He took her elbow and propelled her toward the office tucked into the back corner behind a winding staircase.

She smirked. "A failed strongwoman adrift in the world."

"A strongwoman finding her place in the world." He gave her a crooked grin. "No dropped clown can change that. Your worth isn't tied up in what you accomplish. Nor in how well you perform."

Oh, but Maman's disappointment and Da's expectations . . .

How perfectly wonderful it would be if she could just . . . release it all.

They entered the office, and Mr. Flok rose from the chair behind a desk and opened his arms wide. "My wrestler!"

An hour later, Mabel stood behind a velvet curtain with the museum owner. She peered between the fabric and chewed her lip, counting nine people in the small auditorium. Instead of anticipation, derision and disbelief painted their faces. Mr. Flok paced before the curtain, stopping every few steps to pinch the drapery with his long fingers and snort or sniff. He was a tall man, skinny to the point of looking starved, and as he walked, the electric lights splashed his nervous movements against the scarred oak floor.

"Will more come?" she asked.

Mr. Flok patted her shoulder as he strode by. "I will draw a crowd now."

She watched him leave, then ran her hands over the simple leotard she'd been given for the performance. There wasn't even a length of plaid to break up its plain white expanse. Not one thing revealing who she was . . . or rather, who she used to be.

How she wished for Da. Everything had been complicated by his lies, and Mabel couldn't sift through her memories of him without what he'd done casting long shadows over everything, but she needed him. Had always needed him. Some of her admiration for him had tarnished, but more than anything, she just wished for his presence. His strength. It had always been what held her up.

She peered between the curtains and saw Jake leaning against the far wall, scowling at the trickle of patrons ambling into the room. He would make this work if he could, but he couldn't. There was no one Mabel could lean upon. She was on her own.

What a frightening place to be.

"Come see America's strongest woman!" Mr. Flok's voice called to those who sought the extraordinary.

The claim caught Mabel's fancy. Maybe she wasn't the world's strongest anymore, but America could be a new start.

"Ten dollars to any man who proves me a liar. Raised from childhood to become a warrior!" He was an excellent talker.

Mabel ran her hands over the leotard, following the curves her corset created. She pressed her stomach, wanting to ease the roiling Mr. Flok's hyperbole triggered. What if she failed again?

She peered passed the curtain. The room had filled. Men, women, and children had gathered to see this new aberration of humanity. A female wrestler? What could she possibly look like?

Mr. Flok swept backstage. "We are about to go on," he cried with a wave for her to step aside. He pushed onto stage and introduced her.

A hand pulled at the rope, and she arranged herself on the mark, hands on her hips, chin tilted just so. The curtain opened, electric lights spurring the murky shadows to flight. This was it. The start of a new career. A second chance. She forced her gaze straight, not permitting herself to search for Jake. To confirm he still stood in the room, offering her the strength of his presence.

The audience laughed.

Mabel's scalp prickled and her face burned, and all she wanted was to cover herself. To not have two dozen sets of eyes scanning her body and picking it apart.

"She's not half as big as you promised, Flok," a man with a large beard and belly in the front row shouted.

"She's strong! The strongest woman in the country." Flok paced across the stage, his mannerisms exaggerated, and Mabel didn't wonder why people thought his words were too. Although, how much bigger had people expected her to be? At six feet, she stood taller than most of the men present.

"Flex," Flok spit from the corner of his mouth as he passed by.

Mabel took a few tentative steps forward and lifted her arm, bicep bunching.

The people heckled.

"Get her off the stage!"

"We want to see the Limbless Wonder."

"Ten dollars to the man who can best her." Flok poked her shoulder, forcing her to present her back to the audience. "Look at these legs. Solid as tree trunks. A back able to carry a dozen men."

Mabel's skin burned. She swallowed the lump in her throat and willed away the tears gathering in her eyes. It wasn't that these things had never been said about her before. It was only that they had never been said while she stood there like a cow about to be auctioned to the highest bidder. She'd always been *doing* something. Showing how strong she was. In the circus, it had been about strength. The passivity of this felt more degrading.

Flok leaned close, his steamy breath washing her neck. "You better start moving, or you're done."

Mabel jerked her left arm behind her back and brought her right fist to her head. She tensed her muscles, shaking with the effort to make them look bigger. More impressive.

"Ah, I'm leaving," someone said dismissively.

"I'll take her up on the challenge."

Mabel whirled, and Jake sauntered through the crowd, taking the stairs two at a time. He leveled a steady look at Flok. "Ten dollars?"

Flok narrowed his eyes but dipped his chin.

The crowd hooted. "Are you going to pay us to watch this man throw a woman around?"

Flok offered a tense smile, then glared at Jake and leaned close. "You better not win."

"I never have." He shoved by the showman and shook Mabel's hand for show. "Remember who you are."

"I can't do this. Not without my father. Everyone knows that. I only forgot." She cleared her throat and glanced away. She couldn't cry on stage. Even in her very worst moment, she had never cried.

Da hadn't liked it. *"You are the strongest girl on Earth. The mighty shed no tears."*

But her mother had never come home, and Mabel felt the steady beat of accusation thrum within her breast every time she stood before a crowd and again heard Maman shout those words— *"She's too big, Bram"*—before running from the tent.

"*I* know who you are, Mabel Cunningham. You seem to have forgotten it." Jake released her and stepped back, crouching into a defensive position. He winked. "Come on, darling. Show them what you can do."

It took all of five minutes to lock Jake into a hold he couldn't escape from. The next man took only two.

And somewhere between her husband's flirtatious wink and Flok announcing his money safe, Mabel started to remember.

* * *

"Mabel, you have got to do something about this cat." Jake thrust his shoe beneath her nose, and the scent of urine assaulted her.

She stooped to lift the offender and held it to her chest. The cat vibrated with a gentle hum, and its claws pierced her shirtwaist. "I only want to keep her long enough to give Katie Grace a chance to speak with Alice about her."

"We're going to be stuck with it forever, aren't we?" Jake dropped his shoe beside the bed and glared at the kitten.

Mabel shrugged and set the cat on the floor. It wrapped its tail around her calf and purred as it rubbed against her leg. *He* wouldn't be. Not with Kansas calling to him. "I need to give her a name."

Jake groaned. "We *are* going to be stuck with it forever."

Mabel bit down on a smile. "What do you think about Octavia?"

He held up his arm. "I'll wrestle you for it. I win, the cat goes."

Mabel grasped his fingers, her forearm pressing along the line of his. "Seems fair."

He leaned his forehead against hers. "It's not at all fair, and you know it." Their noses touched, and his breath washed over her lips—cinnamon-scented from the apples at dinner. At her intake of breath, Jake lifted their entwined arms above her head, his body pressing closer, and his lips hovered.

Then he blinked, dropped her hand, and stepped back. The cat gave a yowl when he crushed the tip of its tail, and it leapt up Mabel's skirt.

"Oh, you poor thing. Come here." She lifted Octavia and pressed a kiss to her head. "Let me make it better."

"Not fair," Jake muttered, and her heart stuttered. Not fair that Octavia remained? Or not fair that Mabel kissed her rather than him?

She swallowed hard and stared at him as he bent to retrieve his second pair of shoes from the bottom of the cabinet.

"We should go downstairs," he said, tying the laces. "But first, I have a surprise."

She raised her brows, not certain she could properly form words with how dry her mouth had gone. She needed to find a measure of success and become financially independent, and soon. Because she wasn't sure how much longer she could sleep, eat, and live with Jake before losing all self-control and actually kissing him.

Jake led her down the stairs to Alice and Katie Grace's new, smaller room on the second floor. He rapped on the door, which was promptly answered. Katie Grace grabbed Mabel's hand and tugged her inside. "It's nearly done!"

Jake laughed and went no farther than the door. "You're in good hands. I'll see you downstairs."

Katie Grace stared up at Mabel, her elfin face flushed, the smattering of freckles tripping across her nose distinct against the splash of pale skin. She held her hands in a prayerful position beneath her chin. "Are you really going to *wrestle* in the parlor? Old Mrs. Luvotti is gonna let you? I can't believe it. She's such a pill."

"Katerina Grace Russo!" Alice, sitting on a chair tucked into a corner with the desk, shook her head and stood.

Mabel laughed and touched the child's frizzy crown. "I will be. Mr. Cunningham and I both. And you must admit it was very kind of Mrs. Luvotti to allow us to. She has a very fine parlor." When some of the other boarders discovered Mabel's new position, they had clamored for a demonstration. Mrs. Luvotti had been hard-pressed to resist, and Mabel was certain the landlady hadn't wanted to anyway.

Katie Grace swung her gaze to Alice, eyes wide. "Mam, this is the most exciting thing that has ever happened to me."

Alice laughed and motioned Mabel to follow her toward the bed. "It's over here. I was thrilled when Mr. Cunningham asked me to make it. Though not as thrilled as Katie Grace."

Katie Grace pressed close to Mabel as they followed her mother. "I helped."

"You did?" Mabel asked, perplexed. "I have no idea what it is."

"Close your eyes," Katie Grace said, hopping up and down. Mabel stopped and followed directions.

A moment later, Katie Grace exclaimed, "Open them!"

Mabel did, and when she saw what Alice held, she gasped. She reached for the costume—a bottom made of ruched vermilion silk with an elasticized waist and a blousy top of natural linen.

"Alice." Mabel released a breath as she ran her fingers over the exquisite Irish lace adorning the shirt's neckline and shoulders. "This is beautiful."

"Your husband came to me the day after you secured your position at Flok's Museum. He said the provided attire was too unsophisticated for a woman of your skill."

Mabel glanced up at her friend. "Did he really?"

"Oh yes." Alice clapped her hands over Katie Grace's ears and grinned. "He also said it did nothing to complement your charms."

"Oh, my heavens." Mabel sighed as she ran her fingers over the blouse. "The fabric is very fine. And the workmanship is spectacular, of course. I wonder how he paid for this."

Then she remembered Mr. Flok's narrowed eyes as he and Jake spoke backstage after her performance. The money that changed hands. And Jake's wink when Mr. Flok slipped back through the curtain to announce the next act. *"It's only right I'm paid for my performance."*

"Come on." Katie Grace tugged Mabel's arms. "Go get dressed so you can start."

Mabel did. But back in her room, she took a minute to sit on the edge of the bed, the costume held to her chest, and considered Jake's surprise. She ran over the facts, trying to discard any fancy that didn't align with them.

Jake had thought of her. He had used his money—money meant to see him back home to his family—to buy something she didn't need but would absolutely love. He thought enough of her to consider what would most flatter her *charms*.

In not one of those facts did Mabel recognize a man who didn't care. She wondered if, perhaps, he might.

A knock sounded at the door, and Katie Grace's voice slipped beneath it. "Are you almost ready?"

"Almost." Mabel hurried to remove her clothing. She dug through her drawer for a pair of fleshlings and pulled them over her legs. With the flexibility of her aerialist mother, she reached around her back and fastened the tiny hooks of the Cadolle corselet-gorge she'd purchased in Paris. Unlike a rigid corset, the piece only supported her breasts and left the rest of her free to move and inhale—both things necessary for wrestling. The costume slid over her skin, and she slipped the shirt's buttons through their holes. Leather slippers, supple and soft from use, went on her feet.

"Mabel, why are you taking so long?" The annoyance in Katie Grace's tone earned her a reprimand from her mother and hastened Mabel across the room.

"It fits perfectly." Mabel pulled the door open and gave her hand to Katie Grace. "Let's see who is stronger, me or Mr. Cunningham."

* * *

Jake didn't like this strange sensation of falling—all the time falling—into something deeper and wider and vaster than he'd ever known. He didn't like the way the hairs on his arms prickled when Mabel rolled toward him at night, her even breathing and soft skin doing things to him he'd not felt in years. He didn't like how the audience at Flok's Museum heckled her, laughing and insulting and causing her face to flame red and her gaze to fall as though she weren't higher and better and more than the lot of them. He didn't like thinking of Bram's charge—*take care of my daughter*—which kept him pinned to New York City . . . but really, when he thought on it even a little bit, he knew it had nothing at all to do with that. And he certainly didn't like the way the male boarders sitting in Mrs. Luvotti's boardinghouse parlor stared at Mabel as she entered the room, the costume he'd had Alice make serving only to enhance her curves. Dash it all, but he didn't like a thing about *that.*

Which was stupid, because men all over Europe had ogled and leered, and he never once thought about them. The same had happened with Charlotte, and he'd never once thought of slamming any of them to the floor the way he now considered doing to the mild-mannered architect who lived on the second floor.

Maybe it was because Charlotte sometimes courted that type of attention. Or maybe because Mabel was like the little sister he'd never had.

But that wasn't true. He definitely wouldn't feel such things for a sister. He was honest enough to admit it.

Jake crossed the room. "Do you like it?"

Mabel ran her hands over the shirt and grinned. "I love it. Thank you."

"I helped," Katie Grace interjected, then flopped onto the floor in front of one of the settees.

"Are you ready to wrestle, Mrs. Cunningham?"

"Always."

"Are you really going to trounce a woman, Cunningham?" one of the boarders called—a new one who had only arrived a day earlier. "I thought better of you than that."

"Don't worry." Jake hunkered down and circled Mabel. "Your opinion of me will likely remain unchanged after this. Unless you belong to the variety of man who believes women the weaker sex."

"Aren't they?" another called out.

Jake met Mabel's gaze—clear and guileless but glinting with strength. "Not this one."

He rushed forward, and they met in the middle of the faded Oriental rug, surrounded by the furniture that had been pushed up against the walls and the people who scooted to the edge of their seats.

Circling, hands grasping forearms, breath mingling. Jake grabbed her head and pulled down, his heart thrumming. Because of the effectiveness of his move or her nearness, he wasn't sure.

She managed to escape, and all philosophical ponderings scattered. He couldn't let the match go very long. She knew too much. Was too strong. He only had speed and agility on his side. A measure of surprise, though that was in question. Mabel seemed able to read every opponent's mind. And she'd fought him too many times to be caught unaware.

Jake shot toward her and wrapped his arms around her leg, his fingers slipping over her thigh. Her muscle flexed, moving beneath his skin and drawing his attention. He loved the feel of it. The strength bound up in her limbs. There wasn't a woman in the world like her.

He blinked and refocused. Grabbing behind her knee, he lifted and tried to knock her off her feet. A wordless shout escaped his lips when he nearly did. He'd never gotten even that close to upsetting her. What was going on? Was she unwell? Feverish? Tired?

Someone hooted, and Katie Grace screamed, "Get him!"

He could sense Mabel's will stiffening, and she scooped her arm beneath his and grabbed his wrist, and they found themselves cheek to cheek. With quick movements, she broke his hold on her leg, flipped him over her hip and went down with him.

Scrambling, she threw her leg over his waist and smiled.

Her chest rose and fell with effort. Her eyes danced, and her lovely lips lifted. "Got you."

And he didn't mind in the least.

Didn't give a hoot that he'd been bested by a woman in front of their entire boardinghouse. Didn't care that every man in the room believed him a weakling or a deceiver. Didn't mind that she filled his vision and his mind and his . . . heart? Filled so much that she crowded out every thought of anything else. Anyone else.

A delicious warmth stole through him. Something unrelated to effort. Something hinting at more than friendship. Something that stole the anger that had, for years, boiled his blood. Stole away the image of the one who was the catalyst for it.

And in the space of a lazy blink, Charlotte was there. Reminding him. Filling his veins with ice. Dropping a veil between past love and present possibility.

"Get off me, Mabel."

She frowned and did so. "Are you hurt? What's wrong?"

"Nothing," he said, then offered a tight smile to their audience and practically flew from the room.

CHAPTER 13

ALL MABEL HEARD as Mr. Flok spoke was the battering refrain of *You're not enough. You're not enough. You're not enough.* He didn't say those exact words, of course—but they were close enough that it didn't take much imagination to twist them into a fulfillment of her deepest insecurity.

"People want to be entertained, you see," he said, the electric lights overhead illuminating his waxed hair, "and your wrestling just isn't enough."

"You aren't losing money, though. Not since my husband opened that first match."

"No. You have bested every man and the few women who have challenged you. But that isn't enough. We need something more. Something exciting."

More than her. More than her alone. More than the years she'd dedicated herself to strength.

Tension crawled over Mabel's forehead. She squeezed the

169

bridge of her nose then stretched her thumb and index finger over her brows. "Crowds have been good."

He squinted up at her and rubbed the back of his neck. "Please sit down so I don't have to crane my neck." When she did, he gave an affected sigh and shook his head. "Crowds have been adequate, Miss Cunningham. Average. Nothing like what Mrs. Bluett sees and has seen for months. Her numbers are climbing."

Mrs. Bluett, the Limbless Housewife, ironed, made tea, minded a toddler, and danced a waltz with neither arms nor legs. Mabel had spoken with her only that morning, and the woman was a cyclone of sparking energy. "How does she manage it? What does she do that I don't?"

"She doesn't work alone." Mr. Flok pulled a tattered copy of the *New York World* from beneath a stack of papers and tossed it toward her. "Page 28."

Mabel flipped through. There, on the indicated page, was Jake—and Charlotte—in black and white. His arm thrown over his wife's shoulders, he looked down at her, wearing a smile so wide that his dimples disappeared into the creases. Beneath was an article on his sudden departure from Travis and Wells Circus after her death. Mabel glanced over the print, her gaze snagged back toward the photo in an annoyingly relentless manner. They were so beautiful together that it made Mabel's chest ache.

> The loss of Travis and Wells's most beautiful performer was then matched in bitterness by the disappearance of her husband. Having started in the ring on horseback, Mr. Cunningham soon caught the eye of society's beloved darling, and together they caught the heart of a nation.

She gazed at his image with a frightening hunger, knowing she would have to replace that heat with placid disinterest when she saw him at dinner later that night.

Isabella Moreau, the country's most accomplished aerialist and partner in the act that stole Mrs. Cunningham's life, said the entire circus world grieved—and grieved more still the loss of Mr. Cunningham.

The air in Mabel's nose turned hot and burned its way down her throat at the sight of another woman using her name. Which was unfair, as that woman had laid claim to it first.

She brushed her fingers over Jake's form before laying the magazine back on the desk and meeting Mr. Flok's eyes.

"Am I correct that the Mr. Cunningham mentioned in that article is the same as yours?" Mabel nodded, and he offered her an obsequious smile that did little to settle her tumbling stomach. "I thought he looked familiar when he was here your first day. I hoped he'd come again—"

"He works most days."

His eyelid twitched. "For Travis and Wells?"

She shook her head. "He's not interested in going back to the circus."

"Good." Mr. Flok patted the magazine. "Your husband made Charlotte Cunningham's career what it was. He can do the same for you."

"I don't understand. Both he and Charlotte did trapeze. They complemented each other in a way that he and I do not. I wrestle."

"But you don't only wrestle, do you? From childhood, you worked alongside your father."

"My father was a strongman, Mr. Flok. Jake is an acrobat."

He tapped his fingers against the desk, nails clicking, and his expression pinched. "Use your imagination, Mrs. Cunningham. Surely you have some. Your future with Flok's Museum depends on it."

"He will not want to perform again."

Mr. Flok studied her for a moment, then stood, slowly and

with more grace than could usually be credited a man. He held his hand toward the door. "That would be extremely disappointing."

Mabel left knowing the disappointment would be hers.

✳ ✳ ✳

"That was quite a demonstration last night, Mabel," Alice said. "I'm in complete awe of your strength."

"I don't think Mr. Cunningham likes wrestling." Katie Grace nuzzled the kitten's head and giggled. She and her mother had come to Mabel's rooms when she arrived home from work for a visit with Octavia. "He turned white as a sheet."

"Yes, that was very strange." Mabel shrugged. "It's never happened before."

Katie Grace peered up at them from the floor where she sat beneath the window. "Maybe he didn't like wrestling with you in front of people. It must be very humiliating to be thumped by a girl."

"Katerina Grace, Mr. Cunningham is a professional." Alice narrowed her eyes as Katie Grace pressed the cat's nose to her nose. "Do not grow too attached to that animal, darling. It must go back outside." She frowned, but even Mabel could see there was little substance to the threat.

Katie Grace pouted. "Why? Mrs. and Mr. Cunningham can keep her. Forever."

Mabel raised her brows. "I'm afraid not. Mr. Cunningham is very unhappy that Octavia has taken to doing her business in his shoes." Katie Grace sent her a sharp look, and Mabel held up one finger. "Yes, I named her. Would you like to know the name in its entirety?"

Katie Grace gave an energetic nod, flaxen curls springing around her face.

Mabel used her impresario's voice. Names were noteworthy things. They were wrapped up in all kinds of significance and deserved a grand announcement. "Octavia Maria—for your father's heritage—Shannon—for your mother's—Whiskers. Whiskers is self-explanatory."

"Octavia Maria Shannon Whiskers," Katie Grace said gravely. "That is an awful lot of names."

"She's an awfully important kitten."

Katie Grace glared between her mother and Mabel. "Then shouldn't she have a proper home? Her poor little ear is already mangled." Her eyes welled. "Mam, please."

"Darling, how would I ever convince Mrs. Luvotti that—"

"I'm sure," Mabel said with a wink in Katie Grace's direction, "that Jake could do that inside of a minute."

Alice chuckled. "No doubt." She took stock of her daughter, looking very pathetic and desperate, Octavia Maria Shannon Whiskers nestled in her lap, and sighed. "Very well. But if she begins going to the bathroom in my shoes, we must put her outside."

Katie Grace jumped to her feet, and Alice held up her hand.

"Don't get excited prematurely. Mr. Cunningham must still speak with Mrs. Luvotti."

Katie Grace nodded gravely, but a gap-toothed smile erupted over her face, and she bent to give Alice a kiss. "Thank you, Mam. And she won't go in your shoes. I'm going to bring her to our rooms and make her a bed. And I will teach her, and she will be the best-behaved little cat in all of Manhattan."

"And how will you manage that," Alice said as soon as Katie Grace was out of ear shot, "seeing as how you are not at all the best-behaved little girl in Manhattan? Goodness, Mabel, the child needs a focus. School does not seem to be that for her, and I'm afraid she will get into heaps of trouble. I can't keep her trapped inside our little room all day long—especially now that we've moved to a smaller space. But neither do I trust she is actually making it to school most days. She wanders the streets, and anything could happen."

Mabel shifted on the mattress where she sat beside Alice and patted her friend's arm. "She'll be okay. She's spirited and entirely too interested in excitement, but she's a sweet girl and doesn't have any real intention to get into trouble."

Alice gave her a look of exasperation. "She doesn't need to intentionally court trouble for it to follow her."

The door swung open, and Jake stepped inside. "Oh, I didn't realize we had company."

Alice stood in one graceful movement. "I was just leaving. You'll be happy to know, Mr. Cunningham, that Octavia Maria Shannon Whiskers has found a new home and your shoes are saved." She waved at Mabel and slipped into the hallway.

Jake removed his jacket and hung it on the peg near the door, then dropped his suspenders. "I'm exhausted." He didn't even glance her way as he rounded the bed and flopped onto his stomach, feet dangling off the edge.

"Would you like me to remove your shoes?" Mabel asked.

"Don't bother. I'll only have to put them back on for dinner in thirty minutes."

"Mrs. Luvotti will want you to wash."

He grunted.

"Jake?" Mabel touched his shoulder.

He huffed. "I'm tired, Mabel. Can I have a few minutes of quiet?"

She swallowed hard and moved nearer the headboard, putting space between them. With her feet flat on the floor and her knees pressed tightly together, she picked at the skirt of her violet checked suit. She liked the way the fabric draped her figure. How the belted jacket hugged her waist. She'd entertained the thought that Jake might notice and might even tell her how nice she looked. She lifted her gaze and stared at the wall, noting the whirls in the paper. The little tear near the corner. She sniffed.

At the gentle touch on her back, she looked over her shoulder.

Jake watched her, his head cradled on his folded arms. "I'm sorry. There was no call for me to be so rude to you. What did you need?"

"I only wondered if you were angry with me. It seems you are. You pretended to be asleep when I came to bed last night." He opened his mouth to argue, but she shook her head. "I could tell, Jake." She glanced down at her fingers, woven together in her lap. "You didn't say a word to me this morning, and you can hardly look at me. What did I do?" She shifted so that she could look at him without craning her neck. "Did you want to win the match? It's never bothered you before to lose."

"Of course not. I would never ask you to do that. I don't mind at all that you're stronger than me."

"Or bigger and taller?"

"Not a whit." His voice was gruff, and he cleared his throat. "It's only that . . ." He flipped onto his back, arms folded behind his head, and cast his eyes at the ceiling. "I'm very tired. I work ungodly hours, and it seems as though my pay is gone before it's had a chance to go cold."

"And you want to go home." Her stomach clenched and twisted with fierce dread. She'd been trained, though, to keep her expression passive beneath heavy weight. Despite pain. She'd once done a harness lift of 2,500 pounds with two broken ribs, and no one had been the wiser.

Jake said nothing.

"You need money to pay your way to Kansas, and you don't want to burden your brother."

His jaw twitched. "I left him to that life years ago, digging a living out of cattle and parched land. When I made my start with Charlotte, I sent money. They sent it back. Even though it would have helped. It would definitely help now." He turned to look at her. "I'm not angry with you. Not at all. Not for any reason. I never could be." He held out his arm, and she stared at it. "It's merely a hug, Mabel. I've given you many of those."

Yes, but never so . . . parallel. She leaned into his embrace, and her rigidity yielded to the rightness of it. She bent her knees and turned onto her side, being careful to keep her shoes off the bed. He pulled her nearer, his arm wrapping her back, hand around her waist, and she found her head lying comfortably in the dip of his shoulder.

"I have an idea," she said, "about how you can make more money. Faster too."

"Yes?"

"Mr. Flok told me today that unless I come up with something more interesting than wrestling matches, I will not be working for him much longer."

"You can do many other things. Wrestling was a very small part of your act with Manzo Brothers. In fact, after the first few years, I'm not sure many men were stupid enough to accept the challenge. You've destroyed the pride of more European men than any other woman."

She could hear the laugh in his voice, and she chanced moving nearer. Her body curved against his. She didn't even care that her shoes were on the blanket. "He wants you, though." How she understood the sentiment.

"Me? For what?"

"To do a show with me. He knows who you are, and he knows you will draw a crowd. He thinks I will be more interesting with you."

"You are interesting all on your own, Mabel." His hand slipped to her hip, and he squeezed it. "Anyway, I'm done with that life. It holds no appeal for me."

"But making money and going home does. And it would help me so much, Jake. I'm afraid Mr. Flok isn't very impressed with me. You and I work well together. We could come up with something."

He slipped his arm away, stood, and walked around the bed to offer his hand. He held it between them, meeting her gaze for the first time since the evening before. After a long moment—which felt very short, for Mabel could only think on his fingers woven through hers—his chin dipped. "Only because I care for you and your future. I want you to make a success of this." He released his grip. "I'm going to wash up." At the door, he paused and smiled at her. "You look very pretty today."

When he'd gone, she sank back onto the mattress. He hadn't really answered her question—hadn't told her what had bothered him so much the night before. She didn't believe for a minute that he had been worried about money during their match.

But he was going to perform with her.

And he'd said she was pretty.

CHAPTER 14

THERE WERE TOO MANY people in the elevator to speak freely, but Isabella saw Robert's sidelong glances. She leaned against the wall, relieving the pressure on her knees. It had been a hard show. Travis and Wells had been beset by bad luck since they'd arrived in New York.

Her own, as well as collectively.

Only days after arriving, a runaway elephant had drawn Mayor Gaynor's ire, which only his longstanding friendship with Jerry had soothed. Really, they were lucky Titus hadn't trampled anyone in his bid for freedom. They would have had to put the animal down if he had.

Then one of the lion tamers came down with pneumonia. The lion didn't like his replacement and had taken a sizeable chunk out of the man's arm in front of a terrorized group of schoolchildren the day before their first show. Mayor Gaynor hadn't been happy about that either.

Travis and Wells's strongman had been poached by another

circus—offered center ring and a private stateroom—only that morning, and Robert had spent the afternoon attempting to steal him back to no avail.

Then there were the regular setbacks and troubles—torn costumes, broken harnesses, missed cues—and everyone was frazzled. Discord swept through the performers, tempers short and tongues sharp.

Isabella avoided meeting Robert's gaze. Everything hurt—body and soul—and she only wanted to ice her backside and crawl into bed.

The elevator stuttered to a stop at their floor and quickly emptied. Isabella hung back until Robert followed the crowd.

He tarried, though, bending in pretense of retying his shoelace. "Are you avoiding me?" he asked as she swept past.

Her determination faltered—he sounded so forlorn—and she paused to turn. "No. I'm tired. And I hurt."

"Where?"

"Everywhere." She saw worry dart across his expression, and she reached for his arm. "I'm not injured. Only aching."

Her words were punctuated by the sound of shutting doors and clicking locks. The circus had taken up three entire floors of the hotel, and everyone seemed eager to see the day end. She was, as well, but now she wished she'd joined Rowena and a few other performers on Madison Square Garden's rooftop cabaret to watch a new musical revue. She took a few steps toward her room.

"You've hardly said a word to me in days."

She flipped open her reticule and reached for the key. It was smooth and cold beneath her fingers. "Everyone is talking."

"About us?"

She nodded and glanced at him. "We have been too obvious. My reputation, according to Rowena, is in tatters. I've noticed the stares. And I'm afraid Jerry will hear whispers and I'll be out of a job."

"You're already out of a job. He only extended your time with us because I practically groveled. I reminded him what your mother had done."

The brown carpet, paneled walls, and heavy artwork pushed toward her, and she felt herself sinking beneath the surface of it all. Oh, she knew this heaviness. This desperate hopelessness.

Turning, she pulled out the key and hunched over it, wanting to open the door but afraid if she did, if she released her arms from around her belly, every bit of hurt and fear would tumble over her and she would drown. Swallowed whole and lost to it again.

"I'm sorry," Robert said, his hand warm on her shoulder. "That was unkind of me to say so carelessly."

She turned toward him, more because of fear of what lay inside her than anything else. And when his arms circled her, the scrabbling, clawing, pulsing shadows took flight. "It's true, though, isn't it?"

He didn't say anything.

A door opened down the hall, and the deep sound of men's laughter spilled out of the room. She jerked her chin toward his door, too afraid of what waited in her empty room to want to be alone.

He opened the door and waved her toward one of the tufted chairs flanking the fireplace. When she sank into it, he tossed his jacket onto the bed and sat on the floor, legs crossed.

"What are you doing?" she asked.

He took her foot into his lap and removed her shoe. With sure hands, he reached beneath her skirt and unhooked her stocking, letting it fall around her ankle. As he pulled it off and began massaging her feet, she stared at the top of his bent head. His hair remained as thick as she remembered from their early days with Travis and Wells. It was still dark, though grey had begun to creep up his sideburns, and Isabella clenched her fingers together in her lap to keep from touching it. Touching him.

Her heart tumbled into her stomach, and the blood pumping through her veins spilled hot into her feet beneath his hands. She couldn't want him. Not for any reason except as a way to keep her job.

She couldn't love him.

"Marry me." His words scratched from his throat as though making their way from a place much deeper. He cupped his palms around her calves and pressed his forehead to her knees. "I'm desperate for you. Marry me."

Touching his head, she allowed herself one moment to feel his curls beneath her fingers, then she leaned back and looked up at the ceiling. "I can't."

Robert pulled away. He took a deep, shaking breath and once again set his focus on her feet. "What did he do to you?"

"Nothing." It was true. Bram had done nothing. He hadn't so much as touched her from the moment Mabel was born. Hadn't kissed her. Hadn't rubbed her feet. Tears spilled over, and Isabella couldn't catch them. "It wasn't his fault. I was weak. He was strong. He could have killed me."

Robert's brows drew together, and he placed her foot on the floor before lifting the other. "I don't understand."

He deserved to know, but she had never spoken of it. Just as she'd never told Bram about Paul. Had never said a word about how her first love's death, and the darkness that preceded it, had spilled into their marriage.

But Robert wasn't like Bram. Bram understood the need to keep things buried.

"We will never speak of it again."

Polly had never heard such coldness in Bram's voice before. She had crawled beside him after failing once again to nurse her babe. She needed to succeed at something. Needed to know her body hadn't completely failed her in every way possible.

So she had let the wet nurse carry her child into the adjoining room and had woken her husband with a touch. He'd been deeply asleep, or it would have never happened. It hadn't happened in four months.

"The doctor said not to," Bram had muttered. But Polly never had followed directions. And Bram never could resist her.

She'd nearly gotten what she wanted when he came fully awake, the moonlight bathing his face and the horror scrawled over it. *"He said not to."*

"Please, let's talk about it. He couldn't mean never. Never, Bram? Forever?"

"We will never speak of it again."

Isabella took a breath. "Before I left Manzo Brothers and came to New York, Bram almost lost me. He was big, you remember." She touched her stomach. "And I am very small." Not just in height, the doctor had told her. "Mabel was large. Too large for me."

Robert stood and held out his hand. He drew her toward the bed, where they sat, his arm around her waist, her head tucked beneath his chin.

"I almost died."

A shudder moved through him, and his embrace grew tighter.

"The doctor told Bram another pregnancy would certainly kill me. And then . . ." Then it only got worse.

"But you aren't afraid to be with me."

She hadn't been afraid to be with Bram. She would have sacrificed herself to have a complete marriage with him again. To feel as near to a heart as humanly possible. To have and hold him once more. But Bram had been guided by his emotions. He never could give or take just a little. It wouldn't have been enough for him. His father's blood ran through his veins, and he'd always endeavored to restrain it. "I am well past the age when pregnancy is possible."

"Then why . . . ?"

She shook her head, unwilling to dive further into the sad story. She couldn't bare any more of herself. Couldn't tell him the rest. He had always adored her, as had Bram. And if her husband's opinion could change so entirely with the knowledge of her weakness, couldn't Robert's?

"You have my body, Robert. I can't give you anything else."

"I want all of you. Every bit of you. Your mind and heart and soul. Those are the pieces I want. It's what I've always wanted."

"You want too much." She kissed his jaw. "Besides, there's nothing else left."

※　※　※

Isabella couldn't allow New York to be the end. But if she was headed out anyway, she had nothing to lose.

On the second day of Travis and Wells's New York season, she ignored Robert's demand she perform only those things she could do in her sleep—safe little stunts that would win no one the career she'd had and certainly wouldn't revive it— and, beneath the glare of a thousand electric lights, gave the evening audience a show.

Robert was livid.

"I told you not to do that," he said when she stepped into the dressing room hall, the thundering applause sweeping beneath her feet.

She only shrugged. And then she did it the next afternoon and evening and twice a day until she caught the attention of a *New York Times* reporter.

It seemed her recklessness had paid off. Or not. All she could see was the headline sticking out from beneath a stack of papers on Mr. Wells's desk.

Isabella Moreau Spins Her Way Back into Center Ring

She bit down a smile before looking at the circus owner, who had asked Robert to bring her to his home after the afternoon show. She hadn't seen him in a few years. He'd stopped spending weeks with them at the winter grounds when his wife became ill, passing a year after she took to her bed. And he'd stopped riding the trains with them—in his gilded private coach—even earlier—since Paul had been found washed up on the banks of the Ohio River by Isabella's mother.

"I've had two pieces of interesting news, and both have to do with you." Mr. Wells slid the newspaper, folded over itself, toward her. "This is the first. Would you care to explain?"

Isabella swallowed and pulled the paper nearer. Her eyes scanned the headline again. *Isabella Moreau Spins Her Way Back into Center Ring.* She met his gaze. "That wasn't my intention."

He didn't believe her. She could tell by his raised brows—the only thing breaking his demeanor. Plus, he'd known her a long time. Long enough to remember when she'd wanted nothing more than to prove herself capable.

Not much had changed, though now the need was more desperate.

"Keep reading." Mr. Wells sat back in his chair, leather creaking beneath his bulk.

Robert, sitting beside Isabella, leaned over to read with her. It was toward the end of the article that she realized what she had done.

. . . and it must be said, how far is too far? How far will Travis and Wells go to capture the imagination of the people? How many lives will be put at risk? This particular circus has a history of losing performers to dangerous stunts. One only need go back nine years to remember the great grief felt around the country with the death of Charlotte Cunningham. No one has ever been held to task for that. Likely no one will.

This season alone, there have been multiple mishaps. The elephant Titus escaped his trainers and rampaged 26th Street.

It was called an accident. When a tamer was mauled before a group of schoolchildren, it was said to have been a once-in-a-lifetime incident. But all across the country, all across the world, circus performers are injured because of a lack of safety measures and common sense.

I call on Mr. Jeremiah Wells to no longer put his employees at risk. And on the citizens of New York to demand he be held to task before another beloved performer loses their life to the glitter of his perilous show.

Beside Isabella, Robert blew out a breath. "She didn't intend for this to happen, Jerry."

"Do you speak for her now?"

Isabella didn't dare look at her employer. Instead, she glanced at Robert and noted his red face and bobbing Adam's apple.

"No, of course not."

Mr. Wells tapped the desk, gaining Isabella's attention, and held out his hand. She passed the paper back across the desk. He looked between her and Robert, his expression unnervingly blank. "I have known both of you a long time. You were close with my son." He looked at Isabella. "I valued your mother very much. And for those reasons—for Paul and Hélène—I'm going to pretend I don't see what is going on here. Instead, I want to address the scrutiny you have brought on Travis and Wells, Miss Moreau. This trick you performed had not been vetted. Had not been approved. Had not, as I understand it, even been properly rehearsed."

She shook her head. "I felt I had nothing to lose, sir."

"You value your life so little?"

She heard the pain in his question, and her heart stuttered over Paul's memory. His choice. Over cold ripples of a lake and a moment when shadows invaded.

She dropped her head and picked at the nubby tweed of her skirt. There was a certain disregard all performers—especially flyers—needed to embody so they could do their jobs. They took risks every day—risks others would never consider—and part of being a circus performer meant embracing the inherent danger. She was no different in that way. It was unfair of the article's author to blame Jerry for this. And to bring up Charlotte . . . Charlotte's death had been entirely her own fault.

Her fingers froze in their plucking, and her skin went clammy at the chill filling her veins. She was no different than Charlotte had been—doing something dangerous, something unapproved, to turn heads. To goad the audience to wonder and applause. To make herself relevant. And whether or not the fault lay with Jerry or Travis and Wells, she had brought condemnation down upon them.

"I'm sorry," she said.

"I considered rescinding my previous offer that you can continue working until we leave New York, but I'm fine leaving things how they are as long as you do not pull such a stunt again."

An exhale escaped her lips, and Isabella leaned toward the desk, her hands pressed in a prayerful expression against her chest. "I won't."

"I believe you." Mr. Wells studied her a moment before picking up a pen and tapping it against the desk. "There is one thing more. It seems Jake Cunningham is back in New York."

Isabella gasped and sat up straight, back rigid. She'd never thought to hear that name again.

"I want you to bring him back to us."

"That isn't possible."

"Why?"

"I don't think you understand the extent of his dislike of me." Isabella swallowed. "He blames me for Charlotte's death."

"And were you responsible?"

"You know I wasn't. Charlotte was determined to have her way."

"I want Mr. Cunningham back. Do whatever you must to make it right between the two of you so he will return."

Robert braced his hands against the armrests of his chair. "Come now, Jerry. You can't expect her to induce him to come if he doesn't wish to."

Mr. Wells didn't even blink. "I do expect that." Then he swung his finger between Isabella and Robert. "As for this romance between the two of you . . . make it end or make it right. You are not above the rules, though I'll grant both of you grace because of your long work with us." His gaze pierced Robert. "I am very disappointed in you."

Isabella turned away, knowing she was the one at fault.

A moment later, she and Robert were again in the backseat of Mr. Wells's brick-red Mercedes. She held her hat to her hair as the driver motored down the middle of Fifth Avenue, and leaned against the door, peering out at the horses, carriages, and crush of people.

"It's so much faster than a bicycle," she said, not caring if the wind stole the words before they reached Robert's ears, "but not quite as fast as flying through the air."

His fingers found hers on the seat, and she drew her hand into the safety of her lap. She didn't look at him until they reached Madison Square Garden.

"Well," she said lightly as she let the driver help her from the vehicle, "I have to run, Robert. Show starts in an hour."

She'd taken only three steps before he circled the automobile and met her outside the back door. "Isabella, wait." He ducked to look at her, but she kept her gaze fixed on the shoes peeking out from beneath her skirt. "He said to make it right. Might we?"

"There is no way to make anything right. It's all just so wrong. Every bit of my life. Every bit of—" she looked at him and waved her hand between them—"this."

He blinked, his mouth moving as though around words.

With a defeated slump, he sank against the wall. "This entire time . . . you've been bribing me. You never had any affection for me, did you? I'm a fool."

"No. You're not." Isabella stepped close. "That isn't it."

It *had* been, though, and her breath hitched when she recognized it. She'd thought herself so justified. She'd been desperate, terrified, and she made a living with her body. It didn't seem so far a jump. But she'd hurt one of her dearest friends.

She wanted to touch him. To feel the warmth of his skin and taste his lips. Instead, she pressed her arms to her sides. "I'm sorry. You deserve so much more than this."

"*You* deserve more than this."

He had no idea what she deserved. There was a reason she'd lost everyone she cared about. "Where would it end?" she whispered.

He dropped his hands and reached for hers. "With love, Polly. To know and be known."

She shook her head and tried to push off his grasp but ended up clinging instead. "I don't want you to know me. You've no idea the darkness you'll find."

"Let me help you chase it away."

Bram had promised to love her too. He'd promised to cherish her and protect her.

But promises were as substantial as the gladiolus she'd once made a crown of for her daughter. Dainty, pretty things, but not able to stand upright beneath a harsh wind.

CHAPTER 15

MOST IRONIC ABOUT WORKING for the circus was that Isabella had traveled nearly the width and breadth of the country yet had actually seen very little of it. She'd certainly never seen this particular part of Manhattan, which hemmed her and Robert in with a double string of eight-, nine-, ten-story buildings housing bustling shops on their ground floors. All manner of vehicles—automobiles, carts, carriages, and streetcars—crowded Broadway and threatened every pedestrian arrogant enough to cross the street with bodily harm.

Above them, Flok's Museum rose. Three stories of two-bit entertainment and acts not good or experienced enough to have been picked up by a larger outfit. Except for Jake Cunningham. Why he hadn't gone straight to Mr. Wells, Isabella didn't know. He'd been half of one of the most popular acts Travis and Wells had ever produced. People still wished for his return, even without Charlotte.

"Are you ready?" Robert took her hand, and she let him.

"I have to be." She'd never thought to see Jake again. And with the ugly accusations he'd cast her way the last time she had, she didn't want to now. He'd never wanted to acknowledge anything but the best of Charlotte. But his wife had been reckless and blindly determined. For all her beauty and grace and talent, nothing ever seemed enough for her.

Inside the building, they purchased tickets to the show. People crowded the room, pushing against one another to make their way through the doorway, above which was a lithograph of a rather poor likeness of Jake leaping over a voluptuous woman holding aloft a barbell.

Isabella pointed toward the image. "Is he part of a duo again?"

Robert shrugged and guided her into a small amphitheater. "Maybe that will motivate him to accept Jerry's offer. I doubt Mr. Flok can match us in wages."

Robert clearly underestimated Jake Cunningham's disdain for her.

Inside, they found themselves pressed on all sides by a pulsing, expectant crowd. The room was small and warm. A man bumped against Isabella, and she stumbled.

"So sorry," he said.

She laughed and righted herself. "You must be excited to see the show."

"Oh yes. I saw Jake Cunningham years ago at the circus. Best I've ever witnessed. And now he's performing here every day with his wife."

Isabella blinked. "His wife?" Jake had been so enamored with Charlotte, she never thought he'd marry again. No one did.

The man nodded, his eyes shining. "Mrs. Cunningham is a sight to behold. I've never seen such a woman."

Around them arose excited chatter, and trepidation tugged at Isabella's hope. If Cunningham's act had already drawn such a following in the short time he and his wife had been performing at Flok's Museum, would he be motivated to return to the circus? He could likely find a position at another outfit, and while Travis and Wells was one of the largest, the others didn't come with her.

But Jerry had offered her more than one second chance. She didn't want to give him any reason to regret that decision. To tire of her failures and change his mind.

Robert lifted his arm around her back to protect her from further jostling, and she saw how he looked at her. All tenderness and devotion, despite how poorly she had used him.

But what was his love worth? Romance always came with conditions, and she never seemed to live up to them.

She'd not been enough for Paul. She'd not been enough for Bram.

And she knew, one day, it would become clear she wasn't enough for Robert either.

He guided her to the rows of chairs, and they found two in the middle of the room. The lights flickered just as they sat, and but for the buzzing glow emitted by electric sconces lining the walls, the room went black. A chill skittered across her shoulders. Her first two relationships had ended when shadows proved too much for love to penetrate. Paul's, hers . . .

She leaned nearer to Robert and, concealed by darkness, pressed her arm against his. He stiffened at her touch but then relaxed into it, his body heaving a gentle sigh. She could claim no such contentment. Even in the knowledge that he loved her entirely.

Because beneath the tapping feet and humming excitement, she heard familiar whispers.

She pressed her hands over her ears, sinking as thoughts—unwanted, unformed—battered her. Visions of terrible, violent things. Would she commit them? Could she be forced to? It was why she'd left her daughter with so little resistance. To prevent such a thing.

Greater is he that is in you, mon chou, than he that is in the world. Maman was always saying such old-fashioned things. Isabella wanted to believe it. Wanted it so desperately that the tinny taste of it filled her mouth.

Experience had taught her otherwise. There was nothing in her. Nothing but shifting shadows.

She couldn't hear herself breathe and pressed her palm to her chest to make sure she still did. Robert's arms came around her, and the toneless notes of a calliope filled the room. "Are you well? It is very hot in here."

So very hot. She could almost feel Hell licking at her feet.

A spotlight shone on the showman, and Isabella focused on it. She breathed deeply and counted. *One, two, three . . .* The man wore an ostentatious purple suit and a tall hat. *Four, five, six . . .* When he spoke, his mustache jumped around expressive lips like a marionette. *Seven, eight, nine, ten.*

She sat upright. Gave Robert a nod. "I'm fine. Thank you."

"And now," Mr. Flok said, his voice dripping with theatre, "Mr. and Mrs. Cunningham, recently arrived from the courts and palaces of Europe. Entertainers of royalty now come to delight you. Only here, at Flok's Museum."

With the sparking of lights, Isabella's phantoms fled completely, and she found herself in control once more. Only the slight clamminess slicking her palms remained. "Greater is he that is in me . . ." Her whisper trailed off when she remembered there was no God within her. Not since her mother had received the telegram telling them her father had died in battle and, in thanks for his sacrifice, they were packed off his family farm and handed over to starvation.

Jake Cunningham tumbled from behind the curtain, his legs flipping around his head. Over and over and over until Isabella thought the woman in front of her would faint from excitement. And then there was the strongwoman.

"That is the woman who asked about a position with us," Robert said.

Mrs. Cunningham wore a simple but expertly tailored costume of silk and linen and commanded attention. She herself was the attraction. Nothing was needed—no embellishment or frill—to emphasize her beauty.

"I'm surprised you turned her down. She has a certain quality, does she not?"

"She botched the act miserably, though. I'm curious what she'll do here."

A hush fell over the audience, and even Isabella's own breath straddled between inhale and exhale as Mrs. Cunningham showed the audience exactly what she could do as she lifted her husband. With nary a twitch of her serene expression, she balanced him against her palm and twirled him in dizzy circles above her head.

Jake Cunningham was no insignificant man. Yes, he was a few inches shorter than his wife but strung with muscles and possessing a powerful vitality not at all diminished by his wife's demonstration.

Mrs. Cunningham set down her husband, her gaze settling on him for only a moment. So much could be said in the space of a moment, though, and her eyes were expressive. Snapping with bright energy, though nothing about the rest of her expression gave any indication of the state of her heart.

There were no shadows resting upon this woman.

The couple proceeded through a series of stunts and feats, masculine agility and solid strength perfectly married. They flipped the expectation completely, parting to do separate tricks—Mrs. Cunningham deflecting sledgehammer blows to her chest gleefully swung by Mr. Flok while Jake spun dizzy circles above them on Roman rings—then coming together and sending the crowd into a frenzy of shouts. It wasn't clear, as the strongwoman freed her husband from a tangled loop of iron chains, at what point the audience switched from applauding Jake to cheering for his wife. Where he amazed, she awed.

Isabella tugged Robert's sleeve, drawing his head down. "They are spectacular together, are they not?"

"We were sent to secure a specific acrobat, not an unknown strongwoman."

"We do need one, though, with our strongman's departure."

Robert made a sound in his throat, but his attention was snagged by Mr. Flok's return to the stage, and he didn't respond.

"Aren't they incredible? Newly married and seen only at Flok's Museum." He waved the performers to center stage. "Jacob and Mabel Cunningham!"

And then the veil dropped, and Isabella's hazy memories sharpened. She saw, at once, what years of separation had attempted to conceal. Mrs. Cunningham's black hair, curling around her head like a halo—Isabella reached for the heavy drape of her own, pinned beneath a hat. The strength in her calves and shoulders, a gift from her Scotch father. The gentle curve of her lips, as though kissed by Maman's own.

Mabel Cunningham smiled, and Isabella reached for her, hand trembling and finding no purchase. She pushed from her seat, ignoring the vexation of the man behind her, and tried to stumble past an aisle of skirts and legs. "Mabel!" she called. But her cry was lost to the noise and commotion, and Robert pulled her back down beside him.

Mr. Flok ushered the couple back behind the curtain, and again Isabella found herself cut off from her daughter. They'd taken her, after the birth. Dipping in and out of darkness, she'd heard her baby cry. Had reached for her then too.

"The bairn is well, love. Large. Too large for you." Bram's words had been cloaked in fear.

From the moment her baby had been born, others had been taking her away. The midwife, the doctor, her husband, the wet nurse, the circus, a fractured marriage . . . and Isabella could see now that undergirding all of it had been her own weakness.

Greater is he that is in me . . .

* * *

Jake sank onto a rickety chair pushed into the corner of the small basement dressing room as Mabel slipped behind the screen to change. "This place is beneath you."

She peered around the screen and smiled. "And you?"

"This is temporary for me. Just until you're settled and I've made enough money to return home with something more than contrition. But you could do so much better than this. You *should* be doing something better."

Mabel ducked back and undid the buttons of her costume. It flopped over her hips, and she held her arms wide, letting the stale air circulate around her arms and chest. No baths for the performers at Flok's Museum.

"Did you hear me, Mabel?" The chair thumped against the floor, and Jake's steps sounded as he crossed the room. "Would you like me to speak with the manager at Travis and Wells? I left in the middle of a season, but I don't think he'd hold it against me, given the circumstances."

Mabel's cheeks burned when she thought on those supple, lovely aerialists—so much like Charlotte must have been—dismissing her. How mortifying to have Jake witness that. She wiggled out of her costume, letting it pool around her feet, and pulled on her hose. "No. I don't think they want me."

"Why wouldn't they? I still don't understand why you didn't go when we first arrived in the city. I'm sure they would be thrilled to have you. I read in the paper that their strongman left for another circus. They're probably desperate to fill that space."

Mabel lifted her costume and pressed it into the canvas bag slung over a hook. "They definitely don't want me." She dropped the chemise over her head and pulled on her drawers, then hooked her corset in place.

"How do you know unless you at least try?" Exasperation colored his words. In them, Mabel could hear all the yearning he had to go home and return to his family. She recognized her culpability in his frustrated plans.

She sat heavily on the stool and slid her feet into her shoes. Then sighed. "I did try, Jake. I failed." His shuffling stopped, and she pulled on her shirtwaist and skirt. "I went when we first arrived. Mostly to see if my mother worked for them, but also to see if they needed a strongwoman."

"And they didn't?"

She adjusted her waistband, slipped into her jacket, and slung the bag over her shoulder. "I don't know." She stepped from behind the screen. "I didn't get far enough into my audition to find out. Stage fright followed me from Europe."

He stood like some ancient statue of Adonis. Frozen, one hand gripping the shirt he'd been in the process of putting on, his face carved in gentle benevolence. And then the shirt was hastily pulled over his head, and she found herself caught up against him.

"Why didn't you tell me?" His arms wrapped around her waist, and she wondered how she could feel so safe in the embrace of someone smaller than her, shorter than her, likely not as strong as her. "I'm so sorry."

"I didn't want to disappoint you. I know how much you want to return home. If I'd secured employment with Travis and Wells, you could have left that very evening. And you were working so hard. It seemed a greater weakness to burden you with it than to keep silent."

"Oh, Mabel. Don't think that." He pulled back, his hands on her waist. "The greatest benefit of marriage is *sharing* one another's burdens."

"We aren't married, Jake. Not truly. I have no claim on you."

His brows pinched, and he hugged her again.

She tried to put a little space between their chests. Her heart beat so fiercely that he would certainly feel it, and he would recognize what lay behind its intensity. He'd had great love before and knew the rhythm of it. But his arms slid up her back, hands pressing firmly, fingers following the confluence of muscle and sinew.

Her eyes closed, and she allowed her body to relax against his, head nestled against his shoulder. She pretended, for just a moment, their marriage wasn't mainly meant to avoid scandal. That it wasn't merely a practicality.

"Your heart is beating so fast." His breath wrapped her neck in delicious warmth, and when he dropped his hands to her elbows and encouraged her arms around his waist, she knew there was no extricating herself from the moment. No holding back. No satisfaction in pretense.

She ran her fingers down his spine and, encouraged by his soft inhale, pulled back and met his eyes. She saw something new in their smoky depths. Something that emptied her belly and made her weightless.

"Mabel . . ." And then his mouth was upon hers. "Sweet Mabel."

She had never been kissed and didn't even know where to start. "I don't know how," she breathed against his lips.

"Like this," he whispered and with gentle hands cupped her jaw. "And this." He tilted his head. "And this." He captured her entirely.

A knock sounded on the door, and they jumped apart. As they stared at one another, his expression was arrested by wonder.

But then he looked away and pressed the heels of his palms into his eyes. "I'm sorry. I shouldn't have done that."

A heavy ache filled her chest as his remorse scrubbed every bit of beauty from the moment, and she found herself yanked back to Earth by another knock. "The door."

Jake buttoned up his shirt with fumbling fingers and went to open it.

"There's someone to see you," Mr. Flok said, sounding none too happy.

Jake stiffened. "What are you doing here?"

Mabel craned her neck, but Jake blocked the doorway, and she could see nothing but the top of Mr. Flok's hat.

There came a murmured response—a soft, feminine voice.

"I will leave you," Mr. Flok said, and his hat bounced away.

Jake swung away from the door and crossed the room. He stood beside Mabel, arms crossed, face stony.

"Mr. Pedersen," Mabel said when she recognized the man who entered the room. Her eyes swung to the woman beside him. Tiny—she barely came to the circus manager's chest—and with features so delicate, they seemed made of spun sugar. She looked at Mabel, and then her eyes skittered away.

"What do you want?" Jake asked, and Mabel turned to look at him. How cold he sounded. So unlike himself. And he had shaken off the passion they had shared only a moment ago quickly enough.

"Very good performance," Mr. Pedersen said. "Mrs. Cunningham, you seemed quite capable today."

Mabel flushed at the reminder of her terrible audition. "I find I'm a much better strongwoman alongside my husband."

Mr. Pedersen smiled, affirming her initial positive opinion of him. "Love makes us all a bit better than we are alone, doesn't it?"

"Mabel is the best in the world, with or without me." Offense slid from Jake's words, and Mabel touched his arm, wondering at his barely restrained anger.

"We will get right to it," Mr. Pedersen said. "Wells has sent us to inquire into the possibility of you returning."

"No." Jake retrieved his jacket from the hook on the wall.

"Jake," Mabel said, "you can't mean that. What a wonderful opportunity."

"Then you go. They are in need of a strongman act." He shoved his arms into the jacket. "And it would provide you with a suitable income."

He didn't say that he could then leave. Go home. But she knew he thought it. Her stomach turned beneath a wave of nausea. Had their kiss meant nothing to him? Had he only been overcome with momentary passion? She knew that was sometimes the way of men. But she hadn't thought him capable of such trifling.

"I couldn't do it without you."

The corners of Jake's eyes pinched, and his jaw tightened. "Yes, you could."

"Either way," Mr. Pedersen said gently, "we aren't here to hire a strongwoman. Especially one who requires the presence of her husband to demonstrate strength."

Mabel nodded. She had no defense.

"Robert," the small woman said, "I think you should give her another chance. She just put on a fine show, and she's popular with the crowd."

Mr. Pedersen gave her a tender smile. "Mrs. Cunningham, this is Miss Isabella Moreau. I don't believe you've met. She is already acquainted with your husband."

Mabel shot Jake a quick glance. Of course she recognized the name. Everyone did. But Jake had never mentioned he knew the famed aerialist. And judging by the dark look he cast her way, it seemed he wished he didn't.

Miss Moreau extended a fine-boned hand and touched Mabel's fingers. "It's so very lovely to meet you."

Mabel stared at her, something about her voice tickling loose memories. "Have we met?"

Miss Moreau only gave her a sad smile.

"Jake," Mr. Pedersen said, long-time familiarity and friendship wrapped up in his name, "come back to us."

"I will never work around her again."

Miss Moreau flinched at Jake's announcement but then straightened her shoulders and lifted her chin. "I am very sorry about what happened to Charlotte. You have to know it wasn't my fault. She chose to do the stunt and made unsafe decisions leading up to it. She decided—"

"You encouraged her! Despite knowing I had reservations. Despite the fact that it was too dangerous."

"She was a performer before she married you. You had no right to make decisions for her."

Jake snarled. "Miss Moreau, seeing as you have never had the privilege of being married, I will instruct you in a fundamental part of it—a spouse has every right to raise concerns and questions when the other is pursuing foolishness."

Miss Moreau lifted her hand in entreaty. "And you were right—it was dangerous. But do you really believe, after Charlotte ignored you, that she would have listened to me?"

A muscle in Jake's jaw twitched. "I'm not interested in working for Travis and Wells." Then he glanced at Mabel, and his expression softened. "It would change everything for you," he said softly, and she nodded. He gave a long sigh, his shoulders heaving, then turned back to Mr. Pedersen. "If you allow my wife to prove herself, I will do the show until the end of the New York season. We will put on an act that will draw crowds, and the entire city will quake with excitement." His words and expression were laced with sardonic contempt. "And when she has found her confidence again, I will be done."

"Done with the show?" Mr. Pedersen's brows rose, and he rubbed the fleshy area beneath his chin. "What will you do instead?"

"That is none of your concern."

There was a moment of silence when Jake stared, unblinking, and Mr. Pedersen deliberated and Miss Moreau attempted to hide the fact that she found Mabel a fascinating subject.

Mr. Pedersen held out his hand and clasped Jake's. "I am hoping you'll change your mind and decide to stay on with us."

"I won't."

Kansas beckoned, and neither the promise of fame and fortune—both of which Mabel was certain Jake could reclaim with the snap of a finger—nor an inconvenient wife would keep him from escaping into anonymity.

Mr. Pedersen smiled at her. "It seems, Mrs. Cunningham, that you have found yourself in the position of Travis and Wells's new strongperson act. It is quite clear your husband believes in your competence. Hopefully we will come to agree."

Though Mabel couldn't deny the thrill coursing through her—how she had missed the circus—she was aware, once again, of how very ineffective she was without the assistance of another. Hopefully she could learn to work alone, because Jake, like her father, wouldn't prop her up forever.

CHAPTER 16

MISS MOREAU WATCHED HER. Mabel had caught her staring a dozen times since she'd entered the dressing room that morning but hadn't had the opportunity to address it. Changing performers crowded the space—the three other aerialists who tittered and pointed, acrobats and rope dancers, members of the ballet troupe, and even a female clown who kissed Miss Moreau on the cheek and cast her worried glances.

It had been only two days since Mabel learned she would work for the world's foremost circus, and she could still hardly acknowledge the fact. While the other women flung off bits of clothing and borrowed each other's combs and pots of rouge, Mabel ducked behind the screen and changed into her costume. She ran her hands lightly over the simple bodice with deep reverence for the friendship that had been sewn into every stitch.

Mr. Pedersen had told her when she arrived that morning that she would be fitted for something grander. Something flashier and eye-catching. There were three rings, after all, and one couldn't expect to be noticed by the audience if they wore something so unsophisticated.

She would only have this first show to honor Alice's skill and Jake's thoughtfulness. She tugged the bodice into place and smiled. It would be enough, for both would see it—Jake in the ring with her, and Alice, alongside Katie Grace, on the very front bench, watching.

Katie Grace had been beside herself with excitement when Mabel told her that morning as their belongings were loaded into a cart to be taken to the Hotel Veronica. The news had stopped the tears tracking the child's cheeks.

"We will miss you," Alice had said, squeezing Mabel's hand in Mrs. Luvotti's front parlor. "You must visit. Every time you are in New York."

Mabel stepped back around the screen, pressing her stomach to dislodge the knot of grief settled there. She had become close to Alice and Katie Grace in the weeks since arriving in New York, and she hated leaving them. Always before, her friends had traveled with her. There had not been many good-byes.

The room had emptied while Mabel changed, everyone having gone to watch the show's opening from the wings. Miss Moreau studied her with an unnervingly contained gaze. "You didn't want to go with the others?" Mabel asked.

Miss Moreau shook her head, then bent over the dressing table and shuffled through a collection of jars and bottles. She lifted a sheet of *papier poudré* and pressed it to her nose. "I prefer to stay in the dressing room until it is time to go out."

"I will stay with you, then. My performance is just before yours." Mabel found an empty hook and hung her clothing on it. She turned to find Miss Moreau again staring.

During every minute Mabel had tossed upon the boardinghouse's too-small bed the night before, going over every possible disaster that might happen to cut short this boon to her career—stage fright, injury, poor reception, negative newspaper coverage—not once had she considered she might engender the ill will of America's favorite aerialist before even having had a proper conversation with her.

Was it because she had married Jake? There was certainly palpable hostility between her husband and Miss Moreau.

"You should know," Mabel began, startling Isabella out of her watchful study, "that I don't hold you accountable for Charlotte's death. It seems to me as though it was an accident, though I don't blame Jake for his anger. It must be placed somewhere, and his dead wife isn't a likely subject, is she?"

Isabella paled and stared at her with round eyes. Goodness, she was a beautiful woman. Even now, her youth a memory, Mabel could see why she'd captured the public's regard. Once she'd caught her father staring at a cabinet card of Miss Moreau that he'd picked up in a French *marche aux puces*. He'd turned red as a radish when Mabel mentioned it, but she didn't blame him. Her mother had left over a decade earlier, and he'd never been connected to another woman, despite opportunity.

"I see you watching me." Mabel sat on the settee against the wall, thinking it might settle Miss Moreau if she didn't loom over her. She knew that could be intimidating, though it was never her intention. "I wonder if it's because I'm married to Jake."

"No, that isn't it at all. Though it was quite shocking."

Mabel tipped her head. "How so?"

Miss Moreau paused, then began to move around like a little bird, all nervous, pecking energy. "Only that Jake was so very in love with Charlotte. I never imagined he would move on."

If Mabel had believed Miss Moreau was being completely forthright, she might have been hurt by those words—true though they were—but it would take someone a good deal less observant than she was to miss the telltale signs of dishonesty.

"You seem very happy together, though." Miss Moreau sent

a darting glance toward the empty cushion beside Mabel, then fastened her attention on the wall. "I'm glad for it."

"Would you like to sit down?"

A smile bloomed on the older woman's face, a real one this time. "Yes, thank you." She sank down beside Mabel. "I injured my hip during a show, and it still pinches."

Again, Mabel had the distinct feeling that the aerialist was omitting some part of the truth. Her hip might well hurt, but there was more. Everything she said seemed to dangle unfinished. She spoke in loose ends.

Miss Moreau kneaded her hip with lean, flexible fingers and sighed into the cushion. "Are you very nervous?"

"A little, though I have been performing my entire life. But Travis and Wells is a much bigger outfit than I'm used to."

"Manzo Brothers, correct?"

Mabel nodded. "Once, we were approached by someone from Barnum and Bailey who asked if we would join their show, but Da said no."

"These people here are family," he had said, and Mabel had been glad for it. She'd never wanted to leave. But now she wondered if Da's apathy had resulted in her complete reliance on him and hindered her ability to find success on her own. If they had taken the offer, she would have likely been trained in a solo act— Barnum and Bailey was large, and most performers did more than one—and wouldn't struggle so much now to find her place.

Da had bred dependency despite his constant refrain that she must be strong.

"Tell me about him." Miss Moreau shifted to look at Mabel, and there was something bright and desperate in her eyes.

"My father?"

Miss Moreau nodded.

"He was a strongman. Well loved by everyone and would have been larger than life even without his height, though he was very tall—six feet four—"

"You inherited that from him, then?"

"Yes. My mother was small. I passed her by the time I turned eight. She trained me before that to be an aerialist, but it was soon clear I would grow too tall to continue." Mabel stared across the room, through air and memories. She could shuffle them like cards, pick one out, and likely land on something able to pierce her heart. *"She's too big. She always has been."* Mabel hunched, squeezing her elbows together over her thighs. "How lovely it must be to experience the world from your vantage point. My mother was about your size, and you should have seen her perform. I would sometimes sneak into the audience when I was meant to be in the dressing room or backstage waiting for my act, just so I could experience her the way the crowd did. They loved her. How could they not? She was beautiful and fearless. I may have inherited my father's strength, but I hope there's a bit of my mother's in me, as well."

Miss Moreau's small hand slipped between Mabel's bicep and forearm, warm and comforting. "I think there must be, Mrs. Cunningham."

Mabel straightened, stretching herself along the settee back and working the kinks out of her muscles. "But you didn't ask me about my mother, you asked me about my father. And please, call me Mabel."

Miss Moreau's smile, so engaging and demonstrative, froze into a parody. "I will." She didn't offer the same courtesy.

"My father died not too long ago. I feel a little adrift. It was always he and I. We worked, lived, and ate together. I'm not sure how to function without him."

"Loss is hard. Losing a father is one of the hardest things of all. Mine died in the war, and my mother and I were left without provision."

"That's a common story. My own mother's as well."

Miss Moreau lifted from the settee in one graceful movement. "Well, I believe it's time we get out there."

Mabel followed her down the hall. The nearer they got to the amphitheater, the louder the hum of the audience, the more crowded the path, the harder Mabel's heart pounded, until they were standing between the ring and the dressing room in that undefined space straddling the show and reality. Mabel breathed deeply, but it caught in her chest and wouldn't release. She took shallow, gasping breaths and tried to yawn it out, but still it stuck firmly.

It would be fine. She could already see Jake on his platform high above, rings in hand, waiting for the cue to leap. He would descend as she stepped into the ring and meet her there. She wouldn't be alone.

Still she gasped and blinked against the rimming darkness.

"Are you well, Mabel?" Miss Moreau reached for an errant curl frizzing at Mabel's cheek and pushed it behind her ear.

Mabel closed her eyes as the aerialist's fingers brushed her cheek. "I am beset by stage fright."

"My mother used to tell me to be strong—in all things you set your hands and heart and eyes toward—and all will be well."

The words nestled into Mabel's spirit and dislodged the captive air. "Thank you." She looked at Miss Moreau. A memory stirred, fluttering like an autumn leaf clinging to its branch. She stilled, waiting for it to fall. "My mother used to say the same thing."

Miss Moreau stepped back, her arms going around her waist. "How odd." Something slipped from the hem of her sleeve. A little foot.

"What is that?" The darkness ate again at the fringe of Mabel's vision, and she saw nothing but the dangling white leg and leather shoe.

Miss Moreau poked it back into her sleeve. "Only a little courage." She gave a tight smile. "You better go, Mabel. It's time."

Then Mabel found herself center ring, standing below her

slowly descending husband. She held her arms up by rote and could feel Miss Moreau's stare boring into her back. She could still see the leather-clad foot. A doll's foot. *"Be strong—in all things you set your hands and heart and eyes toward—and all will be well."*

And then Mabel remembered her mother in the dressing room outside some city in Austria, just before Mabel's first act, tucking the doll Isabella into her sleeve. *"For courage,"* Maman had always said.

Mabel whirled and searched for the aerialist.

"Mabel," Jake hissed above her, "get into place."

She lifted her arms and gripped his feet but still searched for Isabella.

At his tap signaling he'd released the rings, she bent her elbows and tossed with all her might. She ignored the crowd's gasp as she caught him. She twirled and faced that in-between space, searching.

Mabel's gaze finally landed on her.

Maman.

✳ ✳ ✳

She knew. Isabella could tell by the tension in Mabel's back. By the way her eyes kept searching the dressing room corridor. She hadn't meant to give it away. Not so soon. Not before Mabel's first performance.

But spending time with her daughter, touching her, sharing with her . . . she'd fallen right back into that familiar role. She hadn't considered that Mabel might remember the doll. That she might remember Maman's proverb. Mabel was so young when Isabella left for New York.

But she was quiet. And observant. Who knew what had worked its way into her daughter's spirit over the years. Isabella could claim only random memories, disconnected from any greater picture, poking through the darkness of her past. She didn't know how many times she had told Mabel to be strong—rotely and without thought because there were no other words, no other feelings, to draw from. She could have repeated it to Mabel at every performance for months and not recalled it, for those days were obscured by wicked, shadowy pain.

She hadn't been a proper mother. She likely never would be.

A band, stretching across the ocean and over decades, tightened around her chest, and as she watched Mabel capture the crowd's heart, she went still. Her heart beat, strong and steady. It forced her blood into a stagnant pool.

Mabel would remember her leaving and promising to return by winter—"*I'll see you in Bologna.*"

She would remember the letters trickling to a stop. She wouldn't know that her own father had been intercepting them. And after their conversation in the dressing room, she knew Mabel likely wouldn't believe it even if Isabella told her.

She would never tell her anyway. If there was a bit of pride Isabella could claim in any of it, it was that she had given Mabel exactly what she'd intended—a strong relationship with her father.

Perhaps that had rooted Mabel in a way she herself never had been. It was a shame her daughter couldn't have had both parents, but at the end of the day, Isabella knew she was weak. Bram had been right about that. And to grow up strong, a girl had to have a strong parent.

Isabella's memories of her own father had been replaced by other, more glamorous ones. She'd been raised by the circus, after all, and as Maman's beauty faded with hard work and grief, her father's image turned into something shadowy and nebulous. She'd tried, in those early years, to grasp for him as the wagons rumbled from town to town, but she never could.

Mabel wouldn't be at risk of losing her own father. Not after years of working so closely with him. And if she had forgotten her mother? Well, that wouldn't be a great loss.

An upright piano was wheeled into the ring, and Isabella watched, chest swelling, as Mabel fit it squarely over her back and lifted, calf muscles bunching, expression as placid as if she were sitting down to tea. Her daughter would not suffer the matrilineal curse. She brimmed with strength. Weakness had no place.

Bram had been right about that too. *"How will you raise a daughter of strength when you yourself are so weak?"* he had asked when Lorenzo, Mabel tucked against his chest, had ushered her back to the circus on that terrible day. Back to her husband. There had been an appalled horror in Bram's voice, in his eyes, and he had palmed his head and muttered something about his mother. His wife.

His words, and the knowledge that she couldn't refute them, had shredded and suffocated. But now, here in front of her stood proof that they had made the best decision. An absent mother beset by weakness was better by far than a present one given to specters and twilight.

"Are you well, Isabella?" Rowena stood next to her. "You're about to go on, and you're very pale."

"I'm not sure. But I will be." She gave a trembling smile as the crowd erupted, feet stomping the floor, hands clapping, whistles piercing, and with a quick glance, Isabella saw that Mabel and Jake had concluded their act. "She's found me."

Rowena stuck a finger into her towering white wig and scratched. "Who has found you?"

"My daughter. She's here." Isabella pointed to Mabel, who strode toward them, a frightening intensity about her.

Before Rowena could respond and before Mabel reached them, Isabella slipped away to scramble up the ladder that would take her above it all. As she clambered toward the wire-and rope-crisscrossed ceiling, her heart leapt and tumbled and took flight. There would be questions to answer. Amends to make. Time to recover.

But her daughter was here.

She reached the platform and took hold of the bar, then glanced down to see Mabel standing outside the ring, staring up at her. Isabella pressed her fingers to her lips and held them out before pushing into the air. Flying. Stomach hurling. Air whooshing past her face and chest.

Alive. Free.

And it was all nothing compared to the knowledge that she had her daughter once more. She was under no illusion that she could make up for the failings of her past. She flipped her legs over the bar and hung from her knees, arms embracing the audience.

But one never knew what the future held, and maybe Mabel had saved a piece of her heart for the mother who'd disappeared as though she'd stepped into a mirror maze.

The melancholy that stalked her always, bleeding into her bits of happiness and blurring the edges of every moment—not as dense now as it had been in the years after Mabel's birth, but still always present—seemed to slide farther from her. Still there, but less palpable.

Isabella laughed and leapt with delicious euphoria for the bar that had been swung toward her. She would reconcile with her lost daughter. Never mind the years that stood between them. Never mind the husband—*husbands*, if she included Mabel's own—who hated her. She would do it with the strength that poured through her now. She would do it.

Her own mother's words spurred her leaping heart.

I can do all things. All things.

CHAPTER

17

"HAVE YOU SEEN ISABELLA?" Mabel gripped Jake's shirt, drawing close in the after-show crush. She had waited in the wings for her mother to finish her act. Talking herself out of scrambling up that tall ladder into the building's rafters, she had pressed her hand against her heart and watched.

She'd waited so many years already. What was another few minutes?

But then the space between them filled with clowns and acrobats and stilt men. A brightly painted wagon, barred and revealing a growling tiger, rumbled past. Women jumped through hoops, their toes gripping the backs of plumed horses. A fire-eater blew flames, red and popping, drawing Mabel's attention for just a moment, and Isabella was lost.

"I've been looking everywhere for her." Someone jostled Mabel, pushing her against Jake's chest, and his hands rounded her back. He drew her toward the wall. "I need to find her. Right now, Jake."

"I haven't seen her."

"She didn't come into the changing room. Where would she have gone? She knows. I can tell she knows I know."

His brows pinched. "Knows what?" Then he shook his head. "I'm sure she'll turn up, but look." He spun her so that she faced Alice and Katie Grace.

Katie Grace's eyes were round and kept pinging from interesting sight to interesting sight. The corridor was full of them—performers and animals being pulled along by their trainers and sideshow entertainers. "I never dreamed," Katie Grace said breathlessly.

Mabel forced her attention off her swirling, desperate thoughts. "Did you enjoy the show?"

Katie Grace hurtled forward, her arms going around Mabel's middle. "Thank you. Thank you so much for letting us come."

"I suppose you enjoyed the clowns best of all?"

"Oh no." Katie Grace looked up at her, little face pinched into serious lines. "Yours was the best of all."

Alice moved toward them and lightly touched Katie Grace's back, and the girl stepped away. "We are very grateful you were able to get us seats to see the show."

"'Specially since this is the very last wonderful thing that will ever happen to us." Katie Grace gave a loud sniff and ignored her mother's shocked "Katie Grace!"

Jake knelt in front of the child. "Why is it the last wonderful thing?"

"We're moving to the Lower East Side into a nasty tenement. There's good news, though! Mama says I no longer have to go to school."

Jake glanced at Mabel, then stood and held out his hand. "How about we show you where the horses are kept?"

Katie Grace gave an enthusiastic nod and skipped beside Jake as he led the way to the staircase that would take them underground. Mabel and Alice followed at a slower pace.

"What has happened?" Mabel asked when they found themselves in the stables and Katie Grace was focused on the magnificent creatures Jake pointed out to her.

Alice watched her daughter as she exclaimed over an elegant Arabian liberty horse. "It just isn't enough. There's nothing left of my husband's savings, and I cannot seem to take in enough work to continue paying for our room at Mrs. Luvotti's."

"And school?"

"I've secured a position at a garment factory. I cannot convince Katie Grace to remain in school, so I think it safer she work alongside me than run the streets."

"Oh, Alice, those places are not safe at all."

Alice looked at her, face pale and chin trembling, and Mabel knew she too thought of the fire that had consumed the Triangle Shirtwaist Factory, which had killed so many people that the papers were still writing about it months later. "What else can we do? I have no money. I begin work in a couple of weeks, and we leave the boardinghouse for our new dwelling Monday." A smile bloomed. "But I'm so very grateful Katie Grace had the chance to see the show. To watch you and Jake perform. It will become a very special memory, I know."

Likely the last for a good long while.

"Oh, that one is the most beautiful!" Katie Grace hung on to Jake's hand as he introduced her to Laura Meadows, one of Travis and Wells's trick riders, who was feeding an apple to her horse, Odysseus.

Laura smiled, then cast Jake a sidelong look, and Mabel recognized the subtle flirtation.

"Would you allow my friend a chance to sit on the horse?" Jake asked.

Laura cocked her hip and stared at him for a moment, then, with a shrug, grabbed a stool from against the wall and helped Katie Grace scramble onto the horse's back.

Mabel ignored the fire in her chest. She would do well to

accept the attention Jake garnered. She couldn't control it and well understood it. Still . . . Her gaze slipped back to Laura, and she took in the woman's neat figure, still clad in her beaded bodice and knee-length, flared skirt. She had smooth, round shoulders and a nipped waist. Shapely legs that ended at well-formed ankles.

Mabel shifted between her own feet, the muscles from heels to knees tensing. Bunching. Her ankles, thick and sturdy, ready for a squat. Laura was so petite and alluring. So very unlike Mabel.

"Mam, look at me," Katie Grace called, and Mabel forced her attention back on the girl, who had kicked off her shoes and now stood barefoot upon the horse's back.

"Oh, that child . . . she terrifies me to death," Alice muttered.

Indeed, Katie Grace had positioned herself in a handstand, skirts flipped over her head and legs making an exclamation mark above a set of lace-trimmed knickers.

Mabel chuckled. "She is a daredevil."

Alice rolled her eyes. "No doubt you will find yourself working beside her one day."

That dropped a thought into Mabel's mind. One that tickled her with possibility, then unfurled as abruptly as a moon-flower. "No doubt." She would say nothing more, for she didn't want to give false hope. "Will you come with me to see our room at the hotel?"

Alice gave Mabel a curious look but nodded. With much cajoling, they convinced Katie Grace to dismount the horse and Laura Meadows to release Jake from her coquetry.

Katie Grace wasn't quite as impressed with the Hotel Veronica as she had been the circus, but she did enjoy the elevator ride, peppering the attendant with questions. When they arrived at the room, Alice arranged her expression into blank appreciation while Katie Grace glanced around, nose wrinkled and lips curled. "This isn't very nice. You're a star, Mabel."

Mabel laughed and went to the dresser upon which sat the pasteboard box. When Jake saw her removing the few coins remaining, his eyes went as soft as a magician's rabbit, and he added to it most of the bills he'd stashed in the top drawer.

"Are you certain?" Mabel whispered as Alice drew Katie Grace to the window. They would find no enticing view. Their room faced the brick wall of the neighboring building.

"Yes. All of our needs are taken care of, and we will be paid soon."

"But Kansas—"

His fingers curled around hers, cupping the money, his thumb running over the bottom of her palm—just above where her hand met her wrist. Who would have guessed what a tender spot that was? What a lovely shiver it would produce?

"I suddenly find myself in less of a hurry to get there."

Mabel pressed her free hand to her chest, certain her heart had fallen to her feet. But no, there it beat. As steady and certain as ever.

"Alice," Jake called, not taking his eyes from Mabel's, "I must head out, but it was very nice to see you." He turned and caught Katie Grace in his arms and flipped her upside down before depositing her on the bed. "You, as well, though I'm not sure this excursion did anything but put lofty ideas in your head."

Then he winked at Mabel and left, preserving a bit of Alice's pride.

Mabel pressed the money into her friend's hand. "Enough to see you through at Mrs. Luvotti's until the end of the month."

"Oh no, I couldn't take this." Alice attempted to give it back.

"Please. I hate to think of either one of you living somewhere crowded and unsafe."

"It will only delay the inevitable."

"I had an idea earlier, but I need a little time."

"For what?"

"I cannot say, but I hope it might offer you an alternative."

Alice glanced at Katie Grace, who was doing her best to execute a midair flip, and her expression softened. "I will accept. But only for her." The gentle planes of her face, the delicately sloping nose and pointed chin, seemed to sketch themselves into an entirely different visage. Something fierce and almost frighteningly determined. "Whatever it is you have in mind, Mabel, I will do it. I will do anything for her."

"Would that every child had a mother like you."

And so clearly it was as though a great hand had come from Heaven and written on the wall in fire, Mabel saw her mother's words. That lovely looping script consigning her to a motherless existence.

. . . perhaps you are right . . . Mabel will find a better life if she supposes I am dead.

Mabel watched Alice and Katie Grace walk down the hall toward another exhilarating ride on the elevator, their arms wrapped around each other's waists, and forced her heart to open. Insisted it not curl in on itself and wither, nor expand and become saturated with the bitterness. Mabel only had one parent left, and the truth always lay somewhere between mirrors and smoke. She would hear her mother's story before deciding what to do with all she'd been told.

And good thing, for the moment Alice and Katie Grace disappeared, Miss Moreau appeared, a timid smile on her lips and Isabella the doll dangling from her fingers.

❊ ❊ ❊

"Isabella."

At first Isabella thought Mabel was speaking to her, but then she saw her daughter's gaze on the doll. She held it out.

"She's so much smaller than I remember." Mabel wrapped her fingers around the doll, and her chin trembled. A tear slipped from her lashes and fell to the carpet. "You left," she said, head still bowed. "You promised to come back and never did."

"I know."

"I thought you had *died.*" There was no accusation in her words. Only pain. Hurt. Confusion. "How could you let him lie to me?"

Isabella's heart gave a violent twist, and she reached for Mabel, fingers barely brushing her shoulder. "It was better for you. I knew that."

Mabel's head jerked up. She grabbed for Isabella's hand and pressed it against her cheek. "How can you say such a thing? Have you any idea how painful it was to lose you?"

"It had to be one of us, and a girl needs a father." Isabella could hardly squeeze the words from her tight throat. They finished on a whisper, and she pressed her palm flat against Mabel's face. How perfectly smooth it was. As unblemished as the doll Mabel held to her chest. "I grew up without one. I know."

"But a girl needs a mother too. Why did it have to be only one of you? Who decided that?"

Isabella said nothing. She would never turn Mabel against her father's memory. Her daughter didn't know how Isabella struggled. How every breath had become steeped in effort. How her soul had been filled with shadows, and even the pricks of light that occasionally managed to break through felt like an assault. How she would spend weeks in their cramped coach, coming out only for shows. How everyone treated her as though she were made of glass—always on the verge of shattering. Splintering into a million little shards that would eventually find their way beneath Mabel's own skin.

Bram had said—and he had been right—that those shards would eventually pierce their daughter. They would have turned her heart toward sadness. Isabella couldn't let that happen. She would sacrifice anything to see that it didn't.

"I don't understand why you left me. What did I do?" Mabel sank to the floor and pressed her head against Isabella's knees. Her skirt billowed around her face and stifled the sobs.

But they still drew Jake down the hall at a run. Isabella heard him, feet pounding, before he appeared. "What happened?" He crouched and, with so much gentleness it hurt to watch, brought Mabel to her feet. She turned toward him, burying her head into his neck, and he glared at Isabella.

Isabella ignored him and touched Mabel's back. "You did nothing. Not ever. Not once. It had nothing at all to do with you."

Mabel's fists gripped the lapels of Jake's jacket, her knuckles white, and released a long, shaky breath. "How can you say that?" She turned. "I remember. '*She is too big. She was always too big.*' Too big for what? I know it was a disappointment when I grew too large to train with you."

"I was disappointed by that, but not in you. Never in you. And I'm sorry you heard those things. I never meant for you to. They were no indication against you."

Mabel shook her head, her eyes glassy. "I don't understand."

"Neither do I." Jake curled his hand around Mabel's waist. It was an intimate gesture. One that proclaimed a greater familiarity with her daughter than Isabella ever could. "What is going on?"

"I will explain everything." Almost everything. There were some things Isabella would never say. Some things Mabel could never know. "But we should go somewhere a little more private."

Mabel glanced around the hotel hallway, color infusing her face as she noticed how public their conversation had been, then pushed into the room. Isabella followed Jake in after her.

They stared at one another, eyes darting, lips pressing into thin lines, hands pushing through hair and worrying fabric. Isabella attempted thrice to begin, but each time she opened her mouth only to find words had fled. Where would she start? What could she say?

Mabel reached across the space between them and tucked

the doll into Isabella's cuff so that only the little legs dangled free. "For courage."

There was a desperate yearning in her daughter's clear blue eyes. So sweet and pure, despite the tear stains streaking her cheeks. She deserved the truth. Isabella would start at the beginning.

"Giving birth to you nearly killed me."

Jake choked, and Mabel looked at him, blinking rapidly as though having forgotten he stood beside her. "Jake, I nearly forgot." She gave Isabella a shy smile. "It turns out I didn't have to look very far to find my mother."

Jake's gaze swung between them, and he paled. "That . . . that can't be possible."

"She took a stage name when she began working with Travis and Wells again. But this *is* my mother, Polly Mac-Ginnis." Mabel hurried across the room and grabbed two chairs from beneath a round table. She brought them over and set them facing each other at the foot of the bed. "Sit. We can talk." She was breathless, her words coming in little puffs, lifting at the end as though weightless and ready to float away.

Isabella took one seat and Mabel the other, their knees bumping. Jake sat between them on the very edge of the mattress, and Isabella spared him only a quick glance before focusing on her daughter.

"Does having Jake here make you nervous?" Mabel asked.

"We . . . have a history." Isabella slipped the doll from her sleeve and pleated its fifty-year-old satin skirt between her fingers. "But if you want him here, I will not object."

Mabel cast Jake a glance. "All right."

Isabella swallowed and tucked the doll into her palm. She squeezed tightly, spending her tension on its sawdust-filled limbs.

If only courage could be found in a hand-me-down toy. *I*

can do all things. She rubbed the doll's head, its halo of hair rough against her thumb.

"You said you nearly died when you gave birth to me." Mabel's voice was like a still stream or lapping lake. Smooth. Inviting.

"Yes. You were very large—almost eleven pounds. I bled for days. The doctor thought I would die. I didn't, but even when I stopped bleeding, even when I sat up and got out of bed, I never felt right again. I couldn't nurse. I hardly had the strength to hold you. For over a month I recuperated. And then, when I was finally able to get out of bed and give you attention, I found myself beset . . ."

Mabel laid her hands over Isabella's, which had become increasingly agitated as she twisted the doll's limbs and stroked its dress, and a stillness settled over her.

"It was dark for so long. Everywhere I went, everything I did, seemed draped in a heavy grey cloud. Including you." Isabella released the doll and turned her fingers up so that she could weave them between Mabel's. Unbearable pressure weighed against her chest, and her nose burned with tears. "I'm so sorry. I didn't know what to do. Your father, the doctor, and every one of our friends all decided I was nothing more than my diagnosis. Puerperal melancholia. I was weak. Incapable. And so afraid, because I felt I was going insane."

"No." Mabel leaned toward her and pressed their knit fingers to her lips. "No, you weren't."

Isabella shook her head. "But I was. I had thoughts. Unbidden and unwanted. Violent, wicked thoughts. They terrified me. Stole my sleep. My breath. Every bit of peace I could claim."

"Did you harm Mabel?"

Isabella had forgotten Jake sat with them, and she gave a little start at his question. "No."

Not intentionally. Not completely. She wouldn't tell that story. She could see that Mabel was draped in fragility. That for all her strength, there was a vulnerability to her that would be easily exploited. She didn't need to know about that time. It was an accident. A result of Isabella's scattered emotions and thoughts.

"I'm sorry you experienced all of that. I'm sorry you were so broken that you thought more brokenness was the answer. I'm sorry you listened to Da and decided he was right about you."

Isabella gave a nervous laugh. "What are you talking about?"

"I found your letters to him. It's how I discovered you were still alive." Mabel again knelt at Isabella's feet and pressed her head into her knees. But there were no tears this time. Only her daughter's shining face and strong arms wrapping around her waist. "But I forgive you. I forgive Da. I forgive every person everything, because I am so entirely happy that I have you once more. That I'm not alone."

Isabella glanced at Jake. His jaw twitched as he watched Mabel burrow against her. Then his enviable posture slipped, head and shoulders and chest sinking, and he left the room.

CHAPTER 18

MABEL WATCHED JAKE STAND at the window from beneath lowered lashes. The morning sun filtered around him, burnishing his bare shoulders and casting his face in shadow. He was all bronzed beauty. She tucked her hand beneath her head and the pillow, her gaze tracing his back.

After he left their room the evening before, Mabel and her mother had talked until the sun completely disappeared behind the cityscape. Then Mabel turned on every electric light and sconce in the room and, forgetting about dinner, they talked some more. Near eleven o'clock, Isabella kissed her cheek and promised to see her in the morning. "You should sleep. You have a show tomorrow," she had said.

But Mabel couldn't sleep. She couldn't shut off the buzzing in her head and flipping of her heart. It was only when her eyes finally began to grow heavy—sometime after one in the morning—that she realized Jake had never returned.

Then she was wide awake once more, sitting with her arms wrapped around her knees and her back pressed against the headboard. He crept in a couple of hours later, hardly looking at her as he pulled off his clothing and slipped beneath the blanket in his drawers.

"Do you want me to retrieve your nightclothes?" Mabel had asked, her voice slicing through the silence between them.

"No." Facing away from her, he'd thrown his arm over his eyes. "You should go to sleep. It's late."

She shifted now, the bed creaking beneath her weight, and she could tell by the stiffening of his spine that he knew she was awake.

"I was worried about you last night," she said.

"I'm fine." His hands, which had been bracketing the window, fell to his sides, and he turned, his gaze landing on hers. "I didn't mean to wake you."

"You didn't." She sat up and caught the blanket against her chest. Her eyes skittered from his. "Have I done something to make you angry?"

He took a few steps toward her, and she raised her eyes. His loveliness struck her fiercely. Not just his fine appearance, but everything about him. His goodness and loyalty and self-sacrifice. She didn't want him to leave. He couldn't take off for Kansas as though she meant nothing at all to him.

He paused in front of her and reached out to touch her jaw. "You have done nothing. I was only shocked. To discover Isabella Moreau is your mother? You, the sweetest, kindest, most gentle woman of my acquaintance, related so closely to that viper—"

"Jake!" She jerked from his touch. "How can you say such a thing about her?"

He sank onto the mattress beside her and, elbows resting on his knees, buried his face in his hands. "It was her fault, Mabel."

She lightly touched his back. "Can you tell me why you believe it's my mother's fault your wife died?"

"Everyone knew how ambitious Isabella was. And she

seemed particularly interested in encouraging married performers always to improve. Always to maintain a level of independence from their husbands so their career could stand on its own. Charlotte thought she had flung stars into the heavens. She was enraptured by her. So taken with the celebrity of it all. And at first, so was I."

Jake rubbed his nose with the back of his hand and looked at her. She'd moved nearer in her attempt at comfort, and now, with her arm draped over him and his face near enough to kiss, she knew there was no way he could end their marriage. Not without it destroying her in the process. She'd thought she could find contentment in having him for a little while, even as a pretend husband. But she now recognized how ludicrous an idea that had been.

"Mabel, I . . ." In one smooth movement, he swept her onto his lap, his arms around her back and his head nestled against her chest. "I'm sorry. I know she's your mother and you're so happy at having found her. But I cannot abide being around her."

"Tell me what happened." She smoothed her hand over his hair. He had to know she loved him. She had never been very good at pretense.

"I didn't want Charlotte to do it at all. Everyone knows the cannonball is the most dangerous circus act. But Isabella convinced her it was good for her career. That she needed to establish a solo act so that, if anything happened to me or between us, she would have an alternative means of providing for herself."

"It's not a bad plan," Mabel murmured.

"No. And Charlotte convinced me of it. My heart seized every time she did the stunt, but after a year, I began to relax. She was good at everything but excelled at being shot into the air. She radiated equal parts strength and grace. Even now, she seems to have been made up of something more than human."

Mabel put her feet on the ground and began to lift off Jake's lap—she hated the way her insides pinched as he praised Charlotte—but his arms tightened around her.

"Stay with me." His voice was raspy. Fractured. It splintered any bit of self-preservation she could claim. "Please."

"Of course." She pressed a kiss to his gathered brow.

"She'd been flying with a net up until that point. I checked it myself every morning because of Zazel's accident years earlier. I didn't trust anyone else to go over it so meticulously—one rotten portion, and Charlotte would die. But she insisted she wouldn't be taken seriously until she did as the other aerialists and trapeze artists did and went without. It was to make her career. Jerry sent out press releases to tantalize the public, and every seat was taken. There were thousands of people in Madison Square Garden that morning." He pulled away from her and sighed. "I wish I had prohibited it."

"How could you? Charlotte was a circus performer, Jake. There are inherent risks involved in such a profession. You know that. She knew that. And she was fearless. It's part of why you loved her. Love her still." And why he likely would never feel the same for Mabel, who drowned in fear every time she stepped foot in the ring. And it wasn't even a reasonable fear. She typically risked nothing more than a sprained wrist or pulled muscle. Her fear was illogical. "What happened?"

"I still don't know completely. I was performing at the same time and only caught parts of her act. But it seemed everything was going the way it should until . . . it wasn't. She was meant to be shot from the cannon and meet Isabella, who was hanging from the trapeze bar. I had just landed on the platform when I heard Isabella shout, 'Charlotte, no!' When I looked, Charlotte was falling through the sky, no net below her."

"Did you ask Isabella about it?"

Jake shook his head. "She'd disappeared by the time the Garden was cleared and they'd taken Charlotte's body to the morgue. I didn't see her for days. When I finally encountered her, I didn't care what she had to say. I only wanted her to know what she'd stolen from me. She said they had launched an inquest, but it seemed to me she was only looking for absolution. I left before it was complete and never saw Isabella again."

"And you haven't spoken to Robert about it since returning?"

"No. I can't bring myself to hear the details." He took a deep breath. "It doesn't matter, does it? My wife is dead, and Isabella was the one to encourage her in the first place."

Jake's argument wasn't fair, but Mabel could see no purpose in pointing it out. More pressing was the "*my wife is dead*" part of his speech. Because though his *first* wife was dead, he had one very much alive sitting upon him at that very moment.

So focused was she on her internal contention, she didn't notice that Jake had cupped her face until his voice, gravelly and taut, interrupted.

"No one would guess how soft you are." Something akin to wonder sparked in his eyes. "Such a dichotomy of strength and grace. So beautiful. It's unnerving, really." His fingers slid down her shoulder and arm, finding a place to rest in the curve of her waist. His other gently pressed the back of her head until only the merest bit of oxygen separated them. And then not even that.

His lips were soft, and Mabel was certain that if she allowed herself to capitulate fully to her enthusiasm, they would disappear beneath hers. He would disappear. So she restrained herself and allowed him to dictate the pace. The intensity.

"How could I know?" he murmured. "I had no idea. All this time." He kissed her lips. Her chin. Her neck. The points of her collarbone jutting above the ribbon of her nightgown. "Do you feel nothing? Are you so unaffected?"

She allowed herself a moment to enjoy the sound of her

husband pleading. Begging for her to meet him in his ardor. That she could induce such desire in a man—not any man, but this particular man—produced a pleasurable sort of gratification.

"Unaffected?" she said with a scoffing sort of laugh. "I have never been unaffected where you are concerned."

He leaned back on his hands and gave her a lazy smile. His eyes grew hazy, full of softened thoughts Mabel wanted nothing more than to explore.

But a knock came at the door, and Jake blinked, all the loveliness she'd seen in his gaze dissipating like fog beneath the morning sun. He looked at her clearly now, and she didn't like it. She knew what lay behind the sharpness and clarity.

"I should see who that is," he said.

She tugged her lip between her teeth and shifted back onto the bed. After climbing beneath the blanket, she pulled it over her chest and shoulders.

Jake coughed as he crossed the room and wiped his hands over his mouth. When the door opened, she saw someone thrust a newspaper through the crack.

"Why aren't you ready? You have a show in an hour. Take this. Where's Mabel? We need to tell her." Robert pushed into the room and stopped when he saw her in bed. "Oh. Well . . ." He ran his hand through his hair, and his mouth tipped into a crooked grin. "You are newlyweds, after all. So sorry." He stepped back into the hall, and as the door closed, his words slipped through, rounded by laughter. "Still, don't be late. There will be a crowd."

❋ ❋ ❋

There is something singularly fascinating about the Travis and Wells duo Jake and Mabel Cunningham. They are a strikingly attractive couple, and one imagines any children born of them to inherit the best of their parents. Mrs. Cunningham, in particular, embodies a startling beauty. With her bowed upper lip, classic chin, and long neck, she might have been hewn in marble by the hand of a Renaissance artist.

As she bends great bars of iron into fanciful shapes as easily as a housewife manipulates bread dough, you are at once struck by the contrast of her unruffled beauty and immense strength. One does not supersede the other. Indeed, hers isn't a brash, masculine kind of brawn—while tall and imposing of stature, she isn't in any way unappealing—but one that would look equally well draped in satin and pearls as standing in a circus ring holding her husband aloft.

Mabel glanced up from the article only when she stumbled over a lip in the sidewalk as she and Jake walked toward Madison Square Garden. There was more. On and on the reporter, who had found himself in the audience the day before, waxed. About her posture, her skin, her "marvelous bosom" and "nicely shaped legs." Mabel folded the newspaper and shoved it under her arm as they crossed the street.

"What does it say?" Jake asked.

"It's a treatise on my beauty."

He gave her a sidelong look and offered his arm as they skirted a table piled high with chard. "Anything about mine?"

"No. He mentions a bit about your athleticism and good humor in allowing me to handle you—also a bit on what attractive children we will likely create—but mostly it's an ode to my bits and pieces."

"You sound unhappy about that."

"There's little to recommend me but what a picture I present. Not really much at all on the show itself. I'm not ungrateful. Truly—I know he didn't have to write anything about it—but it feels . . . demeaning."

She had been written about in such a way before, but not on this scale. Always in small papers with a limited reach, and never more than a paragraph or two because her father's strength absorbed much of the published accolades. But this was the *New York Times*, one of the largest newspapers in the country, and there was something unnerving about knowing that before breakfast, all the men of New York had an image of her in a short skirt firmly implanted in their thoughts.

"You *are* a beautiful woman." It sounded much different coming from Jake than it had coming from the pen of a stranger who knew nothing else about her. "But you are also much more, and it's a crime he didn't note the rest of it. It seems, though, that there will be many witnesses to that fact today." He motioned ahead of them, and Mabel looked up to see a crowd snaking from the Garden's front door. "You're about to become the toast of New York City."

Mabel huffed a laugh. "Surely not."

But Jake was correct, and every show for the rest of the week was sold out. Every seat filled by a person cheering for Mabel and Jake Cunningham. Every front page of every newspaper plastered with an article extolling her virtues. And, thankfully, his as well, though focused on different things. Mabel pretended the discrepancy did not exist, for there was nothing she could do about it anyway, and it seemed a female performer's lot to give up all autonomy over what was said and written about her body.

Sitting beside Alice on a bench between Saturday's shows, Mabel watched Jake play a game of tag with Katie Grace. Spring had come over the city like a tiptoeing child afraid to awaken his father. So quietly, peeking around walls and crouching on the ground, until it suddenly crashed upon them one morning, the last frost melting and the dogwoods blooming, their petals perfuming whole city blocks. Coinciding with the arrival of spring came a note from Alice asking to meet them at Central Park.

"He's just as beautiful as I am," Mabel murmured as Jake grabbed Katie Grace and tossed her into the air. The child's hair flung free of its braids, and she gave a boisterous shout as she flipped and landed on her feet like a cat.

Alice lifted a little off her seat. "Oh, that child. I will die of fear for her one day." She sat back down and glanced at Mabel. "What were you saying? Something about that husband of yours being beautiful."

"I was only thinking of how differently we are written about. The public loves Jake for his talent, but I am reduced to body parts. They are always so quick to point out that my femininity isn't diminished by my strength, as though the two things have not coexisted peacefully together in women for thousands of years." Jake and Katie Grace started their way, and Mabel tracked his loose-limbed stride. "I wonder what would happen if a woman wrote about *his* well-turned calves and tapered waist."

Alice chuckled. "Will you do it?"

"Anonymously, for women aren't supposed to notice such things." Mabel ducked her head, heating filling her face. *She* had noticed. It wasn't the reason she loved him, but it had been what first drew her attention.

Gathering the fabric of her skirt in her hands, she stared at her lap and watched it pleat. Was it sinful to feel such a burning? To watch his back rising and falling as he slept and moonlight stained his skin silver? To think on those two rather nice kisses they'd shared and wish for many more?

"But it isn't wrong to notice such things about your husband. There is a difference between a wife appreciating the physical aspects of marriage and a complete stranger doling out portions of you to a consuming public." Alice took Mabel's hand. "This is why I'm so glad you have found your mother, for you have sorely missed out on that type of guidance and wisdom."

"It's different for me, though."

Alice drew her brows together. "How so?"

But Jake and Katie Grace had reached them.

"We have decided ice cream is in order," Jake said.

"It's too cold for it." Alice straightened Katie Grace's coat and refastened the buttons.

"It's my treat. The circus has been good to us, has it not, Mabel?" Jake held his hand toward her, and she took it and stood.

Katie Grace tugged at her mother, begging and pleading until Alice relented. "From what I've been hearing and reading, you had better not become too comfortable, Jake. It seems your wife has stolen the show. She will be asked to perform solo before too long."

Jake squeezed her fingers, and Mabel wondered how she could feel the heat of them through her glove. He was a fire. A furnace. Everywhere his eyes touched, she burned. Everywhere he touched, she melted.

He winked at her. "That is how it should be."

They found an ice cream man outside the park, and Jake bought each of them a penny lick. Then he purchased another for himself and Katie Grace while Alice grabbed Mabel's hand and told her good-bye. There was a desperation to it, and Mabel knew Alice's bright smile and lively chatter were a show for her daughter. And maybe for Mabel and Jake.

"I'm going to speak with my mother about seeing if Robert can find a place for Alice," Mabel said after Alice and Katie Grace departed and she and Jake walked along Fifth Avenue.

"It would be nice to have them along. I could leave knowing you had a friend." Jake stopped to peer into the window of a stationery store and mutter, "I must write my brother back."

Mabel paused beside him and pretended his words meant nothing at all. "And I have my mother, of course."

"Of course, though you will leave New York, and she will . . ." He looked at her. "Will she stay in New York?"

"I don't know." Mabel swallowed and walked toward the

next shop, a jeweler. "I think I will look in here while you purchase your paper."

Jake's statement, which had struck her so savagely, had been spoken with a nonchalance that bordered on callousness. She would try to understand his position later, but right now, she only wanted a moment away from him.

Inside the shop, gleaming mahogany stands rimmed in gold and sporting massive glass cases boasted of the jeweler's success. Mabel browsed displays of necklaces and tiaras, bracelets and watches, all while working to make peace with the fact that the two people she most loved couldn't abide each other.

As she leaned over the glass to admire a velvet-lined box of rings, someone approached, and his presence destroyed her composure. She sniffed and blinked away the tears that washed across her vision.

"I shouldn't have spoken so carelessly," Jake said, his hand on her elbow. "It will be very hard for you when you are parted from your mother, and I should have been more sensitive to that."

She nodded. "Thank you."

A salesperson approached, reaching for the box of rings before speaking even a word. He set it on the counter in front of Mabel, and his fingers danced over the gold and gems. He plucked out a ring and held it up. "This is the one."

He held out his hand, and it was unthinkable to resist. Mabel removed her glove, placed her fingers in his palm, and let him slide the piece of jewelry above her knuckle.

She admired the three diamonds nestled into the swirling gold setting. "It's lovely."

Jake cleared his throat. "How much is it?"

The clerk named the cost, and Jake's face blanched. It was, she knew, at least what he had saved for his return home. She smiled at him and started to remove the ring, but Jake waved off the clerk and leaned close. "Do you want a wedding band?"

"Of course not." Mabel set the ring with the others. "I couldn't wear it during practice or shows, and truly, what would be the point? It would be a waste to spend so much on something as temporary as our marriage."

CHAPTER 19

Isabella had imagined this precise scenario for decades. Sitting with her daughter while being fitted for a wardrobe. Examining fabrics and trim. Talking with a seamstress about the virtue of particular necklines and sleeves. In most of her daydreams, Mabel was a small child, and they were in some fashionable shop in Europe, not a dingy back room at Madison Square Garden. But that didn't dampen the grin on her lips, nor the lightness invading her limbs.

She felt like a hot air balloon. Buoyant and full of hope.

Mabel ran her hand over the costume's bodice and tugged at the ruffles rimming her upper thighs. The seamstress chastised her, and Mabel's hands fell to her sides. Her eyes landed on the mirror leaning against the wall across the room but quickly darted away.

Annette and Réka Danó entered the room and, with a brief glance at Mabel on the dais, went to a rack of costumes. Hangers scraped the rod, and their giggles and garrulous whispers filled the corners, but Isabella ignored them. She studied her daughter, recalling another incident when Mabel's shoulders had hunched in a similar way. Her eyes flitting here and there, not landing on anything in particular.

"You can't do this," another child of a circus performer had told Mabel just after Bram decided his daughter would train with him. *"You're too big to be an aerialist."* Isabella had said nothing, for that was when she had been Polly and life had been drawn into squares of delineated factions. It was always all or nothing. Black or white. Highs or lows. There had been no balance. No recognition that sometimes things weren't good, nor were they bad. They just were.

Young Mabel's limbs had fallen heavily to her sides, just as they did now, beneath the other child's haughty words. Her shoulders had dipped and her neck curved forward. But she had held in her tears. Isabella could see then that the words had devastated her daughter. And she could see it now. Isabella had done nothing about it then. She'd been too broken to try to fix the mess she'd created. But given this second chance, she would never do nothing again.

Isabella rose from the chair and crossed the room. "Mabel, are you all right?"

Mabel drew her lip between her teeth, then shook her head.

Isabella touched her daughter's arm. "What's the matter?"

"I . . ." Mabel glanced at the seamstress, who was pinning another set of ruffles at Mabel's hips. "This isn't . . ." She waved her hands up and down her torso. "Don't you think this a little indecent?"

"So says the woman who is as tall as a man," Annette said without even attempting to speak in a whisper.

The seamstress jabbed a needle more deeply than necessary, and Mabel jumped. "There is nothing wrong with this costume. It is exactly what Mr. Wells asked for." She had drooping jowls and a featherlike brush of a mustache.

"Oh, there's nothing wrong with it. You are a wonderful seamstress and obviously know what you're doing. It's only that"—Mabel's hands crossed over her body—"it's very revealing. I'm not used to being so exposed."

The seamstress sniffed. "Well, you are a circus performer whose entire show revolves around brute strength. It seems folks would want to see the muscles that lie behind your demonstrations."

"It's more than brute strength." Isabella's pulse galloped, and her face went hot. "Really, you should know how much time and energy goes into training for something like this." No one had worked harder than Bram MacGinnis. Every lift was choreographed. Every moment not in the ring spent training. Not only to increase in strength, but to prevent injury. To grow in poise and flexibility.

The seamstress stood and pressed her hand against the small of her back. She eyed Mabel critically. "Mr. Wells told me to make sure that whatever I put her in, it enhances those things that make her a woman. He doesn't want her looking like a man."

Derisive laughter rose from the costume rack, and Isabella shot Annette and Réka a glare that would have frightened anyone not quite so full of arrogance.

"She never would." Isabella took in Mabel's curves. The fine line of her neck and shoulders. The gently sweeping biceps. The swell of her breasts and the tapering of a decidedly feminine waist. "You could wrap her in a grain sack, and no one would mistake her for anything but a woman."

The aerialists slid past carrying armfuls of chiffon and sequined velvet. "If you paint her grey and give her tusks, people might mistake her for Jumbo." Annette glanced over her shoulder, ostensibly speaking to Réka but meeting Isabella's gaze. "Do you think when she dies, they will stuff her and put her on display?"

The girls disappeared, and Isabella looked at Mabel, who had frozen in place on the stand, her chest not moving with breath and her gaze pinned to the mirror opposite.

"Ignore them. They are small people who wouldn't know beauty and talent if it jumped in front of them and cried 'boo.'"

"They are very much like her." Mabel's eyes shimmered, and she sat on the edge of the dais, her bare legs extended.

"Who?"

"Charlotte." Mabel traced a finger along a tattooed flower. Isabella had seen the edges of it before, peeking out from beneath the hem of her costume, but she'd never asked about it. It wasn't uncommon for circus performers to get tattooed.

"Will you give us a few moments, please?" Isabella asked the seamstress.

The woman sighed, stuck her pins into the cushion attached to her wrist, and shuffled from the room. Isabella sat beside Mabel, allowing their shoulders to touch, and held her breath as she waited for her daughter to pull away.

But she didn't.

"Charlotte Cunningham was lovely."

Mabel nodded miserably.

"She was roundly adored. Talented, beautiful, and irresistible to almost everyone who met her."

Mabel rested her elbows on her knees and buried her face in her hands. "I know."

"But those things are only a small fraction of who she was. Only the most superficial portion of it, in fact."

"But those things matter, Maman."

A sharp intake of breath—Isabella couldn't tell if it was hers or Mabel's—cut between them.

Mabel turned and looked at her. "Is it all right that I call you that once more?"

Isabella merely nodded, though she wanted to dance. "Can

you tell me why you are comparing yourself unfavorably to your husband's departed wife?"

"He loved her entirely. And I am nothing like her." Mabel gave a hard swallow and looked very young. Very inexperienced. Very unsure.

That suddenly seemed the worst thing about Isabella's disappearance. Her daughter had grown up without a mother. With a wonderful, strong father, yes, but without someone to guide her through the complexities of being a woman.

"Why must you be like Charlotte?" Isabella was glad Mabel wasn't. "Has Jake made you feel this way?"

"No. Not at all. It's only that ours is not a genuine kind of marriage, but I want very much to be a genuine kind of wife."

"I don't understand."

"No. I hardly do either." Mabel smiled and stood. She walked to the mirror, examined herself, and turned to look at the backside. "I cannot possibly wear this. It covers even less than a leotard. It's not at all proper."

"I agree."

Mabel's brows rose. "You do?"

"Yes. Even performers should not be required to wear things that make them feel uncomfortable. It isn't good for the show, anyway. If you feel self-conscious, then your act will suffer. I can talk to Robert, if you want." Isabella pretended her offer was nothing special at all, but it was. In it was wrapped everything she wanted to do for her daughter. Everything she wanted to fix and make right.

"I did have a thought about that. You see, I know a seamstress—one of the best—who is in desperate need of a position."

"Oh, Mabel, I don't know. I've heard nothing of them needing another one."

"I know, but her husband recently passed. And she has a young daughter. They have no one." Mabel took Isabella's hand

and pressed it between her own. "Do you remember what it was like with grand-mère? How desperate she was? How the circus saved you? It could save Alice and Katie Grace too."

Isabella did remember. Even now, a lifetime later, she could recall the lean days when her stomach felt as though it was flipping inside out. And the even leaner days when it stopped feeling like anything at all.

"I will speak to Robert."

Mabel grinned and pressed a kiss to Isabella's hand. "Thank you."

"For you, anything." Anything at all. She had so much to make up for.

* * *

Madison Square Garden's rooftop cabaret was said to have the best views in New York City. Isabella couldn't ascertain if that was true or not, for all she saw was a cloud of cigar smoke and a sea of straw boaters and flower-embellished hats.

"What is happening on stage?" she asked Robert with a rueful smile.

He craned his neck. "A couple of skirt dancers are kicking up their heels. You could climb one of the arches." He waggled his brows. "Give the people a real show."

She snorted. All around them, men had darted from their seats at the dozens of small café tables and clambered up the electric light–strung iron arches in an attempt to get a better look at the performers' ankles. They hung from them now, hooting and hollering like monkeys. She lifted her lemonade and sipped. She couldn't see the dancers, but she didn't mind. The pressing crowd created a sense of privacy that suited her tonight.

"Why did you want to meet? And so publicly?" Robert leaned his elbows on the table and studied her face. "This could get us in trouble if we're caught."

"Who would catch us? It's late. Everyone with any sense is in bed resting for tomorrow's show."

Some people liked to talk about the debauchery of life in the circus, but in truth, the rules meant to protect performers' reputations weren't much of a burden. Theirs was exhausting work that didn't leave much at the end of the day to indulge in vice. One had to have a great desire for wickedness to seek it instead of one's bed.

Isabella swallowed another gulp of her drink in an attempt to dislodge the painful lump at the back of her throat. "I just wanted to speak with you about something."

He rubbed his chin, his square fingers burying into the beard he had just begun to grow. Always before he had been clean-shaven.

She reached for his face and rubbed some of the coarse hairs between her thumb and forefinger. "This is new."

"A quick perusal in the mirror told me it was time." He sat back in his chair. "I should have continued performing. Maybe I wouldn't have grown so soft in my old age."

"You aren't soft. And you still look quite handsome."

He lifted an eyebrow in the way he had when they were young and carefree and flirtatious, and she did, quite unexpectedly, find that he was still an attractive man.

"Besides, would you have turned down Jerry's offer to take Paul's place?"

"Of course not. And not only because the work suited me more. I would never have done anything to increase Jerry's burden."

Paul had been filling different roles in the circus since he was old enough to read and write. He'd done everything from clerical work to managing the advance men in order to effectively take over when his father was ready to retire. When Jerry asked Robert to fill that role after Paul's death, there was no question it was more than desperation—it was an honor. Robert paid back Jerry's loyalty by remaining with Travis and Wells even after his entire family left the country to work in Mexico.

Robert leaned his elbows on the table. "This thing you wish to speak about . . . it couldn't be done during the day? Between shows? In one of the hundred moments we find ourselves together?"

A raucous shout erupted from a group of young men standing on their chairs, and Isabella found her attention jerked from Robert's shining face. It gave her a moment to collect herself. To formulate a response that wouldn't hurt him. For thinking a man handsome was an entirely different thing than being ready to give oneself to love again.

"Let's walk." She stood and motioned over the crowd toward the roofline fringed by potted plants and ivy-draped arches. Away from the crowd, she ignored his palpable hope. Ignored the way his arm brushed hers. Ignored her own response. "I was wondering if you could find room to offer a position to a friend of Mabel's. A seamstress."

His steps faltered, but Isabella continued walking as though she hadn't noticed. Her heart pinched. It was entirely her fault. She had given herself to him and, in the process, reason to believe she would also be willing to give him her heart. But he didn't know how shattered it still was. How only thread and paste held it together. If given the opportunity, it would break into a million pieces.

"I don't think we have need of another seamstress." His words were stiff.

They reached the railing, and she gripped it as she stared out over Manhattan. There was no night anymore. Electric lampposts made the city an eternal twilight. Light enough to keep the shadows at bay. She reached her body forward, over her white-knuckled grasp, and let her gaze fall down the side of the building to the street below. Her vision began to swim, and she could feel every beat of her heart. Slow and steady, pushing blood through her veins.

Robert wrapped his arm around her back, his hand resting at her waist. "Don't lean so far over. It makes me nervous."

She stood upright and gave him a rueful smile. "You've seen me dangle from a rope midair."

"I don't like that either."

Stepping away, she pushed herself into the nook where the rail met a smooth pillar. Not as warm and comforting as the arms of a man, but much safer. Directly across from them, on the other side of the crowd, a tower rose. "Have you been up there? I've heard you can see the entire city."

Robert followed her gaze. "Thirty-two stories. It's a marvel. Do you want to go up?"

"No." Even now, many fewer stories high, she'd felt that tug to leap. Sometimes, when she climbed to the top of the ladder, she had an urge to jump free. Without the rope. Without a trapeze. There was always a moment when she thought she might not fall like Charlotte but fly. Her leather-clad toes inching over the edge of the platform, breath a buoy in her chest. And then the crowd's roar would seep through her madness, and she would grab the bar.

Tonight, she wouldn't climb any higher. Standing here on the rooftop with Robert seemed risk enough. "She's a widow. The mother of a young daughter. And Mabel says the most talented seamstress she's ever worked with."

"Why are you doing this? Why try so hard?"

"I'll do anything to recover what I once had with my daughter." No. She wanted more than that. She'd do anything for what she should have had with her daughter.

"I was with you when you received that letter from Bram, Isabella. You were devastated. Don't you remember how it cut you? What makes you think this will be any different?"

His voice was a siren's call. A temptation to creep back

toward safety and protection against hurt. Perhaps it was a prophecy too. All Mabel had seemed to inherit from her was heaps of black hair. Would she wreak destruction as her father once had?

"Mabel isn't Bram. It's not the same at all. She was a child when all this happened. She didn't even know, Robert. She thought I was dead all these years."

"I only want to keep you safe."

"You can't give me that. But you can make me so happy by speaking with Jerry. At least see if Mabel's friend could be brought on."

Robert scrubbed his hand through his beard—Isabella quite liked it now—and groaned. "Fine. Fine. I will speak with him. But I can't promise anything."

She pressed her hands to his chest. "I know."

But Robert would tell the owner of Travis and Wells that Alice was widowed and desperate, a mother, and Isabella would be able to tell Mabel in a couple of days that she'd secured her friend a position. Wouldn't that please her daughter? Wouldn't it make Isabella somewhat of a hero in Mabel's eyes? Strong. Competent. Capable.

Her limbs relaxed, and a delicious warmth filled her, as though she'd ordered a glass of beer instead of lemonade. It filled her up, spilling into her toes and rising to her head, leaving a trail of tingling heat behind. "Thank you."

And without thought, she stood on tiptoe and pressed her lips to his, tasting them through the prickly hair that scraped her skin. When he drew in a harsh breath, she wrapped her arms around his waist.

He pushed her off and stepped back with a swipe of his hand against his mouth. "No."

She blinked. "No?"

"No. I won't. It was wrong of me to allow it in the first place." He turned back toward the edge of the roof and stared up at a sky pricked with silver. "You are starlight. A wisp of imagination. I know I cannot capture you. I should never have even had you. It's not right that I gave you the impression it would be enough. That I would be satisfied with only the very basest version of you." He looked at her again, and Isabella found she could scarcely bear it—his gaze brimming with love and pain and desperation and strength. "As though that's the most important part of you." He shook his head, eyes pinching closed and giving Isabella a brief reprieve. "But it's not. You are so much more, and I want all of you. Or none of you."

"Oh, Robert, I'm not worth it."

And for the first time since Polly Grant had stood beside Robert and Rowena and watched men drag her fiancé's body from the river, she saw Robert cry. Great, quiet tears that fell down his cheeks and burrowed into the craggy hollows of his beard.

Bram had never cried. And he'd refused to comfort her when she had. *"Be strong,"* he would say, then disappear into his memories. An alcoholic father. A bruised and battered mother. A vow made that final time before he'd snuck from the Highland cottage and joined his life to the circus.

He'd made another vow, after Polly had stood at the edge of a Romanian lake, her daughter tied snugly to her empty breasts with a shawl. She'd laid the child on a bed of grass and picked-over wildflowers and then stepped into the lake. *"Our daughter will never be weak like this. Like you. Tears are useless."*

But Robert seemed entirely unashamed.

She stepped away from him. "What are you doing? Stop it."

"I'm so sorry, Polly. I've failed you. I thought, if you realized how much I loved you, you might love me too. But there was nothing loving in what we did. It was idolatry. I worshiped what your body could do for me."

"Robert, stop. Don't say these things." It was vulgar to speak in such a way. Crass and blunt. What had happened, what they did, was all right because it had been hidden. Away from prying eyes. And he hadn't used her. She'd given herself to him.

If anything, she had used him, to induce him to talk Jerry into letting her keep her job.

But it had been so much more than that. It had been anger. Anger at Bram for what he'd done. It had been loneliness. All those years, she'd clung to a sliver of hope, and then, with that write-up of his death, she watched it burn. It had been fear and desperation and maybe a bit of lust. Because it had been so long since she'd allowed herself to feel any kind of desire or attraction. Since before her marriage truly ended.

And to have Robert denigrate the only thing she had to give?

She crossed her arms over her middle and turned back toward the street.

"I'm very sorry." Robert touched her back, and she stiffened.

"Yes, you've said."

"I'll talk to Jerry tomorrow."

She gave a short nod and didn't allow herself to relax until his steps faded and she was certain he'd been enveloped into the crowd. Then she leaned over the railing and watched the shadows play with one another on the street below and wondered if it might not be better to join them.

CHAPTER
20

"I HOPE YOU DON'T MIND, but I invited my mother to join us and Robert." Mabel leaned around the doorframe and saw Maman on a settee with the circus manager. "She won't take part in the interview. I only want to be with her every moment possible."

Jake peered into the room and took a deep breath. Her own hitched. Robert had arranged for a reporter from the *New York World* to interview them. She hadn't considered, when she asked Maman to be present, that Jake would take issue with it. But of course he would.

"I'm sorry. I should have asked you first if it was all right. But I was so happy when she was able to speak with Robert so quickly about giving Alice a position. She will be here tonight, you know, to begin work. I went yesterday after the evening show to tell her, and you should have seen how relieved she was. And Katie Grace too."

"Of course it's all right. I don't mind. She's your mother, and you've wanted to know her for so long."

He sounded perfectly calm, but Mabel saw the tension in his jaw and knew he wasn't as all right with it as he'd said. And for that, she loved him a little more. She didn't fault him his feelings on the matter—his perception had been skewed by grief—but character wasn't in the feeling. It was in the doing. And Jake was constantly *doing* things that cast his in a good light.

She leaned over to lightly kiss his cheek. "Thank you."

"Come on, you two. Time enough for lovemaking later." Robert waved them into the room. He turned to the reporter seated at a square table. "I don't believe we've ever had a duo as enchanted with each other as they are."

"They are newly wed." Maman smiled at Mabel, but it seemed forced. She perched on the very edge of the cushion, her hip pressed against the rolled arm. Robert, too, sported a haggard look—dark half-moons beneath his eyes and a general sense of unease draping him—that was at odds with his typical joviality.

Mabel seemed to be the only one in the room not operating under pretense. She smiled at the reporter—a neat man with very straight posture—before taking one of the chairs across the table from him. Jake sat beside her, and introductions were made.

"Are you aware," Mr. Norris, the journalist, began, "that you are being hailed as America's favorite couple? Mr. Cunningham, did you not enjoy that title with your deceased wife? How do you feel about it?"

Mabel went completely still except for her fingers, which pinched and picked at the fabric of her green linen suit. The weather had warmed enough that she thought it an appropriate choice for the day, with its mother-of-pearl buttons and matching bolero jacket. When Jake saw her after the first show, his eyes had widened, and his dimple appeared. *"How completely charming you look. Like springtime."*

Mabel now berated herself for thinking that portended

a good day. How could Mr. Norris so cruelly bring up Charlotte? As though ambushing a man with questions about his dead wife could ever be excused simply because the ambusher worked for the press. "I don't think—"

"I don't think—"

Mabel looked at Jake, whose words mirrored her own. She hoped he saw the apology in her gaze. His lips curled a little, and his hand found hers, stilling their nervous dance. "I don't think," he began again, "that it should matter. Many men don't have the pleasure of marriage to even one wife so talented and lovely, and I have had two."

Mr. Norris jotted something in his notebook. "When did you realize you were in love with Mrs. Cunningham, the second one? She is different from your first wife. Quite different, indeed, from most women."

"Yes, she is singular." Jake ignored Mr. Norris's first question and, contrary to the heaviness of her heart, Mabel smiled as though it were the very best thing he could have said.

Now she too belonged to this collection of people pretending things they didn't feel. But if everyone else could manage it, she supposed she could as well. Jake thought her singular. There was a certain pleasure in that. At least he didn't believe her ordinary. Though, at the moment, she would give anything for an ordinary marriage. And a definite answer as to when he'd fallen in love with her.

"And you, Mrs. Cunningham, when did you find yourself in love with your husband?" Mr. Norris watched her carefully, his steady gaze likely missing nothing.

"My, you do ask intimate questions." She laughed, airy and light and as false as everything else in the room.

"Readers will want to know. They do love a romance." He put his pen to the paper.

"I . . ." She glanced at Jake. She had never told him she loved him. He likely wouldn't believe anything she said during this interview, for its very premise was built on falsity. But could she lie? She could paint a smile on her lips and laugh and pretend all was as it should be, but could she *speak* a lie? About Jake? "I suppose I've known all along."

"Since you met?"

She nodded and felt Jake's stare. "Now, Mr. Norris, *that* is an interesting story."

Jake snorted, drawing the reporter's attention. "Do you disagree, Mr. Cunningham?"

Mabel chanced a glance at him. Oh, heavens, he was still looking at her. And now she was caught, their gazes snagged, her face as warm as a Christmas fire.

"Not at all, though it doesn't paint me in the best light," Jake said. There were questions in his eyes, deepening their hue. Turning them as dark as the sea during a storm. She wished to drown beneath them.

"How so?" Mr. Norris's question sliced between them, severing the connection.

Jake coughed. "It's not every day a trained athlete is bested in a wrestling competition by a woman." He told the story, ending with a laugh. "She has never lost. But she will. One day. She will lose, and I will be the victor."

Mabel chuckled. "Your optimism is misplaced."

She placed her elbow on the table, and in response, Jake motioned Mr. Norris from his seat and swung into it. Their hands clasped. Their eyes caught.

"The terms?" Jake asked.

"A kiss," Robert called from the settee.

Jake grinned. "If you win, you retain the title of champion." His gaze landed on her lips, and his own softened. Relaxed, as though with anticipation. "If I win, you owe me a kiss."

He called the match just as her limbs went soft as butter. A fraction of a moment too late, she flexed and pushed against his strength. Her arm slammed against the table.

Jake stared at their clasped hands. "What just happened?"

"I . . ." Mabel pressed her free hand to her mouth.

"Have I just witnessed a miracle?" Mr. Norris asked dryly, then began to scratch against his notebook.

"I wasn't ready." Mabel laughed. "I wasn't ready."

Still holding her hand, Jake stood and rounded the table. "I still won. Fair and square." He leaned over her. Brushed his knuckles against her jaw. "I claim my reward."

It was a brief kiss, as kisses went, but Mabel's lashes fluttered against her cheeks, and behind her lids, she saw stars and moonlight.

Mr. Norris cleared his throat, and Mabel sat at the table once more, pressing her palms against her flaming cheeks. "Yes, well . . . it is clear you feel a great deal for each other." His pen scratched over the paper, a stream of tidy words falling upon it. "Mabel Cunningham," he muttered, "the world's strongest woman, has—"

"Atalanta," Robert called from the settee.

Mabel swung her head around. "What is that?"

"Your name. Atalanta, the world's strongest woman. Mr. Wells has decided a woman of your strength deserves an equally strong name."

"There's nothing weak about her name. Mabel. *Ma belle.*" Maman had sunk even further into the settee's corner and crossed her arms over her chest. "There is strength in beauty too."

Robert didn't look at her. His jaw twitched, and he stood. "Her name is now Atalanta. The lithographs will be plastered all over New York City in the coming days, so please refer to her as such." Then he left.

"Atalanta it is." Mr. Norris scribbled upon the paper, slapped his book closed, and gathered his things. "You can expect something at the end of next week."

When he disappeared through the door, Jake following, Mabel sat beside Maman.

"It's only a stage name. I will still be called Mabel in real life. And it's a good one. Atalanta." It rolled off her tongue and slipped over her like a frock. "It's solid, is it not? Sounds weighty and deserving of honor."

"Your father would have liked it." Maman gave a bitter laugh. "Your name was the only thing I had. The only thing he gave me."

Mabel frowned. "I don't understand. It's only an act. Part of being a performer. People often take other names. Don other characters."

"Names mean something, Mabel. They're important. Attached to them are memories and realities and identity." Maman took Mabel's hand and pressed a kiss to her knuckles. "Your name . . . it's the only thing you have of me."

"But . . . you changed your name."

"Yes. Because all of those things I mentioned—the memories and identity—were too painful to move forward with. Polly MacGinnis wasn't strong. She wasn't capable. She was broken and had too many regrets. Every time I heard that name, I would think of all I'd done. All I'd almost done. All that had been done to me. I couldn't have become everything I was meant to be with that weighing on me. My name was a burden. You, though, are none of those things." She sighed and stood. "But no one argues with Mr. Wells, and he's christened you, so Atalanta you shall be."

"Only on stage, Maman."

Isabella shook her head. "It's hard not to change when everyone is cheering for someone else."

* * *

"What do you say we skip the dining hall and grab a hot dog?" Jake asked Mabel after the afternoon performance. "We could walk for a bit. If you weren't planning to return to the hotel for a rest." He pretended to be uninvested in her answer. As though her response made no difference at all to him.

He hadn't been able to stop thinking about their kisses. Hadn't been able to stop thinking about her. And he didn't want to share these few moments between shows with a hundred others.

Mabel, having just stepped out of her dressing room, straightened the cuff of one of her sleeves and smiled brilliantly at him. "Yes, let's do that."

As they left Madison Square Garden and headed down Madison Avenue, Jake scoured his thoughts, trying to find one that would make for interesting conversation. "I think the interview with Mr. Norris went well, don't you?"

Not exactly scintillating. Especially when what he most wanted was more time alone with Mabel. With his wife. With this woman he'd known for years but hadn't really seen.

But to what purpose? He was returning home. They wanted different things from life. They'd already decided on the plan.

And she loved him. She'd said as much in answer to the reporter that morning. Jake supposed he'd always known—Mabel could no more hide her thoughts than her height—but he didn't love her. Not the way a man ought to love his wife. He wasn't sure he was capable of it again. Which meant he needed to be careful with her. He needed to resist this attraction.

Mabel stopped to look into a dressmaker's window, tugging her lower lip between her teeth as she scanned the lines of a fetching walking suit. She sighed. "I don't really need another, do I?"

She started off again, as though not expecting an answer.

"You don't have that many." Charlotte had traveled with trunks of clothing, though she hadn't possessed Mabel's gift for color and cut. Of course, there wasn't much Charlotte didn't look good in, so she could escape the necessity of a more discerning eye.

"But I still need to pay you back, and—"

"You don't need to pay me back."

Mabel raised her brows. "*And* there's no promise of continued work once you leave. You heard Mr. Norris. We are 'America's Favorite Couple.' What does that mean when we're no longer a couple?"

"It means you must develop some confidence in your own ability."

They joined the queue snaking from a cart and were silent until they each held a hot dog, milk buns soft and piled high with briny kraut.

"I suppose I'll miss New York's food most of all," Mabel said when she'd taken the last bite of her lunch. "The pretzels and hot dogs and pizza. Will you miss it at all when you return home?"

"No." He wouldn't miss the food, nor the bustle of the city. Nor the constant moving around and the reminders of what once was and the emptiness that clawed at his belly every time he stepped into the ring. But he would miss her. More than he'd imagined when they left Italy.

They were walking through Madison Square Park now, tracing the winding paths and enjoying the relative silence—only the echo of traffic and crowds whispering through the trees. Jake took a deep breath and allowed the tension to seep from his neck and shoulders.

"I need to talk to you about that. About when you leave and also about a possibility I've just been made aware of." Mabel glanced at him quickly. "Maman suggested a routine. With her clown friend Rowena and me. And . . . you."

"Impossible. I cannot . . . you cannot expect that of me." The birdsong suddenly sounded piercing. They were passing an iron bench set back from the path amidst a blanket of nodding tulips, and he sank onto it.

She sat beside him, her back straight and shoulders stiff.

"It would help me. I need to prepare for your departure, and if I could come up with a few tricks with Maman, it might be enough for me. Robert has already agreed."

Jake's entire body flushed, and sweat gathered beneath his collar. He stared straight ahead, taking in the blooms and greenery. "I'm not sure if I'm angrier that it seems I have little choice in this or because of your persistent stage fright. Don't you think your mother leaving during your most formative years has something to do with your inability to believe in yourself? Why would you trust her with this?"

"My mother left. My father left. You will . . ." She didn't complete her thought, but the words hung between them. *You will leave.* And each time, Mabel was left trying to figure out how to continue on by herself. "I know my parents didn't leave me because of anything I did, but can you imagine how it might feel to a small child? I couldn't continue working with my mother. She went to New York not long after, you know. And after my father died, I failed to fill the very large hole he left behind."

"And me leaving?"

She sighed, staring ahead at a brilliant trio of azaleas. "Well, that *is* my fault, isn't it? I will never, ever be Charlotte."

Thank God, he wanted to say. But how would he explain such a response? "I don't know how I can do this. I accept that Isabella Moreau is your mother. I accept that you want a relationship with her. But I cannot accept working so closely with her."

"You won't spend very much time with her, though. The trick will take less than ten minutes. And only a few hours each day of extra rehearsal until it debuts on Monday."

Jake pushed himself from the bench and took to the trail again. He heard Mabel's steps behind him, but he didn't slow down. She could easily catch up if she wanted to.

That thought fueled his rising irritation. She could do just about anything she wanted to, including preforming on her own. Without him or Isabella or Bram or anyone else acting as her crutch. Mabel was perfectly capable on her own. And now, because of her cursed self-doubt, he was left failing either her or his own integrity. Could he work with Isabella? The woman he was certain encouraged, if not outright pushed, his wife into performing the stunt that killed her. And if the trick captured the audience's fancy, could he leave Mabel to her, knowing she might very well repeat the past?

He paused and waited for Mabel to come alongside him before walking again. "No, I can't do it. It will only keep you reliant on others."

"It's not your responsibility to fix that."

"You can't ask me to work with the woman responsible for my wife's death." He took a few more steps before realizing she no longer walked beside him. Turning, he saw her standing in the path, her gaze pinned to his, eyes frosty.

"Maman had nothing to do with it, and she has suffered enough without you laying the blame for the death of America's Sweetheart at her feet. It has been years, Jake. It might be time to ask Robert what came of the inquest. You cling too tightly to this story you've built up in your mind instead of the truth, and I'm afraid you've become consumed with the lies you've told yourself in order to make sense of such a senseless thing."

Mabel had never spoken to him in such a way, her voice tight and words sharp. Jake thought it likely she'd never spoken to *anyone* that way.

"It isn't your responsibility to fix that, though, is it?" He forced a smile, sure it resembled nothing near one.

Mabel pressed her face into her hands, and the words slipping through her fingers were muffled. "Oh, Jake." She dropped her arms and neared him, taking small, slow steps as though approaching a spooked horse. She caught his hands in hers and pressed them tightly to her middle. "Can you not see I'm trying to make this work the best way I can? The only way I can. I need you right now. I need you to help me."

Jake closed his eyes and leaned his forehead against her shoulder with a groan. How could he refuse her? He could deny her nothing when asked in such a way. She needed him. Not just her mother. Not merely a new act. But *him.*

And then there were her lips slipping over his temple. Her hands releasing his and gripping his shoulders. Her soft murmur brushing his hair.

"Please, Jake."

"All right. All right. I'll do it. Tell me about this trick."

He stepped away from her, unwilling to be trapped even more firmly in her charming, delicious grasp.

❋ ❋ ❋

"I know you don't like this," Mabel said, her voice not carrying farther than Jake, who stood beside her in the ring. "But I'm grateful you're willing to do it."

He didn't respond. There was no time, for Rowena and Maman rode around the ring on bicycles. But something had changed between them after their brief argument five days ago. He'd pulled away. She thought her anger had shifted the equilibrium, or maybe it was how quickly she'd switched allegiance. But what was she supposed to do, caught as she was between a husband who wasn't a husband and a mother who wanted nothing more than to finally be a mother?

She grabbed Jake's hand and, just as Rowena and Maman reached them, said, "I want you both." But the crowd erupted at that moment because Maman had climbed onto the bike seat and begun to flip, and Mabel was certain Jake hadn't heard. Which was just as well. She was growing too bold in her desperation to keep him.

Maman's face glowed as she wove a figure eight with Rowena

around Mabel and Jake. Mabel lifted the specially crafted steel bar at her feet. It had a hook on either end, each made to fit perfectly around the bicycles' frames. She got into position, adjusted the bar, and squatted in preparation to lift. Maman and Rowena positioned their bicycles beneath the hooks, and Mabel stepped forward to catch them.

It was an adequate trick. One that, when Mabel stood upright, engendered a smattering of applause. Tepid. It hardly captured the crowd's awe.

But then Jake rounded them, took a running start, and with a succession of flips, launched himself onto the bar between Mabel's closed fists. She glanced up at him, arms rigid and legs pointing north, his face hovering above her.

He smiled, though sweat dripped from his brow and his body trembled with effort. "Right now, you have us both. Lift."

And to the delight of the audience, she did. Then, when she lowered the bar back to her shoulders, much to *her* delight, Jake bent his elbows and kissed her.

"We didn't rehearse that," she said.

"There are a lot of things happening that haven't been rehearsed."

The clowns spilled into the ring, jumping and pantomiming as Rowena threw her hands into the air and pretended fear. Mabel lowered the contraption, and Jake flipped backward onto the ground. He, Rowena, and Isabella scattered toward their respective stations, and Mabel spent the next few minutes bending iron bars.

Jake was spinning through the air by the time she finished her act and left the ring. She stood outside in the dressing room hall for a few minutes, watching him, until Maman joined her.

Annette, her work complete, slid past them but then stopped and turned. "Is it true that you are her daughter?"

Mabel's mouth went dry as cotton, and she ran her tongue

over her lips. She didn't trust this woman. Manzo Brothers Circus had been a family. Always—always—Mabel had known she belonged. Travis and Wells was a different sort of beast. Jealousies were rampant, and gossip often took an ugly turn. "I am."

Annette lifted her elegant brows and, folding her arms over her chest, tapped her foot as though Mabel were some kind of mischievous child. "And why didn't you tell us?"

"It didn't concern you." Mabel tucked her arm through Maman's and turned to stare again into the heights of the amphitheater. She had little experience dealing with such nastiness and didn't know if being cosseted from it her entire life had been a good thing or not. It did leave her unprepared to confront it, though.

"Well, it does all make sense now." Annette gave a lovely trilling laugh. "I wondered how you'd managed to crawl out of your inconsequential Italian circus right into the best outfit in the world."

Mabel tore her gaze from Jake's athletic form and, despite Maman's pinching fingers inside her elbow, turned back around. "What is that supposed to mean?"

Annette waved her hand. "It's perfectly reasonable. You used your influence to obtain the position, and your mother used . . . hers."

"That's enough." Maman's voice was icy. "Mabel and I only recently discovered our relationship. We don't owe you or anyone else an explanation."

"You should be very careful whom you offend. Not everyone is as accommodating as Mr. Pedersen, and I know how desperately you wish to extend your final few weeks into something more permanent." Annette flounced away, each graceful, prim step a jab to Mabel's vanity.

"Why does she hate us? I'm certain I've never done anything to her." Mabel looked at Maman, who wore a pinched expression.

"She hates everyone who threatens her. You because of your charm and favor, me because I was against the idea of giving her a place with Travis and Wells."

"Why?"

"She reminds me of someone I once knew. Someone ambitious and determined to find fame no matter the cost."

"You mean Charlotte Cunningham."

Maman nodded absently. "Chasing the adoration of strangers. Forever pinning your hopes on the spotlight. It's never worth it."

"Did you do that?"

Maman gave a sad, twisting smile and took Mabel's hand. "Come, let's go bathe and change." After only a few steps, though, she answered. "I did, for a short time. I thought it might chase away my nightmares. But after Charlotte's death, I realized it only bred more."

They reached the private dressing room Mabel and Jake had been given only that morning. *"You have made Mr. Wells extremely happy,"* Robert had told them. *"In just a few days, ticket sales have gone up twenty-five percent because of your act. When we leave New York City, it's almost certain he will give you a small, private stateroom."* A privilege that had quickly become a liability when Robert also gave them both raises. It was enough money to see Jake to Kansas sooner than expected. He would go home after New York and never enjoy that private room. Maybe Maman could join her in his stead.

Inside, a bath had already been filled, and lavender-scented steam rose from it. Maman ran her hand through the water and pressed dripping fingers to the back of her neck. Mabel disrobed, eager for the heat to work its way into her throbbing muscles.

She had only just slid into the water when Maman drew a chair near and began pulling the pins from Mabel's hair. "I love my work, but these days I don't do it because I need validation from the public. I do it because there's nothing else I want to do. Nothing else I can do. And sometimes it feels as though being useful is the only thing keeping the shadows at bay."

"I remember your shadows." Mabel leaned back as her mother began kneading supple fingers over her scalp. "You cried a lot."

"I'm sorry you noticed. I tried to keep it from you."

Mabel craned her neck, the water sloshing over her chest and shoulders. "Why?"

"You were very young. It isn't a child's job to manage a parent's struggles. And your father didn't like it."

Mabel relaxed again and leaned into her mother's touch. "I remember that too," she whispered.

"You will influence her, Polly. Is that what you want? Mabel will become as weak as you." They had thought she was sleeping—they always thought she slept better than she did—but it took much less than their furious whispers to awaken her. Maman's response still rang as clearly today as it had that evening in Bologna. Mabel usually loved the winter break. Other than when the circus practiced, she had her parents' complete attention. But that night they had fought. Maman had cried. Da had sounded so angry, his words sharp and stinging.

"I want Mabel to be nothing like me," Maman had said. That, when it was all Mabel wanted. To be as adored, talented, and feminine as her beautiful mother.

And Da's harsh reply. *"On that we agree."*

Mabel pressed her hands to her eyes. How could she have forgotten?

Maman poured a stream of water over her head, then lifted the hair tonic from the tray and shook some into her palm. She began rubbing it into Mabel's hair, an act so soothing, so nurturing that Mabel's chest constricted and her throat tightened. Tears squeezed from beneath her fingers, and she heard them drip upon the bathwater.

"Darling, what's wrong?" Maman's hands fell from Mabel's head.

"I'm only sorry for how much I loved him. How much I forgot."

"I'm not. I'm glad you loved him. I never wanted you to know some of the things he said. Or did."

Mabel sat upright, her hair falling from its soapy bundle and slipping over her shoulders. She pressed her knees to her breasts and wound her arms around them.

Maman scooted around the side of the tub, her knuckles white as she gripped the rim. "I would give up a thousand life-times with you if it meant my darkness couldn't overshadow your light. You didn't *need* me, Mabel. And if you really think about it, your father was right in knowing how dangerous it was to have me around." She handed Mabel a bar of soap. "Lean your head back." When Mabel did, Maman dipped a dented tin cup into the tub and poured it over her hair. "Did your father ever tell you about your grandmother MacGinnis?"

"Nothing much. She died before I was born, right?"

"Your father believes she was killed. By your grandfather."

Mabel's eyes widened, and she flung her head around, sending a spray of water across the wall. "What?"

"Your grandfather was an alcoholic. And when drunk, he became violent toward your father and grandmother. Your father always blamed her. He thought she was too weak to leave. So, when he had the chance, *he* left."

"He left her alone with such a man?" Would the surprises ever cease? How much farther could Da fall in her estimation?

"He asked her to go with him, but she refused. She gave him all the money she had secreted away, though, and enough food to last a few days." Maman ran her fingers through Mabel's tangled hair, teasing out the snarls and smoothing it beneath her palm. "He wasn't wrong in leaving, but he was wrong about something. He thought your grandmother the weak one, but in truth, it was your grandfather who was weak. Only a very weak man hurts a woman or a child. But, you see, he never reconciled that. His entire life, as far as I know, he perceived your grandmother's refusal to stand up for herself as weakness. He saw her fear as weakness. He saw her tears and reliance on a man and deep desire for a husband as weakness. In me, he saw those same things. And more than anything, he wanted you to be strong. I was in the way of that."

"But now you're not?"

Maman laughed. "I don't think anyone else's weakness can influence you at this point. You are strong in body, mind, and spirit. Stronger than anyone, I think."

Mabel sank back into the water and wished for all the world that Maman was right. But she knew the truth, as much as it would grieve Da.

She wasn't immune to fear and shadows.

CHAPTER 21

AHEAD OF MABEL AND ALICE, Jake walked down the hotel hall toward the elevator, Katie Grace atop his shoulders.

"Would you be afraid if I ran as fast as I could?" He took a few bouncing steps, eliciting a delighted shriek from the child. "I could toss you into the air."

"And I'll flip like you. Then land on my feet like Octavia Maria Shannon Whiskers."

Mabel chuckled. Soon Katie Grace would begin training with Isabella, who had recognized in the child a propensity toward all things acrobatic. Katie Grace had pouted for a couple of minutes, having wanted to become a clown, but after Maman spent a little time with her on the practice rings, lowered to only six feet above the floor, she'd settled.

"He would be an excellent father." Alice took hold of Mabel's arm and squeezed. "Any thoughts on that?"

"Oh no. We aren't . . . No. It isn't likely."

Alice only raised her brows.

"I want children. With Jake." Mabel sighed. She wanted so much with him. "But . . ." She couldn't very well tell Alice that theirs wasn't the sort of marriage that resulted in a child. Ahead, Jake reached the elevator and swung Katie Grace to the ground. The creaking, swaying sound of it ascending echoed up the chamber. "It's very hard, isn't it?"

Alice's gaze settled on her daughter, who was sticking her hands through the grate and wriggling her fingers, slapping at Jake when he attempted to draw her to safety. "It is. But it's also beautiful."

"My mother missed most of the hard and the beautiful." Mabel had shared a bit of her story with Alice after her friend moved into a shared room down the hall from them at the Hotel Veronica. "I'm not angry. Mostly sad. And desperate, I think, to capture every moment and hold it tightly. How do I begin creating those moments with her, Alice? As a mother, what would you have Katie Grace do if there was a world of pain between you?"

The elevator opened, and they didn't speak again until they reached Madison Square Garden and Jake ducked away to spend time in the stables. Mabel found herself standing beside Alice, watching Maman work with Katie Grace in one of the empty dressing rooms. A team of bareback riders was rehearsing in the amphitheater, and nearly everyone else was enjoying the quiet hours between the afternoon and evening shows.

"If I were reunited with Katie Grace after a long absence," Alice said in a low voice, "I believe I would most want to be reminded of the time before. I would want to know that it wasn't all hurt being remembered. Is there a time when you can recall your mother being happy? Of you being happy?"

Katie Grace laughed, the sound bouncing around the empty room. Mabel smiled when Maman pressed her hands against her lips, her feet making a merry dance the way they sometimes had after shows when everyone came together—Lorenzo with his love songs and Giulia and Imilia with their cooing dove voices—and Maman and Da would twirl, his strong arms flinging and gathering. Mabel loved those times most of all. But Maman . . . she loved something even better.

Mabel had held tightly, all these years, to the memory of Maman's laugh. Her approval. Mostly, Mabel remembered her sadness, and that had defined most of their relationship—a vague understanding in Mabel's childish thoughts that something was not quite right—but there had been moments of light. Moments of unrestrained joy. Moments where Mabel found herself snug in Maman's embrace much the way Katie Grace did now. And all of those moments had occurred within the span of five years.

"I think there is something I can do," Mabel whispered. Maybe, if they went back far enough, they would find the healing they needed. Maybe Maman would be reminded of a time before she became entirely consumed by all the things that settled upon her like a heavy weight.

All Mabel wanted now was to help set her mother free. Nothing good ever came of shame. And she so wanted good things for Maman. For them both.

* * *

"Maman?"

Isabella gave a final wave and watched as Katie Grace and Alice pushed through the door, the girl chattering about the ducks at Central Park. Then she turned to look at her own daughter. Now much more grown. No longer placated by a day at the park.

Mabel looked elegant in a handsome walking suit of black and pink stripes that set off her clear skin and startling eyes. Isabella could hardly force herself to look at them sometimes, not only because they reminded her of Bram, but because Mabel often gave the impression of knowing more than she let on. Of looking more deeply than the average person could.

"Yes?"

"I was wondering something. I'm hoping that you could . . ." Mabel twisted her fingers at her waist. "That is, do you remember our routine?"

Isabella blinked.

"The one we worked on before I became too large?"

There was longing in Mabel's words. It tugged at Isabella's heart until she could no longer resist examining memories she'd so long ignored. She closed her eyes and inhaled deeply, almost able to smell the scent so peculiar to Italy. Her daughter's sturdy legs hanging from the practice bar as she pushed herself tall, a wide smile spreading over her upturned face.

"Very good, Mabel," Isabella, then Polly, had said. She'd moved her hand over Mabel's back and supported her middle. *"Now, draw your knees in and push your legs out straight, like you're sitting on a bed."*

It had taken very little effort, for Mabel had been the strongest three-year-old Polly had ever known.

Most of Isabella's memories were like old photographs caught in a fire, the edges burned with regret, all curled up around murky images. But that one stood alone. Pure and sweet and untinged. Isabella had thought, laughing with her little daughter and teaching her the things she knew, that maybe it would be her salvation. Perhaps, in pouring herself into Mabel, she could find redemption from the guilt and regret and shadows that hounded her.

She'd been a fool.

"I remember." She opened her eyes and forced her gaze to meet Mabel's.

"Maybe . . . I was thinking . . ." Mabel pressed her hands to her stomach and offered a quivering smile. "Could we work on something for the show? Together? Do you think Robert would permit it? Would you . . . would you want to?"

Isabella only stared as the emptiness of Madison Square

Garden completely engulfed her. She became lost to its echoes and the ghosts of the afternoon's show. Lost to the applause and stamping feet and calls for Mabel and Jake. America's favorite couple. "I don't understand."

Mabel glanced around. "Can we go somewhere else and talk?"

Isabella nodded, and they left the building and made their way down Park Avenue. Isabella purchased two pretzels from a German vendor who ignored the stack waiting on a rod and pulled warm ones from the charcoal-heated cabinet tucked into his cart.

"This is the best thing about being in New York." Isabella tore off one of the pretzel arms, and they said nothing for several minutes while they wandered into Madison Square Park and enjoyed their snack, the Flatiron Building and Garden's tower hemming them in like twin sentinels.

Mabel tucked the last bit of pretzel into her mouth and crumpled the paper in her palm. "Maman, I *liked* being in the ring with you the other day. When you came out on your bicycle, I felt, for the first time since Da died, as though I could do anything. I sometimes feel so alone that everything I do, everything I am, feels like nothing at all. And I can't do it. I can't do it alone."

"But you aren't alone. You have Jake."

Mabel gave her a pained look. "Do you not wish to work with me? Do you suppose I'm too large? I know I am, but we can be creative with a routine. We can do *something*, right? Something that will use both my strength and your skill."

"Oh, darling." With a gentle touch, Isabella stopped Mabel and drew her toward the side of the path where a dogwood tree, blooms balanced along delicate branches, stood. "I have no doubt that you can do whatever you want to do. But why do you want to, when you work with your husband and the country is falling in love with the two of you?"

"He's leaving."

Isabella shook her head. "What? Where is he going?"

"Kansas."

A curious hollowness filled Isabella's chest, and she recalled another time, another person, who had said a similar thing.

"He wants to move to Kansas to help his brother with the ranch. Can you imagine? Me, on a ranch." Charlotte had laughed, but there was an edge to it. *"I'm not going. He doesn't know it yet, but I'm not giving this up to become a farmwife. He's insane."*

"He loves you. I'm sure he won't insist if he knows how you feel about it. He does know, doesn't he, Charlotte?" Isabella had asked. She knew what secrets did to a marriage.

Charlotte's beautiful face had been as hard as granite. *"I've already seen a lawyer about a divorce."*

"Oh, Charlotte. That's not an answer."

Charlotte had crossed her arms, an obstinate tilt to her chin. *"I haven't signed anything yet. I want him to come around. To see how foolish the idea is. I honestly don't think he cares a whit about me if he's considering such a thing. And anyway, he'll realize tomorrow what a stupid thing he's asking me to do. As if I'm an ordinary woman."*

Jake hadn't had the opportunity to see anything. Charlotte died the next day while trying to prove herself anything but ordinary.

"You don't want to go with him?" Isabella asked, hoping her daughter wouldn't choose work over love. Fame over husband. Her throat pinched, and she swallowed the saliva that filled her mouth.

Mabel glanced at her shoes. "He doesn't want me to go with him."

Everything went dry—her mouth, her throat, her skin, her eyes. Heat poured through Isabella's blood, and if she hadn't been certain she stood in a quiet park, she would have said an audience thundered. It pounded in her ears.

Isabella clenched her skirt and spoke, anger mottling her voice. "Has he met someone?"

"No, Maman," Mabel said in a rush, "it isn't like that. *He* isn't like that. We have an arrangement, you see. Our marriage isn't real. It was always meant to be this way."

"Not real?" Isabella released her hold on the skirt. "What are you saying?"

"We only married to prevent a scandal. It was always the plan to annul it once we reached New York. Once I found you and found work. But Jake used so much of his own money to support us that he needed to work too. He doesn't want to return home empty-handed. He wants to help his family, not show up after all these years and be a burden. And what he makes here, working for Travis and Wells, will be enough to make amends."

"Amends?" Isabella wished the words spilling from her daughter made sense. Their marriage . . . a ruse? She had seen the way Mabel looked at Jake. Had seen what vibrated between them.

"He left home to work in his uncle's wild west show. His father wasn't happy about it, but Jake wanted adventure. And he loved performing."

"Well, what changed that?"

"Charlotte. He loved her very much. And he wanted to have children. To raise them in a home that didn't move every night. To offer them stability."

"And he doesn't want that with you?"

"He doesn't love me."

"Why not?" Isabella crossed her arms. What was wrong with the man? All of New York City had fallen in love with her daughter.

Mabel chuckled and stooped to pull a hyacinth from the soil. She pressed it to her nose and, lashes fluttering, inhaled its sweet perfume. "He's still in love with Charlotte. I am no replacement." At Isabella's disbelieving snort, Mabel handed the flower to her. "When did you stop loving Da?"

Isabella could answer without hesitation. He had been misguided. Occasionally cruel. So determined to prove his daughter strong that he'd sacrificed his marriage. But she loved him still.

Another image replaced Bram's. A smile in place of the hard frown. A flip of blond hair and a jaw that had gentled into maturity. Warm eyes that simmered with restraint. Her breath caught, and her stomach turned. She could not allow such a thing to happen again. With love came pain. With pain came desperation.

"I never did."

Mabel made a sound in her throat as though having made her point and started up the path again. After a few moments, she said, "Jake said you once told Charlotte it was good for a woman to be prepared. To never find herself at the mercy of a husband, for they could always leave. I cannot do my act alone. I have failed at that. I need to have a plan, Maman, for Jake *will* leave. And then what will I do?"

"What do you mean, you cannot do your act alone?"

Mabel stepped beneath the arch that led back out onto the street. They had crossed the entire park and would have to round the block on their way back to Hotel Veronica. Mabel was quiet as they navigated through a crowd of men, all suited in black with matching mustaches and straw boaters. When they broke free, she threaded her fingers through Isabella's. "I've never done anything alone. There's always been someone making decisions for me. Telling me what to do. Making sure all goes well. It's sad, isn't it, how dependent I am on others? But it's always been that way—as far back as I can remember."

Bram's tight script marched into Isabella's thoughts, dark lines slashing across paper that was wrinkled as though crushed by a fist.

Mabel has not handled your abandonment well. She has become consumed by need for you and will not perform, so I've told her you died.

"Since I left you for America?" Isabella asked softly.

Mabel stared ahead and said nothing, but her jaw twitched and her full lips trembled, saying everything Isabella needed to know. Bram hadn't lied, and she thought she might have made the same decision in his position. It must have been easier on Mabel, thinking her mother had died rather than knowing she had chosen to stay away.

"I will speak with Robert." She didn't believe for a moment that Mabel couldn't find success as a solo act, but if her daughter wanted to work with her, who was she to deny it?

And it was clear that when Jake did leave, Mabel would need a distraction from the pain. For the love her daughter had for him was not at all a ruse.

❋ ❋ ❋

Jake paced their small room, rubbing his hands through his hair and over his face. Mabel sat on the edge of the bed and watched, knowing there was little she could do to ease his worries.

"Are you sure it's safe?" He paused midstride and looked at her.

"Yes."

"How do you know?"

Robert had balked too, at first, but Mr. Wells had seen the profit in it. The papers had already gotten hold of the juicy story of Mabel and Isabella's reunion—no one knew how, but Maman was certain it had something to do with a gossip-inclined aerialist. The public loved it, though, so no one asked too many questions. They only sighed over the romance of a long-separated mother and daughter together again, and both at the circus, where they could be ogled and made over. Already Mabel and Isabella had been invited to a ball at the governor's mansion, which had to be politely declined because rest superseded society.

"I'm not going to do anything foolish, Jake. It's only a portion of the act. One stunt. I will climb to the platform, sit on the trapeze bar, and swing. I've done that before with you. I performed most of this trick as a child, remember?"

"But you have never been grabbed onto. And you'll be very high. It's much higher than the tents at Manzo Brothers."

"The dangerous part will be performed by my mother."

His gaze darkened, and Mabel knew he thought of Charlotte, who had taken the more perilous role in her act with Isabella Moreau. "You won't allow her to talk you into anything you don't wish to do, right?"

Mabel lifted from the bed and crossed the room. She took his hands and squeezed them. "It was my idea. Maman has talked me into nothing. I need to prepare for your departure. What will I do when you are gone? You know I cannot do anything alone, and—"

"You keep saying that, Mabel, but it isn't true, and I don't know why you persist in believing it." He lifted their hands and pressed a kiss to her knuckles. "I have enabled you to continue on in it. I should have refused to join you on stage. You would have eventually realized you need no one to prop you up."

"Or I would have been consumed by stage fright and made a fool of myself. I would have failed at Flok's. Failed at Travis and Wells. I would be a laughingstock across the city."

He pulled a hand free and touched her cheek. "You are Atalanta, the World's Strongest Woman."

"I am strong in certain things." She lifted her arm and flexed, her bicep stretching the light fabric of her shirtwaist. "But in those areas where one needs strength of spirit, I fail."

"You are strong in all things." He pulled her toward him and crushed her in his embrace. Pressing his nose against the spot where her neck and shoulder met, he took a shuddering breath as though trying to inhale her very essence. Then he pushed her away and turned toward the window. "You should finish dressing. The doctors will be waiting for you."

Mabel took a moment to collect herself. To bury deep, once more, any fantasy of Jake's kiss. His touch. His complete surrender to her love. As she finished her toilette and fixed her hair, she watched him watching the wall outside their room's window.

They had taken to dressing in each other's presence, backs turned and eyes averted. What would people think if one of them stood outside the door each morning while the other got ready? They had taken to doing a lot of things . . . like cupping their bodies around one another as they slept and kissing various chaste spots in the course of their conversations—knuckles and cheeks and foreheads. Nothing so passionate as the first two kisses that had stolen from Mabel every bit of reserve.

"All done," she said as she poked a final pin into her hair and settled a hat atop. It was a new one. Very stylish and maybe more costly than it should've been, but Mabel had offered to pay Jake back for their boarding at Mrs. Luvotti's and he'd refused. She had no other obligations, and the hat had peeked at her from behind the window of the milliner's, its sweep of violet ribbon and cherry-kissed silk roses defying her to continue blithely on her journey.

It was feminine and bold and everything Mabel hoped to be.

"You look nice," Jake said as he held the door open for her.

"I want to present myself in a way that makes these men take notice."

He raised his brows. "Should I feel threatened?" His laugh told her the question was rhetorical, and she pinched her lips together.

It was becoming hard to keep quiet. Especially because he had to be aware of her feelings for him. And if he already knew, why insist on clandestine glances and silent declarations? Why not just say so?

But she already knew the answer to that. Before the questions became fully formed, she knew she never would. He was allowed the mirage of ignorance as long as she said nothing, and thus nothing had to change. He could continue pretending all was as it always had been, and she risked no rejection.

It was all very safe and pat and clean.

"I only want to best represent Travis and Wells. They have been good to me."

They reached the hotel's tall front door, and as they waited for the doorman to open it, Jake's gaze swept her from head to toe. It was full of admiration, and she allowed herself a moment to enjoy it. She knew her new suit, with its high-necked lace shirtwaist, draped bodice, and belted waist, was particularly suited to her. And for one moment, she hoped Jake tasted a bit of the loss she felt when she thought of his leaving.

The afternoon had taken on a decidedly cheerier note than the morning, which had been spent in a grey drizzle. The sun's warmth scattered her morose thoughts, and everything looked brighter. "Did Robert give you any indication of what they wanted with me?" she asked, lifting her parasol and giving it a little twirl.

"No. Only that they wished to meet you and determine, once and for all, what sort of woman you are." He poked at her with his elbow. "I could have told them the truth of it if they'd only asked."

She laughed and he gave her a flirtatious wink, and ten minutes later, they learned Jake absolutely could not have told them the things they wanted to know.

Mabel stared at the group of doctors—three of them, all very esteemed, with their waxed beards and grave expressions—in the same room where the reporter from the *World* had interviewed her. "You want me to . . . what?"

"Remove your clothing, please." The oldest of the trio pointed toward a screen in the corner. "You will find a garment there you are to wear."

Mabel glanced at Jake, whose pinched brows exposed his own confusion. "Do you feel comfortable with this?" he asked.

"It is completely clinical, Mr. Cunningham." The doctor with a long, curly mustache turned his back to her and spoke to Jake.

Jake ignored him. "Mabel?"

The doctors leveled probing gazes at her. *Clinical*. Very well.

Mabel gave Jake a small smile and made her way toward the screen. Behind it, she found a pile of fabric atop a stool. A simple, satin ruched leotard the color of pearls and pair of gleaming white tights. She donned them and gave the hem a gentle tug, attempting to pull it lower over her bottom before rejoining the men.

She avoided Jake's gaze. Despite the fact that there was no reason for the heat pouring through her body, no reason for the flush crawling up her face, no reason whatsoever for the tingling beneath her scalp and the desire to wrap her arms around herself. This attire was only slightly more revealing than what she wore in the ring, after all. This was no different.

Except it didn't feel that way at all. It felt entirely different.

The doctors studied her as she padded across the room in stockinged feet. "You will don your boots for the photographs," the shortest and youngest of the three said. He had very straight hair. Straight brows that made slashes across his forehead, and a straight nose that ended just above a perfectly straight mouth.

Mabel swallowed and stared at him. Despite his aristocratic looks, there was a charity about him. A benign kind of generosity. "Photographs?"

His brows rose, all in a straight line with nary a hair out of place. "For the medical journal. And the papers. We have been commissioned to study you. To take measurements and determine how closely you come to the ideal beauty."

Mabel couldn't help the laugh that tumbled from her lips. All three men looked at her with wrinkled brows. "But how could you? Who determines the ideal beauty?"

"We do, of course," the oldest one said without a trace of irony.

"I'm going to murder Robert," Jake said, ostensibly under his breath but quite clear to everyone in the room.

The doctors exchanged startled glances, and Mabel shot him a look. "It's fine, Jake. Really."

Mabel pretended detached professionalism as the three strangers manipulated and poked and prodded. They wrapped every part of her with a measuring tape, its brown leather case slapping against her thighs and calves and hips as the young doctor wrote incomprehensible figures—large, loopy, and at odds with his neat appearance—in a small notebook.

When the mustached doctor instructed Mabel to hold out her arms, she complied, and he reached the tape around her back. Jake gave a little growl when he made to wrap it across her bosom, startling the man so that he jumped back, the tape measure clattering to the floor.

"Yes, of course, you should conduct this part," he said, handing over the tape measure.

Which made it even worse. She stared straight ahead at the wall as Jake reached around her, snugging the tape below her arms and pulling it taut over her chest. His fingers brushed the swell of her breasts, and his thumbs met in the middle. He called out the number, and Mabel ducked her head so he wouldn't see her flaming face.

As they all walked in single file out of the room, Jake touched the middle of Mabel's back, but she scooted away, afraid he was looking at her. Studying her. Holding up her body to the numbers recorded in a notebook.

"*I wish I were smaller, like Maman,*" she'd said to her father after learning she would no longer train as an aerialist. "*I hate how big I am.*"

"*There are worse things than being large and strong, Mabel,*" Da had replied.

She hadn't believed him.

It was one thing to be admired and ogled and declared the world's strongest woman. Very much another to be the type of woman a man wanted to marry.

They entered the room next door, where a photographer had set up a backdrop of blurred green and blue ferns and an ornately carved table boasting a profusion of hothouse zinnias. Within minutes, he too had his hands on her, moving her arms this way and that. Arranging her stance and the tilt of her head. His fingers were warm and slim. Foreign. Unwelcome.

Worse, though, was Jake watching it all, his jaw clenching and eyes gleaming. She despised being demeaned in such a way in front of him, but how improper everyone would find it if she sent him away.

The doctors were arranged on the other side of the table. One held a sheet of paper as though studying her measurements with great interest. Another stared at her extended forearm, smooth and pale against the mahogany tabletop. The other, the handsome one, smiled at her, then looked at the photographer. "She is perfect. The numbers prove it."

She flinched, finding no comfort in his statement.

"She is perfect," Jake called from across the room, "but it has nothing at all to do with numbers."

CHAPTER 22

THERE WERE TIMES when Isabella thought, if she squeezed her eyes closed and relied on other senses, the God she wasn't sure she believed in had given her another chance. Sent her hurtling back through time.

A child's laugh. The low rumble of a lion's roar from the barred animal wagons. The soft *shush-shush* as palms slid over the practice bar. In those moments, Isabella could nearly believe he'd heard her desperation and kissed her with redemption.

But then Katie Grace would ask a question, and Isabella would look at her and smile. Give the answer. Pretend she hadn't been somewhere else. With someone else.

"Very good," she said, guiding Katie Grace around the bar. "You're a natural, you know."

Katie Grace huffed and flipped her body into the air, then slapped to the ground with an *oomph* and leapt to her feet, arms reaching for the bar.

Isabella touched the girl's shoulder. "I believe that is enough for now. I'll see you this evening."

Katie Grace eyed the bar. "But—"

"We've been at it for two hours. I need to prepare for the evening show."

"When will I be able to perform?"

"Not this year. Maybe next year they might find some space for you. You'll work hard at the Indiana grounds. Hours and hours every day."

"Promise?"

Isabella laughed. "Yes. You are a rare combination of natural ability and hard work, Katie Grace. I have no doubt you will be up there with me"—she jabbed her finger toward the ceiling—"in a few years."

Her heart gave a little twist. Maybe not with *her*. Though, Isabella couldn't imagine Annette taking the time to train a child. And the Danó sisters were too inexperienced.

Nothing had been said about Isabella's departure since she'd begun working on the new act with Mabel three days earlier, but she held on to the possibility of remaining the way one would hold something delicate. Gently and fearful of shattering it.

It was a simple demonstration, and Mabel had benefited from Jake's occasional training at Manzo Brothers, but still, Isabella had been astounded by her daughter's ability to ease back into the role of aerialist.

They were to debut it this evening, beneath thousands of electric lights and eager eyes. She gazed up at the ceiling as though watching a moving picture play out, and something unfurled in her belly. A hope. A pinprick of possibility. A stopgap.

Maybe one act wasn't a permanent solution, but it could buy her some time. It could send her across America's plains and fields with Mabel. And that, more than continued fame or success, more than money—more than anything—seemed big enough to crowd out the fear, for now, of ending up like her mother.

Before her hope grew too large, she held her hand toward Katie Grace. The girl leapt lightly to her feet. "Let's go find your mother."

"She's working on Mabel's new costume. She said she was going to embroider until her fingers bled."

"I'm sure it will look beautiful." Anything would on her daughter. But Alice had a particular knack for designing pieces that suited Mabel and displayed her singular blend of strength and femininity.

They wound through the Garden's back corridors, Katie Grace darting in and out of rooms and filling the silence with her tireless chatter.

Isabella didn't care a bit. She'd missed so much of this when Mabel was growing up—first because of the distance created by fear and melancholy, then just by distance. Not that Mabel had ever said as many words as Katie Grace just had in the span of ten minutes.

Even so, being in the girl's company held a certain redemptive charm, and Isabella would take advantage of it.

They found Alice in the costuming room at a thick, scarred table, head bent over her work. Katie Grace darted in, braids flying behind her. "Mam! I nearly did a handstand on the bar. Miss Moreau says I might perform next year."

Alice smiled around a trio of pins between her teeth and tucked Katie Grace beneath her chin for a hug.

"Show us what you're making." Katie Grace pulled away and reached for the fabric spread over the table.

Alice pulled the pins from her mouth and gave Katie Grace's fingers a playful smack. "Don't touch, darling. The ruching isn't completely stitched down." She lifted it carefully, and Isabella gasped.

"Oh, it's beautiful." Isabella stepped nearer and peered at the exquisite gold embroidery making fanciful designs against navy satin. She could imagine Mabel standing in the middle of the ring, light pouring from the windows lining the building and falling over her in a spill of heaven. "I'm not sure if she will look more angel or goddess, but the effect will be magnificent."

Alice grinned up at her. "You should see yours."

"Mine?"

"Mr. Pedersen asked that I design you a complementary costume for your new act. He specifically told me to drape you in starlight."

You are starlight. A wisp of imagination. I know I cannot capture you. I should never have even had you." Robert's words, whispered atop the roof that night everything changed, curled up within her breast like a sleeping kitten. How good he was to her, the most undeserving of women. "Starlight."

"He said Mabel was to be the moon and you the stars." Alice pinched her lower lip between her teeth and glanced at the fabric in her hands. "I feel as though I've divulged something I shouldn't have."

Isabella blinked. "No, it isn't that. I'm sure it's fine that you told me. I was just thinking of something. It struck me unexpectedly."

She could love this man. She *did* love this man. She loved him for his steadfastness. For his kindness. For his ability to recognize and repent. Especially for that. He wasn't like Bram. Was so unlike Bram that it made loving him an almost painful thing. But he was Robert. Sweet, always-there Robert.

"Whatever struck you, Isabella, you are gleaming like a star right now." Alice set down Mabel's unfinished costume and chucked Katie Grace beneath the chin. "There is a reason some people achieve stardom. They glow more brightly than other mere mortals." She cast a crooked smile Isabella's way.

The door slid open, and Isabella turned to find Jake standing in it, a newspaper clasped in fist.

"Why don't you go feed Odysseus, Katie Grace?" Alice said, for the expression on Jake's face portended a story. "See if his trainer will allow you to help curry him for the next show."

Jake flicked Katie Grace's braid as she walked past, but the moment her steps clicked around the corner, he faced Isabella, his jaw tense and his eyes grim.

"What's the matter? Is Mabel well?" A needling pain swept over Isabella's chest, and she stood on tiptoes to see over his shoulder.

"She's fine. Resting in our room." His loose-hipped stride ate up the space between them, and he thrust a newspaper toward her. "I wanted, for Mabel's sake, to believe better of you."

"What are you talking about?" Isabella took the paper.

Alice stood and began gathering her things. "I should leave."

Jake sighed and scrubbed a hand over his wrinkled brow. "No. I need your help. I don't know what to do, and I know you want what is best for Mabel." The look he shot Isabella said he didn't believe the same of her. "Just read it," he said, sounding very tired.

"This is the article written by Mr. Norris from the *New York World*?"

"Yes." He took a noisy breath and crossed his arms. "Who would have thought such a small, unimposing man could possess so vicious a tongue? I should have known not to expect anything other than drivel from a rag known for its yellow journalism."

Isabella read, her finger running beneath the small print. "It seems complimentary. I know Mabel doesn't enjoy so much focus on her body, but there's no . . ." The room went hot, then cold. Or maybe it was only her blood changing temperature so quickly. "Oh."

"Yes." Jake's voice was tight. Controlled. But beneath, fury simmered.

She reread the portion that had knocked the breath from her lungs.

In spending time with the couple, there is an unmistakable sense of something amiss. A kind of pragmatism disconnected from romance—oh, there is attraction, make no mistake of that. It hangs about them thick as last January's snow—but it is devoid of the sort of solidarity commonly found in marriages.

Of course, one doesn't expect lasting commitment in these relationships. The circus isn't the place for that. Divorce is as common as apples. When one marriage becomes a little dented or bruised, simply trade it in for a shinier one. But for America's favorite couple, it seems a disenchantment not to be a solid relationship.

Such a disappointment, given Mr. Cunningham's much-lauded previous marriage. There was a sweet truth about that relationship. It was easily understood and equal in standing. This newest one, though, is a mockery of the very institution upon which every good society is built.

Why would such a man, by all accounts still haunted by his wife's ghost, marry such a woman as Mabel MacGinnis?

There is only one answer. Given her perfect proportions and the unholy thing that must be present in the breast of such a woman to keep her in health, I believe it is simple lust that has brought them together.

So do not see them as a replacement for the previous Mr. and Mrs. Cunningham, for there is no comparison. One is an eternal tribute to marriage and the other is a flickering flame. It will likely be snuffed out very soon.

Upon reading the final word, Isabella shoved the detestable thing at Jake. A stone settled in her stomach, heavy and ragged. "Why do you blame me for this?"

"Who else? Mabel told me she's spoken to you of our"—he glanced at Alice—"situation."

"Only just recently, Jake."

He shrugged. "It wouldn't take much for him to change his story."

"You don't believe Mr. Norris is capable of teasing out the truth of the matter? He is a journalist. He understands people."

"You believe I married her for such a dishonorable reason?"

"No. Of course not. But I believe he could have sensed something was not right about your *situation*." She narrowed her eyes. "At least, I hope that is the case."

His cheeks flamed. "Nothing has happened between us, if that's what you're suggesting."

"I'm sorry. Truly." Alice rounded the table and pried the newspaper from Jake's grasp. "But since you have invited me into this conversation, I must understand what it's about."

As her gaze scanned the article, Jake, in starts and fits, explained the truth of their marriage.

"Well, there is something that must not happen. You cannot divorce her after New York. It would affirm this"—Alice waved the paper—"and leave her open to gossip. It could hurt her career. And also her heart." She huffed and slapped the paper onto the table. Then she carefully folded the costume, wrapped it in paper, and set it on the shelf behind her. When she turned back, she gave Jake a hard stare.

"I'm meant to return home. It's been our plan this entire time." He pressed his palms against his eyes.

"You may as well stop lying." Alice approached him, and he dropped his arms. "Everyone in this room knows you love your wife. Your marriage might very well have begun on false pretense, but at some point since, it changed."

"I . . ." Jake's gaze skittered around the room, and then he deflated. Every part of him settled into acknowledgment. His shoulder lifted in a small shrug.

"You were still planning on leaving? Despite how much you care for her?" Isabella shook her head. "Why?"

His eyes were stormy when he turned toward her. "I hate the circus. I hate what it took from me. I hate this particular one even above that." He didn't say he hated her, but she heard it all the same. "I do not want to be wed to it. And I do not want to be wed to a woman whose entire life is it." He lifted the paper from the table and shoved it under his arm. "Say nothing to Mabel of this. I will speak with her about it when the time is right."

When he left, Alice and Isabella looked at one another, saying nothing. But between them sprung a frisson of hope. For if Jake was willing to ignore his hate in order to see Mabel succeed, what could embracing his love accomplish?

❊ ❊ ❊

Mabel turned from the door. "Maman, Robert is here to speak with you."

Isabella stared into the dressing table mirror and kept her breath steady. It had been eleven days since their conversation at the cabaret. Eleven days since he'd sought her out after leaving her alone atop that roof, staring at the electric lights playing with the shadows. They had spoken since, of course. About work only, though. In monotone voices with the fewest words possible, their eyes darting over the other's shoulders, the air between them fraught with tension.

And now he had come to her? With a shaking hand, Isabella pinned another paste diamond into the crown of her hair and took a hitching breath.

"Maman?" Mabel murmured something, and the door slid closed. A moment later, she was on her knees beside Isabella, their hands clasping. "What is it?"

"Whatever has happened, Mabel, I want you to know that my only regret in leaving you is that it hurt you so deeply. But I'm sure you would not have ended up as bright and dear and wonderful as you are had I stayed."

"Don't say that. It isn't true." Mabel dropped Isabella's hands, wrapped her arms around her waist, and laid her head in her lap.

Isabella ran her palm over her daughter's head, careful not to disrupt the arranged curls. "I am a shameful woman. You've no idea the things I've done, and I won't tell you because I want so badly for you to love me. But I have hurt Robert. I have used him terribly."

Mabel lifted her head. "Will he force you to leave? I will stay with you here if he does. I'm certain we can find work with another circus. Travis and Wells isn't the only one."

"I don't think so. He isn't like that. But I feel exposed, and it's hard to endure when I've always hidden my secrets away. I'm afraid he wants to pull them from their pockets and lay them out in the open."

Mabel reached into her sleeve and withdrew the tiny doll. She tucked it between the satin of Isabella's sleeve and her skin. "For courage." Then she went to the door.

Turning back toward the mirror, Isabella rearranged the various pots and vials on her daughter's dressing table. Her heart pounded as Robert's heavy steps crossed the room. She wouldn't look at the mirror, for she didn't want him to see her face.

He stayed quiet as she lifted a box of blotting papers. Put it down again. Replaced the lid on a vial of perfume.

"Polly."

She jumped as though she hadn't known he stood there, waiting for her to speak. Or look at him. Or acknowledge this pain between them.

He slid a small cardboard box onto the table, and she glanced up. "You look beautiful. You're going to go out there and shine so brightly."

She ran her hands down her torso, over the gauzy fabric studded with hundreds of silver sequins. The short blue skirt, the same fabric used for Mabel's, puffed around her thighs. "I'm so happy Mr. Wells saw fit to allow Mabel and me to do this act. It's a dream, Robert. One I don't deserve."

"You deserve much more than you think." He pushed the box nearer with a finger. "Open it."

She pulled it into her lap and lifted the lid. Inside nestled two gold and diamond earrings—stars. Three large diamonds surrounded by smaller ones at the points. "Oh." Her fingers hovered over them, then dropped to her lap. They were beautiful. Too much. Too much for her.

Robert took up Mabel's former position with a chorus of creaking knees and a rueful smile. "We're getting old, Polly." He lifted one of the earrings, his thumb large and clumsy on the delicate post. "Let me."

She offered him her profile and sat absolutely still as he slid it into her earlobe. His fingers swept her jaw as he turned her head and slipped in the other one.

His hands gripping either side of the seat, he smiled. "Let me rephrase, *I'm* getting old. You look as lovely as that last day I saw you in Italy."

She pressed her palm to his dear cheek. "That was a hard day for you."

"Yes." He leaned into her touch. "But why should we continue having hard days? Tell me you feel nothing for me, and I will never say this again, but if you do—if even the smallest piece of your heart belongs to me—then there is no reason we should spend another minute in that place. And make no mistake, every day since you ran away to a different circus has been a hard one for me."

Isabella inhaled, trapping the breath in her lungs. Willing it to be enough to keep the darkness encroaching on her vision at bay. "Don't say it." She squeezed her eyes. "I cannot bear it."

"I will. Only once more." He leaned close enough that his peppermint-flecked breath swept her skin, reminding her of childhood. Of laughter and summer evenings spent running around as laborers tore down tents, and of mornings in Indiana and crunching through the frozen grass on the way to the ramshackle building housing the winter practice arena. Of friendship and years enough and Paul. Of a time before night corrupted the day. "I love you, Polly. I always have. And I want more than your body. I want you. Entirely. You. Always. I want you in my arms at night. I want you at my table in the morning. I want you rightly. Honestly. I want you knit to me—bone of my bone and flesh of my flesh. I want the impossible." He rested his forehead against hers. "To catch a star."

"Oh, Robert, you have no idea—none at all—of the things I've done. Of who I am."

Robert cupped her cheeks in his hands, and his kiss was whisper soft. His words, though, seemed almost reckless in their intensity. "You don't need to be who you've always thought you were. You decide, in this moment, what you can do. Who you can be."

Could she?

"I can do all things." Maman had often invoked this phrase as though it alone had the power to make it so.

Robert pulled back and tipped his head, brown eyes warm. "You say that sometimes, as though it's a talisman, and I remember your mother repeating it, but have you forgotten the rest of the verse? *I can do all things through Christst. . . .* Through him. You do not need to be alone in this."

Those words—*you do not need to be alone*—were a tantalizing possibility. Because she'd never not felt alone. Even in marriage. Even surrounded by thousands of spectators. Even when her daughter had been born. *Especially* when her daughter had been born, the cord sliced through with a scalpel, forever untethering them.

She wondered now if she'd *chosen* to be alone. And if this

was a moment to choose something different. To trust. To share some of her awful burden.

She covered her face. "I once tried to follow Paul."

Her words slid through her fingers, muffled and hardly audible, so she pulled her hands away and said them again. She wanted Robert to hear them. For when he heard, when he knew, would he take back his beautiful earrings and his beautiful words and recognize that the shadows no longer simply chased her but were a part of her?

Was his love what he said it was ... or only sleight of hand?

✻ ✻ ✻

Travis and Wells Circus had been built on a foundation of mesmerizing illusion. Come one, come all. See the enchanting, the impossible, the miraculous. None of it was true, of course. It was only hard work and a little marketing wizardry that made people flock by the thousands to Madison Square Garden to stumble their way through the sideshow and gasp their way through the big top performances. To dream of running away from snug farmhouses and drafty tenements and cavernous Fifth Avenue Mansions.

Isabella had spent nearly her entire life behind the scenes. Every pulled muscle, broken rib, and grueling, sleep-deprived hour proved the circus a fraud in many regards. But there had been moments over those years—few and far between but shining like a lighthouse beacon nonetheless—when she found herself entirely charmed by this life.

This was one of those moments. As she climbed atop the cannon and settled herself inside, arms crossed tightly over her chest and feet planted against the platform spring that would catapult her into the air, an absurd peace slipped over her. It felt warm and safe and right.

"*You must tell her,*" Robert had said in the dressing room. "*Tell her everything.*"

But she had balked. Mabel deserved to know. She deserved honesty. But Isabella had spent so long trying to forget. Could she purposely not only remember, but speak the memories aloud?

Isabella knocked against the side of the cannon, signaling her readiness for the latch to be released. She relaxed her body, and before another thought formed inside her mind, she was flying.

Above her, Mabel grabbed the bar and leapt from the platform. In one smooth movement, she lifted herself onto her seat, legs crossed at the ankles. Just as they'd rehearsed.

Isabella turned a somersault. Then another. A gasp practically shuddered the building as Mabel uncrossed her legs just as Isabella was about to glide past her, offering a handhold. With one powerful movement, Mabel launched Isabella up onto the bar. Her feet gripped it, and the trapeze jerked as Mabel slipped free and dangled in the air.

As they completed each movement—every flip and lift and rise—the ache that had taken residence in Isabella's spirit loosened. The stiffness that held her shoulders straight and rigid released.

She leaned into every beat of the routine and, skin sticky with effort, found something between their entwining limbs and grunts. A shiver of something she'd not experienced in ages.

Joy.

Isabella hoisted herself against the rope and gave Mabel time to position herself. She used her daughter's strength as a backdrop to her grace. Then, the last trick complete, they sat beside each other on the bar, and Isabella laughed. Below them, a thousand bright faces. But Mabel's outshone them all.

They each gripped the rope with one hand, their other braced against the bar between them, and Mabel's little finger brushed Isabella's. "I love you, Maman."

I can do all things. All things. Even speak the truth? *All things through Christ.* Yes. Even speak the truth.

A moment later, they swung toward the platform, and her daughter scrambled down the ladder and into the ring, where she would further prove Atalanta's strength.

I love you, Maman.

Isabella took hold of the trapeze bar. She was not alone.

I love you, Maman.

Her feet slid over the edge of the platform, and she swung around. Ignored her aching knees and pinching side and throbbing shoulder. She positioned herself for the finale.

I love you, Maman.

She soared.

CHAPTER
23

NEVER IN HIS LIFE had Jake considered having lunch above the dead. But here people were, sitting on blankets spread over the grass and graves, eating boiled eggs and pickles. A few children played ring-around-the-rosy with a statue of a cherubim as their parents picnicked nearby.

Jake's chest constricted, and his breaths came short and shallow. Not much stole the air from his lungs, but being here again, hemmed in by Trinity Church and a circle of twenty-story buildings, made him feel the way he had that time his horse bucked him into the air then fell on top of him.

But he'd been in New York for a month now, and Charlotte's ghost would give him no peace, he knew, until he visited. He could hear her voice rush from every alley he passed on his way from Hotel Veronica. In the rafters of the Garden. In Mabel's soft breath as she slept beside him.

*Jake, have you stopped loving me? Why don't you come? Do
you miss me even a little bit?*

Then he would see her pout, the one she'd always used to
get exactly what she wanted from him—from everyone—and
guilt would shred the fragile peace he'd constructed for himself
since leaving everything behind.

Even though he hadn't been to her grave since seeing her
buried, he could pick out the way with his eyes closed. He'd
gone over that day, and the ones preceding it, enough times in
his thoughts that he had worn a track of memories.

Jake paused about ten feet from Charlotte's grave. The tomb-
stone was a ridiculous affair of white marble and tumbling
stone roses. He hadn't chosen it. If it had been left to him, he
would have purchased a simple marker and been done with
it, but the people wanted a place to visit. A place to remember
all she'd meant to them.

A star. America's sweetheart. An angel sent to charm them
every spring.

She hadn't meant more to them than she had to him, and
he knew grief couldn't be measured in outward appearance,
but he had already escaped to Europe when the city contacted
Mr. Wells about erecting a more fitting monument.

There had been a letter, Jake remembered, from the circus
owner, but he was certain he'd tossed it into the fire after
reading the first paragraph. At least, nearly certain. Those first
few months had been lost to too much wine and a few forays
to Marseille's opium dens.

He knelt into the grass above his wife's body. A few brown
flowers, their petals long decayed, were strewn over Charlotte.
Nothing but stems. It was all very desolate and gothic. He
gathered them into a pile and placed them on the grass, then set
about pulling the weeds that had begun to sprout. Charlotte had
hated dandelions. *"Trickery and deceit"* she called them. *"Posing
as a flower but offering nothing except a few bitter salad leaves."*

She'd always loved beautiful things. Hothouse lilies and manicured rosebushes. House of Worth gowns and jewelry from Tiffany's.

"You are the most beautiful of all my belongings," she'd said to him once, and if he had been a less honest man, he would have refuted the claim—he was neither beautiful nor her belonging. But in actuality, he was both.

"Would you mind if I belonged to another?" The question slipped from his lips before he thought to stop it. Before he even really thought it through. And he knew the answer immediately.

Of course she would mind. Charlotte never did like to share. Not her things. Not the spotlight. And certainly not her husband.

Which had been fine when she lived and breathed and walked. But now?

Now he found himself fighting *against* the grief. Wanting to be free of it. Always before he'd wrapped it around himself, resisting its gentle lessening. He would spend hours at night staring at the ceiling of a train car, calling to memory all the beautiful moments. He would press his fingers to his lips and imagine they belonged to Charlotte. He would torture himself until the grief gave up its natural course and flooded him once more.

He had never taken a moment to look up from it. To see that there was someone directly in front of him who might fill the gaping loneliness left by Charlotte.

No, left by the conversation he'd had with Charlotte the night before she died.

"I'd rather live alone with the circus than with you on some dirty Kansas ranch."

The memory of it polluted all the others and cast aspersions on their love. Had it ever been true? Or had she simply picked the most beautiful man? The one who could catapult her career the highest?

And now Mabel. Sweet, lovely, transparent Mabel. Mabel, who would have been content to live out the rest of her days in her father's shadow, traveling with a small European circus— her fame localized to countries the size of New Jersey. Mabel, who had stared at him with round eyes the first time he'd stepped onto her stage and attempted to wrestle her to the ground. Mabel, who never spoke a cross word . . . unless it was in defense of her mother.

The woman who stole from him the opportunity to convince Charlotte he was worth more than acclaim. Worth more than the spotlight.

Maybe that was why he'd suggested Charlotte leave the circus and move to Kansas with him. He knew how much of her heart she'd given the stage. In those rare moments when he allowed himself to look at their marriage unvarnished by romance and glitter, he recognized that she'd earmarked only a corner of it for him. And if they were to have a child?

Jake ran his fingers over the etched letters of her name. *Charlotte Cunningham. America's Sweetheart. Beloved Aerialist.* And below, in much smaller letters, *Wife.* She would approve.

There wouldn't have been anything left for a child.

Unlike Mabel, whose own heart seemed to grow the more she filled it.

Jake stood and left the gravesite. He wove his way through families enjoying the fine spring weather alongside their sand-wiches and lemonade, not realizing until he crossed beneath the stone archway that he hadn't said good-bye to Charlotte.

He considered returning but quickly discarded the notion. He needed to find Mabel and warn her about the article. Then he would discuss with her the train ticket in his pocket.

Alice had said he needed to stay with Mabel or he would prove Mr. Norris right. But he thought it best if he left in the middle of it all and created one big scandal centered solely on him. Mabel would be blanketed by the public's compassion and goodwill. It would only further cement their adoration of her. And in a year or so, she could claim abandonment and file for a divorce, then marry again.

Marry someone willing to spend the rest of his life competing with the circus for his wife's attention.

※ ※ ※

Jake hadn't told her where he was going that morning. They'd slept late, as was typical on Sundays, and breakfasted. Jake had cast her long looks over the cloth-draped table of Hotel Veronica's cozy top-floor restaurant, but every time she raised her brows, he clamped his mouth shut and refocused on spreading eggs across his plate.

Then, just before lunch, he'd left. She shouldn't care—after all, he had no real obligation to inform her of his activities—but she did. She could feel it every moment he was gone. She sat at the window of their room and craned her neck so that she saw past the brick wall of the neighboring building, squinting to see down the slip of congested street.

Did this futile love make her weak? Was it foolish to feel that nothing else in the world mattered nearly as much as capturing that love in return?

There were expectations that came with being the world's strongest woman that had little to do with physical feats. Strength could be demonstrated in so many ways that it seemed absurd to her now to elevate one type so high above the rest.

Jake appeared around the corner of the building across from their window, and his familiar gait ate up the sidewalk. A sigh slid from Mabel's lips, and she watched his progress for a moment more before realizing he didn't walk alone.

She leaned her forehead against the window and blinked. Annette Aubert. She had her hand in his elbow and looked at him—not the street ahead—as they walked.

Numbness stole over Mabel's limbs. Had Jake left to spend time with Annette? Mabel knew the aerialist had eyes on her husband, but that meant nothing. Every woman of marrying age had eyes on her husband.

And until now, Jake had never shown the slightest interest in any of them.

"Calm down. Don't jump to conclusions." Mabel forced her breathing steady, shaking her arms until they began to tingle with renewed blood flow. It might mean nothing. Likely did mean nothing.

But she couldn't help watching as they crossed the street and headed toward the hotel entrance. They were beautiful together. Perfectly proportioned and made to fit like puzzle pieces.

She sat there for a few minutes after they disappeared from view, her thoughts chasing one another. They snapped and twisted until they became a woefully muddled tangle of grief and splintered hope.

The door to their room opened, and Mabel grabbed the mending she'd readied on the seat beside her so Jake wouldn't know she'd been waiting for him. She jabbed the needle through the fabric as he walked into the room and glanced up as though he'd interrupted her chore.

"Hello. Did you have a nice afternoon?" Other questions clawed at her throat, but she swallowed them and offered a placid smile.

He shrugged and sat on the bed but didn't look at her. He only propped his elbows on his knees and buried his head in his hands. He sat like that for some time—long enough that Mabel had mended the hole in his sock, then pulled out the thread, for it had turned out very clumsy and she knew Alice could accomplish much better in less time.

She tossed the jumble of thread and needle back into the basket. "Jake? Is something wrong?" He would tell her, surely, if he had fallen in love with Annette Aubert. He might not love her as she loved him, but he was honorable.

When he looked at her, sweat began to bead above her lip. His eyes were soft. Searching.

"What is it?" she whispered.

"There's something I have to show you, and I hate to do it. I hate to do anything that will bring you pain, but if I don't, then someone else will, and it's better you hear it from me." He stood and went to the dresser. Mabel watched, her brows knitting, as he pulled a newspaper from the bottom of his drawer and approached her. "It's not very flattering, I'm afraid."

She took it and smoothed her thumb over the wrinkles marring the article. As her eyes scanned the words, her body grew ever hotter until she thought her blood boiled beneath the surface of her skin.

"Not very flattering is an understatement," she said. She shoved it back at him and stood. "How long have I been walking around completely unaware I've been made a laughing-stock?"

He folded the paper and tapped it against his thigh. "Two days."

"And how did Mr. Norris come to the conclusion that there is something less than satisfactory about our marriage?"

"I thought it was your mother, but she seemed as confused as I—"

"You spoke with my mother about this before me? And she's seen me every day since and hasn't said a word." Her face flushed. "Who else knows about it?"

"Alice. And . . ." He gripped the back of his neck and stared at his shoes. "Annette brought it up a few moments ago. I'm certain everyone has seen it by now. I'm sorry. I should have told you first."

"Yes. Why didn't you?"

"I wanted to protect you from it. I didn't want it to distract you from your new act."

"Do you think me so feeble?" For years she'd walked around in a cloud of unsuspecting inadequacy. Everyone had been dishonest about her mother. Even her father had conspired against her. She'd been oblivious to the truth. Oblivious to the fact that no one thought her strong enough to handle it. Mabel MacGinnis, capable of mighty feats—she could bend a steel bar at whim and outwrestle any man—but it was all performance. When it came to the things that truly mattered, everyone thought her weak.

"No. Of course not." Jake turned as she walked past him. "I'm sorry, Mabel. Truly. I had no ulterior motive in keeping this from you for so long. I only wanted to wait until the right moment to share it with you. Are you angry at me?"

She stopped at the door, her hand on the knob. "I'm not angry. Only very disappointed."

In him. In Maman. Certainly in Mr. Norris. In Da for not equipping her to deal with such things. And in her own failures.

"Where are you going?"

She didn't answer. She slipped from the room and padded down the hall, head down, until she bumped into someone.

Annette brushed at her skirt as though she'd been toppled to the floor. "Really, Mabel, you ought to pay attention better. You're too large to be careening into unsuspecting passersby."

Mabel made to walk by, but Annette cleared her throat.

"Did Jake speak with you about the article in the paper? How vicious it was." She tapped a finger to her chin in a mockery of deep thought. "Of course, it is very much a family trait, is it not? You cannot help what you've inherited."

Mabel heaved a heavy sigh, loud enough for Annette to hear. "What are you saying?"

"Well, only that it makes sense you've caught a man such

as Jake with your"—her gaze skimmed Mabel from head to toe—"physical attributes when your mother relies equally as much on such things."

Mabel blinked.

"You're confused, I can see." Annette stood on tiptoe, bracing her hands against Mabel's arms, and spoke in a stage whisper. "Your mother is only still employed because of her . . . *particular friendship* with Mr. Pedersen." Mabel recoiled, and Annette stumbled forward. She caught herself with a laugh. "I brought it to the attention of Mr. Wells." She shrugged. "But she always has been a favorite of his."

"I know you don't like me or my mother, Annette, but even for you, this is vile." Mabel began walking again, though she wasn't sure how she managed to lift her feet from the carpet, as heavy as they were.

"I think it's because Isabella was engaged to his son."

Mabel's steps paused, a deep, rhythmic thud pounding against her chest.

"Before he tossed himself into the Ohio River, that is. Your mother isn't very good at keeping lovers, is she? I wonder how long it will take for Mr. Pedersen to realize it."

Something unfurled in Mabel's belly. It poured heat into her blood and filled her mouth with bile. She began once more to walk away, but it spurred her forward, and the doors blurred as she passed them in a jog, her new wing-tip walking boots slapping against the floor.

Still she heard Annette's taunting laugh, like a bell or the soft sound of water running over rocks. Lovely and gentle and everything Mabel was not.

❅ ❅ ❅

Robert hadn't taken back his earrings the way Isabella expected. Not even when she told him her most desperate secret.

She'd thought, when she decided to stay in New York all

those years ago, that she would escape it. That it would be buried so deep in her memories, she would never have to consider what she'd nearly done ever again. But the burden of it had grown heavier through the years until it was almost a relief to tell him.

She leaned over her dressing table and touched the tiny stars. How lovely they were. How lovely *he* was. Running her fingers over her cheek and beneath her chin the way Robert had done the day before after fastening them to her ears, she felt every wrinkle. Every bit of sagging skin. And for once, she cared little about it.

She was loved again.

Could she love in return, when it had always before been entwined with loss? The men she'd chosen ended up choosing other things—Paul, death. Bram, life.

Of course, it wasn't a direct comparison. Bram had chosen *her* life over her, at least initially. Then he had chosen his life and Mabel's without her, as she'd become a liability.

But it all amounted to the same thing—she was not meant for love. She was not enough for love.

When would Robert realize it? Could she bear it? She straightened her shoulders. Robert had pined decades for her. He knew everything—every ugly detail and failure and fear— yet still he remained steadfast.

Her blood turned as warm and thick as zabaglione. It lulled her into a hazy place of possibility. She leaned against the chair, letting her head flop back, and allowed herself to give in to it. Envision a life with Robert. Safe again. Secure in love.

It had been so long.

A firm knock sounded at the door.

"Come in." Isabella turned to look at the door as it opened and sat upright with a smile when Mabel entered. "Darling. How nice of you to stop by."

Mabel crossed the room, her arms stiff at her sides and

hands fisting a fashionable pleated skirt of lavender gingham. Isabella scooted to the edge of her seat and turned to follow Mabel's progress to the window. Her daughter stood there, her fingers on the edge of the open curtain, and peered at the bustling street, shoulders high and straight.

"Is something wrong?" Isabella went to her, drawing back sharply when Mabel shrugged away from her touch.

"Yes." Mabel turned and stared at Isabella, eyes narrowed, lower lip tucked between her teeth. Then she shifted her gaze to the wall over Isabella's shoulder. "Are you . . ." She swallowed hard, and her jaw tightened. "Were you engaged before Da?"

The question came with no warning. No introduction. Isabella could hardly process that her daughter stood before her, asking about Paul. She had never even mentioned the engagement to Bram. Her first fiancé's memory was too tangled with grief and confusion. *"You must tell her,"* Robert had said, and she'd planned to. In bits and pieces, spread out over the years that stretched ahead of them, like morsels of cake fed to a child. Too much at once, and it might make one ill.

"Yes." Mabel's head jerked up at Isabella's confession. "His name was Paul Wells."

"What happened to him?" Mabel whispered.

"He committed suicide. The day after we were engaged."

"Why?"

Isabella shrugged. She had asked herself that question so many times in the days after Paul's death—*Why? Why? Why?*—that the word had ceased to mean anything. Why had darkness so smothered his light that he saw no way forward but out? Why had he proposed, pretended happiness—given Isabella all she'd wanted from the moment her father was snatched away by a Confederate soldier too young for whiskers—then stolen it with one quick leap? Why hadn't she been enough to stay his desperation? His torment? Why hadn't she been strong enough to resist them herself?

There was no peace in *why*. No answers to be had. The question was an eternal torture.

She turned away and crossed the room, her dressing gown sweeping the floor. "Sit with me." She drew the chairs from beneath the small round table in the corner of the room and took one.

Mabel's gaze bounced from Isabella to the chair to the door, but she indulged the request.

Isabella whispered a quick *I can do all things*, adding *through Christ* when she remembered she wasn't alone. Then she launched them into the sadness.

"He had always battled unseen things. Thoughts that tormented him. He was brooding. Serious. Almost fatalistic. And so handsome it hurt to look at him." He'd had eyes shaped like Spanish almonds, hooded and turned down at the corners. She hadn't let herself think on them since that night, consigning the memory of his beauty to the river. "We grew up together, along with Rowena and Robert."

Mabel's jaw clenched. "You loved him."

"Yes."

"Even after you married Da?"

There was condemnation in Mabel's tone that Isabella couldn't comprehend. "What was I to do with it? Shove it in a trunk? That kind of love doesn't just go away. It stays with you forever. It lodges in your heart and becomes a hot, poking prick with every beat. It's *always* there, no matter how far you go to get away from it."

"Did you ever love Da?"

"Of course I did."

"And have you carried that love into this new liaison? Does Da's memory prick your heart when you're with Robert Pedersen? Do you imagine his arms around you instead of the circus manager's?"

Isabella remembered when the water rose back when she

was Polly. She remembered how it spread around her legs and caught her skirt, lifting it so that the fabric ballooned. How its icy fingers prodded her chest, somehow reaching through skin and cartilage and muscle to tighten around her lungs, stealing all her air.

She took a few gasping breaths now and reminded herself she sat in her room. That lake was as far from her as anything ever could be.

But it wasn't. Not really. It never was.

"How do you know about that?"

"Does it matter?" Mabel looked down at her hands, tightly clenched atop the table. "Why would you, Maman? How could you?"

Isabella wrapped her arms around her middle and tucked the dangling sleeves beneath her elbows. "I thought it would save my career."

Mabel flinched. "Jake told me you were solely focused on success. I didn't believe him." She looked at Isabella, her blue eyes as cold as the lake. As deep and unrelenting. "Is that why you agreed to do the act with me? To bolster your sagging career?"

"No! Of course not." Isabella reached across the table and grabbed Mabel's hands in her own. "I wanted to do it because I wanted to spend time with you."

Mabel gave a small shake of her head and pulled her hands away. She dropped them into her lap.

Isabella stared at her own fingers splayed over the table. Thanks to a lifetime of gloves, her hands were still as pale as a tomb, not a freckle or sunspot marring them. But fine lines crisscrossed her skin, bunching up around her knuckles like sagging stockings. "I've always used my body to further my career. I've punished it. Put it on display. Done terrible things to it for the sake of the circus. So it seemed a small thing to give it to Robert. But I never have, and never will, use you."

She reached for the stars in her lobes, which suddenly felt too heavy. She slipped them off and tucked them into her palm, the posts digging into her skin.

"When did it start? While Da was alive?"

"I was faithful to your father until after I learned he'd died." Isabella pressed one of the earrings with her thumb, forcing the sharp end deep. Her roughened skin gave beneath it—an almost audible *pop*—the blessing of momentary release carried by a pinching pain.

Darkness whispered. Isabella's shame could be taken away by the painfully cold water. The abiding knowledge that she deserved nothing else. It was a punishment. A release.

A freedom.

She shook the earring free and tossed the pair onto the table. "If it helps, I regret it fully. I wish I hadn't debased myself so completely. And I'm so terribly sorry, Mabel, that I disappointed you."

"I forgive you," her daughter whispered.

And Isabella's small act of penance seemed very small in the face of such a gift.

"Annette said Mr. Wells has a particular fondness for you and that's why he didn't force you out of the circus."

Caustic heat flooded Isabella's blood, but she took a few deep breaths and focused on the beauty of her daughter. Her gaze traced the handsome lines of Mabel's face, and her heart fell into a gentle cadence. She would deal with the gossipy Annette later.

"Your grandmother found Paul in the shallow water before anyone else was awake. She was with Mr. Wells when he found out about his son's death. He'd come in on the train early that morning, expecting a reunion, but found a body instead. He never knew Paul had proposed to me, though I'm sure he was aware we held an affection for one another. He was always grateful to my mother for discovering Paul's body. And I think he looks fondly on my childhood friendship with his son."

Mabel slid her hand slowly over the table, her finger pushing at one of the earrings. "Mr. Wells likely would have offered you a position, then, even if you couldn't perform anymore. Why not see what he would do?"

"I was afraid. After spending a lifetime doing something I loved, I couldn't imagine being happy doing manual labor, and I'm not qualified for anything else. And I'm vain, Mabel. Proud. Maman's beauty was conquered quickly in the laundry." It was an easy deflection. One readily believed. Mabel's perception of her had been damaged already. She wouldn't tell her that the last time her work had been taken from her, she'd very nearly lost herself to melancholy. "When you're faced with loss, you don't always make rational decisions. Sometimes you do foolish things in the hope that something will fix it, but it only makes it worse."

"Why didn't you tell me about it?" Mabel swallowed hard, and her words were painted with hurt. "I feel very foolish that I had to hear about this from Annette."

"I didn't want to be even more diminished in your eyes. I have done so few things right. And the knowledge wasn't something I wished to burden you with."

"I would have been here for you. I always will be."

"I know that now. But for so long I was alone." Isabella shrugged. "I suppose I became used to trusting no one and doing it all on my own." It was different for Mabel. Whereas Isabella thought she *must* do it without others, Mabel thought she could do nothing without others.

"You don't feel that way now?"

Isabella smiled and scooped the earrings back into her palm. "I've recently been reminded that perhaps I'd forgotten about God." She slipped the posts into her ears and the weight of them settled her. "And now I have you."

CHAPTER 24

FORGIVENESS CAME EASY. It was as simple as recognizing that people often made mistakes and rarely lived up to one's expectations. Mabel had told Maman she forgave her. She'd meant it too.

But that didn't mean she could as easily forget.

When she bumped, quite literally, into Robert Pedersen on her way to the elevator later that same afternoon, she couldn't stop the flush from coloring her face.

He let her enter first, and when she turned to smile at the attendant, her gaze met his. She quickly looked away but could feel his stare on her as the floors slipped past. She hadn't greeted him. That would have been the normal thing to do. But how could she be expected to behave normally with what she knew?

She hoped the floor would open up and swallow her, but the ground remained firm beneath her feet. Only the gate opened.

She rushed from the elevator and hurried toward the front of the hotel, eager to reach the doors.

"Mabel."

Her feet stopped churning, and she paused at the fringed edge of a tired Persian carpet. He would ask her what the matter was. And she would have to explain—

She couldn't explain.

His heavy footsteps sounded behind her. How fascinating that she could so clearly hear them despite the noise of the room—the people chatting in low voices, the crisp *ting* of the front desk bell, the soft *swish* of the great door being opened and closed.

His steps stopped. "Will you walk with me?"

She nodded and, without a glance in his direction, stepped out onto the street.

His stride wasn't as long as hers, but he kept up easily. He said nothing as they traveled down Madison Avenue and the streets became more congested. Automobiles vied for space with handcarts and horses. Pedestrians became more aggressive, paying little regard to either, while elbows jabbed and voices rose. There was a raw energy beneath it all. An anticipation of possibility.

They walked another block until Mabel found herself staring up at a building boasting her own twelve-foot likeness on its side. Her mouth fell open, and she heard a strangled sound in her throat. "What?"

"They've been pasted all over the city," Robert said. "Mr. Wells wants everyone in New York to know about Atalanta. To fall in love with you."

"To fall in love with *her*. That isn't me, Robert."

He lifted his chin and studied the lithograph. "It looks just like you, though. They didn't change anything. They normally do, but everyone has heard you're a paragon of beauty."

"It's indecent." Mabel's gaze traveled the length of her legs, bare but for the slight sheen of tights. The leotard she'd felt so exposed in now gave the entire populace of Manhattan a front-row seat to her décolletage. Her shoulders and arms. The turn of her waist. She had hated the photographs she'd taken for the doctors. Had hated feeling as though every inch of her was being measured. Judged. Held against some standard she hadn't known existed. She hated these garishly colored illustrations that had been made from them. And now that moment she reviled so much was being exploited.

She was being exploited.

And she'd let them do it.

"I've always used my body to further my career. I've punished it. Put it on display. Done terrible things to it for the sake of the circus."

Mabel had settled into a pompous kind of self-righteousness while listening to Maman say such things. But was she any different?

Only in a matter of degree.

"I need to get away." Mabel turned from her image and began pushing through the crowd. She ignored a man shouting at her and ducked just in time to miss being soaked by something tossed out a third-story window.

"Come on." Robert guided her to the side of the street and hailed one of the bright yellow taxicabs. It puttered to a stop beside them, and the handsome driver hopped from his place behind the box. "Bleecker Street," Robert said.

The driver nodded, then gave Mabel a rakish smile. "Ma'am." He pulled open the door.

She glanced inside—a tight squeeze—and back at Robert. "Is it safe?" It didn't look it, with the top half being almost completely encased in glass and nothing powering it—no horse at all—except for whatever made the rumbling sound beneath the driver's seat.

"Perfectly." The driver held out his hand. "The New York

Taxicab Company is pleased to offer Mrs. Mabel Cunningham her very first ride." She shot him a sharp glance, and his grin widened. "I saw you perform three days ago."

Had he seen the bill? Her cheeks heated. When she glanced away from him, her eyes met those of a man across the street, who gave her a lascivious wink. She was certain he'd seen it. Had every man walking by seen it?

Maman had compromised with only one man. Mabel had compromised with the entire population of America's largest city. It hadn't been necessary either. She could have said no. She hadn't been at risk of losing her job.

Robert leaned close. "You're aware you're the world's strongest, bravest, most courageous woman, right? Will you let a taxicab defeat you?"

She chuckled, grateful for his gentle humor. "Very well." She took the driver's hand and allowed him to help her inside before he pressed his gloved fingers to his lips in a romantic gesture reminiscent of Lorenzo reciting one of his poems.

Robert settled beside her. "You have your mother's innate charm," he said after the door had been shut. The conveyance jostled and groaned as the driver climbed back into his seat.

Mabel sent him a sidelong look, then returned her attention to the passing street.

She only had a moment of quiet before Robert spoke again. "Your mother spoke with you."

"Annette Aubert."

"Ah." He shifted, and she glanced at him. "She's felt threatened by Isabella since the first day she started with us."

Mabel raised her brows. "Why? Was she not hired to replace Maman?"

Robert leaned against the seat and stared out the window facing them. "Did you know of Isabella Moreau before you came to New York? Not as your mother but as a performer."

"Yes, of course. Everyone knows of her. I caught Da staring

at a photo of her once. I thought he only thought her beautiful when he hid it in his trunk." She watched Robert carefully as she said it. Looked for a tightening of his jaw or a narrowing of his eyes. To his credit, he only smiled.

"She was beautiful. Still is. But it was always more than that. I cannot overstate how far and wide and deeply she was adored. Possibly the greatest circus performer who has ever been."

"I thought that was Charlotte Cunningham."

He shook his head. "Charlotte was only beloved in as much as she was part of a treasured couple. Isabella was—always will be—set apart. A star glittering in the sky. Almost untouchable. Vibrant. Enough on her own to brighten the darkness. And Annette is meant to fill her shoes. She knows she never will. Someone like your mother comes around once in a lifetime. Once in a century. I've no doubt Annette will be forgotten soon after she retires. Your mother never will be."

"Mr. Wells is ending her career."

"Because he wants to honor your grandmother and keep your mother safe. He had so much respect for your grandmother, you know. She reminded him of his own mother. And she found his son." He stroked his beard, then clasped his hands over his middle. "Your mother isn't young anymore. Every time she climbs that rope, every time she swings from that platform, she comes closer to the moment when she can no longer hold on. Isabella will never admit this, and her career has lasted longer than most aerialists', but she cannot keep up. Age has a way of humbling even the strongest of us."

"You don't seem to mind her age. Her fading strength and beauty."

His face softened. "I have loved her for so long, I only see everything she's always been. And she is still so beautiful."

"You took advantage of her. You knew she was desperate. You knew she felt she had no other choice. That doesn't seem like love."

His shoulders heaved beneath the weight of a sigh. "I know. It was wrong. I thought . . . I thought it might change her mind about marriage."

The rumble of the engine filled the silence. It rattled the windows and buzzed beneath her ribs. "Marriage? Maman said nothing about marriage."

"No. She doesn't feel worthy. It frightens her."

"Why?"

Robert stared out the glass, his gaze tracking the automobile in front of them. "Have you ever been rejected?"

"Yes."

"It's a painful thing, isn't it? It reaches inside you, and no amount of rationale, no understanding that it has little to do with you, diminishes that pain. It weaves itself around your heart, digging deeper and deeper, producing a sharp, stabbing kind of hurt, until you heal *over* it. Until it becomes part of you. The pain becomes a dull ache that can sometimes be ignored but never really goes away. It's still there, except now you can't free yourself from it, so you learn to live with it. You pretend it's not there and that it's bearable. It's not. You've just gotten used to pain. You've forgotten what it's like to not suffer from it." Robert's words trailed off as the taxicab ground to a stop.

Mabel stared at him and rolled the things he'd said around her thoughts. She polished them like stones and tucked them away so she could take them out later and think on them. How long had it been since she'd lived without pain? She hardly noticed it anymore, just as he said. But there it was, crouching within, clawing at her memories and thoughts and the things she believed about herself.

Had it been since she discovered Da's lies? Had it been since Maman left and never returned?

No. It had been much longer than that. She could remember Maman's face—her beautiful lips twisting, disappointment evident as she looked at Mabel. Her lids slowly closing as though she couldn't bear the sight of her own daughter anymore. *"She is much too big. She always has been."*

Since then?

The dull throb awakened. Pinched and poked and burned and came alive once more. Mabel's eyes brimmed with tears as the driver helped her out. He pressed his hand over his heart and bowed.

Robert paid him and then, with a hand on Mabel's back, guided her up the sidewalk until they reached a narrow shop fronted with glass. Mabel blinked and finally noticed where he had led her.

The words *Barsanti Latticini* gilded the glass on both sides of the open door. At the corner, just in front of the *enoteca* tucked beside the cheese shop, a vendor stood beside his flat wagon, shucking clams and handing them to a group of old men sporting wool caps and stained shirts who slurped and sighed.

A shout wended across the street, and when Mabel turned, she saw a sturdy woman, stained apron tied around her waist, yanking at the arm of a small boy who ducked beneath her slapping palm. Lines of carts marched down the street on both sides, hardly far enough apart to allow the customers who squeezed plump eggplants and heads of purple garlic to slide between.

And around it all, between it all, was the music of Bologna. The Italian words settled her whirling thoughts and filled her heart so that nothing was left but the warmth of Italy's sun and cobbled streets and ancient churches. And for the first time since leaving, she missed it.

She looked at Robert and raised her brows.

"Piccola Italia." Little Italy. He smiled and offered his arm, which she took.

Inside the shop, Mabel found herself staring at a glass-fronted case full of the most wonderful delights—soft balls of mozzarella and piles of ricotta, and wheels of hard-rind cheeses stacked atop one another like building blocks.

"Do you want anything?" Robert asked.

Mabel smiled at the man behind the counter. His white teeth flashed, eyes sparking with curiosity. "Can I just have a little *ricotta tutta cream*?" she asked in Italian.

His brows shot to the mass of curls spilling over his forehead, and he quickly scooped a few spoonfuls into a tin cup. After a sprinkle of cocoa powder and a savage whip with a spoon, the snack was presented to her. "You are from Italy?" he asked, and the dimple in his chin reminded her of Jake's.

They spoke of home until Robert cleared his throat and ordered a slice of squacquerone that the cheesemonger wrapped in waxed paper and tied with twine.

"That's Maman's favorite," Mabel said after she finished her cup of ricotta.

"Yes. I try to buy her some when we're in New York. There's a bakery down the street where I can buy *piadina*. I remember the first time we stumbled onto this shop—it was, oh, eleven years ago. She cried all the way back to Madison Square Garden as she ate it."

Mabel didn't say, but she knew why Maman had cried. Every day after a long practice in Manzo Brothers's rickety winter auditorium—really, it was an old mortadella factory whose porky scent never really dissipated—they would stumble from the building all wrapped in thick coats and scarves and, halfway home, stop to buy squares of cheese from Maman's favorite cheese shop. They would eat it with olives and sardines and the unleavened bread Maman loved to wrap around their modest dinner while watching snow fall and blanket the city.

Mabel counted it among her most treasured memories. Maman would too.

They left the shop and started up the street in search of bread. "You must love her very much," she said.

He stared forward, his lips quivering into a smile. "So much. For so long." He patted her hand, which was tucked into his elbow, and gave her a paternal smile. Mabel found she didn't mind it. "It is my goal now to make sure she feels wanted and valued. And so loved she could not imagine leaving it."

They crossed the street beside a boy in short pants and scuffed shoes holding the hand of a young woman, her long dark hair unhampered by a hat.

"*Mamma,*" the child said, "you are the prettiest in the world." The boy turned his face up, and his mother swept him into her arms, eliciting a giggle.

Mabel smiled and watched them as she and Robert passed by. And then another image took its place. Da walking into the yard where Maman had been helping her flip around a bar, his booming laugh drawing Mabel's attention. His open arms pulling her away from practice. Away from Maman.

"*Bram, she must work on this.*" Maman's voice had hit a high note, and she puffed at the hair settling over her brow.

Da had scooped Mabel into his arms and tossed her into the air. "*What say you, my strong girl? Do you want to practice flips with Maman or come with me and learn how to bend steel?*"

"*You.*" Mabel had giggled.

She always chose him. Because she knew she was no good at flipping or swinging. At least, she'd thought so because of the sadness draping her mother, the distraction present in her darting gaze. And besides, bending metal was fun.

She chose Da because he laughed and joked and everyone loved him. Respected him. When she was with Maman, people averted their eyes. They whispered too, though Mabel never heard what they said.

She'd forgotten that. Forgotten all of it but the parts that made *her* feel rejected.

She grabbed Robert's hand. "Maybe, between the two of us, we can help her see how very much she is wanted."

He squeezed her fingers. "Maybe we can."

*   *   *

Jake had never needed much sleep. Even as a child, he'd awaken before the sun and have his chores completed before anyone else got up. If there was even a promise of light, he preferred to take advantage of it.

But since marrying Mabel, he seemed unable to resist the call of their bed. He curled his body around hers, feigning sleep for hours before it finally stole his consciousness. And sometimes he woke early enough that he could watch her at rest, his gaze tracing the lines of her face and neck and shoulders and hips beneath the blankets.

A few times, he'd woken in the middle of the night and felt her gentle touch. She would run her fingers down his back or sweep them through his hair. Once she'd pressed her lips to the naked skin of his neck, her breath warm yet managing to send chills up and down his arms. He'd pretended to sleep then too. Because what would she do if he revealed he knew she loved him?

What would *he* do?

"I'm done," Mabel said.

He turned and watched as she crossed the room, her linen nightgown swishing around her feet. She moved with a grace that belied the power of her muscled limbs. Perhaps from the acrobatic training she'd had as a child and picked up again with him. Or maybe because she was the perfect blend of strength and softness.

She was a delight to watch, and he found himself doing more of it since that interview where she revealed her heart. He'd always before ignored the possibility that she loved him. He'd noticed from the start of their friendship that she favored him, of course. Mabel was nothing if not transparent. She had no idea about the art and artifice of flirtation.

But when he could no longer pretend hers was a childhood fancy, he found his own feelings had changed in the meantime.

How could he have let that happen? Falling in love with a woman married to the circus. Again. He thought he'd learned his lesson.

Mabel settled against the headboard and studied him as he buttoned his nightshirt. "Isn't it funny," she said, her gaze on his legs, "that I wear less in the ring, and much less in advertisements, than I do to sleep? Than even *you* do to sleep? It seems it should be the opposite, does it not? Why should I be trussed up like a Christmas turkey in bed when all of New York has seen me practically naked?"

Her statement sent his mind careening toward things better left unexplored, and he forgot to breathe for a second.

"Would you like to sleep naked?" he asked before he could stop himself, then closed his eyes. "I'm sorry. That was inappropriate."

But when he looked at her again, there was yearning between those thick smudges of sooty lashes. And that was not safe. A man could drown in the promise of it. Could dismiss all inhibitions. Could forget what he hated if he remembered what it was to love.

The bed creaked beneath Mabel's weight, and she sniffed, the sound disrupting the blood pounding in his ears. She'd pulled one corner of her nightgown high above her knee and was tracing the tattooed flower with the tip of her finger. Her quadricep shifted beneath the ink, and Jake forced his eyes off her leg.

Since Charlotte had died, he'd had no issue controlling his passions. No woman came close to tempting him. But now he found himself in the very awkward position of being so attracted to his wife that he wanted nothing more than to hold her. To love her. To give her all of himself. But more than that, he recognized that satiating the physical wouldn't be enough. Not by far. She was so much more than nice legs. He wanted all of her, and how could he do that without destroying her?

Past experience told him it was an impossibility. Fame was a jealous lover.

Mabel sniffed again, and a shaky sigh lifted from her lips.

"What's wrong?" He sat beside her. "What's happened?"

"I . . . I feel as though I've compromised. I've given away my dignity. There are bills of me everywhere, Jake. And they're mortifying in their immodesty. No one thinks anything of it, I'm sure, for I'm a performer and it's a science, isn't it, to study me. Categorize me and break me down into parts. They have a right to my body. They have a right to fall in love with me because of it. I am an oddity, and because of that, able to be objectified in a maddeningly proper manner." She looked at him, those thick lashes wet and spikey. Her cheeks pale except for two spots of color. "It feels as though I'm expected to give my body to the entire world, but I'm not allowed to give it to the one person I most want to. Possibly the only person who really has a right to it."

His mouth went dry. His throat went dry. "I'm moving to Kansas."

"Must you?"

He nodded. Then stopped. Must he? Why? Ostensibly to help his brother. And because he hated the circus. He wouldn't lose another wife to it. He should leave Mabel to her fortune and marry a farmer's daughter. Someone sturdy and good-natured whose only ambitions were home and hearth. "You love performing."

"I do." She reached for his face and laid gentle fingers against his cheek, her thumb slipping over his lower lip. Her skin smelled like oranges. "But I love you too."

"Mabel."

She took his hand and placed it over the flower, and her skin was soft against his palm. She leaned near, her mouth brushing his. "Mr. Norris said you must have married me for lust."

"I didn't." His heart beat against his chest, sharp and incessant in a way that robbed him of breath.

"No. You wouldn't. You had a real marriage once. A complete one. And I'm nothing like her, am I?" She gave a humorless laugh and pulled back, then stood so that her nightgown fell to her feet once more. "I forgot, for a minute, all about her."

So had he. He should feel guilty about it, but he didn't. Charlotte had died years ago, and for the first time, he saw her through the lens of distance. Saw their marriage through the lens of having experienced another—even an incomplete one. It was a betrayal, the things he now thought.

Mabel walked by, and he reached for her, fingers brushing her hip.

"I think I'm going to spend the night with my mother." She didn't look at him. Only started for the dressing gown she'd hung on a hook by the dresser. "I'm sorry, Jake. I don't know what I was thinking."

"Don't apologize. You did nothing wrong."

She shoved her arms into the gown and made quick work of the buttons. "I'm more like my mother than I thought."

"In what way? You're nothing like her."

"You have no idea."

She started for the door, and he was going to let her leave. He was going to let her walk away after exposing her heart, because he was . . . what? Upright. A man of his word. So dedicated to helping his brother with a ranch he'd hated that he was willing to lose this beautiful, wonderful, brilliant woman. Because he was too proud to risk hurt again.

And an idiot. The world's biggest.

Mabel opened the door and stepped into the hall. Jake

leapt from the bed and dashed after her. "Wait. Mabel, wait." He reached her and grabbed the door just before it shut. "Wait."

There was a pause. It felt like eternity. Then she stepped back inside.

He'd spent his entire life taking risks, but never before had he thought he might actually fail. Might actually fall. Until now.

But his blood pumped with risk.

"I do want you. Every part of you." He pressed his hand against her waist and ran it down over her hip. Pulling her near with his other hand at her back, he circled her with his arms.

She made a gasping sound that sent his pulse racing. And then her lips were against his, and he found she *tasted* of oranges too.

"I love you. I tried not to. But you made it so difficult."

She laughed beneath his mouth and kissed him with an abandon Charlotte had never allowed herself. Kissed him with a fervor he never imagined possible. Kissed him until his lips were bruised and kissing no longer seemed enough.

He swept her up, one arm beneath her knees and the other at her back, and pressed his mouth against the gentle slope of her neck, right where it met her shoulder in an enticing curve of bare skin above the lace of her gown. "Are you sure, Mabel? Truly? Because once this happens, we can't go back."

She was silent, and he pulled back to look at her to see if she had changed her mind. If she had come to her senses. It wasn't wise, this wildness, and he was showing his weakness. She was the stronger of them, in every way.

But her eyes were round with wonder, not regret. "You can lift me."

"I've been wrestling you for years."

"But you always lost."

He made a firm pivot and strode toward the bed. "Not this time."

＊　＊　＊

The sound of shouting awakened Mabel. She jerked upright with a gasp, clutching the blanket to her chest.

"I think Katie Grace has lost her cat," Jake said. And then the most delicious feeling shuddered through her as he ran his finger up the center of her bare back. "You are beautiful." His mouth left a trail of kisses where he'd touched, and the mattress shifted as he sat up beside her. "Perfect, really."

"I'm not perfect." Mabel's face flamed, and she ducked against her bent knees.

He swept the fall of her hair from her shoulders, and his breath was warm against her ear. "Perfect. And strong. You are what dreams are made of, Mabel Cunningham. I can scarcely believe they've come true."

She looked at him then, her heart in her throat. In his hands. "I hardly let myself dream at all . . ."

Then his lips were on hers, and she wondered if it would be terribly inconsiderate to plead exhaustion and skip the early show.

A determined knock disabused her of the idea. "Mabel! Jake! I need your help!" Katie Grace slammed her hand against the door. "Octavia needs your help!"

Mabel leapt from the bed. "We're coming."

She set about throwing on her clothes, stopping only momentarily when she caught Jake's gaze as he watched her from beneath hooded eyes. She had no experience in seduction. Maman had left before teaching her how to flirt. And anyway, did one flirt with a husband?

She slowed her frantic movements and took her time dressing. She noticed how his gaze swept her from head to toe. How his bare chest rose and fell with the quickening of his breath. How his jaw softened and his lips parted.

Turning, she reached for the combination settled into a heap atop the dresser, then drew her hair over her shoulder and let her fingers trail over her waist.

Jake watched. He stared. She was almost certain he stopped breathing.

She had never felt more powerful. Had never before, during any lift or trick, experienced such sweeping strength. The thrill of it coursed through her, prickling the hairs on her arms. It made her brazen.

He was her husband. And after the night before, every bit of inadequacy she'd felt, every bit of comparison she'd made of herself to Charlotte's delicate beauty, every bit of timidity had fallen from her as easily as her nightgown. Jake had made it clear he delighted in her. And that filled her more than hundreds of cheering spectators ever could.

With a little growl, he pushed off the blankets, and she shrieked and darted as he gave chase. He was fast. She, unwilling to escape. His arms circled her, and he nuzzled her neck.

Another knock came. "Stop playing games and come help me. I can hear you. I know you're awake."

Jake chuckled. "We've been summoned."

Mabel sighed.

With their demanding neighbor keeping them to task, they readied quickly and met Katie Grace and Alice in the hall.

"Octavia has escaped." Alice blew the fringe from her forehead with an exasperated puff. "I told her to leave the cat at Mrs. Luvotti's. How will she keep track of it? Especially once we leave New York."

Katie Grace glared at her mother, then pointed a finger at Mabel and Jake. "What took you so long?" She shook her head. "Never mind. Just help me find her."

Jake raised his brows, then affected a fanciful bow. "Your Majesty. I will check the ground floor." He set off toward the elevator, whistling a jaunty tune.

"He seems happy this morning." Alice elbowed Mabel. "You both do."

Mabel bit down on a grin and bent to look beneath a table boasting a clutch of drooping flowers. "I believe Jake has decided to stay."

"Not go to Kansas?"

Mabel nodded. Then her stomach did a flip, and she froze, her fingers gripping the edge of the table. He wouldn't. He had to stay now.

Though he hadn't said he would.

Of course, they hadn't said much of anything once he'd carried her to bed. But Jake wasn't the kind of man to abandon his wife. Not his *real* wife.

"He won't go to Kansas," she said, standing straight and dropping her arms. She followed Alice down the hall as Katie Grace plaintively called for Octavia Maria Shannon Whiskers and tried to recapture the certainty and confidence she'd felt only moments earlier.

CHAPTER 25

"Do you want to spend the rest of your life here?"

Jake's question was spoken so softly, Mabel almost didn't hear it in the backstage bustle, where clowns and lions and elephants and jugglers filled the hall. A cluster of ballet dancers warmed up, their supple arms twisting and stretching around lean torsos. Rowena, Maman's dear friend, sprinted between them, her frizzed brown hair puffing beneath a conical hat, a poodle under one arm and a miniature bicycle under the other.

"Here, as in the hall?" she asked with a laugh.

"Here, as in New York." He drew her against the wall. "Here, as in the circus."

"Where else would I spend it?"

"Kansas." She stared, and he grabbed her hands. "I know I have no right to ask you this . . . but couldn't we make a life somewhere else? Together?"

"Why can't we make a life *here* together?"

Someone shoved past her, and she jerked away, hugging

her middle, fingers clenching her sides. Jake stepped so near she could almost hear his heart beating. So near she could almost taste his cinnamon-scented breath. So near her mind was almost entirely filled with moonlit moments from the past two nights.

But Kansas?

"I never dreamed of leaving, Jake."

"I never wanted to stay."

"My mother . . . I've only just gotten her back. I won't leave her on her own now. Especially not with the end of her career in sight."

He looked away and sighed. "Your mother will always have work with Travis and Wells."

"Family is important. How could I abandon her?"

He flinched.

"I wasn't referring to you or the choices you've made," she said. The trick riders pranced down the hall, their horses' hooves clopping an even tempo against the stone floor. They had five minutes before their act began. "I was born into the circus. It's my home. My family. I don't know anything else, and I don't know that I want to know anything else."

"It's Charlotte all over again."

Mabel blinked. "What does she have to do with any of this?"

"She told me she'd rather stay at the circus alone than join me in Kansas. On a dirty ranch, she called it." He stepped away. "And now you."

"That isn't fair. Leaving was never part of the plan. Not for me."

"It wasn't for her either." He gave a humorless laugh.

Mabel grabbed his hand and squeezed it between both of hers. "There are other options. Why does it have to be my dream or yours? We can build a different one. An *our* dream. We can spend winters in Kansas and—"

"Really?" Jake scoffed. "You think Mr. Wells will allow his

biggest star to disappear while the rest of his performers rehearse?"

Mabel lifted his fingers to her lips and gazed at him over their knuckles. "I can commit to performing in part of the show. New York and the East. Some of the Midwest."

"Be reasonable." He shook free of her grasp and flung out his hand. "You know this is a family. A jealous, overbearing, incessantly *involved* family."

People were beginning to notice their desperate whispers. Conversations were slipping into silence, and the nearest performers pretended indifference even as gazes and ears tipped toward them.

"We can find a compromise. We must. Don't you think . . . don't you think we're worth that?"

"Compromise? With the circus?" He gave a derisive laugh and scrubbed his hand through his hair. "I was so struck by you. By wanting you. By loving you. I knew it was foolish. I knew you would never choose me over all of this."

Mabel's nose burned, and a lump settled in her throat. "Why would you, then? Why would you make this so much harder on me than it already was going to be?"

She strode away, not bothering to see if he followed. But of course he did, for they were meant to step into the ring together, smiles on their faces and hands raised in a wave. They would embrace the audience and give everything it wanted. Even if it meant slipping heartache between layers of pretense.

"I'm sorry," Jake said as he positioned himself before her in the ring.

Mabel tucked in her middle and prepared to lift him. "I don't understand how you can hate what I love." She fit her palm around his waist and tried to ignore the feel of his skin shifting beneath the leotard. The sound of his huff against her ear.

"I can't compete with it. You would eventually love it more than you love me."

Mabel stood straight. With one arm beneath Jake's backside, her fingers gripping his hip, she stretched her other arm wide and spun in a circle to the cheers of the crowd. "You're wrong."

She braced her feet against the floor and held her stomach taut, the muscles in her legs flexing in preparation. Jake swung one leg around her neck, got to his knees, and then stood. His hands gripped her shoulders as he raised his legs into a handstand and then, with the force of his training and strength, vaulted upward and forward, flipped, and landed upright before her.

Mabel had believed she competed against Charlotte's beauty. Her charm and sugared appeal. But, in truth, she competed only with the heartache Charlotte had caused.

Even if she followed Jake to Kansas, that wouldn't change. She would forever be proving her love for him. No one, not even she, was strong enough to live beneath that pressure forever.

It would destroy their marriage. It would destroy her.

They completed their act without another word, and when he gripped the trapeze and was hoisted into the air, she watched, chin tilted, hand at her eyes to deflect the glare of the electric lights. An ache lodged beneath her ribs as she took in her fill of him. He was so beautiful.

"Are you all right?" her mother asked.

Mabel glanced down and shook off her melancholy. She couldn't let it overwhelm her now. Not with another act to follow.

Maman smiled, and it reached her eyes, crinkling the corners and brightening her countenance.

"I love you."

"I love you too."

"I won't leave you for anything, Maman."

Her mother's brow wrinkled. "Has something happened?"

"Nothing that wasn't meant to. I only got a little carried away on hope."

It didn't matter, though. Jake could leave just as he'd planned. She wouldn't hold him to their marriage, even though that meant a lifetime alone. She couldn't remarry now. She didn't want to, anyway.

Mabel forced Jake and heartbreak from her thoughts until she stood at the edge of the platform, her hands around the trapeze bar. Looking up as Maman prepped herself, she saw Jake swing through the air above her. He landed on an even higher platform, then looked down at her. She glanced away when he pressed his fingers to his lips, and instead focused on her mother, who was climbing into the cannon down below. But she could feel his gaze on her still. His expectations weighed heavy.

Just as the theatric explosion sounded, Mabel pushed into the air and settled herself atop the bar as she flew through a tunnel of wind and swirling applause.

Maman soared toward her. Then her face pinched and her mouth rounded with a gasp.

Ice flooded Mabel's blood. No. She was too low.

In one smooth movement, Mabel bent to grip the bar and slipped her body over the back of it.

Above her, Jake released a short shout that echoed in the rafters.

As she dangled from her hands, her arms shook, and she breathed a prayer. "Please."

Maman slammed into Mabel's middle, and it took every bit of endurance, every bit of love, to hang on. Mabel's hands slipped a little, the steel smooth against her palms, and she tightened her fists. Maman's clasp dropped.

"Hang on!" Mabel stiffened her legs, and Maman caught them, one hand rounding each ankle. Limbs shaking, Mabel pulled herself up and hooked her arms over the bar so it bit into her armpits. "Maman!"

The crowd gave a collective gasp, as though finally realizing this wasn't part of the act, and then silence fell. Eerie in this place typically filled with the sound of animals, music, and applause.

"I'm here. I'm here." Maman gasped, the air whistling down her throat.

"I'm going to lift you up. Hold on."

Never had Mabel lifted anything so important. Never had so much rested on her strength. She bent her knees, thighs straining and arms burning as she pulled them up, and Maman reached for the ropes attaching them to the rafters, hauling herself the final few inches. There they swung, back and forth over the dozens of people working to open a net, their arms hooked over the bar. Safe. They were safe.

A hush settled over the crowd, and Mabel heard nothing but the creaking trapeze. Maman's labored breathing. Her own heart beating.

Finally they stilled, and Mabel looked up and saw Jake staring at her, his face white, and she lifted trembling fingers to her lips. He crumpled to the platform and dropped his head into his hands.

But she couldn't cry. She couldn't think past what had nearly happened. Who she had nearly lost. "Maman."

"My strong girl. My strong girl." Maman's voice was ragged, each word a stone that slipped from her motionless lips.

A shout from below grabbed Mabel's attention, and she pressed her forehead against Maman's. "You go first. They're ready."

Maman nodded, her nose brushing Mabel's, and she let go. The net bounced beneath her weight but held, and a moment later she slipped to the floor and was caught up in Robert's arms.

When it was Mabel's turn, she first looked up at Jake. He crouched at the edge of the platform, his hands gripping it. "I'm all right," she called, but his entire body shook, and she knew fear would hold him captive until she stood once more on firm ground.

And even then, she might have to accept that Jake clung too tightly to the pain of his past to release it and cling to her instead.

* * *

"The act is done." Robert spoke without preamble. The words made sense in isolation, but Mabel could hardly understand them strung together. Robert wouldn't meet Maman's gaze, though she stood with her hand on the door she'd opened at his knock, his great shoulders round and hunched.

"Come in." Maman sighed as though not surprised or confused by his statement.

She'd been silent since the day before, when Mabel had watched her nearly plummet to her death much the way Charlotte Cunningham had. And this was what she chose to say?

Robert caught up Maman's hands. "You know it has to be over now. You nearly died, Isabella. If Mabel had not been strong enough . . . fast enough . . ." His voice caught.

"I know." Maman sounded so defeated. So accepting of this lunacy.

"No," Mabel said. "It can't be done. Why would you say such a thing? It's a popular act. And I saw the papers this morning—*Atalanta Saves Aerialist.* Everyone is enamored."

She went to the armoire that held her and Maman's costumes. Flinging open the door, she pulled out the two they were meant to wear that afternoon. The stars and the moon. Strung with light and stones. Alice had created magic with her needle, and Mabel knew she and Maman did justice to the work.

What would happen if the stars blinked out and left the moon alone to illuminate the night? The darkness would overwhelm any light it shed. It was not enough on its own.

"I kept resisting this, Mabel. For too long. Robert has known for a while, and so has Mr. Wells—they were kind to allow me to continue working—but I can't ignore the truth of it. I'm too old, darling, to continue."

"But, Maman, it wasn't your fault! They prepped with the wrong dummy." Mabel had watched the workers the day before—stuffing the dummy into the cannon and letting it fly more than a dozen times so that they measured the angle and timing right. But someone had missed a few hours' sleep or had a cold or was worried about a child and misread Maman's weight. It was careless. Dangerous. And it could have ended in tragedy. But why should her mother be punished for another's mistake? "None of this has anything to do with you. None of it—"

"It's all over, Mabel. She's no longer in the show at all." Robert's steps sounded heavy as he plodded toward Maman and lightly touched her shoulder. "I'm sorry."

"What?" Mabel glanced between them. "You're being unreasonable. Both of you."

"I put your life in danger. I promised I never would again." Maman ducked her head, and the hair she'd yet to arrange fell in a shiny curtain around her face. Grey streaked it—thick swaths that Maman had always arranged just so, hiding the evidence of years.

"It has only happened once, though. A fluke."

Maman shook her head. "No, Mabel. It hasn't. Your father wasn't all wrong. What he did, he did for your safety. He knew I was plagued by shadows, and he always worried they would drag me back into that dark place. What else could he do? When I left, he took the opportunity to end it."

"What are you talking about?"

Maman looked at Robert, who nodded, and then she took a deep breath and straightened her shoulders. "I told you that you were a big baby. So big, I was nearly torn in half as you came into the world. When it became clear I would survive, the doctor told me I couldn't become pregnant again. Ever. Your father never touched me after that."

"What do you mean, he never touched you?"

"Just that. He hugged me before I left for New York years later, but until then, our only physical contact was accidental. There was once . . . I tried, but it mattered little. Can you imagine, for a woman whose entire life had been built upon the physical, what it meant not to share that with her husband?"

Maman shrugged. It was a small movement, but Mabel could see everything inherent in it—years of pain and rejection. And what would *she* do, after having tasted the consuming beauty of a whole marriage, if Jake refused her? Never kissed her. Never touched her. Never loved her. If he lived beside her as a husband, but wasn't fully? No . . . she knew too much now to find that a satisfactory arrangement again.

Was it wrong, to put so much importance on that one part? But it was so beautiful. So fulfilling. And it left her feeling safe. Protected.

Without it, she would rather he leave completely.

Love and loss threaded like a generational curse, knotting daughter, mother, and grandmother in a twisted kind of mimicry, and there was a reassurance in it. If she were to have such a passion torn from her, at least she knew she didn't suffer alone. Though she wished Maman hadn't had to.

"Robert," Maman said, "I must tell her."

"Yes." He took her hand and pressed it to his lips. "I will stay or leave. It's your choice. You are stronger than you think."

She pressed his fingers to her heart, and Mabel wondered that she'd remained faithful to Da all the years he lived. She was certain she'd never seen him look at Maman in such a way. With wary uncertainty, yes. Even distant fondness. But with that kind of passion? How had Da been able to tuck it away so completely? Mabel knew a wild, immediate love affair had preceded their marriage. Where had it gone?

"Stay," Maman said.

"What is it?" Mabel's heart picked up its pace and sweat trickled down the middle of her back.

Maman motioned her to the settee. Mabel sat beside her, and Robert went back to his place at the wall. "It's hard to speak of these things—I didn't for so long. I'm not sure why. Shame played a part. I also thought, if I gave the darkness a voice, it was validated and it would gain greater control of me. You may have noticed I'm a little superstitious." She gave a lopsided smile. "But now . . . now I simply want you to love me, and I'm afraid that when you hear what I've done, the things I've suffered, you won't." Tears gathered in her lashes, and she cried silently, as though even her grief didn't deserve to be noticed.

"All I've ever wanted was your attention. Nothing you say now will change my joy at having it."

Maman touched Mabel's cheek. "I'm so sorry you didn't feel as though you received it when you were young." She took a deep breath. "After you were born, it was days before I could hold you. My milk never established itself, so you were given to a wet nurse. Everyone, your father included, treated me as though I were made of glass. And when you were about six weeks old, I sank into darkness. I cannot explain it, except that I knew how Paul had felt. It was with me always. Every moment. I wondered constantly if you wouldn't be better off without me. I knew your father would. I could free him from being shackled to me—a wife whose body almost killed his child. I wasn't the only one who nearly died. When you finally came, there was hardly a breath in your body. The labor had been hard on you too. And I hated myself for it."

"But that was hardly your fault. It was a matter of size."

"Yes, but what happened afterward wasn't."

She squeezed Mabel's hands, and Mabel could feel each fragile bone beneath her mother's skin. It wouldn't take much to snap them—a twist. Maman had always carried about herself the aura of a pixie. How had she survived Mabel's eleven pounds?

"Whatever you have done, I forgive you. I forgive you everything."

"Mabel, you can't forgive before you know what sin has been dealt against you."

"I can and I will. We all have the capacity for mistakes. Wickedness, even. I'm no exception." Maman scoffed, but Mabel shook her head. "What did you do? Surprise me. Shock me. But know you will never lose me."

Maman's chest hitched. She pulled her hand away and passed it over her eyes. "When you were six months old, I decided life was no longer worth the struggle. I hadn't planned it, though the thought plagued me endlessly. But there we sat, beside a little lake outside some town in Austria. It was our Sunday off, and you lay on the grass, pumping your legs. Trying to speak. I just thought, *Someone will be along shortly. She won't be alone very long.* So I kissed your head and walked into the lake. Did you know I can't swim?"

Ice had frozen Mabel. She sat still, eyes wide as the air chilled her nose and throat. She couldn't move her lips, so she shook her head.

"I left you there by yourself. You could have rolled into the lake or been lost until the elements or a wild animal killed you. I thought of none of that. I only wanted it to be over."

"But you didn't die."

"Lorenzo was sitting in a nearby tree, staring at the clouds and writing nonsense. He glanced down just as my head slipped under the water. I awoke as he was pulling me out, and I fought him. I begged him to let me go. But he dragged me to shore, and we saw you . . ." Maman crossed her arms over her waist and bent over them. "You always did things early—rolling, sitting—but I never dreamed you would crawl so soon. I hadn't even seen you rock on your knees. You were very near the shore. So close, in fact, that the water played with your dress as you tried to shove a pebble in your mouth. If it hadn't been for Lorenzo, I would have died that day. You might have too. Twice, I'd put you at risk. First, my body failed you. Then my mind. Yesterday was the final time I will allow it."

Maybe Mabel should have been appalled. Except Maman seemed intent on flagellating herself, and Mabel thought she had suffered enough for a choice made when she hadn't felt she had any other.

"Nothing changes. I still forgive you. I still love you. And even had you succeeded, I would love you. From Heaven or Earth. Love isn't something you deserve. It's something you're offered. It isn't conditional. But, Maman, you can't leave me." A sob caught in Mabel's throat, and she reached for her mother's hands again.

"I'm not leaving you. I never shall again. I am only leaving the show."

"But I can't do it without you."

"Of course you can. You don't need me. *I* have needed you, but you, Mabel . . . you are strong enough to do this without me."

"I couldn't after Da died. And Jake will leave soon. I will be alone."

"Jake is staying." Robert pushed from the wall. "At least until the end of the year."

Mabel blinked. "No. I'm sure he's leaving after New York."

Robert shook his head. "He made it clear that if your mother was taken out of the show right away, he would stay the year." He looked at Maman and gave a sad shake of his head. "I'm sorry, Isabella, but we leave New York in a couple of weeks anyway, and Mr. Wells didn't see a problem in cutting your time a little short in order to have Jake for many more months."

* * *

Jake needed space. He needed a distraction from the churning in his stomach, set in motion the day before when he'd watched his wife tempt death. She'd nearly fallen. Just like Charlotte. And, once more, he'd been powerless to stop it. Everything had rested on Mabel.

Thank God she'd been strong enough to hold on.

But what if she hadn't been?

He couldn't stop the image of her slipping from that bar and slamming into the floor below from battering his peace. It was an easy thing. All he had to do was replace Charlotte's prone, broken body with Mabel's.

He leaned his head against Odysseus's back, desperate to be free of the awful thoughts, and ran his hands over the horse's withers. He missed the animals and wondered why he'd ever given up trick riding.

There was something precious between a man and his horse. And a horse never caused a moment of worry. Never stole his breath and twisted his heart and made him watch, from stories in the air, as life hung in the balance.

Yes, he missed horses, but he would leave it at that. If he delved further, he knew he might ferret out the fact that there wasn't much more about living on a ranch that he missed. And he *was* going home. With Mabel, he hoped. Without her if she refused.

How could he stay and watch as she tossed her life away on a circus that chewed performers up and spit them out as though they were full of gristle and bones?

He pushed away from Odysseus and offered the carrot he'd grabbed on his way into the stables. With a quick rub against the horse's nose, Jake let himself out of the stall and made his way through the stone-tiled room. The animals' gentle snuffles and sighs were wrought with memories. Their musky scent conspired to remind him of his love for performing. Or, rather, what *had* been his love for performing. He might have returned to his uncle's show if it hadn't folded years ago.

But what would he do here? He'd ensured Mabel's safety—as much as was possible in the circus—and now had to finish out the year. That was the deal he'd made with Robert.

"I know you love her," Jake had told the manager the evening before, *"but I don't want another wife dying while working with her. If you drop her from Mabel's act, I'll stay through the year. I'll make Mr. Wells an obscene amount of money."*

Six months and he could leave. Maybe it would be enough time to convince Mabel to go with him.

His steps faltered, and he squeezed his eyes closed, trying to imagine her in the middle of his family's large kitchen, apron tied around her waist and a child tugging at her leg. Her rolling out pie dough like his own mama had done—with a light touch and a gentle smile. But he couldn't see any of it, except maybe the child. He'd watched her enough with Katie Grace to know she'd be a singular mother.

But did that mean she *wouldn't* go with him? Wouldn't find satisfaction in life on the ranch?

With him?

It might not be enough for her. She was Atalanta, bound to the circus and public, with stardust and magic. She was *rooted* to the circus. Generationally, with a family history that knit itself to rings and trains. She was wedded to the circus. . . .

He opened his eyes and stared down the aisle when the door slid open. With it came the click of a switch and a spill of electric light that warred with the sun flooding the dusty windows set high near the ceiling. Jake collected himself and started forward. He needed to rest before the evening show. Already his legs felt heavy and his thoughts fuzzy.

But filling the doorway, dust motes bowing at her feet, stood Mabel, every bit the warrior queen the papers made her out to be. She stared at him a moment, her blue eyes blazing.

"You had my mother removed from the show."

"For your own safety."

Mabel shook her head, undressed waves tumbling around her shoulders in a cloud of ebony. "I am so tired of men deciding what is best for me. First Da, now you. For both, my mother the thing that must be whisked away. How terrifying she must be that not even I can protect myself from her."

"She encouraged you to do that act. The same way she encouraged Charlotte. And she knew how I felt about it both times."

"Oh, Charlotte. I wish you would stop speaking of her as though she had nothing at all to do with the disaster that took place. *Charlotte* chose to do that act. She wanted to, for she knew the danger of it would catch the public's fancy. It would secure her immense fame, just as it had the human cannonballs before her. *Charlotte* knew how dangerous it was. Just as *I* chose to do it this time. In fact, I'm the one who suggested it to Maman." Mabel covered her face with her hands. Her next words were muffled, hardly able to escape the press of her palms. "No matter how strong I am, how much I accomplish, I cannot overcome the perception that I am weak. That I need protection, even from my own decisions." She dropped her hands and stared at him. "The choices you made—just like the choices Da made—have had far-reaching consequences. Maman was not only dropped from my act. She's being retired completely."

"That wasn't my intention."

"But it's what happened."

"I only asked that she be pulled from your act."

"As though that interference is such a little thing."

"You're angry."

Her brows jumped over that lovely smooth forehead. Every bit of her looked sculpted from marble at the moment. Cold and unyielding. Very much unlike her.

"What did you expect? My entire life, I've wanted my mother back. You just ripped her away."

"From the act, Mabel. Not from you."

"And when we leave New York at the end of the week? Will she sign herself up as a washerwoman? Break her back and consign herself to an early death?"

Jake scoffed. "Surely it's not as dire as that. There must be something she can do that wouldn't require physical labor."

"For a woman?" She took a step toward him, and her voice dipped. "Have you any idea how few options we have? My mother is a performer. What else can she do? She's had no education or experience in anything outside of performing."

"She can be a ballet girl or—"

"She's fifty years old, Jake. Think."

He threw his hands up. "Well, why can't she marry Robert? God knows he's asked her enough times."

Mabel crossed her arms and studied him, making him feel as though the inches between them were actually feet. Her father had claimed the same gift—able to make a person feel small with one look. He'd never expected to see it on her face.

"So a woman without options should marry? The way a woman wishing to protect her reputation should?" She took another step toward him. "How very modern of me to believe marriage should be based on mutual affection. But I suppose a man so easily willing to end his own has already shown what a dim view he takes of the relationship."

"That isn't fair. Ours was a different kind of situation. It was a tool. We never intended to make it permanent."

"But I hoped. I dreamed. I wished. That you would love me. That you would want to stay with me."

"I do. I've told you that. I would spend the rest of my life with you."

"Just not here." She swept her arms wide.

Why did he have to give up his . . . not dream, exactly. It wasn't his dream to return home. It was more a desire to escape with nowhere else to go. But why did he have to give up his plan? His intention? "Not here."

"I suppose I should get used to performing alone, then. Since Maman is no longer permitted and you shall not be here. Why you think it so much more important for me to learn to work alone than for you to learn to work with others is beyond me."

She turned and ducked away so quickly that Jake hadn't even a moment to process what she'd said before her steps clattered down the hall.

Very well. Alone to Kansas it would be.

CHAPTER

26

IN THE SPAN OF A MOMENT, everything Isabella had worked for, striven toward, obsessed over, and relied on had disappeared. Her life as she'd always known it was gone.

Well, not as she'd *always* known it. There were those early years during the war, before the sound of the calliope had ever called to her, of starvation and want. Grief and loss. But that was a life she hardly remembered. Now there was nothing else outside of the circus.

The doorknob of her room jiggled, and Isabella pulled the blankets more tightly over her head. She inhaled the stale air and watched shadow and light play through the fabric. Rowena typically never returned to her room between shows. She would eat lunch with the other performers and then spend the next couple of hours exploring the city.

"Get up. We're going." Rowena's voice was demanding. Almost strident.

Isabella squeezed her eyes shut. "No."

"Will you stay in bed until the circus leaves town and the hotel kicks you onto the street?"

"If I must."

Rowena sighed. "Get up."

The blankets were torn from Isabella, and she found herself tugged onto the floor. She glared up at her friend. "That was uncalled for." Her nightgown had puddled around her hips, and she tugged it down her legs, then drew her knees to her chin. "You have no idea what this feels like. I have nothing. I am nothing." The truth of it clawed the back of her throat, and she pulled her body into a ball.

"You have plenty." Rowena crouched before her, and her steady hand found Isabella's shoulder. "I know, right now, you cannot see clearly. So I am going to be your eyes. I am going to be your reality. And this is what I know to be true—you have friends who love you, a man who wishes for nothing but your happiness, and a daughter who needs you. You have your health, a working mind, and a heart that has suffered much worse. All you don't have, Isabella, is a job." She stood and went to the wardrobe. Pulling out a skirt and shirtwaist, she held them up. "Let's go eat. Everything looks much better on a full stomach."

Fifteen minutes later, and not quite sure how Rowena had managed it, Isabella found herself walking briskly down Fifth Avenue toward the dumpy tearoom where her friend, for some ungodly reason, enjoyed taking lunch.

Isabella wrinkled her nose as she stepped through the Mad Hatter's front door. Inside, they were seated on benches at one of the thick, scarred tables, and Rowena ordered for both of them.

"Really," Isabella said as a wide-lipped bowl of pea soup was set before her, "you prefer this over whatever they were serving in the circus dining room?"

"I prefer the company." Rowena raised a brow and offered a cheeky smile. "Don't be so snobbish."

Isabella pushed aside the bowl and drew her teacup forward. Lifting it, she inhaled the fragrant steam but set it back on the table without bringing it to her lips. "I'm not hungry." She wasn't anything. Emptiness yawned like a cavern, consuming everything inside her.

Of course, Isabella could appreciate on a surface level that Rowena was right. She knew there were people who cared for her. She knew her daughter loved her. But if she *knew* a thing, why could she not *believe* it? Why the looming depression that colored everything in grey mist? The gaping darkness that wanted to swallow her whole?

She could never escape. She'd tried once before, but even that had ended in failure, and she didn't think she was brave enough to try again, for if she knew but couldn't believe in the temporal, she certainly couldn't believe in the eternal. And when knowing and believing were locked in such a battle, the clash of it became a great, deafening commotion imprisoning her thoughts.

Rowena dipped her spoon back into the bowl but left it there and patted her lips with a napkin. "What are your plans?"

"I will see Mr. Wells later this afternoon." Isabella gave a tired shrug. "I plan to throw myself upon his mercy."

"I guess that's something." Rowena pinched her spoon between her fingers, stared for a moment at her soup, then glanced up. "And you won't marry Robert?"

"I was considering it—don't look at me like that. It only just recently occurred to me that it wouldn't be as dangerous as I supposed."

"Dangerous? Isabella, it's *Robert*. He's a Teddy bear."

"I know. But Bram seemed a Teddy bear too, until he was faced with the 'for worse' and 'in sickness' parts of a marriage. For so long I just wasn't sure I could trust Robert with my heart. It still feels so broken. It wouldn't take much to demolish me completely. Bram never really knew me. He didn't know much about Paul or anything at all about my father." She reached for her ears and pushed against the diamond stars. "Robert has seen me and known me through some of my very worst moments. And I realized the other day, when he gave me these, that though my body was always safe with Bram, my heart is safe with Robert."

"So you *will* marry him?" Rowena slid the spoon through her bowl and took a hearty bite.

Isabella sighed. "How can I?"

Her friend tossed down the spoon, and a few patrons at nearby tables glanced up at the clatter. Rowena waited until they returned their attention to their own affairs before responding with a hiss, "How maddening you are! What do you mean?"

"I never told him I was considering marrying him, and if I do now, he will only think it is because I have no other choice."

Rowena gave a disbelieving grunt. "Why do you think he would care?"

"I care. I never want him to suspect my motives. I've been married and felt unloved before. It is something that eats away at your peace and joy until you can no longer experience either in anything else."

"What is your plan, then? Never marry a man you believe you love, one who can provide for you and keep you from hard labor or poverty? Will you do the wash like your mother and work your fingers to the bone? Or maybe, with Mabel's success, comes enough money for you to retire comfortably. Will *she* care for you?"

Isabella shook her head. "None of those things. I'm not sure what I'll do."

Rowena snorted. "Why must you overcomplicate things? It would be easy enough to tell Robert you love him, and if there are doubts, so be it." She sat back in her chair. "But I suppose I understand. And even should you convince him of your feelings, you would never be content as a housewife. The circus is in your blood. You would never give it up."

"That's true."

But more than that, with Mabel set to leave with the show at the end of the week, Isabella needed to find a way to stay on. Rowena had said earlier that Mabel needed her, but the truth was reversed. For as much as giving up the circus seemed unthinkable, giving up Mabel would be impossible. Isabella wanted to stay with the circus. She *needed* her daughter.

Mabel tethered her to everything good in life—all those things she could sometimes only see as shadows and light playing on the other side. If she found herself torn, once more, from her daughter, she was afraid she might become completely unmoored.

* * *

Mr. Wells had always been an intimidating man. Even having been married to Bram—the world's strongest—Isabella found herself cowering before her first love's father.

He wasn't even particularly large, and he very much resembled the Santa Clauses who graced the paper cards housewives handed out at Christmastime. Maybe it was how closely stitched he was to her history. Or maybe it was the fact that he held her career—her future—in the palm of his hand, with only a rusty obligation to the friendship Isabella had with his long-dead son binding him to it.

She stood in the doorway of his Fifth Avenue mansion's library beside Robert, her heart in her throat.

"Come in. Come in." He rose a little when they were announced and waved them toward a matching pair of chairs on the other side of his wide mahogany desk. He steepled his fingers and waited until they were settled, then cleared his throat. "I have a proposition. We are expanding the show. Has Robert told you about it?"

She shook her head, and Robert reached for her hand. "We haven't had the chance to speak of it," he said.

Mr. Wells made a low sound in his throat, his gaze dropping to their clasped hands. Robert withdrew with a jerk. "Well, we are. And I've noticed how well you've been working with the little fatherless girl—"

"Katie Grace," Isabella said. She wouldn't allow the child to be defined by what she'd lost.

"Yes, Katie Grace. I was at the Garden last week, and I watched you working with her between shows. She shows great promise."

"She is very hardworking and naturally talented. I'm sure she will go far."

"*You* show great promise, Polly."

Her head jerked up at his use of her former name. Robert sometimes slipped back into childhood, usually in moments of great feeling, but coming from Mr. Wells, there was a poignant sense of homecoming wrapped around it. Isabella glanced at Robert, and his eyes were like summer—warm and touched by gold.

Mr. Wells cleared his throat. "I know there has been some concern that you would be without a means to support yourself, but I promised your mother you would always have a place with Travis and Wells."

Isabella frowned. "What?"

Mr. Wells had snapping, intelligent eyes crowned with magnificent grey brows, but they turned dark and fathomless as he studied her. He took a steady breath and spread his hands over the whirls and wax of his desk. "She found Paul. She could have let the water sweep him away, but she didn't. She pulled him to safety and saw that he was cared for . . . and then she found me. I will never forget the comfort of being with someone who had experienced such a loss." He folded his hands together and leaned forward. "But more than that, my son loved you. Enough to want to marry you."

Isabella drew in a breath. "How do you know that?" She'd never intended to tell him. No one but Robert and Rowena knew, and Rowena wouldn't have said a thing. She looked at Robert, but he seemed unfazed by Mr. Wells's admission. Not at all burdened by guilt.

Mr. Wells pulled open a drawer and withdrew an envelope, her name splashed over the front of it in Paul's tight handwriting. *Polly, my love.* Her skin tingled as gooseflesh sprang out over her arms and back. It was Paul calling from the river. His last words to her a ghostly whisper in ink.

"When will we tell the world?" Polly had asked, admiring the ring upon her finger. Three diamonds in a burnished setting.

"Soon. When we arrive in Ohio. Father is coming, and we can tell him in person, Polly, my love."

Mr. Wells stared down at the letter. "I found this, alongside one addressed to myself and his mother, in his chest. I read it. I'm sorry for that and for never having given it to you, but I was so ashamed by his decision. So bowed by guilt at not having seen the seriousness of his affliction. I knew he suffered from melancholy—he had since he was a boy—but I never imagined . . ." He slid the envelope across the table. "I should have given it to you years ago, but I put it away and pretended it didn't exist."

Hand trembling, Polly took it. She slid her finger beneath the flap and withdrew a single sheet of paper.

Sometimes the darkness overwhelms the light. I cannot go on pretending as though I see a spark. It is too heavy a night. This has nothing to do with you, my love. Nothing at all to do with anyone. I wish we could have a future together. I am afraid, though, that my dark thoughts will eventually shadow your light. And I am so tired of fighting them. Keep the ring. Think of me fondly.

Poor Paul. He hadn't thought. Only allowed that moment to overcome all others. And there had been no Lorenzo to rescue him. Maman had come by too late, while Polly had still been asleep upon a narrow cot, her dreams chasing romance.

"I'm sorry if this reopens old wounds." Mr. Wells sounded tired.

She shook her head. "Thank you for giving it to me. I'm not upset that you hid it." She refolded the letter, slipped it back into its envelope, and set it on the desk.

"I will always honor my gratitude for your mother, Polly, and I will honor my son's love for you. I do believe it's time for you to retire—I would not be honoring anyone if I allowed you to continue in a job that has become too dangerous—but I hope you will stay with Travis and Wells anyway, because we could use your expertise."

Polly's mouth went dry, and her throat tightened. "With the laundry?"

Mr. Wells chuckled. "No. With the children. Katie Grace to start. Our bearded lady's son is nearly six and ready to begin his training as well. There are a few other children of performers and a few more coming when we winter." He sat back and folded his hands over his belly with a satisfied grunt. "I want you to train them and help them discover their place in the circus."

She hadn't much experience with children, having left her own so early on, but she'd enjoyed working with Katie Grace—though she wasn't sure it was any less exhausting than flipping around on the trapeze. But this was a job she could find purpose in and enjoy. It was more than she had imagined being offered. "Of course."

"Then it's settled." Mr. Wells stood and rounded the desk. Robert and Isabella followed suit. "One more thing. I wasn't happy to hear of your lapse in judgment, and I expect it not to happen again. However, that doesn't mean I disapprove of the two of you together. My son loved both of you. I hope you honor that in regard to how you move forward in your relationship."

"There isn't one," Robert said quickly and sent her a reassuring glance.

Isabella said nothing as she followed Mr. Wells toward the door. She had a job. One that would keep her traveling with the circus, remaining with Mabel, not growing bent beneath hard labor and becoming a burden to her daughter. She didn't *need* Robert now.

Which changed everything. She could finally admit she *wanted* him.

She glanced over her shoulder and paused until Robert reached her. "We will certainly take your advice, sir."

Robert's steps faltered, and his gaze shot to hers. Then his mouth curled, and he reached for her hand.

CHAPTER 27

SHE COULDN'T DO IT.

She'd thought she might be able to. In those moments after she'd spoken to Jake the day before, when everything fell into place with stunning clarity, Mabel had seen how she needed to distance herself from him. Both professionally and personally.

"We can continue the ruse until Travis and Wells is headed to Indiana for the winter," she'd told him last night as he lay in bed, both of them squeezing their arms tightly to their sides in an effort not to accidently brush against the other. "But I don't want to perform with you anymore. I don't think I could bear it." Being so close to him, touching him, pretending to be completely happy, knowing it was all for the sake of the audience. None of it real. None of it true. None of it lasting.

He hadn't said anything. Only rolled away and pressed the pillow over his head.

Mabel leaned against the wall just outside her dressing room and stared down the hallway. There was nothing but the usual crowd of performers milling about, checking costumes and stretching taut muscles. Everyone waited for their moment.

What was a circus performer who couldn't perform? She'd thought she could do it without him, and maybe a part of her had wanted to punish him for making it so she couldn't do it with Maman, but the truth settled between every rapid beat of her heart. "I cannot do it."

Maman, standing on one side of her, glanced at Robert, who stood on the other. "Cannot do what, darling?"

"Go on. I cannot go on. I cannot." Mabel spoke with short, airy breaths, and her words rattled inside her chest. "I will fail. Without you, without Jake . . ." She whirled toward Robert. "You must let Maman go on with me. Her costume is just inside, and it will not take long for her to change." She grabbed his hands. "Please. I need more time to prepare."

"Do you want me to find Jake? I'm sure he is willing to—"

"No. Jake is not an option." She couldn't be so close to Jake and not have him. She wouldn't go back to Mrs. Luvotti's drawing room, their interactions heavy with want, unable to commit to more than what they'd decided.

It had proven a disastrous decision the first time they chose to ignore their original plans. She couldn't do it again.

"What is the difference," Robert asked, "if your mother is with you in the ring or standing mere feet away in the hall? You've done plenty of tricks on your own, and you haven't added anything new to the routine. You've only expanded what you already do."

His words made sense, but it mattered little how logical they sounded. Jake had said so many words beneath the Manzo Brothers tent, and still she'd failed. Still she'd made a fool of herself. Still her face flamed when she thought of the tittering laughter and pointed fingers. And still she felt the stalking fear, like flames, licking at her arms and legs. Singeing her hair and searing her skin. Turning her thoughts to muddle, her muscles to mush.

"I . . . I cannot do it."

What would happen if she never conquered her fear? What if she had another public failure, this one in front of a New York crowd? Mr. Norris had already proven there were those waiting for her to disappoint everyone. Waiting for her to show she wasn't what everyone thought.

Atalanta, stripped down. Exposed.

Who was she without her title? What was she if not the world's strongest woman?

"I cannot. I cannot." She groaned, and soft hands came around her waist and pressed against her spine. Maman's head rested against her chest.

"I know this feeling," Maman said. "I know the attraction of surrender." Her voice turned harsh. Demanding. "But, Mabel, do not yield. You are stronger than it."

"I'm not. I never have been. Maman, I failed. Every time I've tried to do anything on my own, I've failed. After Da died. In the ring. When I tried to find a job. In my marriage."

Maman grabbed Mabel's hands and looked up. "I'm sorry for my part in making you feel as though you are incapable. I'm sorry your father and the circus made you feel as though you need others to prop you up. I'm sorry for so many things, but you don't need to be who you've always thought you were. You decide, in this moment, what you can do. Who you can be."

Mabel gave a harsh shake of her head, but the burning in her chest began to ease, and her breathing fell back into its normal rhythm.

"You call yourself weak and have determined you cannot stand on your own. I called myself useless without my work and decided my entire worth was wrapped up in what my body could give. We believed lies. Decide, right now, that you are more than what you've told yourself. You can do this. Not because you are a strongwoman, but because you have a strong heart and spirit."

For so long, Mabel had defined herself by loss. She'd resolutely clung to a story written by broken people, and it had brought her nothing but insecurity and self-doubt. Perhaps it was time to try something different. Perhaps it was time to learn from her mother's mistakes, not just adopt them.

"I can do this alone?"

"You don't have to. If there's anything that gives me comfort, it's knowing you have never been alone. Even when I wasn't present. Even when your father died." Maman pressed a hard kiss to Mabel's hand. "Even when you cannot see him, God is there. You don't need to rely entirely on your own strength. You don't even need to rely on others. You can do all things *through* Christ, Mabel, including overcoming your fear."

Something warm and certain filled Mabel's veins. More than Maman's words, her own change—the confidence with which she spoke—convinced Mabel of the truth in it. Maman had been so determined to be self-reliant. So driven to prove herself strong and capable. For her to admit relying on someone else—even if that someone was God—was more than a little persuasive. "I can do this."

Maman beamed. "Yes. More than anything else in the world, I believe you can."

As Mabel stepped away from the wall, Jake ambled down the hall. Their eyes met, and his steps faltered. He shifted from one foot to the other, and the way his shoulders stretched his leotard showed just how exacting an artist God was. Beneath the fabric and flesh and muscle, though, lay a heart Mabel hadn't been able to wrestle for herself. She'd lost that match.

"Are you well?" he asked. So stilted. So formal.

"Yes."

He came forward another few steps. "Do you need anything? You aren't struggling with stage fright?"

"I think I'll be fine. I must be. You're leaving." Her fingers itched for his skin, and her heart beat an almost painful cadence. "I'm very sorry I had to lose everything in order to shake off the burden of dependence. I can do this, Jake. Thank you for believing it this entire time."

Then she turned and walked into the amphitheater.

Lights swung and spilled over her. Two clowns stumbled as they rolled a piano into the ring and, feigning fright, darted away. Mabel played a few notes, the tinny sound, out of tune and out of place, pinging round the building. Then she rounded it, placed her arms through the straps, and launched herself up straight.

The audience erupted, calling her name. She walked the instrument in a circle and settled it down again. Looking up into the sun-hazed rafters of Madison Square Garden, she saw Jake stepping off the ladder and striding across his platform toward its very edge. He was all brilliance and beauty, and her knees nearly buckled.

She *could* do it alone.

But she didn't at all want to.

* * *

Jake couldn't keep his gaze from its traitorous journey back toward Mabel, where she held court at Jerry Wells's mansion, surrounded by a ring of fawning, adoring, well-heeled devotees.

He hadn't wanted to attend this spring fete meant to show off Travis and Wells's newest stars, but he had no suitable excuse when he'd brought up the possibility of skipping it to Robert. Wanting to avoid the torture of being so near his wife likely wouldn't be an approved reason.

They'd already eaten dinner—a lavish affair of more courses than Jake could count—while he and Mabel attempted to pretend nothing more than a plate of *filet de boeuf* stood between them. Now everyone gathered in groups of three or four, conversing around the fine parlor furniture about dull things he cared little about. He swallowed a yawn. The mantel clock beside his head ticked away the minutes. Ten o'clock. He was normally asleep by now.

Or staring through the murky darkness at the ceiling, trying to ignore the fact that the loveliest woman in the world slept inches from him and he couldn't do a cursed thing about it. From the very beginning, their marriage had been pocked with pretense. And he'd spent too much time going over everything—every word spoken, every promise made, every fevered touch—hoping to unravel how his brittle, closed-off heart had become so entwined with hers.

His gaze slid over the floor and ferreted her out. There, near the corner of the room, her mother and Robert beside her, along with a woman in pearls and a man with heavy lids Jake didn't like the look of.

Never had Mabel looked more alluring than she did tonight. The fair expanse of her décolletage was accentuated by a draped gown the color of wine. It swept below her bust and fell to the floor in a gentle column, black beads swirling from hip to hem. Every curve highlighted.

Not one other woman in the room could touch her.

"She is something." Mr. Wells slid up beside him. "We're very lucky Miss Moreau insisted we hire her alongside you. Think what the show—the country—could have missed out on."

"Yes. She is one of a kind. Likely one in a generation."

Mr. Wells lifted his glass and stared into it as though assessing business possibilities instead of port. "And you're with us for the rest of the year, Robert tells me. I cannot induce you to commit yourself longer? We would make it worth your while."

The man eyeing Mabel said something, and she laughed, the thick, husky sound of it wrapping Jake's chest in a noose and tightening until he was forced to inhale deeply. He swung his gaze from his wife and pinned it to the circus owner. "No."

Mr. Wells brought the drink to his lips and took a sip. "Horses."

Jake blinked.

"I'm growing the show. Taking on twenty more horses. Six more acts, half of those equestrian. And children."

"You're putting children in the show?"

"We've brought in the new seamstress's daughter. But there are others—five, actually—children of performers who will begin their training over the winter. A couple have been working hard for years and will be ready to launch their careers next season. The others are just starting out. We're doing Arabian Nights."

Jake scratched his temple. The room had grown stuffy, dinner sitting in his stomach like lead, and Mabel's low murmur and sporadic laughter taunted him. And now he had to make sense of the disjointed ramblings of an ambitious businessman when all he wanted was a warm bed. His wife beside him.

"It's going to be the biggest show ever seen. And you need a lot of horses for Arabian Nights. You also need people to perform on those horses and someone to choreograph for those performing." Mr. Wells's hand found Jake's shoulder. "Your skill is wasted flipping off platforms. I need someone who understands horses. Someone with the experience to help me create a show that will astound the world."

"The world?"

"After next year's run, we're headed to Europe again."

"And you want me to be part of it?" Jake's gaze made its way back to Mabel. He narrowed his eyes at the sight of her, arms wrapped around her stomach. Closed off and made small. Smile stiff. Something was wrong.

"I want you to manage it."

Jake swung his head around. "What?"

"It'll be too big a show for just Robert, and he's going to be a little distracted, I think, for some time come winter. I want you to handle the equestrian portion of the show. Manage the acts, train the performers, hire those needed to care for the horses, and organize the advance men."

"Not perform?" Something soft and warm unfurled in his belly, spread over his limbs, and filled his veins.

"You are one of the greatest acrobats we've ever seen." Mr. Wells's lips tipped into a crooked smile. "Not, of course, a once-in-a-lifetime sort of performer like your wife, but close enough." His palm cupped Jake's shoulder, and his expression turned serious. "But I see it all the time—a performer who no longer enjoys performing. Who works from habit instead of passion. You've been clear since we hired you that you weren't planning to make this your permanent home. You lost your joy in performing after Charlotte's terrible accident, and it doesn't seem as though it ever returned."

"I hope I've not disappointed you in any way. I have given the show my best."

Mr. Wells waved his hands. "No, not at all. Your acts have been faultless. But I've been around a long time, and I can read a situation. I thought maybe we could induce you to stay with a change of focus. I will throw a stateroom into the deal—private enough for you and your wife. And you can work with us—with Robert and Isabella—to make Travis and Wells a household name, not only here in America, but everywhere."

The pleasant heat slipping over his skin turned cold. "Isabella?"

"She'll be working with the children."

Jake turned his gaze toward his mother-in-law. Beside her, Mabel stood stiff, her scarlet face a beacon for his concern.

"If you'll give me a minute," he said and strode across the room. He slid into the conversation just as easily as he took her hand. "Are you well, darling? It's quite hot in here." A way out, should she need it. The gardens were lovely. He had spied a profusion of early spring blooms aglow beneath the moonlight outside a set of French doors.

Mabel pulled her hand free. "I'm fine. Please . . . continue your conversation with Mr. Wells. You needn't leave the party on my account."

He clenched his jaw and gave a quick bow of his head. "Very well."

She'd made her wishes clear. Despite Bram's final concern, Mabel MacGinnis had little need for him. Little need, it seemed, for anyone. She'd finally gotten what she wanted: the confidence to step into the ring—and into life—on her own.

✻ ✻ ✻

Mabel watched Jake return to his conversation with Mr. Wells across the room. For a few moments, she pinned her gaze to his back, willing him to turn around. To offer his protection again. But he didn't. And why would he? She'd rebuffed him as roundly as possible.

She returned her attention to the conversation happening around her. To the wealthy businessman who spoke blandly of the coming heat and the escape he planned to his Newport cottage. Nothing about Mr. Jonas Moore initially struck her as anything but middling—his age, his build, his looks—but it took no more than ten minutes to recognize the lust in his gaze as it swept over her.

He was attentive to his wife—a slight woman with mousy brown hair and jumpy smile—but the moment someone else began to speak, he took to admiring Mabel in a wholly inappropriate manner.

"I see Mrs. Baum over there and I wish to speak with her, so I will take my leave." Mrs. Moore slid away. Her husband's eyes, though, stayed put. Firmly planted upon Mabel's breasts.

She glanced down at the swell of them, ensconced in satin, and heat spilled into her blood, mottled her chest, and crept up her neck. She crossed her arms over her waist, noting Mr. Moore's gaze had slipped south.

The dressmaker—New York's very best—had assured Mabel that this gown was the height of fashion. *"You will be the toast of the city in it, with your magnificent figure,"* she'd said at Mabel's final fitting. The neckline was low, but nothing shocking. Every woman in the room wore a similar style.

Perhaps she shouldn't have, though, for no other woman in the room was as well-endowed. No other woman in the room had been plastered all over New York in papers and upon bills. Every man in the room had seen Mabel's legs. They could close their eyes and recall her bare back, flexed for the camera. They knew intimate details about the length of her arms and circumference of her waist—the very area Mr. Moore seemed quite incapable of removing his eyes from.

It was science, after all.

Mabel moved closer to Maman, and her breath released as Mr. Moore swung his lecherous gaze toward Robert, and they spoke of his "very generous" investment in Travis and Wells's expansion.

"I think I should like something to drink," Maman said. "Will you join me, Mabel?"

"Don't leave just yet, Mrs. Cunningham. I'd like to discuss an opportunity with you." Mr. Moore touched Mabel's bare arm with dry fingers. "It will be worth your time."

"I think I will attend to my mother." Mabel swallowed and didn't meet Mr. Moore's eyes. Instead, she searched the room for the only man whose hands she wanted upon her. But Jake was deep in conversation with Mr. Wells near the fireplace. Not that she wished for him, at the moment. She would die if he saw another man take such liberties.

Maman waved her hand. "Don't trouble yourself, Mabel. Robert will come with me."

They walked away, and she considered following, but Mr.

Wells had been a kind, generous host, and she didn't want to treat one of his guests—especially one with such deep pockets—with blatant rudeness. Despite his own.

"What is it, Mr. Moore?" Mabel turned back around and saw that he had taken a few steps nearer to her. She backed up, but a pedestal table sporting a large enamel vase of sweet peas and anemones stopped her.

"Did you know I own the largest cigarette manufacturer in the country?" He puffed out his chest.

"No, I wasn't aware of that. Congratulations."

"A few years ago, a competing brand hired Fatty Arbuckle for a series of advertisements, and it proved extremely successful."

Mabel nodded.

"I'd like to hire you, Mrs. Cunningham, for our print ads." His gaze swept her. "What does the World's Strongest Woman smoke?"

She raised her brows. "Nothing. It isn't legal for women to smoke in public in New York."

"That doesn't mean they don't in private. And you have captured the nation's fancy. Imagine how much influence you have. Why, you could snap your fingers and have every woman in the country purchasing Moore Cigarettes."

"Why would I want to use my supposed influence to do that? I don't smoke." Da had, on occasion, puffed at a cigar, and though Mabel enjoyed the earthy, old-book scent, she'd never cared to try one for herself.

Mr. Moore leaned close and whispered a number in her ear. "That is what we'll pay you."

Mabel's eyes widened. It was nearly half what she could make in an entire year of performing.

"We would provide everything, as well. Your costume should demonstrate why you are the world's strongest and most beautiful woman. Something similar to the one you wore in that lovely photograph the *New York Times* published." His gaze slipped low, and he wet his lips with his tongue. "I would also be on hand should you need anything. Anything at all."

"Please, Mr. Moore, you are standing very close to me. I am not comfortable."

"A woman of your talents and freedom? You have found yourself close to many men, I imagine. I read that article, and I wonder, is it true? I believe so. Your . . . charms are considerable."

She sucked in a breath, and her hands balled into fists at her side. "You are being extremely inappropriate and insulting. I think I will get a drink with my mother, after all." Her chest rose and fell with labored breathing, once more drawing Mr. Moore's eyes.

"Come now. I'm a longtime investor in Travis and Wells. And despite Jerry's insistence that his show is family friendly, I'm quite aware his performers are less so." He barked a laugh and threw a look around, and then his fingers darted between them, and he gave her breast a quick squeeze.

For years, Mabel had ignored articles that turned her into a sideshow oddity. She'd pretended indifference as her marriage was sacrificed upon the altar of lewdness disguised as public opinion. And she had allowed a trio of strangers to measure and parse and study her. All because she resided within a body that was a little outside of ordinary but entirely God-given and designed. Was she so bizarrely knit together as to elicit such horrid behavior from people? Was she so weak as to allow it?

No more.

She kicked at the table behind her, stepped back, and swung.

She'd never punched a man before. She'd wrestled and subdued and lifted, but punched? She'd never had to, for if any man at Manzo Brothers had been tempted to do such a thing as the rooster-like Mr. Moore, Da's towering presence would have dissuaded even the stupidest.

Mr. Moore slumped to the ground like a sack of dropped potatoes.

Silence fell over the room. Mabel swallowed, then looked up at the white faces and hanging mouths.

"I'm so sorry, Mr. Wells," she said, gesturing toward the toppled table and water seeping into the carpet, "for making such a mess. It couldn't be helped."

Then she spun and escaped into the hall.

She heard the eruption as she raced over the parquet floor and found the doors leading into the garden. Her heart pounded with each step and didn't calm down until she settled upon a small stone bench nestled beneath a flowering dogwood, its pink blooms blushing in the moonlight.

Someone approached behind her, and she pressed her palms to her hot cheeks. "I'd rather be alone right now."

There was a brush of steps against grass, then a pause before whoever it was came forward again. She threw a glance over her shoulder and, seeing Jake, dropped her head into her lap and wrapped her arms around it, fingers knit behind her neck.

He settled beside her, his leg rustling her skirts. "Mr. Moore is alive, though I'm not sure how. I don't think I would survive such a knockout."

She huffed a choked laugh and sat upright.

"I'm sure he deserved much worse."

"He said vile things to me, then . . ." She circled her arms around her chest.

"I can deduce. I saw what filled his eyes."

They sat silently for a few moments until Mabel began to uncoil and relax in the safety of Jake's presence. He lightly touched her hand, which rested on the bench beside his own.

"I'm sorry. For everything."

"For having Maman fired?"

"I can't apologize for that. I was only trying to protect you." Her throat thickened, but she forced her gaze upon the low stone wall facing them until her tears became memory instead of possibility. "I believe I proved tonight that I don't need your protection."

He nodded. "You're right, of course. I've always said that. I do wish, however, that you wanted it." He stood. "We will have to pretend for a good while longer, Mabel. But as soon as the circus heads toward Indiana, I'll go home. You will not be granted an annulment, but I will take all the blame in the event of a divorce."

She listened to him walk away and used every bit of her strength to remain seated. To keep from chasing him into the house and begging him to stay. To love her. To make their marriage work. *"You will need no one, my girl,"* Da had always said. And it seemed he had been prophetic.

Need and loss were so entwined, though, that she wasn't sure she could find it within herself to thank him for the lesson.

CHAPTER 28

A PORTER HAD BROUGHT the trunk to her room, along with Rowena's, so that they could pack before Travis and Wells departed the city. Their final show was tomorrow evening. Then they were off, their days spent building up and breaking down. Nights spent rocking to sleep on a berth nailed to the floor of a train as they made the country a patchwork of canvas and dreams.

Isabella sat on her knees, dressing gown tucked beneath her legs, and pulled out the cigar box. Its enamel lid was smooth beneath her skin.

With clumsy fingers, she pulled out, one by one, her haunting treasures—Maman's wedding ring; a brooch made of gold, her father's hair caught within like an insect in amber; an infant's lace cap, its silk ribbons gone yellow.

She ran her thumb over the length of satin and let the strings pool in her lap. She had tied the cap upon her daughter's head the first day she'd been strong enough to hold her.

She'd pressed her finger to Mabel's sweet nose and puckered lips, kissed the little points of her ears, and pressed her face to the bottom of her baby's wrinkled, curled feet. They had been wide and square, the little toes like buds on a rosebush.

She lifted a photograph from her wedding day—Bram's wild hair as unrestrained as his smile and her eyes shining. Free at last. So she'd thought.

He had been a beautiful man. Generous, passionate, optimistic. And then life met his past, and he never seemed able to untangle the two. She pressed the picture to her lips and sighed a kiss over it.

Good-bye, my love.

Isabella picked through the box, pushing aside a clutch of early advertisements, creased and gone velvet with age; a bag of pebbles she, Rowena, Robert, and Paul had collected along a creek in Tennessee as children; a sheet torn from a magazine boasting a photograph of Bram and twelve-year-old Mabel, each lifting a barbell above their heads. She'd never looked at another circus magazine after that, afraid she'd stumble on an article or photograph of them. It had proven too painful to remember.

She lifted a handkerchief sporting Paul's initials. He'd given it to her on a Sunday when she'd tripped and scraped her palms. Rusty blood streaked it still. As she unfolded the fabric, the ring he'd given her tumbled to the floor. She slid it onto her finger and acknowledged its weight. Then she pressed the tip of her finger against the diamond, much the way she'd once done to Mabel's infant lips and nose.

She covered the ring with her other hand and closed her eyes.

Good-bye, my love.

Then she repacked it all, settling everything back in the bottom of the trunk. She eased the lid closed and glanced over her shoulder at Rowena, who was still in bed, breathing with gentle sighs.

Isabella tightened the sash of her gown and rebraided the fall of hair over her shoulder. Then she crossed the room, working through all the reasons she shouldn't do what she was about to do.

They fell like rocks around her, soft thuds echoing in the silence.

One thing seemed to answer them all.

"Love isn't something you deserve. It's something you're offered."

How could Isabella accept less than what others were willing to offer? Was it loving to reject them? To reject their forgiveness? Their grace? To hide the light of their love beneath the shadow of her guilt?

"You don't need to be who you've always thought you were." Why should she continue believing the worst about herself? It had brought her nothing but heartache. She could become the mother Mabel deserved. The woman Robert already saw her as. She could do all things.

But not on her own. She was no longer on her own.

She slipped through the door, careful to close it with a soft click behind her, and moved down the hall toward Robert's room. It was barely morning, and everyone with an ounce of sense was still in bed.

But Isabella couldn't wait. Once the sun splashed watery rays over the Brooklyn Bridge, the day would bustle with things to do. A trip to prepare for. Shows to complete.

She knocked, a gentle *rap rap rap* that wouldn't disturb him if he wasn't already awake.

The door opened, and Robert stood there in a pair of midnight-blue pajamas. He blinked. "Isabella?"

"Polly."

His smile curved. "Polly."

"Hello, my love."

He held out his hand and pressed her fingers to his lips.

There was a moment during every show, when she reached

for the trapeze bar and positioned herself to jump, that her body froze. It was an unnatural thing, leaping into the air, knowing that if anything went wrong—a lapse in timing, sloppy rigging—death was the most likely outcome. And she stiffened now, recognizing the importance of the moment. Knowing that if she didn't jump, if she stood there frozen by fear, she would never fly.

"I've come to tell you yes. If you'll have me."

Her fingers curled around his as he lowered her hand. "Truly?"

She nodded.

The flame that lit his eyes promised a lifetime of shadow chasing. But he needed to know and be prepared. They still crouched, waiting.

"Robert, I can't promise only beauty. The melancholy is diminished but not gone. It may never be."

"I will take you however you come." He stepped into the hall and gathered her close, wrapping her body, battered and small, in his wide embrace. He was not as strong as Bram, but she'd never felt safer. He was not as young as Paul, but she could finally see a future. "I will love you, Polly, in sickness and health. In darkness and light."

She lifted onto her toes and cupped his dear, familiar face in her palms. And when his mouth found hers, there was more than promises. More than passion. More, even, than love.

There was acceptance. And the certainty that her shadows, whenever and wherever they appeared, would not frighten him away.

✻ ✻ ✻

Their final day in New York began overcast and dreary. Sunlight, too weak to do much but cast hazy rays over the hall, filtered through the windows lining the upper balconies of the Garden.

Despite the clouds, no rain was forecasted, so the skylight was open, and a dim rectangle illuminated center ring. Polly watched Jake swing through the rafters, his arms and legs stretched long. He was as graceful and powerful as a leopard, and his movements were explosive. Exact.

Mabel stood nearby, awaiting her cue to enter the ring, pretending disinterest in the act flying above their heads.

"He really is a talented man."

Mabel made a noncommittal sound in her throat and yanked her gaze toward the tumble of clowns in one of the smaller rings.

Polly straightened the wide cuff of her new jacket. She'd never imagined she would be standing outside the ring, watching it all, wearing a smart suit instead of a costume. She definitely never imagined she'd be all right with it. No, more than all right. Content. "It's a shame he hates the circus so much that he's running all the way to Kansas to get away from it."

Mabel sighed and slid her eyes toward Polly. "What are you doing, Maman?"

"I only want to make sure you're not giving up too soon."

"I don't see how a relationship can work when one person hates what the other loves."

"Are you referring to the circus . . . or me?" Polly offered a smile for levity, but her belly knotted. She hated the thought of being at the center of another failed marriage.

Mabel didn't answer.

"Are you all right to go in there on your own?"

Mabel nodded. "You were right. I'd been holding so tightly to who I thought I was, I hadn't allowed any room to grow into the person I could become. I'm capable of doing what needs to be done, in and out of the ring. Even when what needs to be done is hard. You showed me that. You've done so many hard things, and I've always wanted to be like you. And you reminded me that even when it looks like it, I'm never alone. In the ring or anywhere else."

Polly's chest filled with lightness, and she thought she might lift off the ground. She never imagined her life could be filled with such beauty and honor. "And you proved it the other day with Mr. Moore. You took care of yourself well."

Mabel gave her a sidelong look. "I never apologized to Mr. Wells about that. I suppose he's very angry."

"Robert saw what happened. If you hadn't hit that man, he would have. Mr. Wells was livid. He's responsible for keeping the performers safe, and he's sorry you were put in such a situation."

"Did Mr. Moore pull his investment?"

Polly chuckled. "He doubled it. When Jake returned from following you outside, he lifted Mr. Moore from the ground—"

"He was still lying there?"

"I think he would be still, had Jake not returned." Polly watched Jake descend the ladder, act complete. "He lifted Mr. Moore, who seemed ready to faint, and whispered something in his ear. Ten minutes later, Mr. Moore, a piece of meat slapped to his eye, told Mr. Wells he would be privileged to double his investment. Then he left."

"What do you think Jake said?" Mabel shifted her attention and followed his progress toward them.

"I imagine threats were involved." Polly pulled the doll Isabella from her jacket pocket. "I know you don't need her anymore, but I hope you want her."

Mabel took the doll and pressed its tiny head to her lips. She slipped it beneath her sleeve, little legs dangling. "Thank you, Maman."

Mabel pulled Polly into a hug, her firm embrace squeezing out the years of hurt. Polly thought it just might chase off the regret, as well. She pulled back. "You are strong, Mabel, in all you set your hands and heart and eyes toward. I'm proud of you."

She watched Mabel stride toward center ring as applause rained down around her, filling the amphitheater and Polly's heart. As Mabel stooped to lift a barbell, as beautiful and graceful in movement as Jake had been while soaring, the clouds parted, and a glowing ribbon fell upon her daughter and sent the shadows made by ropes and rigging fleeing.

Around Polly, the other performers were all dressed up like players in a fever dream. Up close, one could see the cracks in their thick makeup. The sweat dripping from temples and noses, staining armpits and backs. The way age and injury and labor stamped itself upon faces. Bodies. Spirits.

But there was also perseverance. Friendship. The knowledge that a day's work meant delight to children and adults alike. The circus was dream and nightmare all wrapped up together. But so, too, was most of life.

Jake slipped into the hall and walked along the wall hemming in the thousands of spectators. Every few steps, he would glance at Mabel, and as he drew nearer, Polly could see the naked yearning on his face. He strode past, and she followed him through the jostling crowd of performers. The back corridors smelled of sweat and horseflesh and the distinct odor of a big cat having marked its territory.

Ahead of her, Jake pushed at the door to the men's dressing room, and she hurried.

"Jake. A moment."

He paused, his hand still on the knob, and his shoulders rose and fell in a deep sigh. "What is it, Isabella? I really want a bath and a change."

"Polly," she whispered. "I've taken back my name."

He dipped his chin, then turned, his gaze steady and cautious.

"I want to exhort you—" A whooping laugh erupted behind them, and Polly looked over her shoulder. The lion tamer and his assistant were striding down the hall, their tall, shiny boots eating up the space. "Could we go somewhere more private?"

Jake swiped at his forehead. "Fine. But let me at least change."

She nodded and pressed against the wall, watching for Mabel's appearance and hoping Jake hurried so she could usher him away before her daughter's act finished.

The moment he stepped through the door, she started off, her shoes clicking against the marble floor with punchy doggedness. She turned right when the corridor split and led Jake into the concert hall. This room, used as the sideshow, was mostly empty. The spectators were watching the show, and the oddities—the bearded lady and tallest man and conjoined twins and contortionists and all the rest—were in their dressing rooms, touching up makeup and resting.

Only one person was present—Tom Cotton, the human skeleton—and he sat folded in a chair nearly hidden in the corner, reading a novel and eating a sandwich. Polly waved to him as she and Jake circled the room, peering into the enclave-like rooms created by scaffolding and painted board.

"What do you want, Polly?"

"I want to convince you to stay."

His steps faltered, and he paused beside a small stage set with miniature furniture. He crossed his arms, and his face turned to stone. "Why?"

"You love my daughter." His expression softened just enough to encourage her to continue. "And I know you despise me."

"I despise all of this." He threw out his hands. "It stole Charlotte from me and destroyed my marriage."

"No, it didn't. I know you don't want to hear this, but you owe it to Mabel to make a decision informed by truth." She reached for his arm, wanting to soften the delivery. Not knowing how she possibly could. "Charlotte was never going to move with you to Kansas. She told me so the day before she died."

"She told me too, but if we'd had the time, I could have convinced her to come with me."

"You couldn't have. She'd already seen an attorney and wanted a divorce."

Jake jerked away. "You're lying."

"I wish I were. But Charlotte didn't love anyone more than she loved fame. I can tell you the attorney's name, if you wish to speak with him."

He shook his head, and his nostrils flared white. His lips pressed into a line. But still his eyes turned glassy, and Polly's own eyes pricked with tears.

"Why are you telling me this? Why now?" he asked.

"Because you've built her up to be something she never was. You've turned a fictionalized story of her into a wedge that is driving you and Mabel apart."

He dropped his arms. "I only wanted to take Charlotte home because I saw her slipping away. The circus was stealing her, and I wanted to take her far from it. I wanted my wife back."

"I don't think you ever had her, Jake. She was desperate for the public's adoration. It led to her death."

"Tell me." His voice was flat. Resigned.

"She wasn't meant to wear that costume—the white silk one that revealed her legs. She had already asked Robert, who refused because it didn't fit with the show's theme. Do you remember it?"

"The Crusades."

"She was Florine of Burgundy. Dressed in red and gold with a flowing chiffon skirt and long tight sleeves. *That* costume was pounds heavier. Not as flattering to her figure. The skirt and gem-encrusted bodice slowed her ascent."

Jake's face blanched. "God, Charlotte. What a foolish thing to do."

"She wore the costume she wanted—the white one—beneath the other and stripped it off right before she climbed into the cannon so that no one would see. She didn't think to have everything recalibrated. I knew right away—the moment she burst from the cannon—that she was going to go too high. She would miss the bar, and I couldn't do anything to change it. I'm so sorry."

She had called out and Jake's shout answered her own. When she had looked up at him, standing on the platform above her, shock and disbelief etched his face. She knew what would happen. So did he. She heard the crowd's gasp as Charlotte flew headfirst into a truss. Another one as she fell.

And Polly had closed her eyes, gripping tightly to the steel ropes that held her aloft.

"I had no idea."

"Mr. Wells wrote to you, to tell you what came of the inquest."

"I tossed it in the fire."

She nodded, understanding the grief that would cause someone to ignore the truth. "Mabel isn't Charlotte."

It was a presumptuous thing to say. Disrespectful, perhaps, to the dead. But it needed saying.

"I know. She loves completely." There was a little-boy yearning in his voice. An undercurrent of desperation and loss that pierced Polly's heart and made her want to tuck him into a hug.

But he was not a little boy, and grown men didn't need coddling. They needed the truth. They needed to move on from their pasts and confront the future they'd been given.

"Bram wasn't willing to fight for me. For us. Please don't make that mistake with Mabel."

✳ ✳ ✳

If Jake were caught, he'd likely be released from Travis and Wells, and he might very well be brought up on charges. But he needed space. Quiet. And the only way he knew to find it, short of stealing Mr. Wells's fancy Mercedes, was with a horse.

He didn't know this one's name. It was a handsome animal—a black-and-white Appaloosa with a calm demeanor and insistent nicker—and Jake thought he'd seen it in the ring beneath one of the trick riders. He'd only chosen it because it was in the stall nearest the double doors leading out of the stable.

Jake eased the animal onto 26th Street and passed Madison Square Park, which wasn't big enough for his purpose today. On Fifth Avenue he trotted down the middle of the road, steering clear of the chugging automobiles and trolleys. New York was too congested. He'd always preferred it when the circus left the city and gave them something to look at besides miles of skyscrapers and the backs of the people walking in front of you.

"I hate the circus." He tried the words, but they tasted foreign on his tongue. Kind of bitter, and not for the reason he would have suspected fifteen minutes ago, before speaking with Isabella. Polly.

He'd said them so often, believed them for so long, he'd forgotten to evaluate them for truth.

He didn't hate the circus. He hated what his wife had allowed it to do to her. Though maybe even that wasn't right.

He hated what she'd allowed her quest for significance to do to her. And she'd used the circus as a means of attaining it. He couldn't deny Polly's claim. He'd known Charlotte wasn't happy with him, and it had started long before he suggested they move to Kansas. They'd been brilliant together, but nothing could last very long in the face of Charlotte's singled-minded focus. Their marriage hadn't been the only thing burned.

Ahead, Central Park loomed, and he urged the horse forward until they found the bridle path. After galloping a few minutes, he gave the horse its head and allowed the animal the freedom to fly. It would have been impossible with a typical horse, for the trails had been created in a way that dissuaded races, but circus horses were not typical, and the animal's speed and agility meant Jake could shake free from the clamor of the city.

He could breathe.

He didn't think he'd been able to take a full breath since that second kiss, when he realized Mabel meant much more to him than the daughter of an old friend ought to. And as they'd packed their trunks the night before, only the sounds of creaking steps and clinking latches breaking the unnatural silence, he'd thought he might suffocate with the weight of the knowledge that she was leaving. Or he was. *They* were leaving each other.

And why?

The lake appeared, winking through a drape of velvet leaves, and Jake pulled on the reins. Ahead, a little girl in a red coat and beribboned straw hat bent to float a paper boat in the water. The small boy beside her poked a stick at it, and they watched it drift away. They never would be able to get it back. The breeze was light but enough to send it over the rippling water, where it would sink. Jake tracked it until it dipped and disappeared. The children, bored of their game, wandered off in the company of a grim-faced woman, and Jake dismounted and walked the horse to the water's edge.

"Why you think it so much more important for me to learn to work alone than for you to learn to work with others is beyond me."

Mabel's words, the ones she'd spoken with such precise certainty that day in the stables when he'd had Isabella let go, played over the water. Why indeed? She was a capable woman, perfectly able to perform on stage without anyone holding her up. But had he been so focused on her discovering it that he'd somehow missed his own weakness?

What would it look like if he stayed? If he didn't leave Travis and Wells and didn't go home to Kansas and didn't blithely hand his wife a divorce as though it meant as little as changing one's shoes?

And had he really, from the very start of his relationship with Mabel, spoken so lightly of the same thing that had, only an hour earlier, made his insides twist with violence when hearing how easily Charlotte had considered it? How could Charlotte have loved him and been so eager to see him on his way? Because they hadn't wanted to sort out a difference in opinion on where they lived?

It all seemed so wasteful now. So childishly self-absorbed.

And wholly unnecessary to repeat. Mr. Wells had offered him an escape. A chance to leave the work he no longer loved but still remain with the woman he adored. A chance to retire from the rings and work with horses.

The Appaloosa snuffled restlessly, and a goose landed in the water with a splash and a honk.

What an absolute fool he was.

But there was no reason he couldn't turn things around.

Jake urged the horse back into a trot. The shop he wanted was just on the other side of the park, and he wasn't going to spend another minute pretending he didn't love Mabel enough to rejoin the circus.

❊ ❊ ❊

Mabel missed her father. Missed him without any rancor or twisting doubts about his affection. He'd been a flawed man, made more so because of the fears shaped by his childhood, and he'd made choices she could see, in retrospect, were wrong. But he'd made them with the best of intentions. He'd wanted her protected and to grow up strong. He'd simply had the wrong idea of what strength actually was. She hoped, if God allowed him a moment to watch from Heaven, that he would see her conquer this last New York show and be proud.

Overnight, it seemed, the city had been plastered with new bills—*Atalanta to take on the Bridge of Zeus in her final New*

York show. It was her father's trademark. A trick no woman had ever attempted.

She wasn't sure she should. The last time she'd tried, she'd been too daunted to even position herself. It was the trick she and Da had been perfecting before he died. *"Ah, love, you are everything I've ever wanted in a daughter,"* he'd told her when she crawled from beneath the curved wooden bridge. *"The world isn't big enough for you."*

She wanted to see this through and finish what they'd started. She wanted to prove, if only to herself, that she could.

A quick glance at the dressing room hall showed Maman and Robert standing as close together as two people possibly could in public. Robert bounced on his toes and rubbed his hands. He'd been in the circus business long enough to know when something was going to be well received, he'd told Mabel before she stepped into the ring for the evening performance.

She would do well to trust him. And she did. But her stomach turned a somersault, and as she positioned herself beneath the tall wooden structure draped with aerialists, she glanced around for one man. She wanted to draw strength from his presence. She needed to see that *he* approved.

But Jake was nowhere, and it was just as well. With bent knees, she centered herself below Réka Danó and, bracing the crossbar over her shoulders, sprang up straight, her middle tight and muscles rigid.

It was an easy trick. A warm-up. The real event came next.

Before she felt entirely ready, it was time, and she lay back against a low stool specially made to cradle her shoulders and support her back. With knees bent and feet secure against the floor, she braced herself for the weight.

A few laborers, dressed in red and white ceremonial garb and sporting helmets fringed with scarlet feathers, arranged the jointed bridge over her middle, supported against her chest and knees. She took a few deep breaths and had no problem sucking air into her lungs or expanding her chest. There had been time for only one rehearsal, but she didn't need another.

The music changed, and two by two they came—a dozen men in all—dressed as armor bearers and soldiers. They carried pennants and swords with jeweled hilts and instruments that looked as though they might have been played in ancient Persia. They marched across the bridge held aloft by Mabel's torso and stood along it, all twelve of them at once, pennants held high and voices lifted in what Mr. Wells thought a good approximation of an ancient battle cry.

And she breathed. With every inhale, strength filled her veins. With every exhale, certainty enveloped her thoughts. She would be fine. It would hurt, she knew. She would miss his voice. His touch. But she could survive without a husband.

Her mother had. Her grandmother had. She was made of the same ilk.

She wouldn't force him to stay with her. She couldn't anyway, despite the claims splashed across advertisements and papers. *Atalanta, the strongest woman! Capable of great feats! Able to bend steel and the will of men!*

All but one.

The soldiers high-stepped off the bridge, and then came the horses. Three in all. One at a time, thank goodness. Their shoes clicked sharply against the wood, and Mabel sucked a long breath into her lungs. The first horse and its rider crossed.

She pressed her fingers against the edge of the bridge, slivers of wood sliding into her fingertips. Squeezing her eyes shut, she saw a younger version of Maman staring at her sadly. *"She's too big."* Lorenzo tumbling from her grasp, his body making a dull thump on the ground. The audience hissing and shouting in derision. The papers. The doctors. Mr. Moore with his grasping hands and vile tongue. Jake.

Oh, Jake.

Then those images were replaced by others. Da catching her

in his arms and swinging her high. Katie Grace, eyes wide, after watching the show for the first time. Maman sitting beside her on the trapeze bar, their pinkies touching. And Jake . . .

Oh, Jake.

There were too many things to remember in regard to him. It was better she didn't at all.

She set her jaw and opened her eyes to see the second horse's swishing tail. The third came, its prance high. The rider stared straight ahead, his helmet slightly askew. He turned and looked down at her, then leapt onto his mount's back, supple feet gripping.

Every bit of Mabel's exposed skin prickled when he flashed a dimple. She laughed when he tossed the helmet away and flipped. Once. Twice. Three times.

The audience cheered. Above them, high in the rafters, the acrobats and aerialists stood on their platforms or hung from their bars and watched.

Jake slid from the horse and slapped its rump, sending it trotting away. His knees bumped against the bridge as he knelt above her, and his gaze was a caress. Then he pulled something from his pocket, and it glittered in the glow of electric lights. "Will you marry me?"

Her heart thrummed a tarantella. "We're already married."

"For real this time."

"It's always been real for me, Jake."

His grin could put the sun to shame. He hopped off the bridge and, with a great heave, shoved it off her, then took her hand and slipped the ring—*the* ring!—on her finger, but she only had a moment to admire it for he brushed his lips against her cheek.

The audience sighed. Then they clapped and pounded their feet against the floor.

"I'm going to run away," he said, his words nearly lost to the buzzing excitement.

"To Kansas?" She wrapped her arms around his waist. She wouldn't let go for anything

"To the circus."

She pressed her face against his shoulder. "Really, Jake? Are you staying with us? With me?"

He pulled back and pushed a curl behind her ear. Then he grinned in a way Mabel felt down to her toes. "I'll tell you what, how about we wrestle for it? You win, I stay. I win, I stay . . . and you give me a kiss."

She drew her lip between her teeth as though deep in thought, then, as Jake stared at her with stars in his eyes and memories on his lips, she swept her foot around and caught the back of his legs, and he toppled to the ground with a grunt. She knelt beside him.

"Not fair," he said with a laugh. "I wasn't ready. I wasn't ready for any of it."

"But I won." She bent over him, lips hovering. "I think I might give you that kiss anyway, though."

And she did.

❋ ❋ ❋

Sundays were meant for rest. For worship and family—whether forged in blood or stitched in crisscrossing train tracks. Sundays were meant for sleeping late and laughing hard. For reading novels that passed through a dozen hands as Travis and Wells scuttled over a map of towns and cities and states.

Sundays were for weddings too.

On this first Sunday since leaving New York, Mabel sat on the bottom bunk in the berth Maman had shared with Rowena for so many years and watched as she prepared to give her heart to the man who had so longed for it.

"Tell me about your wedding, Mabel," Maman said as Rowena twisted her hair into curls and pinned them in a cascade. "I'm sure it was a bit fancier than what Robert and I will have."

Mabel laughed softly, remembering the ancient chapel, its sagging roof and faded murals. It had turned out to be a poor portent of her and Jake's newly vibrant relationship. But she thought on the memory fondly, grateful she could look at it any time she wished. "Not at all. It was very simple. Only the two of us, in fact, were present." Maman would be surrounded by friends. By family too, since she and Jake would be in attendance. "There was nothing about it that would inspire Lorenzo to poetry."

Maman's eyes went soft. "We will see him, you know, when we go to Europe next year. Robert says Mr. Wells has already been in touch with Giuseppe."

"Are you all right with that? Seeing the people who conspired to keep us apart all these years?"

"They did it out of love. They wanted to protect you and honor your father. And I've been granted an enormous amount of grace. How could I show any less?"

They said nothing else about it because sometimes the only thing one could do when badly wronged was forgive. Move forward with living. Allow the hurts of the past to find healing in the promise of the future.

"I think you're ready." Rowena clasped Maman's shoulders and kissed her cheek. "Robert will fall over at the sight of you. I'll go find my seat."

When Rowena left, Mabel admired her mother's ivory wedding gown, accentuated only by a fall of lace and silk rosettes down the bodice. Alice had worked day and night to complete it in time. "You look beautiful."

Maman smiled and blew out a gentle huff of air. "I guess it's time." She stood and ran her hands over the skirt, and her gaze bounced around the room as though looking for escape.

"Are you all right?" Mabel asked. She knew Maman's ghosts hadn't been vanquished. They likely never would be completely. Sometimes one needed to stand alone, but other times . . . well, there was freedom in finding yourself knit to others. Allowing them to hold you up when your legs went weak in the face of a battle. Mabel was discovering how to determine which was called for.

"I'm scared." Maman began to tremble, her entire body taken over by the fear that had held her captive to lies.

Mabel wrapped her mother in an embrace. "I will hold you until you no longer are."

"I never thought I would marry again. Not even after I discovered your father had died."

"It is worth it, though. There is such beauty in what lies ahead." Mabel pulled back a little and grasped her mother's arms. "And Robert is not Da."

"Oh, but—"

"No. Do not make excuses. I loved him. I know you loved him. But he allowed his own fear to destroy you. To destroy *us.* Robert won't. He will love you in weakness and strength. He will never sacrifice you to his fears."

Maman's trembling subsided. She took a deep breath and shook her arms. "You're right. How did you become so wise?"

Mabel smiled. "I just recognize what is in front of me. I don't believe I've ever seen a man so in love as yours."

"Well, there is yours." Maman blinked, and a wrinkle of worry appeared between her brows. "Do you suppose Jake will ever forgive me?"

"There is nothing to forgive."

She had spoken about it with him only the night before, bringing it up in the afterglow of the love they'd shared, hoping the loveliness of that moment would soften the poke of bad memories.

"Your mother had nothing to do with Charlotte's death. I recognize that, but she's been entwined with my grief for so long, I'm not sure I can force my heart into compliance."

"I only ask, for my sake, that you try."

"I would do anything for you. Even that."

He'd already proven how much he would do for her—giving up his plans to move home and live quietly on his family's ranch. He didn't love the circus the way she did, but she hoped, with this new position out of the spotlight and working with the horses he adored, he would come around to it again one day.

The sound of a cornet wended toward them. A tuba joined its mellow call, followed closely by a French horn.

"Jake will come to love you as I do, I'm certain." Mabel stepped away and smiled. "Are you ready?"

"I believe so."

Mabel took her mother's hand and led her from the train car. Up ahead, the tent rose. It had been decided they wouldn't tear it down after the previous night's show. *"Mr. Wells said he will make an allowance for the wedding if everyone is amenable to doing a little work on a Sunday evening,"* Robert had told them.

And everyone had been. A wedding in the circus was no small thing, and joining one of its brightest stars with the man who kept everything running seemed a big thing, indeed.

They crossed the trampled field somewhere between Durham and Raleigh, arms wound together, and when they reached the canvas, Maman took a deep breath.

"Do you need Isabella for courage?" Mabel asked.

"No." Maman pushed open the flap. "I have you. And that is more than enough."

Something poured into Mabel's belly—a heavy, weighty, joyous, buoyant, almost painful thing that made her feel as though she were rooted to the ground and flying through the air all at once. It strengthened her spine and turned her knees soft as jelly. It made her want to laugh and cry. Dance and rest. Throw her arms wide and stand perfectly still as heaven's whisper bathed her in promise.

That was the thing about love—the unimaginable became reality, and every dream proved more than possibility.

"It's time." Maman entered the tent, and Mabel, all her childhood hopes converging in this one spectacular moment, followed in her steps.

A NOTE
from the AUTHOR

THERE ARE SOME THINGS we should talk more about. Like women who pursue traditionally male-dominated careers, or couples who flip gender expectations (for instance, a heroine who towers over the hero), or how completely exhausting and crushing postpartum depression and OCD are.

I know. I have four children and suffered after each was born. The first two in silence because no one wants to hear about the darkness that can envelop a woman during what is supposed to be the happiest time in her life. The next two a little more vocally because I was tired of pretending all was well.

And during my last struggle, I thought, gosh, it's hard *now*. When we understand hormones and sleep deprivation and have Zoloft. What was it like for women a hundred years ago? How did they make sense of it? How did they cope?

I wanted to tell the story of that woman and her daughter. This book is for all of you I've talked to who feel reduced because in books and movies and on television shows and social media, you don't see your stories represented. It's still a hush-hush thing we're afraid to talk about because we never want anyone to question how much we love the little baby tucked against our breast. But let's talk. I think, in sharing our experiences, we'll come to discover we are much less alone in them than we thought we were.

I had no intention of having a backstory of suicide. No plans to give Isabella that past. But like so many families, ours has, more than once, been touched by it. It's not an easy thing to write about and an infinitely harder thing to walk through. But darkness flees in light, and it's worth flipping the switch. It happens to us. To Christians who trust God. To parents who love their children. To spouses who tried so hard. To friends who had no idea anything was wrong. I only want to say, I see your pain. You're not alone in it.

A few years ago, I listened to a *History Chicks* podcast episode on Katie Sandwina and fell completely in love with her. She inspired Mabel and parts of her story (some of her tricks, how she met her husband, the scene where she's measured by the doctors and called the most perfect female). Katie Grace was named in honor of her.

Isabella's signature act was based on Lillian Leitzel's plange. And, yes, circus performers could become very popular and incredibly wealthy. They were the Hollywood stars of their day.

Travis and Wells is made up but loosely based on an amalgam of various large circuses during this time. Barnum & Bailey kicked off their season in New York City and spent a month performing at Madison Square Garden. (The second one. We're currently on the fourth.)

It was fun setting this book in my home state of New York. Only a few years after Isabella and Mabel's story, my own grandmother, from an Italian immigrant family, would walk those same streets. Maybe she saw the circus at Madison Square Garden. Perhaps she bought cheese at one of the shops in Little Italy. Maybe she rode bicycles at Coney Island and ate hot dogs and soft pretzels while walking in the park and stood in a rooftop cabaret and looked out over the city. I love thinking that Nanny might have passed Katie Grace or Mabel or Isabella on the street.

Well, if they had actually been real. Sometimes I forget my characters aren't. I hope, while reading *The Weight of Air*, you forgot too. I hope, if you identified with their struggles, you also found hope in their answers. Mostly, I hope you enjoyed this story of two women caught between love and fear. I loved getting to know Mabel and Isabella, and it feels particularly hard this time to say good-bye.

ACKNOWLEDGMENTS

My biggest, most heartfelt thanks go to everyone at Bethany House. You have been a dream to work with, and I've enjoyed every moment of it. Especially to my editor, Jessica Sharpe, who just might believe in my books as much as my husband does. I don't take you for granted.

Thanks to Karen Solem, who represented this book. And to my new agent, Rachel McMillan, who has gone above and beyond. I'm so grateful for your support and expertise.

To my readers, who have given these worlds I've dreamed up their time, money, and pieces of their hearts. All the big hugs to you! It's such a privilege to be able to do this, and I'm thankful to each one of you.

To the History Chicks, who have offered me endless hours of entertainment during the many (many) hours I've spent driving my kids all over the city, and who made history come alive for my teenage daughters in a way no textbook ever could.

Thanks to Sarah Monzon, who made sure Jake and his horse didn't do anything ridiculous and unhorselike, and to CW Briar and Jacob Hunter, who made sure physics was honored.

To my writing partners—Lindsey, Kristi, Leslie, and Hope.

As I wrote this book, I tried to keep in mind what Kristi wrote in big letters at the top of our brainstorming pad—*No one dies of cholera.* She said nothing about a cannonball stunt gone wrong.

To my husband, who has always loved me unconditionally, even during my darkest moments postpartum. Who has never been threatened by strong women. And who enjoyed it immensely every time I told him we needed to practice one of Mabel and Jake's wrestling scenes (maybe even more than the kissing scenes).

To my children—Ellie, Grainne, Hazel, and August. You are worth every struggle. Every fight. Every moment shadows fell. God has used you to pierce through darkness. You are my starlight.

To the God who has loved me so well. I am never alone. I am who you say I am. I can do all things through Christ. Praise Him.

Kimberly Duffy is a Long Island native currently traveling the globe by way of Cincinnati, Ohio. When she's not exploring places that require a passport, homeschooling her four kids, or stuffing just *one more thing* into her carry-on, she writes historical fiction that takes her readers back in time. You can find her at kimberlyduffy.com.

Sign Up for Kimberly's Newsletter

Keep up to date with Kimberly's news on book releases and events by signing up for her email list at kimberlyduffy.com.

More from Kimberly Duffy

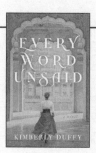

As the nation's most fearless travel columnist, Augusta Travers explores the country, spinning stories for women unable to leave hearth and home. Suddenly caught in a scandal, she escapes to India to visit old friends, promising great tales of boldness. But instead she encounters a plague, new affections, and the realization that she can't outrun her past.

Every Word Unsaid

You May Also Like . . .

When a stranger appears in India with news that Ottilie Russell's brother must travel to England to take his place as a nobleman, she is shattered by the secrets that come to light. But betrayal and loss lurk in England too, and soon Ottilie must fight to ensure her brother doesn't forget who he is, as well as stitch a place for herself in this foreign land.

A Tapestry of Light by Kimberly Duffy
kimberlyduffy.com

Determined to uphold her father's legacy, newly graduated Nora Shipley joins an entomology research expedition to India to prove herself in the field. In this spellbinding new land, Nora is faced with impossible choices—between saving a young Indian girl and saving her career, and between what she's always thought she wanted and the man she's come to love.

A Mosaic of Wings by Kimberly Duffy
kimberlyduffy.com

In 1865, orphaned Daisy Francois takes a housemaid position and finds that the eccentric Gothic authoress inside hides a story more harrowing than those in her novels. Centuries later, Cleo Clemmons uncovers an age-old mystery, and the dust of the old castle's curse threatens to rise again, this time leaving no one alive to tell its sordid tale.

The Vanishing at Castle Moreau by Jaime Jo Wright
jaimewrightbooks.com

◈ BETHANYHOUSE

More from Bethany House

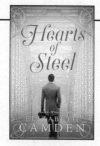

When successful businesswoman Maggie Molinaro offends a corrupt banker, she unwittingly sets off a series of calamities that threaten to destroy her life's work. She teams up with charismatic steel magnate Liam Blackstone, but what begins as a practical alliance soon evolves into a romance between two wounded people determined to beat the odds.

Hearts of Steel by Elizabeth Camden
THE BLACKSTONE LEGACY #3
elizabethcamden.com

During World War II, when special agent Sterling Bertrand is washed ashore at Evie Farrow's inn, her life is turned upside down. As Evie and Sterling work together to track down a German agent, they unravel mysteries that go back to World War I. The ripples from the past are still rocking their lives, and it seems yesterday's tides may sweep them into danger today.

Yesterday's Tides by Roseanna M. White
roseannamwhite.com

With a notorious forger preying on New York's high society, Metropolitan Museum of Art curator Lauren Westlake is just the expert needed to track down the criminal. As she and Detective Joe Caravello search for the truth, the closer they get to discovering the forger's identity, the more entangled they become in a web of deception and crime.

The Metropolitan Affair by Jocelyn Green
ON CENTRAL PARK #1
jocelyngreen.com

BETHANYHOUSE